Gilligan's Table

A Caribbean Cruise Mystery by

SANDY CARES

GILLIGAN'S TABLE: A Caribbean Cruise Mystery
by Sandy Cares

Published by Treasure Isles Press

First Edition, January 2021

Copyright © 2021 Sandy Cares

Author Services by Pedernales Publishing, LLC.
www.pedernalespublishing.com

Cover by Jana Rade

Library of Congress Control Number: 2020925951

ISBN: 978-1-7364124-2-8 Paperback Edition
ISBN: 978-1-7364124-1-1 Hardcover Edition
ISBN: 978-1-7364124-0-4 Digital Edition

Printed in the United States of America

To Mom and Dad.
A kid should be so lucky.

Chapter One

Day One: February 3, Wednesday
Miami, Florida, USA
Partly Cloudy: High: 81ºF/27ºC. Low: 65ºF/18ºC.

4:42 AM SETH CALLED AND SAID he would not be joining me on the cruise.

"Good timing, Seth," I said. "I'm standing here in my foyer waiting for the cab that's supposed to plow through this Michigan blizzard so I can meet you at the airport in thirty-nine minutes just like we've been planning since Thanksgiving. What the hell is going on?"

He hemmed and hawed. I knew that if I could have seen him, one foot would be twisted behind the other ankle and he'd be leaning on the fridge holding the cell phone in the crook of his neck and combing his long fingers through his thick brown hair. He tried to sound manly. "It's over, Marianne. I've moved on. I'm really sorry. I just didn't know how to tell you any sooner, but I thought if I told you now, at least you could enjoy yourself on the cruise, even if I'm not going with you."

It sounded like he'd been rehearsing all night.

"Even if?" I asked. "Do you hear yourself, Seth? Even if? Shouldn't it be 'especially since,' if you're pulling this on me? Seriously, Seth, is this some kind of joke?" I was standing up straight and felt taller than my five-foot-two stature. I felt myself stiffening, my tight fist digging sharply into my hip. Of all the last straws he'd ever managed to come up with in the past, this one had to take the prize. Here he was telling me he was through as calmly as if he were telling me the price of gas.

"Oh, by the way, Marianne, I was driving by the gas station today and I noticed that gas is down a couple cents. And oh, by the way, I'm moving on and not joining you on the cruise we've been planning since Thanksgiving."

I'd forked out nearly a thousand dollars for my half of this pleasure junket, I suddenly remembered. Underneath my freshly cut bob with kitchen bangs because the stylist had convinced me they were in style again, my head was spinning dizzily out of control. It felt like I'd been sucker-punched in the gut and then kicked in the head for good measure. I didn't know where this sudden change of heart in Seth was coming from or even how to react, and there was no way I could remain calm and collected. It was too early in the morning for this. I felt like I was collapsing inside, and my familiar world was deflating and caving in and dismantling and unraveling and disintegrating.

"You are a genuine first-class no-good low-down creep!" I yelled, feeling warm spit shoot through my front teeth. I recall using a stronger word than "creep." I was way past tears and fast approaching murder mode. We had spent a lot of money, argued over excursion options, bought a lot of resort wear – even some his-and-hers – and, hardest of all to reconcile, we had looked forward to our trip together so many times since booking it the day after Thanksgiving. It was supposed to be our romantic Valentine's Day cruise. So why was he blowing it like this?

Seth stumbled on, explaining and apologizing clumsily. He said it wasn't my fault, it was his, and a lot of other blah-blah that didn't mean a thing except that he was taking the easy way out.

I said goodbye and clicked off the phone as the driver emerged from the taxi in the swirling snow, his silhouette blocking the headlights as he came to collect my suitcase and load it into the trunk. Before running to the warm shelter of the cab, I shut off the lights and locked and double-checked the front door. I checked that the timer on the table lamp was set so the house wouldn't appear vacant at night while I was gone. I knew the drill about fending for myself since my divorce about ten years earlier and at that moment it was looking like I might be alone again.

My relationship with Seth up until now had been rocky, to be truthful, and we had had our share of ups and downs and breakups and makeups in our almost one-and-a-half years together. More than one person had advised me that it couldn't last. But no, I had to go and fall in love and listen to my stupid heart. Everyone could see that we weren't meant to be. Truth be told, if I'd been perfectly honest about it, I could see it too, but sometimes you cling just because you've come too far already, and you do everything you can to avoid having to start over with someone else.

I guess you could say we were infatuated from the start. But, as I already said, most people looking from the outside said we were too different for it to last. We surprised them when somehow we scraped and crawled our way across the finish line of our first-year marker. Then our respective friends could only fall back on the old default that we were living proof of opposites attracting. We decided to go for it and booked a Caribbean cruise. We were ecstatic at the prospect of our first real getaway together, and we delighted ourselves by imagining the fun we would have snorkeling in warm water along palm-fringed beaches, hiking through rain forests as toucans flew between banana and mango trees, and dancing by moonlight to a steel-pan band under the shimmering glow of tiki torches with oversized piña coladas in our hands.

We even enrolled in a six-week intensive ballroom dance class at Starz Dance Studio to perfect some of our favorite moves and learn some fancy new ones for the cruise. By New Year's we had researched, discussed, argued over and finally selected and booked our shore excursions. The cruise would take place in the days leading up to Valentine's Day, and I had every reason to believe Seth intended to take the opportunity to pop The Question, mostly because I told him that would be the ideal time to do it. Many times. I even splurged on a special red dress for Valentine's Day, anticipating a Valentine's Day dance on the ship. As I recall, it was he who had pushed so hard for us to go in that particular time frame. I swear it wasn't my doing.

I was relieved the driver was not one of those talkative types, and as he approached the airport, the snow was so thick that light from the terminal building appeared murky and dim. He asked me where he should stop, and I told him the American Airlines terminal. A few minutes later, I was shoving off my sneakers with my feet while removing my jacket and sweater and belt and clearing security. I kept trying not to stare as a security woman who could have been Paul Bunyan's fraternal twin, sideburns and all, patted down an old lady who could barely sit up in her wheelchair and probably weighed less than her oxygen tank.

5:48 AM I bought some coffee at Gabby's, remarking to myself how the airport coffee shop always smelled like burnt toast early in the morning. I found a seat at my gate and checked the clock. The flight would not board for another hour and a half, so I pulled out my Kindle. I couldn't read. None of the words in front of me made any sense or even stood still and my mind rolled back over the last year and a half and, more specifically, over the last few months to dig out and turn over any clues or red flags that should have warned me. Even with our turbulent track record, I had not foreseen the end of our relationship coming at me like this, and to be truthful, I don't think there was any way I could have predicted it or prepared myself. Nothing had seemed any different over the last few weeks, so no clues there. I couldn't even take a stab at who it was he'd moved on with, leaving me alone here at Gate B4 with my head pounding like a Tlingit drum in a Raven and Eagle ceremony and my heart twisting in the wind like the last dried-up apple dangling from a tree after the snow started to fly. There were no answers and too many questions.

A gray and snow-swirled day was just starting to break outside the airport window. Anyone looking at me could not have guessed that my life was in a state of upheaval as I sat calmly by myself in the hard, molded-plastic airport chair with a corner chipped off. But there I was, awaiting the same flight that would have taken both of us away to a blissful, romantic vacation, and now would jet me off to celebrate Valentine's Day alone. Some cruise this was shaping up to be.

7:21 AM Tucked into seat 27C with my neck snuggled into one of those ring pillows that looks like an inflatable toilet seat, I had plenty of time to mull things over on the flight from Michigan to Miami. Seth was the kind of man every woman wanted to run away with into the sunset. Well, at least from a distance. Let me start there. But then there was the inevitable encounter with all his former exes who always seemed to pop out of the woodwork when you least expected it. He was very tall and willowy, but athletic and graceful in his movements, which must have come in handy with his job as an emergency medical technician. He had thick brown hair and steel-gray eyes that locked onto mine whenever we talked. He lived in the small house he'd inherited from his parents on the other side of town about a twenty-five-minutes' drive from me. We had never lived together because, even though he had invited me to move in with him a few times, truth be told, I just liked my house better. That was something we always left for a future discussion.

Seth was adventuresome and creative and spontaneous. I was cautious and practical and methodical. He rode horses as a kid while I was cloistered in our study at home learning to play the cello. He was effortlessly charismatic. He walked into a room and everyone crowded around him. I wasn't popular. Throughout school, I'd always been the last one left to fill a team, after everyone else had been chosen.

And boy could that man dance! I wasn't half as good a dancer as he was when we met at a singles dance on Labor Day. But I worked at it and he was a willing instructor. I had no end of ferocious competition from the other women who knew him; a mind-blowing array of ex-girlfriends, ex-dance partners, moms to his kids and an ever-expanding posse of fans and groupies and other hangers-on, all of whom wanted him – without me. I could have sworn they were conspiring to keep me away from Seth, and they used dancing to accomplish that end because they were all fiercely competitive and Seth only danced with the best. But I kept at it and the struggle made me stronger. I got so good that we danced our way to winning a respectable number of competitions at rodeos and charities with country music bands and even raised eyebrows in the ballroom of the Grand Hotel on Mackinac Island one time. That was when he spun me so high over his head that I barely missed taking out the disco ball and the next morning a new rule posted on the ballroom door stated that dancers had to keep at least one foot on the ground. He laughed and called it a proud moment.

While a part of me was in disbelief that Seth had ended our relationship, there was another part that didn't understand why this meltdown hadn't happened sooner. There were so many things about us that clearly didn't fit. What was obvious to our friends and families we simply refused to admit. I kept to my work routine, workouts, and stayed on a budget. He could let the spirit of the moment take him spontaneously to spend the afternoon fishing with a friend or taking his snowmobile for a long ride into the countryside or going to the horse auction and buying an antique horse cart he could hardly afford. Or even buying a twenty-one-hand Belgian horse, which he honest to God did one time.

Then there were our differences of opinion about everything from the best way to slice pickles to the quickest route to the Upper Peninsula. We could agree without a second thought on momentous decisions about life and then start a war over where to put the log pile. Come to think of it, maybe we both knew deep down this day inevitably would come. It probably was destined to happen sooner or later and maybe this was the best way for it to go down.

On the other hand, I suddenly thought, maybe it was all going to work out for us after all. Maybe Seth was going through something I couldn't understand right now, and when he came to his senses, he would catch up with me at Virgin Gorda or St. Lucia. Maybe he was planning a surprise all along! As the plane taxied to a stop in Miami, my heart skipped a beat hoping he was at this very moment on his way to another airport to catch up with me in a romantic overture, there to greet me at the bottom of the gangway as I walked off the ship – alone – at St. Lucia or Tortola or St Bart's. There had to be airports in those places, I was certain, and he might show up and make it all right. My head didn't really believe what my heart wanted so badly to embrace. I felt gutted. I felt abandoned. I felt confused. But I needed to cling to some particle of hope, or my heart was going to burst.

2:47 PM I signed all the requisite forms and presented my passport and credit card at the cruise terminal registration desk for check-in. "Welcome aboard the MS *Minerva*, Miss Milliner," the smiling receptionist nearly sang as she handed me a welcome letter, a map of the ship, and my credit card receipt. I walked up the gangway to board the ship with my newly minted ship pass card. A photographer directed me to a screen in front of which two yellow footprints painted on the floor showed me where to stand for my official welcome-aboard photograph. I couldn't smile and I was sure I blinked when the camera clicked. I was about to embark on an adventure that was already more than I'd booked. I didn't have to look in the mirror to know my brown hair looked more like a robin's nest from wearing my knit cap all the way from Michigan. My lipstick was worn off and I probably looked like I'd been crying. I dreaded the very real prospect of spending an entire cruise alone with no one else to share the sights and experiences. I tried to squelch the dismal thought of spending Valentine's Day alone in my room while other couples were out and about with flowers and chocolates and corsages and champagne, dancing to a live steel-pan band on the pool deck under a full moon. The worst part was, I was out of phone reach of Seth, so I had no way of talking with him, of hearing his voice, of telling him how much I was hoping he'd find a way to catch up with me.

On second thought, maybe that was a blessing.

I felt myself smile slightly for the first time all day when I opened the door and walked into my suite. This would be my own little space for the next couple of weeks and already I liked how it was laid out. It seemed welcoming and efficient. It was small, but as I explored, I discovered cubbies and nooks in clever places. The bed was tightly made, and everything had been thoroughly cleaned. The television was on with a ship officer in his crisp dark blue uniform pointing out the various safety features of the vessel. An ice bucket with a welcome bottle of champagne, a basket brimming with fresh fruit and a box of chocolates crowded the small coffee table invitingly. The first order of business was to empty my suitcase and organize my belongings. This didn't take very long because I hadn't brought much with me. That is, of course, unless you counted the three dozen pairs of shoes, sandals, sneakers, surf socks, Crocs, hiking boots, pumps, and dancing shoes I had jammed into every available corner of my suitcase. I lined them all up neatly, heels against the wall and toes facing out along every available wall in the room. Then I took my ship pass card that also doubled as a room key and left to explore the ship. I went through what anyone who has ever been aboard a cruise ship already knows: exploring the ship is a whole experience in its own right and takes a little doing to get a lay of the land because cruise ships are so big.

A group of passengers was following a hefty woman wearing black pants and a colorful silk blouse. She acted like she knew what she was talking about, so I nonchalantly followed them, just close enough to hear her, but not close enough to commit to belonging to the group. It was a delicate maneuver. She explained that all cruise ships have designated passenger decks and common areas on other decks. A main lobby, or centrum, in the center of the ship hosted a reception desk, shore excursion desk, port shopping expert's desk, and concierge desk, as well as offices for the cruise director, general manager, cruise salesperson, purser, security and other administrators. Throughout the ship were lots of sitting areas, bars, and game rooms and lounges for mingling, munching, drinking or reading, and music venues for evening entertainment. Of course, there was a huge theater for the nightly shows, occasional movies, lectures, and group games like bingo and trivia. Then there were the spas and recreation areas, the boutiques, and of course dining rooms and restaurants and swimming pools and hot tubs. There is never enough time on a cruise ship to experience it all and do everything that is offered.

The woman explained that our ship, the MS *Minerva*, as one of the largest ships of its kind, had too many recreational offerings to explore right then. A list of venues tumbled out of her mouth including stores and boutiques, theaters, restaurants, art galleries, demonstration kitchens, even a rock-climbing wall, skating rink, and classrooms for arts and crafts and cooking, not to mention a pool deck with two giant pools and several hot tubs.

It's like summer camp for grown-ups.

These ships are so big it takes most people the entire cruise to figure out where things are. My incidental guide kidded that people go back and forth trying to remember if their room is on the starboard side aft or the port side fore or midship or wherever, and a comical but common sight in the first few days of any cruise is watching people scurrying in the opposite direction they should be going. "We're late for dinner," says a woman dressed in a long evening gown hanging on the arm of her tuxedo-clad husband as the couple rushes straightaway from the direction of the dining room and headlong in the exact opposite direction toward the ship's infirmary!

I parted from the group on the top deck of the ship and worked my way down all the decks. I stopped to consult the ubiquitous deck plans showcased in mounted frames in the elevator areas and staircases. I moved at a leisurely pace, alternating between the inside and outside decks. It was a pleasant distraction meeting people along the way who were doing the same thing.

It was a balmy February day in Miami, a far cry from the Michigan blizzard I'd left behind. I had already shed my sweater and was enjoying the feeling of the tropical breezes wafting through my tee shirt as I walked across the pool deck to climb up to the sports deck and check out the miniature golf course and basketball court. Only one other couple was there, holding hands and gazing over the railings at the view of the busy dock beneath, but curiously, seeing them embrace did not upset me or make me long for Seth. Perhaps there is something about physically departing from a place that helps one leave the memories behind as well, I mused.

I descended to the promenade deck where couples were walking laps to get in their daily "steps" trying to pre-empt the onslaught of calorie-laden temptations awaiting them at every meal and as many snacks for the next twelve days. A posted placard said a mile was equal to five times around the track, and I made a mental note to add a morning walk to my daily regimen. At least my intentions were noble. I slipped inside a door and walked the short distance to the fitness center, spa, and salon services and peeked inside. Some passengers were already pounding away on the treadmills and elliptical machines, hefting the dumbbells to the point of sweat. The view of the ocean outside was enough to lure me into the fitness room every day. I was beginning to feel excited and already thinking less and less about Seth.

By the time I returned to my room, I had poked my nose into one of the three levels of the main dining room, walked past the library, inquired about a Pilates class in the fitness center, pressed my face against the sparkling windows of the three boutiques and a couple of the gift stores, checked out the theater, peeked at the climbing wall, walked into the bowling alley, watched roller skaters on their way to the rink, and nearly collided with a "Kids' Club" parade, the knee-height revelers wearing paper hats and blowing noisemakers. I ate a panini on perfectly crusty Italian bread and some pasta salad up on the Lido deck, polished it off with a soft ice cream cone, walked through at least four different lounges and the casino, looked into the computer room and studied the ship's projected itinerary on the wall-sized television screen in the main lobby beside the reception desk. Summer camp for adults, indeed!

3:33 PM An announcement for the four o'clock safety drill blared through the ship's loudspeakers, so I had some time to kill. Back in my room again, I took my life jacket down from the closet shelf and laid it on the bed in preparation for the muster drill and then sat on my veranda and watched the bustle of activity on the port several decks beneath me. I watched as immense containers were being laded off cargo ships and piled neatly on the dock, the same corrugated containers stamped with names like Crowley, Dole and Hapag-Lloyd I often saw whisking past me while waiting in my car at a railroad crossing.

At five minutes to four, the voice that identified itself as our cruise director made another safety drill announcement, only this time she emphasized twice that no one on board the ship was allowed to skip the drill. She instructed us to take our life jackets and report to the muster station number printed on our ship pass card. My muster station was A04, so I headed for the main theater two decks below. A few minutes later, the ship's alarm sounded seven short blasts and one long one. That, she said, was the international emergency signal and time for everyone to get to their muster stations for the actual safety drill. The stairway was already crowded with guests being organized and directed by smiling and well-trained crew personnel who stood at their posts in bright lime-green caps and neon-orange life jackets with the ship's logo prominently displayed. The muster drill lasted about twenty minutes, during which time we practiced putting on our life jackets. The loud and clear voice of our cruise director coming through the ship's loudspeakers told us to dress sensibly and in layers in a real emergency, emphasizing the need for socks and sneakers. Perhaps of most importance, we were told to wear a hat because it can be very cold and much of your body heat escapes from your head. In case of an emergency, we were told to wait for instructions from the crew and refrain from panicking. It was also important to remain quiet because the crew would be trying to get information that might be hard to hear over the walkie-talkies or whatever they had to use in an emergency. The cruise director's voice continued, stressing several times the importance of limiting smoking to the designated areas on the ship and explained that fire is the biggest threat at sea. After a pause, she added that MS *Minerva* had a zero-tolerance policy for anything thrown overboard and we were made to understand that infractions would be enforced with severe penalties, including fines and disembarkation at the next port. The room grew quiet as that information was absorbed. A long blast of the alarm signaled the end of the muster drill. I returned to my room and placed my life jacket back on the closet shelf, hoping I would not need it again. I tossed my knit cap up there too actually glad I had brought it along.

When the next announcement from the cruise director came into my room, her tone was decidedly different. In a very cordial and gracious tone she welcomed everyone aboard the magnificent MS *Minerva* and read off a list of activities for the evening, starting with the sail away party up on the pool deck.

I hurried up to the pool deck to join the action. The ship was glistening white and sparkling from all the lights as a brass band dressed in tropical shirts played Bob Marley and Jimmy Buffet music. Waiters were serving champagne, umbrella drinks and wine from silver trays. Tables festooned with garlands of flowers held assortments of hors d'oeuvres and sweets for the taking. Nautical flags spanning the entire ship's length fluttered festively over the entire scene. With three loud blasts of the ship's horn, we peeled away from the pier and headed out to the open sea. There was something exhilarating about watching as the lines were lifted and the ship started to depart from the dock.

It occurred to me right then that we were really leaving the security of land behind us as our floating resort would become a self-contained community on the open waters. Earlier that afternoon, I'd discovered that the boutiques and casinos don't actually open until the ship is a certain distance from port. I imagined it had something to do with not competing with local businesses onshore while the ship was in port. As if a guest could dive off a cruise ship and swim back to Walgreen's for a better deal on a tube of toothpaste!

5:38 PM By the time I returned to my cabin, I was feeling a little groggy and blamed it on the seasick patch I'd put behind my right ear before I'd boarded the ship. This prescription medication looks like a round bandage and is placed on the soft skin behind the ear. It can affect people differently and made me drowsy. I fell into a deep sleep on top of my bedspread.

Later, I was rustled from a coma when I heard someone tapping on the door. As I gradually came to,

I tried to get my bearings and remember where I was in the pitch-black room. I heard the door crack open to reveal the silhouette of a man. He softly introduced himself as Kulit, my Indonesian steward from Java. I turned on the little reading lamp over my bed and saw a very thin and tall young man with a wide smile that bespoke a ready sense of humor. He looked like one of those Javanese shadow puppets, all skinny and joints and gesticulating in every direction at the same time while smiling nonstop. "Miss Marrriannna?" he ventured, politely rolling the r and n for dramatic effect.

"Yes," I answered, wondering how long I'd been asleep.

"You are missing dinner," he remonstrated while shaking a long and knuckly finger at me in a comically parental fashion.

"I was planning to skip it anyway since it's probably too late," I said, not wanting to admit I was too depressed to venture out anymore. "Don't you think I'm too late anyway?" I added, expecting him to agree.

"No!" was his resounding answer. "You should at least go to the dining room and meet your dining companions. Hurry and go right now," he urged, flapping his hands at me. "Hurry, hurry! You still have time. The chef will cook you a good dinner. Very good. Yes, you will see.

"And this message was on your door," he said,

handing me a sealed envelope as I walked toward the door and turned on the overhead lights. Suddenly I was wide awake as I tore open the envelope completely confident that the letter inside was from Seth and would tell me at which upcoming port I could expect to be reunited with him. I removed a letter folded neatly inside. It was written on the ship's stationery, the kind they leave in your drawer. I tried to collect myself and as I read it, I needed to lean against the doorjamb. I read the letter over again. It was not from Seth. Kulit was staring at me with a strange expression, but then turned to leave, stating he would return later to neaten my room and turn down my sheets.

I dabbed on some lipstick and threw on one of my dresses knowing only that I had to get down to the main dining room. Seven years earlier, on a safari in Botswana with an old boyfriend, I had met a couple from Kentucky: Donna, a professor, and her husband, Fred, an engineer. We had stayed in touch occasionally for a couple of years after that. Then one day I received an email from them saying that Donna had been diagnosed with a rare disease of the nervous system and they were moving out West to be closer to a doctor that specialized in treatments for her particular malady. After that, I never heard from them again. Now I was stunned to read that Fred was on the ship and had recognized me from across the room during the muster drill and sent me an invitation to join him for dinner. Ominously, the note didn't mention Donna.

6:48 PM I made my way bobbing and weaving along the corridors that felt like a carnival fun house as the ship bumped and crashed its way through the waves. The ship was picking up speed, apparently making up for lost time while sitting around port all day. No one was in the hallways, and the odors of vacuumed carpeting mingled with varnish, room service coffee, and something that smelled like curry permeated the air along the way. Finally, I found myself facing the maître d' at the dazzling entrance to the dining room. He wanted to see my ship card. No one goes anywhere or does anything on or off the ship without that essential piece of identification. I showed him my card and he asked where my traveling partner was. I told him I was traveling alone. I showed him Fred's name on the letter in my hand and asked where he was seated so I could join him. He looked at the name, consulted his big computer screen, and told me that Fred had not registered with the dining room. He added that I would be seated at my assigned table with my new dining companions, and before I could respond, a formally clad waiter took me by the elbow and guided me to a table at the outermost edge of the room. I was already learning that whatever my plans might have been, the cruise ship's plans prevailed. Aha! I thought as he pulled out the upholstered chair for me, placed a napkin on my lap, and handed me a menu. Table 1A. The last bastion of the Lonely-Hearts Club. Not even Table 1. Had to be 1A like a misfit trying to squeeze into the mainstream.

"May I present Miss Marrriannna," the waiter announced dramatically to the diners. Another r-and-n roller, I observed. Either this was in their training manual or the waiter and my room steward came from the same neighborhood in Java. I looked around me. There were six people seated at the table, already enjoying appetizers, a fact that surprised me, as I had been certain they would have been wrapping up dessert and coffee by now.

As I was settling into my seat, another waiter glided over followed by a young couple and a girl about ten years old. The waiter looked at his chart and realized he had brought them to the wrong table. The little girl spoke up, insisting this was the table she wanted to join. The waiter patiently explained that there was no room for three more diners, but the girl pled. Finally, her parents stepped in and explained that if they were to take our table, they would have to split up, at which the girl offered to sit there herself and let her parents sit elsewhere. The girl's mother gasped audibly. The waiter, sensing a family argument in the brewing, simply apologized to us and headed to a nearby table, giving the family the option of following him or not. All three of them followed him to the table and were seated.

In the split second before she walked away, the girl looked at me with an expression I could only describe as eerie and intense that conveyed an urgency to communicate something. I felt sure I'd seen her somewhere before, but I could not fathom where.

Gilligan's Table

I picked up my leather-bound menu as I simultaneously scanned my dining mates who were continuing their conversations. An older couple was seated across from me, he in round tortoiseshell glasses, a white shirt with a navy blazer and solid blue ascot, she in a lavender chiffon dress with sparkling rhinestones covering her décolletage, with an outdated hairdo that looked like the stylist had made overuse of one of those rat-tailed teasing combs popular in the Beatles and Barbie era.

Next to me was a buxom woman in a low-cut moss-green cocktail dress with puffed-up henna-dyed hair that she'd sprinkled with glittery highlights. Her nail polish was the color of Bazooka bubblegum. Two men on my other side were immersed in a spirited conversation, ignoring everyone else at the table. From what I could hear, they were discussing an invention. They had turned a napkin into some configuration or other and were in a debate over something. Finally, there was a lone reclusive man wearing a beige sweater vest over a collared shirt, a look you'd hardly expect to see on board a fun Caribbean cruise headed for beach destinations and Margaritaville parties. His was the image reserved for the stereotypical nerd which, judging from his pocket protector, he clearly was.

Gradually, the chatter wound down and the older couple greeted me first: she, smiling shyly behind shiny but crooked teeth, and he, telling me I looked horrible. At least he's honest, I thought. Not feeling a need to explain to a group of complete strangers everything I had been through that day, I blamed it on the scopolamine patch behind my ear. Taking charge, the older man boomed: "Pull the damn thing off!" I could have sworn it was Mr. Magoo's voice if I'd closed my eyes.

The glitzy lady with the bouffant ginger-orange hair was fidgeting and kept looking at Mr. Magoo whenever she talked, as if they were the only two people at the table. She was persistent about soliciting his attention, and once she had it she held it tenaciously. She had a strong German accent; I couldn't be certain, but I would have guessed she was flaunting it.

At one point, she leaned over and whispered conspiratorially into my ear that the couple across the table were "millionaires," as if there was a pressing need for me to know that, but I only found her interest in it amusing.

"Have you sailed the MS *Minerva* before?" It was the buxom lady asking the millionaire.

"No," he answered. "This is the first time for us. I don't know if I like it," he said as he looked around dismissively. "The décor in this dining room is positively hideous," he shouted. "Look at those atrocious clusters of grapes hanging down from the ceiling." He pointed with one hand to the chandelier behind me and I turned around and looked up to see what he was talking about. "I don't know if I can stand to sit here night after night and look at that ugly thing.

I'm worried one of those vile grape clusters will fall and smash my waiter's head before the night is done. And I won't get my drink."

"Well," the curvaceous lady wrinkled her nose, "I have been on the sister ship, the MS *Cleopatra*. It was much more beautiful and there were no grape clusters hanging from the dining room ceiling, I can assure you of that."

"Well, that's a relief!" Mr. Magoo said, wiping his hand across his forehead to dramatize the point. "I hope there weren't any deadly asps coming out of the walls, though," he added, chuckling heartily at his own joke.

The voluptuous woman laughed mirthfully and sipped from her wine glass as the waiter deposited her dinner in front of her. "It looks very good," she said to her plate, sounding genuinely surprised.

"What did you order?" the older of the two inventors asked, craning his neck to get a closer look at her plate.

"Osso bucco," she replied, taking up her silver knife and fork.

"I didn't know what that was. I ordered something I could identify. Prime rib and mashed potatoes," he said as the waiter reached around him with an enormous plate.

We went around the table announcing our first names to each other, having made an executive committee decision to save our last names for later in the cruise when we got to know each other better. After all, we had twelve days together, so we could take our time getting to know each other and we wouldn't remember everyone's last names anyway.

The millionaire started first, continuing to take the lead in everything like a self-appointed jury foreman. He stood up and announced importantly, "I am Marshall Mooney the Third and my wife is Lorelai. We're from Hollywood and I alone may call my wife Dovey. The rest of you may address her as Mrs. Mooney."

"And what do you do, Mr. Marshall Mooney the Tird?" the buxom lady asked, her accent causing an embarrassing mispronunciation.

"Oh, ho, ho," he answered. "We'll wait for another time to discuss things like that, won't we? Suffice it to say it's what I've already done that explains how we can afford to be here. Isn't that right, Dovey?" He looked down at his blushing bride of seventy-something who giggled and hid her mouth with one hand.

"Well, I am sure you are a very substantial pillar of the community," Mrs. Buxom said approvingly, never taking her eyes off his expensive blazer and ascot.

"I may as well introduce myself now," she announced to the table and half the dining room as well. "My name is Ginny. I'm from Austria, but now I live in Boca. I used to be an actress you see." She paused dramatically and batted her eyelashes for extra effect. "I starred and sang and danced my way across the stages of Europe in my day," she gloated. "They tell me I have a beautiful voice. I could have gone on to sing opera. La Scala, *Aida, La Traviata.*" She was mixing up operas with opera houses, but who was keeping score? "When I was young I married a Greek god. But he turned out to be a god-damn Greek," she said, laughing. "So now I am traveling the world alone and must say I am enjoying it so far."

"You sing?" the younger of the inventors asked. "Maybe you'll sing for us on karaoke night," he added.

My turn. I didn't stand up. I didn't see the need to stand for the six other people gathered around one table. I simply said I was Marianne. I was from Michigan, and I was happy to be on the cruise, which wasn't totally honest. I didn't say anything about Seth or bring up the fact that I was feeling very seasick. Everyone nodded politely but seemed unimpressed. I was relieved no one asked what I did for a living.

Next it was the two inventors' turns.

"I'm Skip," the older man said. He had a very jolly smile. He pointed at his younger companion and said, "And this is my son, Denny."

I was momentarily distracted from my seasickness. His son? I had all I could do to see one scintilla of evidence that they shared the same genetic code. The father was pale and paunchy and freckled and nearly bald but for a handful of lonely strands stretched over the top of his pate from his right temple to his left ear. The son was skinny and scrappy, and his dark beady eyes darted back and forth around the table like he was suffering from a bad case of separation anxiety from his video games. He looked out from under a knife-straight edge of black bangs more popular in the sixties than in the present decade. He must have been in his early twenties.

"We're from Cleveland," Skip added as an afterthought. "We're going to do a little deep-sea fishing together. M'boy here, Denny, just graduated and starts his job when we get back home, so we thought we'd come on a little cruise, the two of us together. You see, his mother just remarried, so Denny can't live with her anymore. He'll be moving in with me once we get home from the cruise on account of his job is right on Lake Erie. Looks like m'boy's going to follow my footsteps in the family trade. I'm retired Merchant Marines and Denny here has joined the Coast Guard."

Everyone nodded in passive approval. Then we all turned our attention to the nerdy guy as the waiter replenished the bread baskets.

"I am Dr. Feerum," he said formally and succinctly, rolling a chopstick from his pad thai between his thumb and forefinger. "I am a professor."

There was a shocker.

That was all he said. I figured he was either shy or conceited. There was a long pause while we waited for him to elaborate. Even Ginny started asking something but thought better of it and stopped mid-sentence. That was all we got from the professor, so we murmured our pleasure at hearing this and gratefully looked up when

Marshall Mooney the Third took the metaphorical mic again.

"Well, here's to twelve days of camaraderie and good times and high adventure among friends on the good ship MS *Minerva*," he said. "Let's all toast to Table 1A!" With that, we raised our glasses in unison and chink-chinked one another all around. As I looked about me, something was becoming crystal clear. I was sitting with a cast of characters I'd known from way back when, in the earliest days of my childhood. There was a skipper, his sidekick, a millionaire and his wife, a glitzy one-time actress now decades past her sell-by date, and a professor. It was then that I had to face what there was no denying. I was sitting at Gilligan's Table. And if this was Gilligan's Table, then I guess that made me, and here's the kicker - the girl next door, Mary Ann.

After picking at a dinner of shrimp cocktail and a Caesar salad followed by bow-tie pasta swimming in buttery garlic sauce with portobello mushrooms, I went back to my cabin for a good swirl of Listerine and grabbed my sweater. A few minutes later, I found myself thirteen rows back in an aisle seat in the chilly theater waiting for the night show to begin. It was something called "Neon City" and turned out to be a lively cabaret revue with leggy dancers and young energetic singers with perfect hair and teeth all moving and dancing in practiced synchronism. Lights strobed and changed colors even as they splashed angular patterns and rays across the stage floor and foreheads of the singers and dancers who stomped and strutted their perfect bodies in shimmery costumes for forty-five high-energy minutes.

At the show's conclusion, Pearl, our gracious cruise director, took the microphone to introduce herself and acknowledge the band and performers and stage crew. Her dark chestnut skin glowed warmly in the bright spotlights as she stated that she proudly hailed from the beautiful island of Jamaica. This cruise would not go there, but she asked us to consider booking a future cruise to Jamaica while on board, and she would be sure to invite anyone who did so to lunch at her home overlooking an idyllic Jamaican beach. The audience applauded in enthusiastic approval. Then she greeted everyone officially and promised the cruise of a lifetime with more spectacular shows, guest entertainers, and recreational and social events to fill the next twelve days aboard the beautiful MS *Minerva*. Finally, she invited everyone to the Paris Lounge on the top deck for some after-the-show dancing and two-for-one drinks.

By now I figured I had nothing to lose, having survived a traumatic day and still standing up. So, I crammed myself into an elevator bulging with about a dozen other passengers and we ascended skyward to the top deck where the lovely Paris Lounge awaited us with subtle lights and a dance band and a singer already in the process of crooning "Smooth Operator" while a few showoffs glided effortlessly across the polished parquet dance floor. It didn't take long for someone to tap my shoulder for a dance. He introduced himself as Roy, the assistant cruise director. I remembered him from Pearl's introduction just a few minutes earlier in the theater. The band had switched to a slow rumba, and for at least the duration of the dance I felt like I could go on and dance without Seth in my life.

After about an hour in the Paris Lounge, I headed back to my suite. On my bed, Kulit had left two chocolate mints, a bingo card, and the ship's daily newsletter, *The Tides,* that listed all the events for the following day. I climbed into bed and read it from cover to cover, circling the activities that looked interesting to me, including a morning workout, a lecture, a dance class, a computer class, a digital camera class, a trivia game, a belly-flop contest, and a cooking demonstration, knowing full well I would never get to do them all. As I turned to switch off the light, I noticed something new in my room: a monkey cleverly made from white towels was dangling playfully from the curtain. It was no doubt the handiwork of Kulit, who it appeared was also an expert in towel origami. I smiled as I tumbled headlong into my disheveled dreams.

Chapter Two

Day Two: February 4, Thursday
En Route to Spanish Town, BVI.
Weather updates will be given in the morning by the cruise
director and midday by the captain.

MORNING BROKE LIKE A LASER BEAM across the proverbial bow, with a blindingly radiant sapphire sky reigning over a brilliant turquoise sea. That's how it is in the Caribbean. One minute it is dark, and the next minute the sun is up and everything is drenched in brilliant, blindingly bright daylight. I hung off my balcony railing breathing in the sea air and watching the waves break and splash against the fast-moving hull of the ship several decks beneath me. A little while later I was sitting in the deck chair rereading *The Tides* when there was a rap on the door, and in walked Kulit.

"Ah! Good morning, Miss Marrriannna!" he greeted me. "Did you have a good dinner last night?"

"Yes, thanks. I was just reading this newsletter." I held up *The Tides* as I arose from the deck chair and went into the stateroom. "There are so many activities while we're at sea today, I don't think I'll have time to do everything I want to do," I said. "There are aerobics classes and lectures and ice sculpture demonstrations and belly-flop contests and a computer class and a lecture and a chef demonstration and trivia and afternoon tea, and a show tonight and even dance classes. Not to mention swimming and miniature golf and bowling and climbing the rock wall and shopping and just sitting right here on the balcony and reading a book from the library." It was as if the offerings had expanded overnight.

"The cruise ship is a very busy place," Kulit said, smiling and wagging a finger at me, which statement was probably going to be the biggest understatement of the day. He looked around the fairly neat and organized room, focusing on the sixty-seven pairs of shoes that lined every available inch along the baseboards. Obviously, I didn't bring enough shoes because I was standing there in bare feet.

Kulit said excitedly, "Breakfast is served now, Miss Marianna!" You should go to the restaurant and the chef will make you something very special. What do you want? An omelet? Pannycakes? Lamb chops? Order whatever you like. It's very, very good. Or you can go upstairs to the Lido deck and help yourself at the buffet and sit outside. Very nice too." He smiled. I felt he was hinting that he wanted to get started cleaning up my room and needed me to get out of there. I told him I'd be ready in a half hour. I'd slept in too late to attend the morning stretch-and-tone session in the fitness center, so I showered and dressed and hustled to the Lido deck for some coffee and breakfast. I was no stranger to living alone and was beginning to appreciate the beauty of cruising alone by not having to coordinate with anyone else. I also appreciated the flexibility to change plans on a dime with only myself to notify and approve the change.

Up on the Lido deck, I strolled among the tempting breakfast offerings lined up in appetizing displays along the twenty-mile serpentine counters garnished with tropical fruits cleverly carved to resemble playful monkeys and fish and tropical flowers. The endless variety of offerings sated my eyes so completely that when it came right down to it, I couldn't decide and ended up taking my usual everyday breakfast at home: some oatmeal and fresh fruit. Then I went to find an empty table on the outside veranda. Oh, and I grabbed an iced carrot muffin on the way. Cruises are for splurging, after all. I plunked myself down at a table set for four under a sprawling sun umbrella. A waiter was pouring me some coffee when Skip and Denny from Gilligan's Table the night before came by and asked if they could join me. "Please do," I said, pointing to the empty chairs.

"We didn't want to say anything, but Mr. Mooney was right, Marianne. You looked pretty uncomfortable last night. That seasickness can really get to you. Are you better today?"

The mere mention of seasickness brought it to the forefront of my consciousness and suddenly I could identify a dull not-quite-rightness in the pit of my stomach that wasn't made any better by looking out at the water dipping and bobbing beyond the edge of the deck. In the time it had taken me to shower and come up to the Lido deck, the water had turned from lapis blue to battleship gray. The sun was no longer shining, having been replaced by a low ceiling of threatening clouds. That is how it is in the Caribbean. Blissful and idyllic one minute and a pitching and roiling tempest the next. I thought about a meadow of peaceful daisies blowing in a gentle wind on a familiar Michigan hill and tried to stay calm, persuading myself to believe that the scopolamine patch was hard at work keeping me steady.

"Thanks for the reminder," I said, careful not to turn my head too fast for fear of barfing all over them. I was really beginning to feel the sea rise in my stomach just then.

"So, you are traveling all by yourself?" Skip asked with a little too much interest. "I mean it's none of my business, but I know it's not the easiest thing in the world for a single woman, or a woman without someone like a guy to travel with. I always told Cindy, that's my daughter, to travel with a friend before she got married. Now her husband can tell her that," he said and elbowed his son as they laughed at what apparently was a family joke. He was eating a hefty Western omelet with abundant helpings of link sausages and home fries swimming in ketchup and an assortment of toast, donuts, muffins, and other pastries on a separate dinner-size plate. Denny was focused on something approximating an Egg McMuffin.

"What'd you think of Dr. Feerum?" Denny suddenly asked, looking up at me. "Now that guy is hiding something. Probably killed someone and hid the body under his front porch," he said, which caused the first visible reaction from Skip who started snickering while smearing grape jelly on a banana muffin.

"Denny and I were thinking we're going to keep an eye on that one," Skip said resolutely. "And you ought to stay away from him, being single and alone and a mighty pretty lady at that," he added.

Denny looked at me with a goofy expression and I decided he was the one I should avoid at all costs. The jury was still out on Dr. Feerum. Peculiar, yes, but not in a threatening way. Earlier I had been toying with the notion of changing to another dinner table or switching from early to late seating to avoid that gang altogether, but now I wanted to stay right where I was at Gilligan's Table, reasoning I'd run into goofballs everywhere else and at least mine were the devils I already knew. I had a strong hunch that these characters would provide me with automatic nightly entertainment, and I wanted to see it through.

"Well," I said, again careful not to turn my head too fast, "I have to excuse myself and get ready to go to the lecture. I think it starts in about fifteen minutes and I want to find a good seat."

"Lecture?" Skip asked, sounding interested.

"Yes," I said. "It's listed in *The Tides*. There's a presentation this morning about snorkeling in the Caribbean. If you're planning on doing any snorkeling, it might be interesting," I added helpfully.

"You interested?" Skip looked at his son.

"Sounds good, but I signed up for a tour of the bridge," Denny said. "You can come with me or go to the lecture because I think they're at the same time, Dad. I'm going to sit here a while and watch for whales," he went on as he integrated his spoon in the seesaw game he was already playing with his fork and knife over his Egg McMuffin. Skip thought about it and decided to join Denny for the bridge tour.

I GOT TO THE THEATER EARLY and selected an aisle seat in the ninth row. Close enough to take it all in, but with access to a quick escape at the end. People shuffled in and took their seats, steadying themselves from the ship's sway, the aisles filling up faster than the center seats. The room took its time to fill up with couples and kids and most people coming alone because their spouse was at one of the other events going on simultaneously like the Caribbean Gems talk where you could win a tanzanite bracelet for being one of the first fifty people to attend, or bingo in the Pirate's

Den, or an art talk followed by an auction in the ship's gallery. A few people waved at others they recognized, but this close to the beginning of the cruise, there wasn't too much familiarity yet.

As the room quietly filled, the speaker stood at his podium talking with the lighting technician while the sound technician taped a little microphone wire to his cheek and clipped a battery pack to his belt. The white movie screen suddenly lit up with a colorful title, "Snorkeling in the Caribbean," in bright teal blue with the speaker's name and website prominently displayed at the bottom. A photograph filled the background with some stunning red and purple corals being visited by delicate translucent fish with diaphanous fins fluttering like silk in the iridescent blue waters. Some music was playing lightly in the background, Super Mario Brothers' "Underwater Theme," I thought. The lighting man went back to his post in the rear of the theater and the speaker tapped the podium to get everyone's attention. By now the room was over half full and people were streaming inside trying to take any available seating they could find in the dark.

Just then, the ship's loudspeaker crackled to life and the voice of Pearl the cruise director bounced through, welcoming everyone to a brand-new day of endless fun and entertainment aboard the beautiful MS *Minerva*. She reported the temperature followed by a rundown of the morning's activities and events. Someone distracted me with a tap on the shoulder. It was Marshall Mooney the Third. "Good morning," he said cheerfully. "Nice to see you are up and looking better. Mind if I sit here?"

"Be my guest," I said, wondering just how badly I had looked the night before, as he squeezed over my knees and dropped into the empty seat to my left. Leaning over, he whispered at my face, "Dovey is already hard at work at bingo this morning. Couldn't drag her away from it, as I'm afraid it's where she will be for the duration of the cruise. Well, either there or in the casino," he chuckled. Then, looking up at the stage and around the fast-filling and nearly darkened auditorium, he asked, "So what is this all about?" as if he had just dropped in from the moon. I was about to explain the self-evident when the speaker tapped his podium and then tapped the business end of his microphone and cleared his throat saying "testing" at the same time. The background music faded away and a spotlight illuminated his face and suit and tie as a new slide flashed on the screen behind him. With a distinctive French accent, he introduced himself as Dr. Remy Pinot, and joked about growing up in France with the name of a wine. He thanked everyone for coming when they could have been up on the pool deck watching the sexy legs contest instead. The audience laughed at what must be the oldest opening line on a cruise ship stage. He explained that he was a retired professor of comparative literature from the Sorbonne in Paris. But a lifetime of recreational travel and diving had brought him to the point where he found a niche in presenting educational lectures on cruise ships. When he said he was a personal friend of the Jacques Cousteau family, you could hear people mumbling as they leaned in with renewed interest.

Dr. Pinot plunged headlong into his subject, flashing a high-powered laser pointer at pictures of things like coral and sharks and turtles and seahorses on the screen. He started with a general background about the geological origins of the Caribbean islands, pointing out that the seven thousand or so Caribbean islands are naturally divided into three major groupings, including the Bahamas chain, the Greater Antilles, and the Lesser Antilles. Pointing to a geographical map of the region on the screen, he explained that the Greater Antilles grouping is made up of continental rock and is considered a subdivision of the North American continent. It includes the Caribbean's four biggest islands: Cuba, Hispaniola, Jamaica, and Puerto Rico. This grouping also includes the tiny archipelagos of the Cayman Islands. He informed us that all the Greater Antilles islands combined contain the lion's share, something like ninety percent, of the land mass in the Caribbean. By contrast, the Lesser Antilles, he said, is a string of smaller islands that forms a gentle arc from the Virgin Islands to Venezuela, defining the eastern edge of the Caribbean Sea. He said these islands are volcanic in origin, and many of them still exhibit volcanic activity including active calderas, underwater hot springs, and volcanic eruptions in recent history. He showed us on a map of the region how this volcanic necklace was a continuation of the Colombian Andes mountain range running right under the sea.

Dr. Pinot said he would have more to say on the individual islands in due time, assuring us that our itinerary would take us to islands in those three major groupings.

His talk made an exploration of everything under the water's surface too tempting to pass up. He was encouraging enough to persuade even the most reluctant passenger to consider snorkeling. He offered practical information about the best beaches for snorkeling and scuba diving along our itinerary, how to fit and use the snorkeling equipment safely, and encouraged first timers to dive right in, so to speak. At the end of the presentation, he opened the floor up to questions, but I took full advantage of my quick exit seat and dashed up the aisle and out of the auditorium, this time heading for the library.

One thing I always insist on no matter where I am is a good book by my bed. If there's a rainy day or even a half hour of down time, nothing beats reading a chapter or two from a novel or mystery or especially a book written by a local author about the local vicinity. The library, I learned, operated on the honor system, so I had access to any of the books at any time as long as I returned them by the last day of the cruise. Inside, cushy upholstered chairs were arranged in clusters between polished wooden bookcases with glass fronts and crystal knobs. Little hidden nooks isolated couples sitting on brass-studded leather chairs reading and sipping espressos together. I drooled over the tempting titles, wishing the cruise was twice as long for all the good reading there. I selected a book from the "Caribbean Favorites" shelf entitled *Two on the Isle* by Robb White, an author I hadn't heard of. It sounded interesting, and the dust-jacket description promised an adventure set on a tiny island near Tortola, one of our ports-of-call.

While I was in the library, a uniformed staff member was busy shelving books and answering occasional questions, mostly about where things were on the ship. She introduced herself as Angela and stated that she was the ship's social hostess. She asked if I was traveling alone or with someone else.

"As it turns out, I am cruising alone," I answered truthfully, not wanting to go into the details of my recent break-up. She didn't seem interested in an explanation anyway, and simply reported that she was planning some get-togethers for solo travelers throughout the cruise. Would I be interested in joining such events? She upped the ante with a promise of free wine. I hadn't considered myself single for a while, but I guess that officially described me now. "Sure," I said, giving her my room number so she could add me to the invitation list. I asked how she became a social hostess, and she explained that she started out on ships as a dancer and singer. I could believe it, judging from her tall and svelte figure. I asked what a cruise ship social hostess did exactly, and when she described that her function was to organize and host social events, like cocktail parties and dinners – drinks included – to promote safe meeting and mingling on board, I joked that she should sleep with one eye open or I'd be after her job! I meant it to be funny and really kind of a compliment, but she copped an immediate attitude, snapping back that she would send me an invitation to the next solo traveler event, and then she went back to filing books, never cracking so much as a smile.

SINCE I HAD MISSED my morning jog around the deck, I opted for the dance lesson to get some exercise and headed to the cha-cha class. As is always the case with social dance classes, the majority of participants are women because even the married ladies can't always sweet-talk their husbands into taking a dance class. So, adding the single women to those who couldn't drag their husband or partner along resulted in about two-thirds women with never enough unattached men to go around. Roy, the assistant cruise director who had danced with me the night before, was teaching this class. Soft-spoken, and keeping everything light and humorous, he soon succeeded in having the few men who were there actually doing a respectable cha-cha.

A few minutes into the lesson, a solitary figure

appeared at the back of the room and stood there watching the activity. It was none other than Dr. Feerum from Gilligan's Table. Thank goodness, I thought. We needed all the men we could get. Apparently Roy had the same thought because as soon as he noticed Dr. Feerum, he invited him to take one of the many solo women as his partner for the next lesson. Dr. Feerum extended his hand to an attractive Asian lady standing near the edge of the dance floor. Maybe it was the lighting or the music or the fact that I was not as tired or seasick as I had been earlier, but on closer inspection, Dr. Feerum was not so bad looking. He had a thick shock of wavy bisque-colored hair. He wore glasses that looked like they were borrowed from T.S. Eliot and a shy smile fixed on his mouth. He seemed to be in pretty decent shape and was wearing leather-soled shoes, as if he'd brought them along specifically for dancing. He swept Minga off her feet with an ostentatious flair that left everyone else looking on in admiration. Roy clapped and went over to shake Dr. Feerum's hand, then took Minga for himself. Dr. Feerum came over to me and took me in his arms very naturally. I noticed he was a good dance height for me. Truth be told, I always had to reach up to Seth when we danced, something that was always just uncomfortable enough to be on my mind. We hustled through the cha-cha, and then as if he were hired to do so, Dr. Feerum thanked me and moved on to the next single lady, leaving me to dance on my own, something I had not done in a while. I was already looking forward to dinner at Gilligan's Table that night so I could strike up a conversation with Dr. Feerum, knowing we had something in common.

By the end of the lesson, I had danced mostly on my own with a few spins around the floor with Roy and Dr. Feerum intermittently. Once while dancing with Dr. Feerum, I mentioned that we were assigned to the same dinner table, and he looked at me strangely as if he had not noticed or did not believe me and moved quickly along to the next lady. Maybe he just didn't care. When the forty-five minutes ended, Roy stopped the music and said something motivating and complimentary that made us all clap for our great efforts. Then he invited us to join him the next day for another dance class and to keep Valentine's Day in mind because there would be a dance contest with prizes. Everyone laughed at the mere suggestion that a couple of spins through a cruise ship dance class could qualify anyone to enter, let alone win, a dance contest. Before Roy dismissed us, he handed the mic to Angela, the social hostess, who looked just as glum as she had when I'd left her in the library earlier. She announced that the grand prize for the Valentine's Day dance contest would be a bottle of champagne and offered entry forms for any interested couples.

From the dance class, I made my way back to the theater which was filling up with people forming their own small groups. This was the trivia crowd, a venerable tradition on these ships, usually hosted by the cruise director. Trivia is one of the biggest sea-day events because it is very social and lends itself to lots of interaction, heated debate and, more often than not, passionate arguments. Okay, out-and-out fights. By the end of the cruise, trivia has usually risen to the level of blood sport. Teams gang up on each other and even attack the trivia host, disputing the correct answers. Cruise directors that serve as trivia hosts endure boos, attacks on their intelligence and, from time to time, well-aimed shoes. Normally civilized people run amok. I figured I would stick around for trivia and fall into a group in need of more players. Pearl entered the theater and started organizing her notes at the lectern. She was smiling and exuding a real party spirit while the stage manager discreetly slipped a microphone over her head, taped the speaker part to her cheek and hooked the battery pack to a hidden pocket. She was wearing a brightly colored caftan in a distinctive African print batik that suited her personality and conveyed confidence and control. She lived every inch the image of "the woman in charge" while remaining gracious and cordial.

From what I could gather, these trivia players were such experienced cruisers that Pearl didn't even have to give any instructions or explain what was going on. The newcomers simply learned by osmosis. Players formed teams that would become cohesive units for the rest of the cruise, and reputations and friendships would rise and fall along with their teams' daily successes or failures. As Pearl called out for team names around the room, the team names were lobbed at her so she could record them. They were clever names like Battle the Bulge, Seas the Day, Cruise Control, and Nautical but Nice, that one from an all-women team. Pearl played along, giggling and cracking jokes in response as she worked the room. Once the team names were registered, Pearl started the game by asking a series of questions, giving each team a few minutes to discuss its official answer before writing it down.

I took it that no one on our team was an educator, professor, author, former ambassador, rocket scientist, doctor, rock star, judge, CEO, journalist, ex-parolee, or anyone with a specialty in anything, so we fielded the diverse questions from the wide and varied landscapes of our respective life's experiences. We didn't do too badly on the questions about celebrities and pop culture, mostly because of our youngest member, Meredith, who was an assistant marketing executive for an advertising agency in Wichita. But we were stumped on just about everything else. I mean, "How many earths could fit inside the sun?" Really? Who would go around with that little nugget of trivia stuck in their back pocket? The answer was one-and-a-third million, but we didn't come close. We could have used an astrophysicist for that one. And "What percentage of speeches in Shakespeare's plays is recited by women?" Who comes up with this stuff, anyway? Well, we didn't know the answer was seventeen percent, but you can pretty well bet that's one thing I will never forget from now on.

After twenty questions plus one bonus, meaning one free point for everyone, Pearl asked the teams to switch answer sheets with a nearby team to score each other's. Then as she publicly asked for the team scores, she made sure to add humiliation to injury by pointing out exactly where each team was sitting for everyone to see. Our team came in pretty close to rock bottom. I didn't want to commit to playing with them again, so I thanked them all and said I might have to play on another team next time, figuring any new team would be an improvement. I know that's probably not the best attitude, but a girl's gotta do what a girl's gotta do. Besides, I was meaning to ask Gilligan's Table if they wanted to form a trivia team. Or at least, that's what crossed my mind just then.

Still in my dance shoes from the cha-cha class, I slipped back to my stateroom to change them and consult my to-do list. It was already lunchtime and all I had accomplished since breakfast was attending the snorkeling lecture, finding a library book, taking a dance lesson, and suffering an abysmally embarrassing and public loss in trivia. I decided to skip the computer and camera classes, reasoning that I should go up to the pool deck since the day was turning beautiful and sunny. I changed into my bathing suit and cover-up and headed for the pool. On my way, I passed two young women talking intently with each other on the staircase landing. Each spoke English in a different accent, and both were gesturing wildly. They seemed dreadfully agitated about something and one was even sobbing. When I stopped to ask if there was anything I could do to help, I realized from their name tags that they were crew members. The sobbing one looked at me with an expression of pure agony. Her huge brown eyes were accentuated by perfectly shaped eyebrows and smudges of eye shadow applied artfully to the outer corners of her eyes. Her lips were full and pouting as she tried to smile at me while holding back her tears. "We play in the string quartet. My name is Danita," she said as she offered her hand. "And this is Valetta," she said, motioning to the other young woman, a startling redhead with steel-gray eyes and flushed cheeks. Valetta offered her hand and smiled bravely.

"I wish I could help you," I said in earnest. "Is there something I can do?"

"Only if you know how to play the cello," Valetta burst out, her shoulders suddenly convulsing with uncontrollable shaking. Danita then explained that they had not been able to find their cellist anywhere on the ship after it had sailed from Old San Juan the day before the present cruise began. There was great concern that the missing woman, Sabrina, may either have left the ship in Old San Juan and gone AWOL, or missed it by mistake, or had fallen overboard or worse. Nobody knew where she was, and an intensive search was underway behind the scenes. The musicians were very worried about their friend while simultaneously trying to figure out how to perform until she, or a replacement, could be found. Danita touched my shoulder and apologized for bringing me into a crew dilemma on my vacation. But I told her that, as it turned out, I actually knew how to play the cello, having been forced against my will to take cello lessons when I was young, my youthful protestations falling on the unsympathetic ears of my parents who were determined to cram some semblance of culture and civility into the cracks and crevices of my otherwise misspent youth. I offered to help if I could, never dreaming they might actually take me up on it.

Danita and Valetta both looked at me, tilting their heads quizzically in opposite directions. Valetta's mouth was open, her sparkling white teeth glistening between her bright coral lips. "You can play Haydn? Bach? Mozart?"

"Yup, Yup and Yup," I answered. "Vivaldi, too, and Brahms. Not as well as you can, I am sure," I laughed. "But I took lessons until I went to college, and I still play from time to time for the fun of it. I'd need to practice up a bit, but I can at least try to help you."

The women thanked me profusely, asked for my stateroom number, and ran off, gesturing and talking together. I expected they would call me back to thank me and report happily that Sabrina had miraculously reappeared. But when I returned to my room after my swim, I found a white envelope in the message placket on my door. Inside was a very nice letter from Pearl, the cruise director, accepting my offer to play the cello with the string quartet until Sabrina was located, with the promise of a free cruise of my choice in the future. It sounded like a fair exchange to me, and when I called her at the number she had provided, she asked me to meet her in her office directly.

Pearl's office was very efficient and surprisingly stark. The office was nothing like the public part of the ship with its plush carpeting, warm curtains, tapestries, and dark wood accents. This was an antiseptic workspace with metal file cabinets and a metal desk, bulletin boards crowded with reports and graphs and charts, and a bare hard metal floor painted white enough to make you sneeze. The lighting was not the warm lighting in the public part of the ship, but the intensely bright light of a hospital surgery unit. There were no cozy pictures of family or doggy or warm-and-fuzzy mementos cluttering Pearl's desk. This was all business; everything in front of her was there to help her direct and schedule the ship's entertainment.

I knew that Pearl was tall from the way she'd looked on stage the night before and again while she was hosting the trivia game, and now standing next to her, she absolutely towered over me. Her hair was tucked up in a beautiful batik turban that made her beautiful amber eyes the first thing you saw in her wide and open face. She was extremely gracious, keeping a professional demeanor at all times, and even though we both knew she was a very busy lady with a million things to juggle, she treated me as if I were the only person in the world, leaning in when we talked, and focusing directly on my face. Her eyes never darted at the clock or at her watch or out the window or at anything on her desk. She seemed relaxed and engaged in our conversation, and she really made me feel important, thanking me for even considering helping out by joining the quartet on my cruise. She said there'd be no hard feelings if I wanted to back out. But I was determined to keep my promise. Besides, adventures like this don't come every day, and one thing I've learned in three and a half decades is that you never know where an adventure will take you, especially one that comes out of the blue. After discussing the details with Pearl, I signed some papers and asked for a rehearsal and performance schedule as well as the sheet music I would need.

Just as we were finishing up, Danita entered the cruise director's office as if on cue with an armload of sheet music. She assured me that if I couldn't play everything perfectly, not to worry. The string quartet musicians would help me and could even modify the program if necessary. Then she led me to the rehearsal room where Sabrina's cello was stored in a closet and told me I could practice there any time. I looked at the schedule she handed me and noticed that the quartet was scheduled for an afternoon tea performance at four o'clock with no rehearsal beforehand. I was relieved, however, that the pieces planned for teatime included music I already knew and could perform with minimal practice, so I went upstairs for some lunch and then returned to practice until half past three. When the group met me in the practice room, they brought a gown for me to wear that matched the other girls' gowns. After I changed, I followed them upstairs to the Paris Lounge where our music stands were set up.

I HAD BEEN TO HIGH TEAS before, but few were as extravagant and tasteful as the scene set before me. Small tables were draped with spotless white tablecloths, each one provisioned with polished silverware and creamy white porcelain teapots. A bud vase with real flowers added color to each table. Tuxedoed waiters circulated among the tables pushing trolleys and creating a hubbub of activity at each table. The trolleys were laden with scones and bowls of fresh clotted cream and fruit preserves and finger sandwiches and platters showing off tortes and pies and cupcakes and chocolate éclairs and apricot-filled pastries and cookies and miniature cheesecakes and sandwiches. The variety was as irresistible as it was endless. The waitstaff was cheerfully proffering selections from the heavy trays of the sweets while offering tea selections for the piping hot water in the teapots. Guests sat formally around the tables in a mellow delirium of merriment, a low-volume chatter filling the room as silver clinked against china. Elegant women in dressy hats caught my attention. These were not sun hats, but statement hats: feathered and bowed and beribboned hats that could have turned heads at the Kentucky Derby. Amidst all this, I noticed the couple and young girl who had nearly been seated at our table. The couple was sitting with another couple while their daughter sat on the floor nearby beneath a window, absorbed in a book. I thought that was refreshing: a young person surrounded by a cultural event, reading. It was certainly a far cry from the usual scenes of kids today, with their heads bent over a device playing video-type games.

Mario, the only male member of the quartet, gave the nod, his chin planted firmly on the bottom of his violin, and we all started playing Pachelbel's Canon in unison. I kept my focus on the sheet music and concentrated on blending in with the other musicians, grateful that there was so much else going on around us to distract the listeners from any errant squeaks from my cello. It went very well considering, and after an hour of playing a classical medley that included Beethoven's Ode to Joy, Handel's Chamber Suite, Vivaldi's Concerto in D Minor, and Corelli's Concerto Grosso #10, we took our music off the stands, collected our instruments, and headed downstairs to the rehearsal room to put everything away. As soon as my borrowed cello was safely stowed in its closet, Mario announced that we'd have a long rehearsal the next morning in preparation for the captain's reception in the evening. Already this was beginning to feel like a real commitment, but I welcomed the adventure and wanted to see it through.

The other musicians dispersed to attend to other duties on board the ship as I reverted to being a passenger again, returned to my room, and changed for dinner.

The red light flashing on the phone heralded a message from Angela inviting me to join the solo traveler group for a brief cocktail reception at the Mar-teeny Bar before dinner, apologizing for the short notice. I checked the clock and guessed the reception was still in progress, so I went directly to the Mar-teeny Bar. Right away, a couple of people recognized me from the string quartet, and I had to refrain from mentioning the missing musician when asked how I came to join the quartet. I simply said I had been invited because I play the cello and left it at that. Most of the conversation was about the ship and its stunning amenities and friendly crew, and people were already comparing notes about their respective shore excursion options. With free cocktails providing all a person needed to visit and linger, I circulated, talking with nearly everyone there. I met a woman from England who spun wool from her own flock of sheep and told me about anthrax, a man who restored old wooden airplanes somewhere out East, and a woman whose King Charles Spaniel had been a contender in the Westminster Dog Show the previous year and she had all the pictures and a bottomless bag of stories to prove it. Just as I was about to leave, my eye took in a man talking with a woman who'd told me earlier that she was a foot model. We'd talked about what a great gig that was. You could show up for work, hair in curlers and wearing a bathrobe as long as your feet were clean and you had a fresh pedicure. She was wearing open-toed sandals and her feet were truly exquisite. She said her employers flew her everywhere, especially to beautiful tropical beaches, because people love to see pretty feet in white sand along the water's edge. It puts them in a good mood, and they buy the nail polish and foot products to perpetuate that nice feeling.

But my attention was focused on the man talking with her. He looked vaguely familiar. Suddenly it hit me like a lightning bolt, and just as I realized who he was, he looked up as though he had been keeping me in his peripheral vision. He walked over, flashing a wide smile. Looking a little older and maybe less springy than the last time I had seen him, he still had the unmistakable sparkling eyes that I remembered. It was Fred, the engineer I'd met along with his wife Donna on that safari in Botswana, the man who'd sent me the note the night before. I'd forgotten all about him in the excitement of meeting everyone at Gilligan's Table, my seasickness, and joining the string quartet. But here was Fred. Donna wasn't with him, so I knew he was going to start with some sad news. I braced myself.

"Marianne!" His voice was a little raspy and now it was all coming back to me.

"Fred!" I responded, not knowing where to take it from there. "I got your note last night, but when I arrived at the dining room they said you hadn't registered there yet, so they took me to my assigned table." I didn't know if it was appropriate to interject a little levity just then and describe my dining partners, but I thought better of it. Fred made a shooing motion with one hand and took my hand with his other one and said it wasn't important. He hadn't been able to bring himself to go to dinner and had ended up at the Crow's Nest Bar all evening. He laughed and said, "Well, I guess you could figure out Donna's not here."

"I'm so sorry, Fred," I said. "You never told me – I mean wrote, and I was too afraid to inquire." Then I stammered through something that I couldn't even figure out myself that must have sounded very awkward.

"No, no. It's okay, Marianne," he said reassuringly. "Really. I'm doing my best to pick up the pieces and move on now. I was surprised to see you traveling alone this time," he said, then quickly added, "I didn't ask, honestly, they just told me that automatically when I asked them to deliver that note."

Nice as Fred was, I was hoping that he didn't have me in his crosshairs because, really, he wasn't my type and I was in too much relationship turmoil to start anything right then. I would have to be very gentle and kind, not exactly my forte, and make it crystal clear from the start that I was not interested in anything more than just being a friend. I didn't know if this was the time to draw that line but, fortunately, I didn't have to.

"As a matter of fact, I met someone very nice after Donna . . ." he let the rest of the sentence trail off. "Donna and I had booked this cruise a couple years before everything happened, and we never canceled just because we kept hoping she would be okay. It gave us both something to look forward to. I wasn't going to come, but about six months ago, I met Stacey and we decided I should come, and she will join me in a few days when we get to St. Lucia. I know it must seem sudden . . ." he started to apologize.

"Oh, Fred, that's great to know. I mean about Stacey coming to join you," I said with

maybe too much relief. "I really look forward to meeting her, and maybe we can have drinks together."

"I'd like that a lot, Marianne. I think you'd like her very much. Anyway, that's what's been going on with my life. How are you doing?"

I didn't want to bring up all the recent Seth drama and couldn't honestly remember if I'd even mentioned him in any of my emails to Fred and Donna. I downplayed my own life's saga at that point, not wanting to have to perform any damage control in the future for anything I might say at that moment.

I simply told him things were going really well with my work and this cruise was a nice and badly needed diversion. We hugged lightly and went our separate ways and I headed to the dining room. We had not made any effort to join each other for dinner, and I was a little relieved. Not that I wouldn't enjoy some time talking with Fred, but more because I was eager to get back to Gilligan's Table and discover what had transpired with my friends during the day.

I ARRIVED TO FIND a newcomer at our table. I was the last one to show up and the waiter was already taking everyone's orders by the time I had settled into my seat. Skip and Denny sat next to Mrs. Mooney, and Ginny and I sat across from them with the new guy occupying the seat next to me. I'd been hoping to start a conversation with Dr. Feerum, but everyone was curious about the new man who introduced himself simply as Wink. He was medium build and dressed nicely with a blue-striped shirt, navy blazer, and tropical-print tie. He looked like he could have been a lecturer. I guessed his age to be between forty and fifty. He told us that he used to work on cruise ships, adding that he was on board the MS *Minerva* in a consulting capacity for shipboard compliance issues, whatever that was supposed to mean. Then he asked us all how we had spent our first day at sea. I started to talk, intending to ask everyone at the table if they'd like to form a trivia team. But Mr. Mooney took the allegorical mic to announce to everyone that he'd seen me at the snorkeling lecture that morning and added that I'd suddenly run off, leaving him in a cloud of dust afterward. Whether he was amused or insulted, I couldn't tell. Instead of asking me where I had gone in such a big rush, he changed the subject to his and Mrs. Mooney's other activities.

Mrs. Mooney had not won at bingo. They had both played bridge in the afternoon and met someone or other they had cruised with on another ship a few years before who had since split up and was back on this cruise showing off his new "child bride" as Mr. Mooney disparagingly described it with a gruff snort. I got the feeling that for these frequent cruisers, the matter of running into each other on other ships with other itineraries was not as noteworthy as the drama that filled their lives during the interims between cruises. To them, it was like coming back to their favorite country club.

Skip had foregone the tour of the bridge with Denny, and instead had entered the belly- flop contest on a whim. He was disappointed to only come in second place and elucidated every detail of his belly flop, assuring us that his exhibition had been superior to the contestant who had actually placed first. He patted his protruding stomach and said it was probably because the winner had more "ballast" and then set right out to do something about making up for his deficiency by ordering two appetizers and two desserts. Denny recounted his tour of the bridge and described the amazing technology that steers, guides, and navigates the ship, leaving in the dust the old-world methods that used astrolabes and compasses and stars as navigational aids. He said he got to meet the captain and passed around his smart phone photo to prove it. Everyone admired the picture and voiced approval as his phone made its way around the table.

Suddenly, Ginny turned to Wink and introduced herself. "I don't believe we've introduced ourselves to you yet, Wink," she said. "Please excuse our terrible manners." Again, she spoke loud enough for our half of the dining room to hear her. "I'm Ginny," she said, smiling and offering her right hand.

"I think Ginny is right and it's high time we make proper introductions all around to Wink," Mr. Mooney's voice boomed as our appetizers arrived. "I'm Marshall Mooney the Third, and this is my wife Lorelai. Only I can call her Dovey," he repeated from the previous night's introduction, holding up his wine glass as if making a toast. "We hail from Hollywood, but there was a time when we lived in Texas. And, yes, we had oil in our backyard. And lots of it!"

Ginny, who was obviously impressed enough to forget about Wink temporarily, held up her own wine glass. For the first time I noticed her wrists were weighed down with glistening bracelets and rings that appeared to be made of diamonds, sapphires, emeralds, and rubies, probably heirlooms, and convincing enough to look real. In her bid to show off her finery to Mr. Mooney, she had dropped the ball about introducing herself to Wink.

Skip picked it up without missing a beat. "Well, I am Skip, and this here is m'boy Denny," Skip said to Wink. He added that he had served in the Merchant Marines on the Great Lakes and now lived in Cleveland with Denny who would be working on a ship for the Coast Guard. Denny stared straight ahead beyond the dining room windows and the setting sun at the water's edge and rocked back and forth impatiently.

Dr. Feerum introduced himself and then suddenly arose. "I'm Dr. Feerum, a professor," he said simply. "I must excuse myself now," he said politely. Then he bowed, pushed his chair in, and walked to the exit. It suddenly was apparent why he had ordered only an appetizer and nothing else. Once he was too far out of earshot to hear me, I looked at the others and asked, "A professor of what? Did he tell anyone?"

Ginny looked up from her gazpacho soup. She took her time answering. "Well," she said, as if trying hard to remember the pertinent conversation, "Dr. Feerum is a professor of literature, I think. No, maybe he said marine biology. Or engineering. I don't remember now," she said, flapping her hands in frustration. "He's very nice, though." Then she added, as an afterthought, to me, "You should get to know him. He's single, too, you know."

I must have involuntarily blushed because Skip pointed at me and laughed. "Ha! You better stay away from him," he blasted and quickly looked behind him as if The Professor might be coming back to the table. He lowered his voice and looked at me conspiratorially. "I mean, I'm not sure he'd be right for you. You're, uh, normal and sociable. He's like a recluse. There's something suspicious about him," Skip finished, diving into his second shrimp cocktail.

"He's okay, Dad," Denny suddenly countered. "I talked with him today and he likes to fish. If you want to date Miss Marianne yourself, Dad, why don't you just ask her instead of beating around the bush and hiding behind Dr. Feerum?" He looked straight at his father and there was no question that all pistons were firing. The entire table drew a collective gasp of horror, anticipating an out-and-out fight between the father and son. I was beginning to see Denny in quite another light. Mr. Mooney cleared his throat and asked if anyone knew why Dr. Feerum had to leave so abruptly. Denny knew the answer. He told us that Dr. Feerum was organizing notes for a talk he was going to give the following day on the indigenous people of the Caribbean. Denny explained that while Dr. Feerum was not the official lecturer on this cruise, he had offered to give a talk or two, and Pearl was happy to add him to the agenda.

"Does anyone know about the original inhabitants of these islands?" I asked, remembering my first impressions from reading James Michener's *Caribbean* several years earlier, but not able to remember many of the details. No one admitted to knowing much about the subject, but everyone agreed it might be fun to attend Dr. Feerum's talk, and Skip said we should all sit together to show him our support. I knew the talk conflicted with my rehearsal schedule, so at that point I felt it incumbent on me to explain my new role as honorary cellist in the string quartet. All the same, I restrained from leaking any word about the poor missing cellist so as not to start rumors or incite alarm throughout the ship. I simply said I was filling in temporarily and they all seemed satisfied with that. At least no one followed up with any more questioning. They were fascinated that I could play the cello and asked when they could see me perform with the string quartet.

"Tomorrow evening at the captain's reception," I said. "You get to see Dr. Feerum give his talk tomorrow morning and watch me perform tomorrow evening," I said triumphantly. "Much as I'd like to, I won't be able to join you for Dr. Feerum's talk because our rehearsal is set for that time. So, don't assume I am passing up Dr. Feerum's talk for wine tasting or an origami workshop."

"Capital!" boomed the voice of Mr. Magoo. "Let's toast to the abundant talents here at Table 1A."

Everyone murmured approval and clinked wine and water glasses. As the chatter subsided, I quickly introduced myself to Wink, aware that I had not done so previously.

Strangely, I felt as if he already knew me. No one asked any more questions or seemed curious about me, so I was able to keep Seth and my livelihood under wraps for at least another day. I'd also missed my chance to bring up the trivia team proposal, but things being what they were, it didn't look like I'd have much time for trivia this cruise anyway.

BETWEEN DINNER AND THE EVENING show I had a few minutes to myself, so I walked upstairs and out to the pool deck for some fresh air. A stiff wind was battering things around, and I had to hold on to the railing with one hand and keep pushing my skirt down with the other. Some couples were leaning against the railings looking at the faraway lights of other cruise ships, majestic and barely moving over the oil-black water, but the wind kept their vigils short and they turned around and headed back inside. My eyes swept upwards to the sports deck where a solitary figure stood with his back to me. He was looking over the railing at some faint flickering lights on the water that may have been from a distant lighthouse or island. I noted he was wearing sunglasses and assumed he'd been out there watching the entire sunset and forgot to take them off after dark. Suddenly, he looked down at me, and as soon as he saw me looking at him, he turned and ran to the nearest exit. He was barely discernible in the growing darkness, but I sensed that he did not want to be seen. I glanced around at that point and realized I was the only soul on the entire deck as well as the deck above. The wind rose to a fury, so I found the nearest door and went back inside the ship and downstairs to the theater for the evening presentation.

The show was one of those all-out big musicales with colorful larger-than-life costumes and singing and dancing about love lost and found and happy endings. Beautiful young people with sparkling eyes and glue-white smiles and perfect legs and long ballerina necks danced and sang and made everyone feel like part of the fantasy. They sang age-old love songs about memories and hopes and better days to come. Some in the audience stood and swayed with the music and no one minded in the least. One or two couples even got up and slow danced in the back of the theater. When the curtain came down forty-five minutes later, the audience leapt to their feet and cheered. Pearl took the mic in hand and strutted onto center stage to thank the performers and the band and the stage technicians and especially the audience for appreciating the performers' hard work so much. Then she reminded everyone to reserve the following evening for the captain's reception and to consult *The Tides* before going to bed to help plan the next day's activities as we were to be at sea another day. Finally, she invited anyone who still had a little steam left to come upstairs to the Paris Lounge for more dancing, or alternatively to join Piet in the piano lounge for a game of Name That Tune, or to make their deposits in the casino, and with that the auditorium quickly emptied out.

I knew the smart thing was to go to bed and be well rested for the quartet rehearsal the next morning. But I wasn't tired enough to retire for the night and, still going strong on adrenaline, I strolled upstairs, walking up the stairwell instead of riding the elevator to avoid the crush. Midway up the stairs I thought I saw someone standing in the corridor entrance on deck nine, but when I passed the corridor on my way up there was no one, so I assumed it was just a figment of my imagination or someone heading back to their room. I walked all the way up to the fifteenth deck and found a single seat toward the back of the Paris Lounge to watch the dancers. I had no intention of dancing myself. When a waiter came by, I asked him to bring me a minty mojito. A few minutes after my first sip, someone touched me on the right shoulder. I looked up to see Wink standing there. He pointed to the dance floor, gesturing for me to join him, so I left my minty mojito and handbag on the little round table and we glided out to the floor where the band was playing an irresistible rumba. He was a good dancer, not smooth like Roy, but fun enough, and I was happy that I'd decided to come upstairs after all. The physical movement and music rejuvenated me, and I suddenly was feeling more awake. I asked Wink if he was working on the ship during this cruise and he said he was. He added that he was looking forward to seeing the quartet perform again at the captain's reception which told me he had already seen us play at afternoon tea that day, although I didn't recall seeing him there. As his eyes panned back and forth across the Paris Lounge, he suddenly chuckled. "I can't stop myself from looking around to see if anyone else is here from Gilligan's Table." A little involuntary squeak escaped me when I heard him say "Gilligan's Table." I asked him if he had been thinking what I had been thinking, and he stopped dancing and walked me back to my table and sat down across from me.

"Did you see the makeup of that table?" he asked, laughter in his eyes. "I mean, Mr. Mooney IS Thurston Howell the Third, that crazy guy and his son are the Skipper and Gilligan, and you are the perfect Mary Ann. We've got an absent-minded professor, and what do you think about the frustrated movie star, Ginny, with her ginger-orange hair? I suppose in her day she may have been a bombshell."

We both laughed over that and I agreed ours was a colorful group of characters and told him I too had concluded after the first dinner that I was seated at Gilligan's Table. "All we need now is to get stranded on an island," I giggled. "I hardly think we could survive three hours together." Then I changed the subject.

"So, you're in the security detail? What do you know about the missing cellist?" I asked.

I knew that came tumbling out too fast, but it was

too late to retract it. I have a track record of talking before thinking. Wink was quiet and didn't respond for a moment. Apparently I wasn't supposed to have asked that.

"It's true, I'm part of the security detail here on the ship. They assigned me to your table because it's way back in the outermost corner which gives me the best view of the dining room. Everyone is supposed to think I'm a passenger. I'm to look for any unusual behavior and to keep my eyes and ears open for anything that might help discover the whereabouts of that missing musician. I shouldn't be telling you this, but now that you are honorary crew, I suppose I can, and anyway, since you are replacing Sabrina, I have to keep an eye on you too for your own safety. At this point, we don't know if she is still on the ship or back in Old San Juan or if she's being held hostage on or off the ship or if she fell – or someone pushed her – overboard. We haven't heard anything from her, and no one has seen her in Old San Juan or the ship, so we are not ruling anything out."

Now it was my turn to be thoughtful. I asked when she had last been seen, and he replied that people had seen her on the ship just before it arrived in Old San Juan one day before the present cruise started. According to the security records, Sabrina's ship card was swiped off the ship in the late morning and she apparently returned to the ship by swiping her card back on the ship in the middle of the afternoon, but in fact she had not been seen on the ship since she'd left it. It could simply mean she had left again without the card being swiped, or that someone else had used her card and she had never left the ship in the first place, or that she got off in the morning and someone else came on board in the afternoon using her card. Or, worst case, she had been on board the entire time and was being held hostage somewhere, hiding on her own, or somehow went overboard. But the bottom line was that she was missing, and they had to find her.

"Did you know her personally? I mean, did you ever see or talk with her?" I asked Wink.

"No, I have never met her. I joined the ship yesterday in Miami when you did. People who knew her said she was a quiet type. Shy. She was from Mexico City. She was a bit younger than the others in the quartet as well as its newest addition. She started only a few months ago to replace Thalia who left the group to get married last fall. This was only her second contract with the fleet. Her first contract was on the MS *Athena,* our sister ship. Sabrina was a very good musician and got along well with the group. It's a bad situation, but we are trying to keep it under wraps so as not to upset the passengers. I was glad you didn't tell anyone about it at Gilligan's Table tonight," he said.

"Are there any suspects?" I asked.

"No suspects, no motives. Nothing at all. But the entire string quartet might be at risk, so stay alert and if you see anything suspicious, let me or anyone on the security staff know immediately."

Until now I had not even considered the possibility of being in any kind of danger myself. If anything, I was the most innocent of bystanders. Just a passenger on board for fun and fantasy for a few days and then – poof – back to my humdrum life with only the memories. I didn't see how my participation in the quartet could put me in harm's way, but deferred to Wink's expertise in the matter and promised to stay on my toes. "So, you are a permanent employee aboard the ship?" I was still trying to figure it out.

"Permanent for the company, but I work across the fleet," he answered. "I oversee security personnel training at headquarters in Miami and go from ship to ship to inspect procedures and offer suggestions for improvement," he said. "It's uncommon for me to sit in the dining room with the passengers, but this is an extraordinary situation."

"I see," I said, starting to make sense of it all but, more importantly, I decided I liked Wink's blue eyes. I said I would do whatever I could to help with the investigation, but didn't think I had much to offer. He said to keep my eyes open and that I might be in a better position to see something than I might realize since I was seeing things through a fresh set of eyes. As Wink finished his drink, he said he had some business to tie up in his office and excused himself.

Just then, Angela announced to the room that she

had entry forms for the Valentine's Day dance contest. Two couples drifted casually by to take one. I approached Angela and told her I would like to enter, but that my partner had bailed before the cruise started. I asked if she could match me up with a partner. Without even looking at me, she dismissively said she didn't offer that service and I should ask around on the ship and try to find someone on my own. The dance floor was thick with couples right then and they all looked pretty good. For the first time since coming on board, I felt a sense of real loss at the prospect of missing out on participating in the dance contest with a steady dance partner. It was one of the things I had been looking forward to more than anything else; that, and the rosy promise that Seth would propose to me on Valentine's night. Now it looked like both dreams were dashed.

Someone tapped me on the shoulder. It was the assistant cruise director, Roy. We went on the dance floor for an East Coast swing that morphed into a salsa as the music changed. My mood lifted and I was having a lot of fun. Roy was really good. Better than Seth, I thought. Probably from teaching classes all the time. As we danced, he told me there were some dance hosts on board who would be happy to dance with me, but he saw my question coming and cut me off at the pass, adding that the dance hosts were not eligible to enter the contest, so I was on my own there. Still, knowing there were people to practice with was somewhat reassuring.

It was late and on the way back to my stateroom I stayed away from the outside deck, even though I could have used a good gulp of fresh air. Back in my room, I tried opening the sliding door to the balcony but the strong wind was squealing so much that I left it closed. I turned around, and that was the first time I noticed the red light blinking on my phone. I picked it up to hear a sinister, scratchy, and barely audible voice utter: "SOMEONE IS MISSING. ARE YOU NEXT?"

I didn't know if I should panic or report it or just ignore it and go to bed. I thought pranks were probably common fare on these big ships and figured it was not a cause for alarm. Just in case, though, I checked in the closet, the shower, and under the bed and tumbled into bed leaving the light on.

Chapter Three

Day Three: February 5, Friday
En route to Spanish Town (Virgin Gorda), BVI
Weather updates will be given in the morning by the cruise
director and midday by the captain.

THE NEXT MORNING'S REHEARSAL was scheduled for 8:30 to 10:30. It was another day at sea, so I had no pressing matters other than the rehearsal and a couple of activities I wanted to attend before reporting for duty at the captain's evening reception. I started the day early with a half hour on the treadmill, then showered and breakfasted on the outside Lido deck at a table under a sun umbrella. The sea was pitching and heaving even more dramatically than the previous day, so I was fighting a little nausea and hoping the rehearsal would distract me enough to overcome it. My wish came true because the rehearsal proceeded straight through like a tour de force and was so rigorous that I forgot all about being seasick. I had all I could do to keep up. I had been able to glide my way through most of the program at the afternoon tea the day before on the strength of my familiarity with the pieces in that program. But the program for the captain's reception was more challenging, and we would be playing for nearly two hours straight. Thankfully, Danita, Valetta, and Mario were very patient and accommodating, offering helpful hints, and even going so far as to rearrange some measures to help me navigate the patchy musical terrain, and in the end I felt confident enough to make a good show of it that evening. I had the rest of the day to do as I pleased before reporting to the Paris Lounge dressed up and ready to perform where our chairs and music stands – and my cello – would be awaiting us at five o'clock, in time for the five-fifteen reception.

As anticipated, I had to forego Dr. Feerum's lecture on the indigenous peoples of the Caribbean, but I did make it to the chefs' cooking demonstration after rehearsal ended. There were two chefs, an Italian and a Frenchman. They duked it out like dueling piano adversaries I saw one time, spouting off at each other with slapstick gusto, beating eggs, beating pans, and beating up on each other's national cooking traditions, each belittling the other with wagging fingers for using butter when the other used cream for the same recipe, and carrying on as they peeled, diced, heated, poured, measured, sifted, browned, tasted, and garnished to the delight and entertainment of the audience.

I decided to take advantage of a little physical

activity with the dance class and then went back to the theater for another round of trivia. My team arrived in unison and we each sat in the same seat we had sat in the day before. If I'd had any misguided hopes of latching onto another team, they were hopelessly dashed as this group adopted me. I figured I may as well surrender. Besides Meredith, the Wichita marketing assistant executive with the skinny on all the celebrity and pop culture trivia questions, there were three couples. Kate and Barry, the youngest members of our team, were on the cruise to celebrate their first anniversary. The oldest couple was Mildred and Stan. The third couple introduced themselves as Karla and Patrick and called each other "So-So's" for "Significant Others." They had met online and were not married or planning to at this point. They joked that SO could also work for SOS and laughed that their relationship needed it some of the time. They informed us that they couldn't be sure about keeping up with trivia for the rest of the cruise because they didn't like to come back to the ship early on the days we were in port. I thought about inviting Fred and Stacey to join our team after our St. Lucia stop when Stacey was supposed to join Fred. Fred was pretty smart, being an engineer and all, and we could use his help. I had no doubt that Stacey would prove to be intelligent too.

Pearl reported to duty at the lectern and began shuffling papers and offering golf pencils and scratch paper, smiling at everyone around the room as she checked to see if all the teams were in place. From her calm and gracious demeanor, you'd never guess that she was thinking about a million behind-the-scenes fires to put out. A few new people wandered into the room, and she assigned them to smaller teams that needed players or combined teams to make new teams altogether. For her first question, Pearl asked how many virgins the Virgin Islands was named for. After a pause, she said it was a trick question and then reminded everyone that the answer to it and a lot more information about our first port of call, Virgin Gorda, would be presented by the guest lecturer, Dr. Pinot, at quarter past two o'clock. I glanced at my watch and made a mental note to come back for that talk. The rest of trivia was almost as brutal as the day before, but our score was better by one, so at least we were moving along the right trajectory. I was beginning to enjoy my teammates' company, even if we were not the brainiacs on some other teams. We were stumped on every history question, every quantum physics question, every word origin question, and only redeemed ourselves with the pop culture questions because of Meredith. We scored one wild card answer because Barry somehow knew that the Pittsburgh Penguins were NOT one of the original six NHL teams. Way to go, Barry!

After trivia, it was a pleasure to return to a stateroom that was sparkling clean and freshly made up for me, and I thought that this turn of events – ending up with my own room – was becoming more pleasant with every passing day. I doubted if Seth would have joined me for the chefs' demonstration and could fairly guarantee he wouldn't have touched trivia. I felt adventurous and lighthearted stepping in and taking on my "honorary crew" role with the string quartet. I never would have seen this side of a cruise if Seth had been with me, because it wouldn't have been an option. I popped off my shoes and dropped on top of the smoothly made-up bed just as I noticed the message light on the phone blinking its red eye at me. I picked up the receiver and dialed the number to retrieve my message. Half expecting it to be Mario or one of the girls with a last-minute reminder about something for the reception performance, I was stunned to hear a scratchy and barely audible voice come through with well-paced words spoken slowly and threateningly: "YOU'RE PLAYING A SOUR NOTE: GO HOME! AND DON'T REPEAT THIS OR ELSE!" Then the message clicked off. I played it two more times trying to figure out if I could identify the voice at all, my first person of interest being Denny, although I couldn't explain why. But it was not a voice I had heard before. I wasn't even certain the message was meant for me in the first place; I thought it might have been intended for Sabrina, the missing cellist.

But then I wondered, could this voice belong to that solitary figure I saw way up on the sport deck the evening before? Could it belong to the shadowy figure I thought I saw lurking in the corridor on my way up the staircase? Could those persons be one and the same? And the scariest thought of all, could someone be after me? I wondered if the message had recorded a stateroom number, but when I checked for it, only the word "Unknown" appeared in the little frame. No, I concluded with dread, this message was intended for me and me only, and whoever sent it wanted me off the ship. I wanted to tell Wink, but because of the final threat, I decided to hold off for the time being.

A sharp rap at the door startled me out of my thoughts, and I looked through the peephole. The big fisheye staring back at me belonged to Valetta who, assuming I was looking at her through the peephole, ruffled a sheaf of papers into my view. I opened the door and invited her inside. In broken English she explained she had the music scores I'd need for the duration of the cruise and quickly added that we would only be performing for the afternoon teas from here on out, so I was free to enjoy my time on shore and join any shore excursions as long as I was back on the ship in the Paris Lounge and in my chair with my cello at three forty-five every day. She went on to say there had been no progress in locating Sabrina, but urged me to keep an eye out for anything unusual and to tell her about anything or report it to the security people on board. She asked if I had met any of the security detail, and I told her straight out I thought Wink was a security man before thinking I might have been better off keeping that to myself. Valetta said "everyone" across the fleet knew Wink worked security and he was as good a person as any to report anyone or anything that might be of interest. She also mentioned that, according to a memo she had received, in the next two days there would be a full-scale interrogation of all the members of the quartet that would have to include me, even though I had just joined the group. I was beginning to realize that I was being drawn deeper and deeper into this imbroglio. While she was in the room, I showed her the two evening gowns I had brought along. She said they were beautiful, but they wore costumes to coordinate the group for each performance and I could wear Sabrina's. Sabrina was taller than I, so I knew there would have to be some temporary adjustments for the length. Valetta said not to worry, that the costume coordinator would handle it. As she left, she noticed the phone still blinking and nonchalantly remarked that I had a message waiting.

After she left, I thought about what to tell the investigators and reasoned I should tell them about the phone threats and even the shifty character I had seen on deck, but at the same time I did not want to put myself or anyone else in harm's way. I was almost contemplating leaving the ship at the next port and taking the very next flight home. But that would never do; after all, I had already been through so much and couldn't stop in the middle of an adventure. Besides, the more I thought about it, the more I could convince myself that the messages were pranks.

At a quarter past two, I returned to the theater for Dr. Pinot's presentation, and took the same seat I'd used for trivia. I noticed others were doing the same thing. People can be such creatures of habit. The theater was filling up as passengers poured through the doors, most everyone smiling and talking quietly. Dr. Pinot had a lovely photograph of the famous Baths at Virgin Gorda projected on the screen with the title "The Plump Maiden: Virgin Gorda" splayed across it. He waited until the very last moment just after the lights were dimmed to address us from the lectern. He tapped his mic and started right in explaining that there are two groupings of Virgin Islands: the U.S. Virgins that include St. Thomas, St. John, and St. Croix; and the British Virgins that include Tortola, Virgin Gorda, Anegada and dozens of tinier islands with whimsical names like Salty Dog Cay, Dead Chest Island, Prickly Pear, Fallen Jerusalem, and Sandy Spit. Columbus named the entire group of Virgin Islands when he came through on his second New World voyage in 1493. All the beautiful islands he saw, one after another, reminded him of St. Ursula and her eleven thousand handmaidens on the way to St. Ursula's wedding in Germany, where she was supposed to meet her fiancé. I imagined a wedding party with eleven thousand blushing bridesmaids and chuckled at what a feat it would be to outfit all those women. The memory of St. Ursula is alive and well in the British Virgin Islands; she serves as the star of its coat of arms and the object of the annual St. Ursula's holiday that commemorates the naming of the Virgin Islands by Columbus on October 21, 1493. Little wonder St. Ursula is a favorite in the region: she is the patron saint for educating girls, and education is something these islands take very seriously, insisting that all their students wear uniforms, for starters.

Following Columbus, the islands attracted the Spanish for a short while, but when they found no resources of interest to them, the Dutch and English came sniffing around, battling for control, until eventually the archipelago ended up in the lap of the English. Pirates came and went all along, using the many islands to clean, or careen, their ships and found countless nooks and crannies in the islands to hide their treasure, the holes they dug near shore serving as an early version of the modern deposit bank. The British Virgin Islands is a British Overseas Territory that uses the U.S. dollar as its official currency as a concession to a tourist-driven economy. Sugar and cotton production took place in these islands long ago, and African slaves were imported and distributed across the West Indies, leaving a legacy of majority African-descended populations. Today the British Virgin Islands enjoys a booming economy by other Caribbean standards, on the strength of tourism and offshore financing.

Dr. Pinot switched his attention to Virgin Gorda and described the house-sized boulders that create mysterious pools and eerie grottos at the famous

Baths. He displayed photographs of serene beaches and warned us to avoid the poisonous manchineel tree which can seriously burn one's skin. He provided lots of beautiful photographs and told some amazing stories about these islands, with advice on where to find uncrowded beaches, botanic gardens, horse-riding paths, local rum distilleries, and some enduring tourist favorites like Sunny Caribbee's and Pusser's.

At five o'clock, I was dressed in an elegant black gown seated front and center with the string quartet group as the captain and his chief officers formed a reception line leading from the open glass-paned French doors into the gracious lounge. For the occasion the lounge had been festooned with Chinese vases and waist-high urns containing opulent bouquets of freshly cut and artistically arranged tropical flowers and greenery. The captain's reception was as gala an affair as any I had ever attended, and after the captain made his welcome speech and each of the officers introduced himself or herself, champagne flowed and hors d'oeuvres floated around the room on silver trays for a couple of hours as we played classical pieces. I didn't have a chance to look up much from my music, but caught patches of this and that and stored them away in my memory to try to make sense of later. I noticed at one point the ten-year-old girl reading quietly on the floor beneath her favorite window. No one seemed to pay her any mind, and her parents were in a deep discussion with other guests at a table a short distance away. When the reception ended and our part was finished, the band took over and started in with some dance music. A foxtrot led to familiar ballroom standards until the floor was packed hip-to-hip with dancers in elegant evening gowns and sharp black tuxedos. I was about to head back to my room with my music when I felt a tap on my arm. "Let's dance?" were the words I heard as I turned and saw Roy holding his hand out to me.

"Sure!" I said. And without a word we floated out to the dance floor for a rumba, a tango, and a waltz.

I danced so much that I ended up skipping dinner altogether that night, not returning to my room until after nine thirty and too tired to venture back out. Besides, the dining room was well on its way to wrapping up the second seating by the time I left the dancing, and Gilligan's Table would by now be occupied by another group of diners altogether. I showered, slipped into my nightgown, and drifted off to sleep looking very much forward to our first shore stop at Virgin Gorda where I would join an excursion to the famous scenic Baths.

AT MIDNIGHT, I sat bolt upright in bed wide awake. Realizing I was very hungry, I could not get myself to relax and fall sleep again. I got out of bed and pulled on my jeans and a sweater and sneakers and went up to the pool deck for some fresh air and to look for something to eat. The night was warm but humid and foggy and droplets of moisture were precipitating on the wooden handrails. No one was on the deck, and the dim glow of a nearly full moon fought its way past the bright lights illuminating the outline of the ship. I thought about the fact that I had a full excursion day coming to me with only the obligation of an hour of playing for the afternoon tea. Even before Dr. Pinot's lecture, I had seen photographs of the imposing rocks clustered on a tantalizing beach and had heard about the mysterious pools and caverns within those behemoth boulders and could only imagine what it would be like to wade inside and see for myself.

Determined to find an all-night pizzeria or ice cream dispensary on board, I turned to walk to the other side of the ship, hoping some leftovers from the midnight buffet might still be available in the cafeteria. Now was as good a time as any to find out. Just as I was right about midship, a stiff wind riled up as the ship heaved suddenly, and I quickly grasped the nearest handrail to steady my balance. As I did so, I felt someone push hard against me from behind, shoving me into the railing. It felt like the person was trying to wedge me between the gaps in the railing. I gasped in surprise and looked down at the black waves smacking against the ship and breaking into white foam. I tried to get a glimpse of my attacker, but all I could see was a tall, shadowy figure. I pushed back against it, but I was facing the railing and had no way of seeing who was behind me. My heart was racing uncontrollably. It seemed as if the sudden wind, the unsettling heave of the ocean, and the mysterious push had all happened simultaneously and, remembering Wink's warning, I was palpably shaken.

As I was trying to make sense of it, I felt a big hand grab my right arm and pull me away. I saw the shadowy figure of someone tall and thin running away while the big hand maintained a firm grasp on my arm. In the dark, I couldn't make out who was holding onto me, but when he started to talk, I recognized Skip from Gilligan's Table. He asked if I'd gotten a good look at my attacker, but I said I had not, and he said neither had he. I asked what he was doing up so late and he replied that he was looking for anything left over from the midnight buffet. I told him that had been my intention too. Skip guided me back inside the ship to a little area set aside for the staff and crew where coffee and cookies were available around the clock. A few late-working crew members were seated together around a table talking and laughing. He asked if I was okay and if I wanted anything to eat, but I was pretty shaken up and wasn't hungry anymore. I told him I just wanted to return to my room, so he walked me to my room on his way back to his own. I was back in the safety and shelter of my room, my hunger replaced by fear.

Wink may have been correct to warn me that someone might want to do me harm, but I didn't know how to tell him that I had gone on deck in light of the awful threat left on my phone. I admitted to myself that I had been careless by going on deck all alone late at night and that if Skip had not arrived when he did, for all I knew I could have been boosted over or pushed through the railings and even now I would be struggling alone in the dark waters below as the ship sailed on. During all the times I had spoken with Wink, I had never asked for, and he had never offered, his number to call him in just such an emergency. But even so, I was inclined to keep my experience to myself for now. What a pickle I was in! I determined to find Wink on Virgin Gorda the next day and tell him everything.

Chapter Four

Day Four: February 6, Saturday
Spanish Town (Virgin Gorda), BVI.
Partly Cloudy: High-81ºF / 27º C. Low 73ºF / 23º C.

HOLDING MY BREAKFAST DISH, I stepped onto the terrace deck to find a table and straightaway saw Dr. Feerum sitting alone at a table for four. I sat down across from him without asking if he would mind my company. I was going to sit there whether he liked it or not.

"I'm sorry I couldn't make it to your talk yesterday," I said. "You should have told the table that night why you left us early. We only learned about your talk from Denny after you left. They all planned to go, but I had to rehearse with the string quartet."

"You did very well at the captain's reception," Dr. Feerum said, breaking the top of a soft-boiled egg with his spoon. "That is interesting how you are taking on the responsibility of a staff person. I hope they are compensating you or have commuted your fare."

"I get a free future cruise in exchange," I explained. "Besides, if the other cellist reappears, I still receive the free future cruise and am relieved of the duties. I really don't mind either way since I already know how to play the cello and I always welcome a little adventure." I almost choked on my bran muffin when I realized how easily I'd let slip out the fact about the missing musician.

"Oh, do tell," Dr. Feerum said. "So, there is a shipboard mystery?" he asked, looking up at me with renewed interest. He didn't miss a trick.

"Oops. I wasn't supposed to let that out, so please keep it to yourself, Dr. Feerum," I said. "I'm a little distracted because I've been warned I could be in some danger too."

"And you're also distracted because you have reason to believe the danger may be more imminent than you previously thought?" he asked, taking a tidy bite from the corner of his whole wheat toast.

"Maybe," I offered. "But I don't want to read into things," I said, secretly wondering if he had any way of knowing about the telephone threat I'd received or the attack on the deck.

"Do you have plans today?" he asked, changing the subject. "I am taking the deep-sea fishing excursion," he went on as if I'd asked. "I always do some fishing at least a couple of times whenever I cruise in the Caribbean."

"Virgin Gorda's Baths await me," I said. Then I

told him how Seth and I had researched and booked the excursions in advance and how he more or less left me at the altar the morning of the cruise. I immediately regretted it.

Dr. Feerum was very quiet. "That's quite a story. Perhaps some time I'll tell you my own story. But we'll need more time. A lot more time," he said with a slight smile as he wiped his mouth. There was a very small scar above his right lip. Probably a souvenir from a schoolyard fight, I thought. He had kind eyes, I decided, which made me rule him out as a suspect behind the phone threats. He was wearing a tan safari shirt and his pocket protector was distinctly missing. I plunged ahead with my burning question. "Dr. Feerum, you are a professor of what?"

"Astrophysics and astronomy," he answered, almost shrugging off his expertise. I immediately thought how much we could use him on our trivia team.

"So, you gave a talk on the indigenous people of the Caribbean?" I squinted my eyes just a little to convey my confusion.

"It's a passion," he said. "Studying indigenous histories in places I travel. And scuba diving. I also enjoy ballroom dancing, thanks to Mom who dragged me to Fred Astaire dance lessons when I was a kid. I earned my way through college and grad school teaching ballroom dance. I always pack a pair of dancing shoes because there are always women needing dance partners. And I bring along a couple of Power Point lectures in my laptop in case the cruise director can use an extra activity in the program. I've sailed with Pearl before and she appreciates a little extra to offer the guests."

THERE IS NO PIER big enough for cruise ships at Virgin Gorda's little capital of Spanish Town, so the ship anchored farther out, and we tendered into Spanish Town over clear and playful waters beneath a blazing Caribbean sky. Our brief tender ride took us past rows of luxurious yachts whose ports of registry hailed from the world's four corners. Reaching the pier area, we boarded graffiti-splashed open-air safari-style buses, with reggae music blaring wildly from the speakers. We took in the sights along the fifteen-minute ride up a narrow stretch of paved road edged on both sides by brilliant bougainvillea, with self-righteous chickens strutting around on their way to important chicken appointments. The weather buoyed our already high spirits. We were all very happy to be off the ship and on dry land on an alluring tropical island. The view from the parking lot at the top of the Baths tempted us with glimpses of what awaited us below: enormous, house-sized boulders toppled helter-skelter in boisterous blue waters surrounded by bobbing yachts at anchor.

We walked down a natural trail with gnarled roots protruding between slippery rocks that caught us off guard like landmines. About a half hour later, the trail spilled out into a small but spellbinding beach with impossibly turquoise water and waves slapping dramatically against the boulders. A local watering hole, Poor Man's Bar, stood sentinel over a handful of local vendors displaying their wares on rocks, tree stumps, or on the white sand of the beach. A small table under a tree held handmade jewelry and was loosely attended by a young girl and her "auntie." A tall dark-skinned man wearing a knit cap in red, green, and yellow stripes was selling beach towels hanging from a tree branch. Salt-and-pepper dreadlocks dangled to his buttocks, and he explained to anyone who asked that the red, yellow, and green stripes on the towels and on his knit cap were the colors of Rastafari. Tubs full of faded snorkel masks, tubes, and flippers were at the ready for rent.

I followed the direction of an arrow with the word "Grotto" hand-painted across it to explore firsthand this natural marvel Dr. Pinot had urged us to visit and see up close all the pools and caverns underneath the toppled boulders. Entering the grotto was like going through a looking glass into another world. Inside, a silence and kind of light made us feel like we were being admitted into a secret watercolor painting. A luminescent pool of clear aquamarine water lay under gigantic boulders so tight upon each other they only allowed narrow wedges of the sapphire sky and glinting sea to enter. Voices echoed eerily, muffled by the thick and sticky air as people took turns photographing each other, posing from all directions to include backdrop views of the boulders, the pools, the sand, and the narrow glimmers of the beach outside.

A series of guide ropes and wooden ladders leading up to platforms and catwalks allowed tourists to transit from one part of the cavern to the next, moving in single file and waiting to allow people coming through from the opposite direction. The tight passages forced some to turn around without venturing any further. I slung my beach bag over my shoulder, backpack style, and concentrated on gripping the guide rope across the broad breasts of the rocks. I took my time going up the wooden stairs, grateful I was wearing surf socks for extra grip. Going down the steeper stairs, I shimmied down on my fanny.

I emerged onto a breathtaking beach named Devil's Bay on the other side of the grotto just as a sudden and random cloudburst thoroughly doused the beach. I walked the rain-spattered beach for a while, considered taking shelter under a nearby copse of trees until I recognized the red paint on them, signaling they were the dangerous manchineel trees to be avoided. With no end in sight to the rain, I scurried back into the shelter of the grotto and clambered through in reverse direction until I emerged on the original beach, Spring Bay, where once again a bright blue and sun-filled sky greeted me.

I was about to head back up to the parking lot

and browse in the gift store I had seen earlier, when I spotted two familiar faces. Skip and Denny approached me from the opposite side of the beach, flailing their arms to get my attention. They had been snorkeling, judging by the masks and flippers dangling from their hands. "Have you been to the grotto?" Skip asked excitedly.

"Yes, I have, and it was unbelievable," I said, pointing behind me. "The Devil's Bay beach on the other side is magnificent, and I would be there still if it hadn't started to downpour. Now I wish I'd stayed a while longer."

"What are you talking about?" Skip asked, incredulous. He pointed in the opposite direction, saying they'd seen the grotto and it was just a pile of big rocks blocking passage along that side of the beach and not very impressive.

"The grotto is in that direction," I countered, still pointing behind me, "and it was amazing. If you want to see it, I will go back with you right now."

"That'd be great," Skip said, brightening up. I noticed he pulled in his stomach a bit too.

We entered the narrow opening, and Denny whistled in amazement at the sight of the first pool. From there it was a repeat of the tour I had just taken, yet every bit as mysterious and amazing as before. Now, the addition of the men's comments and expressions of fascination and delight made the second trip even more pleasurable. As portly as he was, Skip was actually quite agile, and Denny, who was scrappy and scrawny, was downright athletic.

"Did you play sports in high school, Denny?" I asked.

"Tennis and track and field," he said as he hoisted himself up the side of a rock, bypassing the guide rope. "Actually, I was hoping there might be a rock-climbing excursion along the way, but this pretty much gets it out of my system."

"You've probably booked yourself on the zipline and ocean kayaking tours," I mused.

"Actually, yes and no," he answered. "Zipline for sure, but I opted for the waterfall and river tubing instead of the ocean kayak at one of our stops."

"Not me," Skip interjected. "In fact, I won't be surprised if you and I see each other on some of these trips. I'm mostly here for beaching and sightseeing," he said.

"I have a few of those lined up myself, some snorkeling and a rainforest hike and, believe it or not, I'm on the zipline one too!" I answered Denny.

"Then we'll have a lot to talk about over dinner that night," Denny said. I scooted ahead of them, eager to find the path for the exit to Devil's Bay. Suddenly, I turned around and found myself standing all alone in a dark cavern in a small but deep pool that came up to mid-thigh. Light seeping inside through cracks between the rocks illuminated the top of the cavern and reflected eerily on the pool below, providing just enough light for me to see around me. I left the cavern, heading in the direction I thought I had come from, but instead I found myself in a bigger cavern. I seemed to be alone here too. I listened, but could hear no voices, only water gurgling in and out between the rocks.

I systematically looked between all the rocks in the perimeter of this cavern for a way out, but all I could see was the darkness of hollows and the brightness of the Caribbean shining through the narrow cracks. I tried to backtrack my steps but could not find an exit. As I came to the realization that I was lost in the grotto, a foreboding sense of panic and despair tugged at me. I shouted, but only heard my own echo blending in with the crash of the surf against the rocks on one side of the cavern and the water bubbling and gushing in and out. I ran to that side and looked around for anything bigger than the narrow spaces between the rocks and finally found a gap between two rocks I judged myself able to squeeze through.

I spent what felt like an hour grappling with the slippery boulders trying to secure my release to freedom. At one point I underestimated the distance and moved too forcefully against a rock, scraping my leg. I watched as a thick stream of blood smeared its way down the rock and dissipated in an incoming wave. I held my breath and managed to force my way through a very narrow pass and emerged on the surf side where crazy rough waves slammed violently against the rocks. I had succeeded in extricating myself from the prison of the cavern, but now I was at the mercy of a manic current spewing dangerous waves in every direction, with not a human soul in sight. Holding my breath again, I steadied my beach bag over my shoulder and carefully and deliberately crawled my way up to the top of the rocks where I was hoping to figure out a way back to safety. It took all my energy, strength, and focus to heave and shimmy and worm my way up to a high point where the view encompassed only the tops of more slippery rocks, more gaps for the voracious tides to smash through, and views of the beach that seemed farther away than ever.

An all-out rush of panic welled up inside me when I realized I had no idea of the time and had to be back for the last shuttle ride to the tender station in time for the string quartet's performance at afternoon tea. My mind raced in uncontrollable directions and leapt from missing the tea to missing the last tender to even missing the ship altogether! I was almost starting to hallucinate. To add to my consternation, my beach bag had been caught and swallowed under one of the errant waves, and while it was now securely over my shoulder, all its contents, including my camera, were completely waterlogged.

Suddenly, the scratchy message on my phone came to mind. I started to panic as I heard my own voice saying things like "I'm a cooked goose," and "How could I let this happen?" Against the relentless pounding of the spray on the rocks I kept walking in no particular direction until a hand appeared a few feet in front of me. I grabbed it gratefully, and it steadied and pulled me up over the last rock and guided me to the safety of a nearby platform between two boulders.

The hand was attached to Wink. "What are you doing here?" we asked each other simultaneously. He was soaked and not smiling.

"I was making a second round to show Skip and Denny the ropes and . . ." my voice trailed off as I tried to hold back tears.

"Good thing they told me you were lost," he said. "Those two never would have figured out where to find you. This place is so dangerous, Marianne. You have to stay with the group here."

"I meant to do that," I said, even though I really hadn't.

"Well, you're okay now and that's all that matters," he said, wrapping his towel from the ship around me. "Let's get back to the shuttle now before the tender line gets long."

Along the path going up to the parking lot, a woman standing on one of the rocks and waving a kerchief nearly shouted with delight at the sight of Wink.

"Wink!" she cried. "You are here!"

We both turned to see a bewitching siren of the sea, if ever there was one. Tall, wrapped in a gorgeous pashmina shawl that exposed perfectly tanned thighs and a seductive pile of red hair that spilled over her shoulders, a woman stood barefoot, her toes meticulously polished to match the shimmering copper-red lip gloss on lips that framed her gleaming white teeth. She held a pair of espadrille sandals in one hand, and a big, oversized satchel was slung over her other shoulder.

"Hello, Sorrenta," Wink acknowledged, seeming to be equally happy to see her. "I haven't seen you around the ship. Been busy in the kitchen icing our desserts all this time?" Evading the question, she said she had come down for a quick swim at the Baths but was now on her way back to the ship. She spoke with a lyrical accent that could only be Italian.

"Come on," Wink said to her, "I'm just going back now." I noted he did not say "We." He held out his hand and helped steady Sorrenta along the path as she reached out and grabbed his other hand. I was starting to hate her. We trudged back towards the shuttle, my morning's excitement now a distant and insignificant memory, and I felt like an appendage all the way back to the tender platform. I stared out at the scenery as Wink and Sorrenta chattered on.

As if suddenly remembering I existed, Wink turned to me just as we were boarding the tender and said, "This is Marianne, Sorrenta. Marianne, this is Sorrenta."

We nodded at each other. The brief tender ride back to the ship was scenic over calmer waters than before, and with stunning views of the yachts anchored in the harbor or skimming over the water heading to new destinations. When we stepped off the tender and climbed up the metal steps to the security entrance, Sorrenta suddenly yelped. "Wink! I can't find my ship card." She opened her oversized bag and swirled her hands inside, pulling items out and dropping them back in. I thought it curious that she had what appeared to be a week's worth of clothes in what looked like a carry-on satchel for an hour or two at the beach.

"Did you check your pockets?" Wink asked.

"I only have two," she said. She felt them and said it wasn't there.

"Don't worry," he said. "Come with me and once you're on board you can get them to print you a new card. Then he proceeded to lead the way into the ship, followed by Sorrenta who took his hand again, I noticed. I trailed behind like a puppy, wet and cold, with Wink's towel still around me.

"She can't find her card, but she's with me," Wink told the uniformed security guard who let them both go through, swiping Wink's card as he dashed away.

I STILL HAD TIME to join my trivia team before reporting to duty with the quartet. Even if we weren't doing much better than before, the game was growing under my skin, and I could understand why people carved out an hour of their afternoons for the game. It was social, fun, and engaging, and Pearl did a really wonderful job of making people laugh and enjoy it. When teams challenged her answer, she just laughed and said this was no democracy and her answers stood, even if anyone thought they were wrong. Some people took offense, but most people kept it in perspective and enjoyed themselves.

The one thing that was shaping up to be a constant was the winning team. It was the same team every day and they were good. I figured they must be professors and doctors and lawyers. But the scuttlebutt was that they were all very frequent cruisers who got to know each other over the years and whenever they happened to be on the same cruise, they got together and formed a team. By now they either knew all the answers or knew how to stack their team with people who could cover all the different trivia categories. The team called itself the First Mates and from what I could see, the team leaders were a smart-looking couple, Dutch and Mavis. Once again, our team was skimming rock bottom, but we did get an unexpected point because Karla just happened to know that Abraham Lincoln's dog was named Fido. We got nearly everything else wrong and our final score wasn't much better than the day before. I was considering trying to meet Dutch and Mavis to tap them for some hints.

Afternoon tea came and went without incident, and by now I was feeling pretty comfortable with my place among these incredibly talented musicians. The routine was giving my day some welcome structure, too.

No one mentioned the missing cellist or asked if I'd noticed anything amiss, so the subject was conveniently avoided for the day. I did make a point of watching for the frosted cakes at the tea and couldn't help wondering if they were examples of the allegedly exceptional cake-decorating skills of Sorrenta. The cakes looked amazing! I wondered why I hadn't noticed the frosting before as I watched the ten-year-old girl sitting beneath her favorite window, licking a mile-high dollop of light-green frosting swirled artfully atop an oversized cupcake held in one hand. Her other hand was busily typing something in the tablet lying on her lap.

I was looking forward to having dinner with the gang that evening and sharing my adventure in the Baths now that it was a few hours old. When I arrived at Gilligan's Table, however, there were other plans in store for the evening. The table had been decked out with some props. A lorgnette, magnifying glass, a Sherlock Holmes cap, a roll of yellow crime scene tape, a police investigation pad, some handcuffs, and a murder mystery jigsaw puzzle formed a centerpiece in the center of the table. A booklet of game rules lay at each place setting. It was Murder Mystery Dinner night, and everyone was going to play a role as each table tried to unravel a separate mystery.

The rules called for up to eight characters. Since Wink was absent, there was a role for each of us with one to spare. Someone among us was the murderer, and the challenge was for that person to keep his or her identity from everyone else as long as possible, while everyone else tried to figure out who the murderer was. The rules were easy to follow and we each assumed an assigned role and played with levity and hysterics between mystery-themed dinner courses and with frequent toasts of wine as the mystery unraveled.

Diners at the other tables were enacting murder mysteries of their own, and the level of chatter and laughter and ching-chinging from toasting glasses was noticeably higher and more boisterous than in previous evenings.

The setting of our table's mystery was a riverboat on a Rhine tour. A woman was found dead in the theater and it was determined she had been poisoned. The motive was to obtain her jewelry, and the suspects included the chef, the chief purser, and three random passengers. We were all suspects for one reason or another and the mystery unraveled among the crowded stalls of Cologne during the Christmas Market. A descriptive tour of the cities along the Rhine accompanied the shadowy backgrounds of the suspects involved, and everyone had personal anecdotes or memories of travels in that region to share as we worked our way through to solving the mystery. In the end, Dovey was the murderer. She was smoked out by Ginny who solved the mystery and stood up to curtsy. More toasts ensued all around, and we settled into our espressos and desserts feeling satisfied after a job well done with a fun game. For the first time, I examined the icing on my dessert cake and noticed that it was appreciably thicker, more decorative, and richer than on any of the previous nights, which made me half wonder if Sorrenta had just joined the ship that day.

Then, while everyone at our table was considering sitting together at the evening show, Ginny turned to me out of the blue. "Well, we have solved one mystery here, but it seems there is another one left to solve, right here on the MS *Minerva*." She looked expectantly at me and paused dramatically while everyone else, including Dr. Feerum, looked on in anticipation of an answer. "I – er – I don't know what you mean, Ginny," I stuttered innocently. She put down her glass, turned to face me directly and said more slowly and dramatically, "You are not telling us everything you know. I think there is something going on right here on the ship involving a murdered cellist that would explain why you joined the string quartet."

Dr. Feerum cleared his throat and started to say something, but Denny interrupted and admitted he thought there was something fishy about how I took over a staff position suddenly and wondered if Ginny was right. When Skip said it sounded too unbelievable to believe, Denny agreed with him too. Ginny took the opportunity to drive her point home and faced me squarely again. "I think something has happened here that is very, very bad, and they are not telling us. We need to know so we can help solve the mystery of the dead cellist right here on the ship."

It felt like they were all ganging up on me. I vehemently denied anyone was dead or murdered, which only accentuated the part that someone was missing. That admission was not lost on Ginny. I was also keenly aware that I had spilled the beans to Dr. Feerum that morning and hoped he would have the tact and discretion to keep our conversation private. Ginny took a bite of her piña colada sponge cake and then scooped up an extra-thick dollop of the frosting, swirling it on her fork luxuriantly. She thought about what I had said. Putting her fork down, she looked at me again and said she was going to be watching me closely because she feared for my safety. Dr. Feerum was making no effort to break into the conversation. He sat quietly, not paying attention to anything at our table. Instead, he was focused intensely on something or someone in the dining room a couple tables behind me. Suddenly, I was very curious about who was sitting behind me. I asked Dr. Feerum what he was gazing at and as I did so, the rest of the table craned their necks to look in the same direction. There was a birthday celebration at the table behind me, and we watched as the waiters carried over a spectacular birthday cake, aglow with candles, led by Sorrenta wearing a tall chef hat and an immaculate white apron.

Even from where we sat, I could see the luscious frosting that waved and laced over the cake. It was garnished with fresh raspberries and sugar leaves, and the frosting around the sides had been textured into an intricate basket weave. It was too beautiful even to eat. I glanced at the lucky recipient of this cake, but the elderly "birthday boy" was sitting with his back to us. What I did notice, however, brought on a sudden and unexplainable pang. There was Wink, sitting at the birthday table! Suddenly, the waiters circled the table and struck up a jolly rendition of "Happy Birthday." When the last note of the familiar tune drifted across the room and diners at the birthday table ooohed and aaahed over the cake, the clattering started up anew. We watched as Sorrenta sliced the first piece of cake and the waiters cut and served the rest, and then we all looked at each other with blank stares.

"What is Wink doing at that other table?" Skip asked, in a tone implying that Wink was cheating on us.

"He probably wanted some of her frosting," I answered before thinking.

When I left the dining room after dinner, I glanced over at the birthday table. Wink was still there, but he was not eating frosting. He was having a heated conversation with the little girl who spent her time reading and typing at high tea.

Chapter Five

Day Five: February 7, Sunday
St. Bart's (Gustavia
Partly Cloudy. High 81° F/27° C. Low 75° F/24° C.

THE OCEAN MUST HAVE BEEN more turbulent than it looked, because the tender service was delayed. Passengers heading down the stairway to the tender platform spanned five decks, and more pressed into the line on every deck. No one moved forward, but the heaving and swaying of the ship caught several people off guard who nearly fell down and had to grab a handrail or a person to steady themselves.

Some passengers found it more comfortable to sit right there on the steps. We were all tolerating this extreme discomfort for the chance to get to solid land. Conversation and sudden bursts of quiet laughter showed that, despite the delays, people were optimistic and determined to set foot on St. Bart's eventually. In a general announcement, cruise director Pearl advised that anyone with mobility issues might want to reconsider their plans and wait until the ocean calmed down. She offered an alternative activity, inviting guests to the Paris Lounge for a game of Pictionary. She added that some excursions might be canceled and advised us to check with the shore attendant as soon as we got off the tenders on the other side.

Finally, there was a sign of progress and the line poked slowly ahead, the stair squatters inching down a step along with the rest of the standing crowd.

I was booked on something called the Yellow Submarine Underwater Adventure, and people talking about it opined that it was probably going to be canceled, which would have been okay with me. I can get claustrophobic in cramped quarters, and I could only imagine how I would feel in a cylinder under the water without much room to move and no way to escape. Booking that excursion had been the brainchild of Seth, anyway, and by now I was counting the benefits of his absence rather than missing him. I would have been happy to spend a day on the beach, but Seth had wanted the submarine experience, so here I was about to go unless it was miraculously canceled, and I'd be off the hook.

It was finally my turn to board the tender, and from my vantage point at the top of the scaffolding stairs on the ship, I could see why the crew was taking its time with the tenders. The waves were smacking and hitting the tender hard, pushing it against the ship's side. People inside screamed with every hard thwack, and the crew was taking one person at a time and hoisting each one carefully and safely right over the tender's opening and planting them individually on the benches inside. Just as I was escorted to a bench, what felt like a rogue wave caught the tender and slammed it fiercely against the ship, lifting people quite literally out of their hard fiberglass seats. I had a flash fear of vomiting before my brain settled down and rewired that thought into something akin to a carnival ride. All of a sudden, I started laughing inexplicably like a kid in a bumper car.

The ride to the shore was turbulent. But if you have ever looked closely at tender boats, it's easy to see why those things cannot sink. They might take you on Mr. Whale Tail's Wild Ride, but they won't go down. They just keep bobbing up again no matter how hard the water batters and tosses them. The plastic window shields were rolled up and open, allowing a strong breeze and cold spray to splash on us in waves that were either horrific or spectacular, depending on your viewpoint. I was still laughing when we arrived at the tender station twenty minutes later. The best way to ride through turbulence is to hold on and relax. Let yourself bounce around and don't brace or tense up.

We got off the tender and I went straight to the information booth where a friendly woman with a strong French accent greeted me. Sure enough, the Yellow Submarine was canceled. She offered me an alternative ATV adventure that I turned down. But the

Bell Helmet Diving option sounded promising when she assured me it would take place in a very calm and protected cove. It was the shortest excursion as well, leaving more time for a beach break, so I took it.

The boat ride to the cove was brief, and the orientation and safety review took only about fifteen minutes. Most of that time was spent signing our lives away with a ream of waivers. Then we walked to the business end of the short dock where we boarded a boat to a place that was promised to be full of fish and coral and underwater magic. The staff placed huge helmets over our heads which held a bubble of air inside a glass front for viewing out. The helmets were open to the water around our shoulders – you could put your hand under the helmet and scratch your nose if it was itching.

The staff lowered us with a rope into the water one at a time. As soon as I hit the surface, I could feel the water come up to my neck and stop right there even as they dropped me below the surface until I was totally submerged. The sensation of being underwater but with air inside the big helmet over my head took a little getting used to. The sounds were what impressed me first. Inside my helmet, I could hear the air circulation system which kept introducing fresh air and made a dull sound like a little fan. But even more noticeable than that were the pings and pongs from the boat hovering above us and the noise from the activity of my fellow divers. I wondered if any of the sounds I was hearing were from whales calling to each other far off in the ocean.

We followed our French guide Gaston on a path along the sea floor as we held onto the guide rope. Once everyone in our group was situated under the water and we were all holding the rope and ready to walk in a line along the ocean floor, the guide swam by to get our attention and we formed a circle around him. What they forgot to tell us in the briefing was that everything was miniaturized to a Lilliputian dimension through the glass bubble window of the helmet. I held my hand out and it looked like the size of a doll hand. Gaston was only six feet away, but he looked like he was only a few inches tall. The fish were so small I could barely even make them out.

As we started walking along the path, I looked down at my tiny feet and suddenly my mind couldn't grasp that those little feet were holding up my entire body. The whole experience – the sounds, the small appearance of everything and even the very strong currents – were all converging in my head in a way that produced one big, unexpected, annoying and embarrassing effluence of vomit.

Once I threw up, something even stranger and more surprising happened. Someone reached under my helmet and slapped my face. Slap! Slap! Slap! It tingled and felt sharp like a million tiny razors, and I immediately concluded that Gaston thought I'd fainted and was trying to revive me by slapping my face.

I looked around and people were pointing and laughing at me. Even the guy with the video camera came over and zoomed right on my face. What!? I thought. They have the audacity to laugh at my suffering? What kind of people are they, anyway? This was the hardest thing to understand. Here I was, my stomach tied in knots, my feet barely able to support me against the strong currents pulling me in all directions, unfamiliar sounds pulsing through my ears, and everywhere I looked the world was so small that I had lost perspective of my own size. I was horrified! Confused, embarrassed, and seasick right there underwater, if it's possible to be seasick in the sea, and humiliated by my own friends, or at least by my fellow excursioners. It was all I could do to give them a piece of my mind, but this was underwater, and they wouldn't have heard me anyway.

Gaston motioned in a way I knew was asking if I wanted to go back up to the boat. One thing they told us beforehand was that when you gave the thumbs up sign, they would take you back up, and there would be no coming down again. I might have been in pain, but I was going to get my money's worth, so I waved him away and soldiered on.

I think there are some days that are meant to go in one direction no matter what your intentions or how much you will it otherwise, because we were no sooner moving away when it happened again. I felt my stomach go queasy and something rumbled its way from my gut to my throat and blaaa, out it came again. I looked around and couldn't believe how much there was to throw up. I hadn't even had much for breakfast. But there I was, barfing underwater all over again. Slap! Slap! Slap! There it was once more, followed by the million little stings on my face. Only this time what I realized in horror and total amazement was that this stinging sensation was not caused by any slap from Gaston but rather by thousands of little fish with sharp gills swarming inside my helmet to scoop up my mess. Once the slapping stopped and the evidence of my regurgitation was gone, the whole thought of it got me so sick to my stomach – I can't make it up! – I actually did it again. By now I was getting used to it and my stomach was settling. For the third time the clean-up crew filled my helmet, forming a silvery cloud and wiping my face like a scaly piscine napkin with more Slap! Slap! Slap! My fellow excursioners, now reassigned to the category of former friends, were still laughing at me, even more so than before and, even more abominably, that shameless video guy swam by me again with his diabolical camera and took more close-ups.

I was good to go, though. My eyes and mind were finally on the same page with this miniature world. There was nothing left to expel, even if I tried. The worst was over. Determined to get my last dime's worth from this abysmal experience, I motioned to Gaston that I was ready to proceed. Problem is, in my haste to convey my message, I gave him the universal "Okay" thumbs-up signal, which of course in his world was the signal to send me back to the surface and the awaiting boat. I tried to cancel that message, furiously shaking my head and giving the "Okay" sign with both hands but it wasn't enough. My fate was sealed.

Gaston swam over to me and stuck his miniature face directly in front of my helmet and pointed upward, showing me in no uncertain terms that that was where I was headed. The guy with the underwater video came by again and the other members of our group were still watching and laughing. Forget about the octopus, shark, squid, seahorses, corals, conchs, sea turtles, and all the other underwater denizens. Apparently, I had provided the best entertainment of all.

All my efforts to stay with the group were in vain as I felt myself being pulled from the depths. Up, up, up I went as I tried to pantomime to Gaston that I was really okay now and wanted to go on with the excursion. Up, up, up I went as the heartless Gaston didn't think to take into consideration that thumbs up, in the rest of the world, meant "good to go" and that that is what I'd meant to say. Apparently, I was too much of a distraction and they had to get me out of the way. Next thing I knew, two staff persons met me at the surface, took the dastardly helmet off, and guided me up some shaky stairs into the boat. I took the dry towel they gave me and literally threw myself on the floor of the boat where I wanted to lie alone and wallow in my bad luck. I could smell the foul odor of vomit mingled with the diesel fumes coming from the engines. The boat crew brought me a can of Coke which I used as a mouthwash to get rid of the taste in my mouth.

An hour later everyone else who, I'm quick to add, got their full money's worth from the tour, was clambering back on board laughing and chatting excitedly and we were on our way back to the pier. The laughter started up anew when they asked me what it was like to have all those fish descend on me like that. I didn't realize it yet, but when I got back to my room later and looked at myself in the mirror, I saw that the gills of the fish had made millions of minuscule little cuts all over my cheeks and chin. It looked like a bad shave with a dull razor.

I asked Gaston why he hadn't warned us in the orientation that everything looked tiny through the bell helmet and that was what triggered my nausea. Everyone looked at me in disbelief. No one else had experienced that, and I could tell they were really wondering about me. I didn't know how to convince them that I knew what I had seen; that everything appeared to be in miniature, and that was what made me nauseous in the first place. They probably figured I'd had a couple mimosas with breakfast.

So, the Bell Helmet Dive adventure was a bust. And yet, they still got an additional eighty-five bucks out of me for the video that captured me in all my upchucking glory. Yup, that's right. After all that, I went and bought the stupid video anyway. Sucker.

When the shuttle returned us to the tender platform, I inquired about the nearby beaches. It was still early and growing hotter by the minute and I needed to redeem the morning. A nice beach would be the best answer! The same woman in the tourist kiosk was all too happy to direct me to Seashell Beach, assuring me in her lovely French accent that it was very scenic and unspoiled and within easy walking distance.

I strolled along the boardwalk, taking in a gorgeous view of yachts in the gracious harbor to my right and small, red-roofed houses tumbling up the hills that ringed the shallow and protected harbor, or careenage. Nearly everyone knows that St. Bart's is the playground of the rich and famous. The French Caribbean's answer to St. Tropez, it feels more European than Caribbean. It is also trés expensive because everything is first class – no junk here, and everything has to be imported. Visitors are considered "high end" tourists and are held up to that expectation. Bargaining is not the custom in St. Bart's as it is in the little public markets throughout the West Indies. For some people, St. Bart's is too "sanitized," but for most visitors it is paradise.

I approached the far end of the boardwalk and walked around a delightful open-air bistro where patrons munching on crispy baguettes and drinking coffee were enjoying the picturesque view of the boats in the careenage. Clearing that, I saw a small park dominated by a huge anchor that jutted unexpectedly up out of the grass and was impossible to miss. Somehow this anchor had been dragged to St. Bart's from St. Thomas by a captain in the 1800s, although for the life of me, I can't imagine how a captain wouldn't notice somewhere along the ride that he was dragging a few extra tons along behind him. I crossed the very wide street and ascended the stone steps of the St. Bart's Anglican Church, built in the mid-nineteenth century. With its wooden pews and open jalousies inviting the tropical breezes to flush through, it lived up to every expectation of a quaint tropical island church. The road in front of the Anglican church took me a couple short blocks to a corner displaying a sign with an arrow pointing left. The sign said "Plage," and I knew enough French to understand that was the direction to the beach. I noticed two street names on every corner, one in French and the other in Swedish. That's because St. Bart's, while named for his brother by Columbus, was later settled by the French in the early seventeenth century but handed over to the Swedes who held it for nearly a century from 1784 to 1878 before it reverted back to the French. The French and Swedish street names live in harmony to prove that the French and Swedish people always enjoyed a harmonious relationship regardless of which nation was the landlord. Today, St. Bart's enjoys a relationship with France (its official flag is the French flag), but it also enjoys its own island government. French is the language, and the euro is the currency, but in a place like St. Bart's, you're probably better off with a credit card. If you have to ask how much it costs, you probably can't afford it.

Making my way along the path to the beach, I glanced left at an intersection. Two structures caught my attention. One of them was the Catholic church, a large gray building with a unique rounded stone staircase leading up to the entrance. The building dates to about the same time as the Anglican church, mid-nineteenth century. Farther down the same road, a square little tower with a pointed rooftop stood out from the surrounding buildings. I climbed the dilapidated stone staircase leading to it and found myself facing a tall pyramidal stone structure with a wooden door painted green and white on a diagonal. The door was painted by a local artist who happened to be there when the sun cast a shadow against the door, which she retained by painting the two parts of the resulting diagonal green and white. A big round clock high on the tower faced the Caribbean. Originally a Swedish bell tower, a big bell inside once rang every day at dusk to remind the children to empty the chamber pots. In 1918, when the gift of the clock from Kaiser Wilhelm arrived in St. Bart's, the people of Gustavia converted their bell tower into a clock tower.[1]

---

1   The clock ticked over the town for 99 years until the high winds from a hurricane named Irma peeled it off in 2017.

Gilligan's Table

I returned to the beach road where I could see Caribbean-style open-veranda houses embellished with colorfully painted friezes of tropical flowers. Ornate bannisters and wide wooden window shutters confirmed the French influences from its earliest settlers and even brought to mind images of New Orleans. In short order, I was standing in front of a spectacular beach. Seashell Beach was comprised of minuscule seashells right down to the water's edge. A stir of activity centered around a woman in a bathing suit posing against a stunning backdrop of yachts in a jewel-blue sea. It turned out to be a shoot for a fashion magazine cover.

Several women were sprawled out on towels, oiled heavily and sporting nothing on top. One woman I would describe as happily endowed, situated where she was partially hidden among some boulders, was heaving two heavy rocks in a methodical sequence that was likely part of her daily workout regimen. I guessed those boulders she was pumping weighed about twelve pounds apiece and concluded she must have worked up to that, judging from her size triple-Ds. Maybe she was on to something. I found two stones of about a pound or two each and stashed them in my bag to start my own boulder-heaving regimen. Maybe in time I could work up to those twelve pounders and achieve some triple-Ds of my own. Anyway, a girl can dream. I saw a few people from the ship on the beach that day, but for the most part I spent my time alone on my towel alternating between watching the scene and taking refreshing dips, the memory of the morning's bell helmet disaster long gone.

Dr. Pinot, the ship lecturer, was walking along the shore and came over to chat. He told me he had seen some beautiful purple fish in front of a prominent cluster of rocks further down the beach. When he noticed I did not have any snorkeling gear, he offered me the use of his own mask and tube, pointing to the spot where I should swim to see the fish. I told him about my experience with the bell helmet dive earlier that morning, and he assured me that nothing would make me dizzy in this protected cove and urged me to go in the water for a few minutes and enjoy the peaceful world. I took him up on his offer and availed myself of the magical underwater world that lay just beyond the shores of this incredible shell-laden beach. The delicate waving corals, the schools of glittery little jellyfish, and the iridescent purple fish seemed to live and play together in a silent and magical universe of their own so detached from the world beyond the water's surface. I emerged feeling better about everything and returned the mask and tube to Dr. Pinot who moved along to talk with another couple sitting farther down the beach. I started collecting my beach stuff while contemplating a little window-shopping when a familiar woman's voice hallooed me. I turned around to see Ginny waving her arms and running up the beach toward me. She was wearing a colorful sunhat with a wide brim. A colorful scarf of tropical flowers tied the hat to her head.

"I thought that was you," she said brightly. "Isn't this beautiful?" she added.

"I just went for a little snorkel, courtesy of Dr. Pinot," I told her.

"I don't like to get my hair wet," she said resolutely. "Anyway, I saw a wonderful French bistro with a view of the marina and was going to stop there for lunch. Do you want to come along?"

I had not been planning on eating on shore, but it sounded like fun and I still had plenty of time for lunch and some shopping. "Sure," I said. "Sounds like fun. If it's the same bistro I saw on my way over, the view from its tables is lovely. Let's go."

"Good," she said as we headed up the beach. "I have to ask you some things anyway."

I knew plenty well what "things" she had to ask me about and made a mental note to keep my resolve and not tell her anything. Besides, there was really nothing to say. So far, there had been no interrogations or even casual questioning by the security. Not of me, anyway. For all I knew, Sabrina had been located and they were keeping me out of the loop. Maybe she'd run off with one of the sous chefs.

We approached the same little bistro I had noticed earlier and snapped up the tiny table for two at the edge closest to the front of the patio for some shade and with the best view of the marina. The waiter handed us menus and described the special, a seafood crepe Suzette. Ginny ordered that and I ordered a Niçoise salad with fresh tuna. The waiter then brought a crusty baguette and iced teas and scurried back into the kitchen, leaving us to enjoy the gorgeous view of the mega-yachts.

"You were right about that girl not being murdered, or at least as far as anyone knows yet." Ginny jumped right in and took off as if we had been discussing the subject for days. "I've done a little poking around myself. That musician was very young. Most of the staff members don't remember her well because it was her first assignment on board our ship and she was spending most of her days practicing."

A sudden pang of something, maybe guilt, stung me as I considered the notion that perhaps I should have been practicing a little more than I was.

"No one had a motive to do her in, and maybe no one needed to kill her at all," Ginny went on. "Not as far as I can see. But someone must have needed to get her out of the way. That's what I am thinking, anyway. Usually, these things can be traced back to jealousy over a man," she went on as if she were practicing her closing argument to a jury. "And I don't think she had any money to speak of, so we can disqualify that as a motive."

She was speaking as if I were automatically agreeing with everything she said so far, and I felt the need to break in and try to distance myself from the whole mess. "I don't know anything about all this,

Ginny," I said. "They just asked me to fill in for a while since I play the cello. For all I know, the girl sprained an ankle running back to the ship in Old San Juan and missed it as easily as that. She's probably safe with her relatives right now looking forward to rejoining the ship when we return to Old San Juan again."

"That would make sense if she had communicated with the ship in all this time," Ginny argued logically. "They would say she is safe, and she just missed the ship and they could arrange to fly her to the next island to meet the ship. But I think there is a poor girl somewhere out there, either drowned overboard or taken hostage to keep her out of the way of someone who is up to no good . . . and I believe that someone is on this ship!"

"You are very good at solving mysteries, just like you figured out it was Mrs. Mooney who was the murderer at our murder mystery dinner last night," I said. "But this is real life, and the investigators and security people are all over it. They don't need us to fill in the gaps with speculation and hearsay."

"Then you just be very careful, Marianne," she said, looking directly at me. "You may be at risk of danger too because whatever happened to that girl happened because she was in a position to see or know something and now you are in her exact position. And whoever was involved might think they didn't complete the job and try to finish it with you. You never know about these things." Then she added, "If they are making you wear Sabrina's things for the quartet, you should insist on wearing your own. You have your own black dress. You can wear that and put a different scarf around your neck. Sabrina's dresses may mark you and you could be taken for her by mistake."

"Well, that would only be the case if more people are involved than are on the ship right now as well as if the people who meant to do Sabrina harm don't know that I am not Sabrina," I explained, starting to second guess myself.

Ginny completely dismissed my argument and startled me with, "Has any stranger contacted you or left any threatening messages for you?"

I wished Wink had asked me the same question as point-blank as Ginny was asking me right now. Of course, the answer was a resounding yes. But if I told Ginny this, I would be admitting out loud that I had never told Wink about the threatening messages even though he had told me explicitly to report anything untoward to him. I could almost set my watch by Ginny telling Wink what I should have told him myself, so I did not answer her question.

"Please," I begged, "can we not talk about this anymore, Ginny? I don't feel comfortable saying anything at all right now."

"Whatever you wish," she said, picking up her fork as the waiter emerged again and placed our lunches in front of us.

After a delectable lunch and light talk interrupted

by pleasant banter with some other folks from the ship who recognized us as they passed by, we sauntered along the main street for a little window-shopping before returning to the tender station. I saw a cute black dress, simple and accessorized in a very French way with a yellow straw bag and beaded scarf and went in to try it on. Over two thousand euros! I wasn't sure how much that translated into American dollars, but I was pretty sure it was over my budget. And that didn't include the straw bag or the scarf! Ginny laughed and offered to buy it for me in a magnanimous gesture that was more show than substance. I put aside any aspirations to update my wardrobe on St. Bart's, resolving that my own black dress would do just fine a little longer.

BACK IN MY ROOM on the MS *Minerva*, a crisp white envelope lay on my bed, contrasting with the dark green bedspread. I opened it to find a note reading, "Please meet your security team for an update and questioning that may help us resolve the unexplained absence of Ms. Sabrina Verbena. We request you report to the ship's security office, next to the infirmary on Deck 4, directly following afternoon tea. Thank you." It was signed by Peter "Wink" Tasker, Officer in Command, Security Detail. I had no idea if it would be a group interrogation or if they wanted to see me alone. I didn't know if Wink would conduct the interview or whether there would be an entire panel of interrogators. Either way, I decided I would tell everything I knew, straight up with no holds barred, even the fact that I had let the cat out of the bag with Dr. Feerum, and that Ginny was asking nosy questions. It almost seemed moot because the entire Gilligan's Table already knew about the missing cellist and for all I knew, so did the rest of the ship. For the first time, I was regretting my involvement in this saga, but I was in too deep and there was no way out.

I couldn't resist another go at trivia and had just enough time to make it to the theater to join my group. Somehow, the team was crystallizing as my refuge against the onslaught of endless questions and intrigue over the missing cellist from my companions at Gilligan's Table. My trivia partners were already seated, in full throttle, talking up a storm, when I took my seat. Pearl started in at that very moment, telling us that the day's theme was transportation. I almost groaned out loud when the first question was, "How many ships pass through the Panama Canal every year?" No one on our team had the slightest idea and we settled randomly on five hundred, which was a far cry from the answer of fourteen thousand Pearl was looking for. The next question was no easier. "How many planes were grounded on 9/11?" We didn't have a clue and guessed a thousand. We were a mere three thousand shy of the correct answer. But we did score one point for the answer to the world's busiest vehicular bridge, thanks to Kate who painted lighthouses for a hobby. She once painted the Little Red Lighthouse at the foot of the George Washington Bridge in Manhattan and learned at the time that the George Washington Bridge was the busiest vehicular bridge in the world! Amazing! When Pearl gave the answer, she also added that the bridge sees a yearly volume of over a hundred and four million vehicles. Of course, I don't have to tell you it was the First Mates team that placed first once again. And they had only six people on their team. One couple wasn't even there.

The afternoon tea recital went swimmingly, considering how little preparation I had put into it. We played classical versions of Broadway musical theme songs. While the room was by no means packed, as people were still shopping and enjoying the beaches on St. Bart's, the guests who attended seemed to love the fun twist to our usually classical format. A solitary figure sat beneath a window focused on her book, but this time her parents were nowhere in sight. She was immersed in her book and had on her lap a china dish with a wedge of frosting-topped cake. I looked at the desserts across the room and had to admit they all looked exceptionally luscious. I reluctantly credited Sorrenta. I still hated her, though.

Directly after the tea, I was knocking on the glossy white metal door of Wink's office, tucked back in the furthest corner of the fourth deck between the infirmary and a door ominously labeled "Brig." Danita and Valetta had already been interrogated separately and had filled me in. Mario had been his usual man of few words and had little to add. His interrogation was scheduled for after dinner.

Valetta and Danita told me they were asked when they last saw Sabrina, whether she had any enemies they knew about, if there was anyone she didn't like or talked about on this cruise or any prior ones, and if either of them knew her friends or family back home. They were asked if they had anything to do with her disappearance and asserted that they had nothing to do with it and only wished she would come back to rejoin the quartet. They had seen nothing unusual or suspicious on board, and since both of them remained on the ship in San Juan, they did not know where Sabrina had gone that day. Neither one knew whether she had been planning to get off the ship or visit anyone in San Juan. They told me all this, assuming I would be asked the same questions. I knew how to answer those questions, and as I waited for Wink to answer his office door, I hoped he would ask me if I had received any mysterious messages just as Ginny had asked me at lunch that day. But, whether he asked or not, I was determined to come clean and tell him of the threatening messages I had received.

When the door opened, Wink led me inside the stark and antiseptically white office. Nothing but a lamp, a pen, and a computer were on the metal desk, behind which was a well-used office chair. A file cabinet and chair were the only other pieces of furniture in the room. No vase of flowers, no pictures of girlfriends or dogs, not even a coffee mug. He drew the extra chair up for me. I sat down and said, "I already know what you are going to ask me, and I'm sorry but I don't know anything about this case. I don't even know what Sabrina looks like. To be honest, I regret jumping in because I never dreamed it would end up pulling me into the investigation like this. I mean, how could I have anything to do with Sabrina's disappearance? What do they think, that I did her in just to have a chance to spend my holiday working on the cruise ship?"

"Well, that plus a free future cruise," he said and winked.

"Oh, you got me there. That would certainly seal the deal then," I joked, feeling a smile break across my face.

"Listen, Marianne," Wink said, "I know you didn't have anything to do with Sabrina's disappearance just as much as I know those other girls and even that kid, Mario, are innocent. But on a ship, any irregularity like this is considered a crime. Everyone is suspect and we don't stop our investigation until all stones are turned and every possible line of inquiry is followed. Thoroughly. Sabrina's room has been closed off and is considered a crime scene until we reach Miami where the authorities will come on board and take over if she hasn't materialized by then.

"Right now, I am investigating Sabrina's job orders and itinerary from the ship itself. It doesn't happen often, but sometimes these things can be traced back to a simple screw-up on a work schedule. With thousands of these kids running around doing all kinds of jobs on the ships and transferring from ship to ship and needing time off for this and that, schedules can get messed up. For all we know, Sabrina was issued the wrong schedule and is just waiting for her next assignment, thinking she finished the last one in San Juan. Or she might have received a directive to report to another ship by mistake, even from another cruise company, or from a different agent. She might even have ended up on the wrong ship somehow without realizing it until it was too late. Besides the MS *Minerva*, the MS *Athena,* our sister ship, was also in San Juan that same day. The ships are virtually identical, and she may have mistakenly boarded the other ship and didn't realize it until it was too late. She simply may be too embarrassed to admit it to anyone and is hiding out with a sympathetic crew member until that ship returns to San Juan or even Miami. I know that's a long shot, but it's more plausible than the thought of someone trying to knock that poor kid off. I mean, she's twenty-two years old, has no enemies, and certainly no money. There just isn't a motive."

"Except of course a free future cruise," I snickered and heaved a sigh of relief.

"I don't need to interrogate you at all, Marianne. What you're doing is a wonderful thing here, and if no one has thanked you on behalf of the ship, then allow me to be the first to do just that. Your talents are amazing, and your grace and magnanimity are arguably bigger. You've swept in and answered a need that no one else could fill, and you've been keeping a hectic rehearsal and performance schedule at your own sacrifice. I only hope you're finding some time to enjoy yourself. That is, besides getting lost in the grotto the other day and nearly getting yourself killed on those rocks. What were you thinking, girl?"

"Uh," I started in, "it was, well, I had just been in the grotto a while before and I thought I knew my way around. I guess I wanted to show off to Skip and Denny. They were so amazed by the place. It felt kind of nice to be their guide. Then I don't know what happened, but I looked around me and I was all alone. It was awful until you found me."

"Why are you here alone, Marianne, I mean on this cruise?"

I looked at Wink in disbelief. I didn't know what had put him up to that question. I didn't want to flatter myself by thinking it was his way of showing an interest in me. After all, he was all about Sorrenta. She was his focus of interest, not I. Besides, coming from anyone else, that question could be taken as a little scary, or even as a red flag.

"I don't know what you mean," I said and put on my best quizzical expression.

He dropped his head into his hands propped up on his elbows. He said nothing and waited. I caved. To this day I don't know why I did so, but I recounted the last year and a half of my life with Seth and how he backed out of the trip at the last possible second. In a way, it was the second time in one day that something had poured out of my mouth uncontrollably. I told Wink that on one hand I had been surprised at our break-up while on the other hand I was surprised it hadn't happened sooner. I told him how I had thought it would be hard to get over Seth, but how quickly I actually did get over him here on the ship. If Seth meant to be cruel, maybe it backfired on him because it was turning out okay for me. Wink stopped me cold when he suddenly asked if Seth posed any threat to me. I wondered why he would bring that up and what it had to do with anything. "There's no reason I can think of," I answered, "unless he took out a life insurance policy on me, but we're not married and never even cohabited, so I don't know how he could do that." I was half joking, but Wink started jotting things down on a small pad he pulled out of the drawer in his desk. "No, Seth wasn't violent or vindictive. If we weren't soulmates, at least we weren't out to kill each other either. Nothing like that. In fact," I added, "if I have to admit something, I'm still secretly hoping he will show up and surprise me on one of these islands."

Wink looked at me for a very long while. Then he spoke slowly and deliberately. "Marianne, I need you to listen to me and take everything I say very seriously." His eyes blazed into mine like lasers. "I want you to look over your shoulder when you are alone. I want you to tell me anything you see or hear that is menacing, threatening, or even just a little odd. Here is my card; you can always dial my pager at 5111, even if it's late at night. And speaking of that, I don't want you to be going up to the deck at night anymore. You almost became shark food Monday night." If I'd been against the wall, Wink's eyes would have been nailing me to it. "And you didn't tell me about that, so now that I have you in an official interrogation, I am commanding you to tell me anything else about that incident. On pain of being disembarked. This is serious. It is for the safety of you as well as the other passengers."

"How did you know about that night on the deck, Wink?" I asked tremulously.

"There's a little thing we call cameras all over the place. The only thing we couldn't get a good reading of was the attacker's face because he was wearing a mask. And we lost his trail once he got back inside the ship and got lost in the crowd. We don't know if he is a crew member or passenger or even an officer. He may not even be on the ship anymore. He could have disembarked in Virgin Gorda or St. Bart's. There are guys who get on these ships and run around attacking people and robbing staterooms and even pushing people overboard, and they disappear as suddenly as they appeared, only to be found on another ship."

"Scary," I said. "They sound like pirates."

"Very much so," he agreed.

I cleared my throat and told him about the messages left on my machine. He shrugged and didn't sound surprised that I'd kept something from him. "Did you save them?" he asked flatly. I could see the blood pumping through his neck veins.

"No. I was scared, because it warned me not to tell anyone. I didn't even think about saving it. Do they get saved automatically?"

"I'll check your message recordings in our database."

"Messages," I cleared my throat.

"Messages," Wink repeated. "More than one." Long pause. "Was it the same voice both times? Was it familiar?"

"Yes and no. It was the same voice, but not familiar. In fact, it was muffled like he was talking through thick cloth stuffed with steel wool."

"And what did they say?"

"Leave. Go home. The second one said not to tell anyone 'or else.'"

"The more I am hearing, the more I am inclined to think you may be in even more danger than Sabrina who is probably safe at a relative's or on another ship right now."

"Well, I hope she is safe," I said. "Has anyone tried calling her emergency contacts?" I tried to offer helpfully.

"Someone did place a call to her mother, who said Sabrina had sounded fine when she called her from

San Juan. They'd planned to talk again the next day when the ship was in Miami, but when Sabrina didn't call, her mother was not overly concerned because it was only a day later, and she knew sometimes Sabrina couldn't leave the ship."

"It must be hard knowing someone who lives on a ship and living with uncertainty about when they can reach you," I said. I had never really thought about the logistics of working a long-term contract at sea, and how it affects lives back at home.

Then Wink said more lightly, "I'll have to miss dinner, so save me a seat in the theater for the comedy act tonight and I'll join you there right after I interrogate Mario. If you get any hair-brained ideas about strolling the outside decks after dark, I will let you do so under one circumstance: that you call and wait for me to join you. Oh, and one more thing," he added, as if the thought had just come to him, "if you are wearing Sabrina's gowns for the quartet, stop doing it. I'll tell the rest of the quartet too. Wear your own clothing, whether you match them or not."

I felt like telling him I'd already been warned about that. I got up to leave the office, but he had more to say.

"Oh, and one last thing before you go," he said, just as I was reaching for the door handle. "The night you skipped dinner, the rest of us at Gilligan's Table decided to book an excursion in Dominica. It's the Champagne Snorkel and we're hoping you can join us." His expression changed and he was smiling. "It should be over in plenty of time for your afternoon tea commitment. Stop by the excursions office and see if you can book it, unless, of course, you have already made other plans for that day that you'd rather do."

I let myself out of his office and stopped directly at the shore excursions desk to book the Champagne Snorkel Tour on my way to the dining room. With the diversion of the murder mystery dinner the prior evening, all of us gathered around Gilligan's Table were looking forward to sharing two days' worth of our experiences on shore. Dr. Feerum was the only one missing.

"Wow, Marianne!" Skip said excitedly. "That was some close call yesterday. We thought we were going to lose you for good. Why'd you run away from us down there? Those were some rogue currents you got yourself caught in! You could have been grabbed by one and pulled out to sea without anyone ever knowing what happened to you."

Ginny looked on in stunned silence as she lowered her wine glass without taking so much as a sip. "Is someone trying to kill her?" she asked menacingly to no one in particular.

"Yesterday," I clarified for the rest of the table, "I met Skip and Denny at the Baths on Virgin Gorda, and while we were going through, I shot ahead to scout out the trail and ended up getting lost in the grotto. Then I had to squeeze my way out and ended up on the surf side of the rocks. It nearly did me in, but I was able to climb up a rock and that's when Wink saw me and guided me to safety. And no, Ginny, there is no one trying to kill me." I hoped.

Mr. Mooney cleared his throat and proclaimed what a mahhhvelous day he and Dovey had had on St. Bart's. They had gone shopping in the boutiques, and Mrs. Mooney showed off her new watch and ring and bracelet, bragging that she had paid for them with her winnings from the casino. "She's at it all night long, the old girl," Mr. Mooney boasted as his wife smiled and nodded her bobble head in consent.

"What do you do besides gamble?" It was Ginny asking a question in her very direct way. Somehow, she could get away with it because of that strong German accent. If I had asked the same question, I'd be lynched along with my Midwest twang.

"Dovey is a damn good gambler, and pretty cute too, I might add." I closed my eyes and was hearing Mr. Magoo's voice. I opened them and there was Thurston Howell the Third. Mr. Mooney went on to announce to the table how in Dovey he had married the goose that laid the golden egg because for as long as he'd known her, she had been a gaming enthusiast. "She's even figured out how to do it on our computer at home," he added proudly. "Imagine how clever she is for that!"

My eyes turned to Ginny's who caught mine and then darted to Skip, while Denny and I made simultaneous big eyes at each other and then Skip and

I matched eyes while Denny and Ginny did. It was like toasting and cross-toasting across the table only with eyes instead of wine glasses. Only the Mooneys seemed oblivious. Before the moment became downright awkward, Dr. Feerum joined the table, filling the empty seat between Mr. Mooney and Ginny. He smiled at everyone and sat down. He looked very smart in a white shirt behind a crisp burgundy blazer mercifully lacking that pocket protector.

"So, how did you enjoy St. Bart's?" Dr. Feerum asked no one in particular as he settled into his seat.

Ginny spoke first and recalled how she'd spent the day on Seashell Beach and then commandeered me to join her for lunch at the French bistro. She conveniently omitted the whole part about grilling me over the missing cellist. She passed around her smart phone with a picture she had taken of the beach showing her manicured pink toenails posed delicately among the seashells and described the sight of the shell-covered beach with enthusiasm as everyone admired the picture. Denny turned to Dr. Feerum and asked if he had gone on the deep-sea fishing expedition and hung on the professor's every word as he related the stories about the enormous snappers and tuna and swordfish they had caught and released. Denny nearly clapped his hands in approval and said he and Skip were looking forward to their turn in Antigua. I wasn't sure but thought that might be the same deep-sea fishing expedition I had booked with Seth. Skip and

Denny talked excitedly about their ATV adventure on St. Bart's, adding that their first choice, the Yellow Submarine Adventure, had been canceled due to the rough waves.

"I was booked on that one as well," I said. "They offered me the ATV alternative, but I went for the Bell Helmet Dive Experience instead." I smiled and spared them the details. Not exactly dinnertime conversation, if you know what I mean.

"The ATV was a fun way to see the island," Skip said. "I wish you had come along with us. It would have been nice to have you with us."

"I'm inclined to agree," I said, and wished I'd opted for it instead of the Bell Helmet Dive.

The ship's chef had concocted a typical island seafood dinner as the night's special that included a fisherman's sampler platter piled a mile high with fried, baked, broiled and poached fish, scallops, mussels, lobster, crab, squid, and shrimp, and served up with a pail of coleslaw and French fries and corn muffins. Everyone ordered the special except for Mr. Mooney, who ordered a plain hamburger with French fries which was his usual choice. The fisherman platters arrived so much higher than promised that they were served atop large chargers to collect everything that was falling off the pile. Bowls of ketchup and tartar sauce and cocktail sauce and platters of lemon wedges were passed around the table enthusiastically.

"Does everyone know that the karaoke contest is

tonight?" Ginny asked between satisfying mouthfuls of coleslaw and fried shrimp.

"Are you going to enter it, Ginny?" I asked.

"I was going to ask if you were," she answered without missing a beat.

"I hadn't thought about it, but I suppose I could go up and check it out after the comedy act. I don't have anything ready, though."

"You must have a nice voice," Ginny said. She always had a way of deflecting one part of the conversation to start it going in another direction.

"Well, it's not bad, but I've never taken my singing very seriously," I answered truthfully. "I'm more of an instrument-playing kind of music maker."

"What about anyone else?" I asked, looking around with interest at the other members of Gilligan's Table.

"I can sing 'Monster Mash,'" Denny offered.

"Oh, for heaven's sake. That's not for karaoke," Ginny protested.

"Well, I heard someone sing it at a karaoke bar in Cleveland one time," he said defensively.

"It must have been Halloween night," Ginny said. But it's not for karaoke on the MS *Minerva*."

"Believe it or not," Skipper said, opening the top button of his shirt and clearing his throat, "I was the lead in my high school musical. *Fiddler on the Roof*."

"Oh! That is so funny," Ginny looked up and started to laugh. "You aren't even Jewish! How did they choose you? Weren't there any nice Jewish boys in your high school?"

"Well, if you must know exactly, I was actually the understudy. The main guy was Herb Greenberg."

We all threw back our heads and laughed. "Can you remember any of the songs?" Dr. Feerum asked.

"Yes, I had to know them all because there was a bad case of mumps going around that year. Some of the kids in the high school were stricken and I had to be ready in case Herb came down with them. In the end, they never needed me, but I did learn to deliver a resounding rendition of 'If I Were a Rich Man.'"

Everyone laughed again.

"Then you should enter the contest tonight," Ginny said like it was settled.

"I might just give it a try," Skip said. "But I'll need a cheering section, so I expect you all to be up there with me. First one up there after the comedy act has to save seats for the rest of us. Last one buys our drinks. Hey, Ginny, since you brought it up, are you going to sing too?"

"Oh yes," she said, flirting her eyes at him. "I sang and danced for years. I was very popular on stage. I know so many good karaoke songs."

"I bet you have a great voice. I can picture you in an opera."

"Why are you saying that?" Denny chirped up. "Because you think she's the fat lady?" He was referring to that old opera joke about the fat lady singing.

"Ohh!" Ginny winced.

"No, no, no! Denny! That's awful. Apologize to Ginny right now. I was just commenting that she has the look of an actress. She could be on stage like a movie star."

Ginny made no pretense of hiding her pleasure at the flattery. She paused and then announced to the table and our entire half of the dining room that she would be singing the song that is her country's national anthem and her personal specialty, 'Edelweiss.' We all agreed to meet upstairs after the comedian's show, and as soon as we lapped up the last of our hot fudge ice cream sundaes, we scooted off to find seats in the theater before the comedy act started.

I split from the rest of the group and took two seats near the aisle, sitting in one and draping my sweater over the one next to me. As the house lights dimmed, a finger brushed lightly across my back. Wink found me and laughed heartily when I relayed the dinner conversation. We laughed through the comedian's show and then took the elevator upstairs to the Paris Lounge for the karaoke contest. Skip and Denny had beat us to the punch and had pushed some chairs close to a loveseat so we could all sit together. Ginny bounded in, followed by Mr. Mooney, who was without his lovely Dovey.

"Dovey is feeling lucky tonight and will join us in a while. She wants to try her hand at the craps table," he announced. He ordered a vodka martini from the waiter, who stopped by and deposited a bowl of salted nuts on the table.

Skip was the first one called up to the microphone. The music started and he belted out the words to 'If I Were a Rich Man' and wasn't half bad. He wasn't altogether in tune, but the drinks were two for one and no one complained. His accompanying antics must have been stored in his long-term memory from his high school days, and he was entertaining. He received a rousing ovation from our corner and sat down satisfied with his efforts. Denny leaned over and patted his father on the shoulder with approval.

A string of other contestants followed, none of whom excited the audience as much as Skip. Denny made a debut with "Monster Mash" that left the room in helpless laughter. Even Ginny was laughing in uncontrollable fits, and Skip said he swore she was going to wet the floor.

It was all fun and the talent seemed to deteriorate with each succeeding contestant until Roy, the assistant cruise director who was the karaoke emcee, introduced Sorrenta, who appeared from the shadows wearing a dazzling cream-colored sparkle-studded gown that showcased her voluptuous figure and her coppery-red hair mounded in luscious heaps atop her head. She took the mic and sang her heart out to "La Habanera." If I were totally honest with myself, I would have admitted that she looked better than Sophia Loren and sounded at least as good as Maria Callas. The girl has one set of lungs, I told myself, not able to restrain myself from glancing at Wink, who made no attempt to hide the sheer pleasure on his face. When she finished, Roy took the mic back from her, explaining that Sorrenta was more of a "guest appearance" and not part of the karaoke contest, but they liked to slip her in anyway because it was such a treat to hear her sing. The room exploded with applause and, blowing a kiss directly at Wink, Sorrenta disappeared as quickly as she had appeared.

"Well, that's not really fair to those of us following her," Ginny said with a huff. And as if there were demons intentionally trying to play out a self-fulfilling prophecy, Roy announced right then, "Now we are pleased to present to you Ginny who will sing 'Edelweiss.'" Ginny rose and, acknowledging the audience with imperial grace, walked to the front and took the mic for herself.

"Dovey's missing a good show," Mr. Mooney said as Ginny returned to her seat later, positively glowing. She looked as if she had just won an Oscar. She seemed to be thoroughly pleased with her performance, smiling through the beads of perspiration on her forehead and fanning herself as if she had just been standing in front of the spotlights on the stage of the Met. She sank into the upholstered chair and rewarded herself with sips of the melon martini a waiter had brought to her while she was on stage. We piled genuine compliments on her.

By the time the winner was announced, it was

already a few minutes past midnight. We were all surprised because the winner was a woman who had sung a song about wind beneath wings made famous by Bette Midler and she had sung it a bit flat. But Roy rewarded her with a fanny pack embroidered with the MS *Minerva* logo. Wink asked if I had any plans to go out on deck at that hour and offered to accompany me if so, but I assured him I was heading right back to my bed for a good night's sleep. He told me to call immediately if there was a message on my phone and we parted ways for the night. Nothing was waiting for me in my room except for an octopus made from a towel with eight towel-tentacles spread out on my divinely comfortable bed.

Chapter Six

Day Six: February 8, Monday
Roseau, Dominica
Scattered Showers. High: 82°F/28°C. Low: 70°F/21°C.

I WAS ALREADY UP and starting the day with an early breakfast when the loudspeaker crackled to life. Instead of Pearl, it was the captain's husky voice that filled the air. He stated that the ship had made an emergency stop at St. Martin during the night to disembark a passenger who had suddenly taken ill. Consequently, our arrival time at Dominica would be at noon instead of eight in the morning as scheduled, but instead of departing at six o'clock in the evening, we'd stay there until eleven o'clock at night. Immediately following the captain's announcement, Pearl came on to say that the excursions team was already hard at work rearranging all the tours in Dominica. They would go on as planned, she assured us, but just later than originally scheduled. Since we would be in port until night, the staff was planning a fun deck party with the band playing calypso, soca, reggae, and some line-dancing music for the die-hards, with Caribbean drinks and snacks served, all starting at eight thirty at night. She added that afternoon tea was canceled as most guests would still be on their excursions. When I got back to my room, a revised edition of *The Tides* was already awaiting me in the message slot on my door. Inside my room, I walked over to the desk to pick up the blinking phone. The message was from the excursions department informing me that the Champagne Snorkel excursion would now start at three o'clock. Without tea scheduled that day, and with a lot of time between noon and the excursion, I would have time to explore the island on my own.

A morning trivia game was starting up, so I headed to the theater and met with the three other people from my team who had bothered to show up. I was happy Meredith was there. I was happy to see Mildred and Stan too. They hadn't really contributed to any points so far, but they were pleasant enough company. They brought their own coffee and Danish and settled right into the upholstered chairs.

Pearl shuffled her papers around as she offered golf pencils and pieces of scratch paper to those that came without their own.

"Today," she said, "I'm using the subject of fear for our trivia theme. You need to decide what the phobia is from the word."

Okay, this sounded intriguing. I felt a little bump

of confidence. But when we were done and the answers were read, our little team looked more deflated with every passing answer. Once again, we had tanked. I mean, who knew that monophobia meant fear of being alone? We thought it was fear of mononucleosis. Ecophobia meant fear of houses, not fear of recycling.

Triskaidekaphobia? Fear of the number thirteen. I feared just trying to pronounce it! And pathophobia meant fear of disease, not fear of hiking trails as we'd reasoned. But at the very end of the list, a miracle happened, at least that's how we explained our unexpected point. It was for the word chrematophobia. We were ready to write down a fear of whipping cream, but Mildred kept insisting it meant fear of money instead. Who would have known that? We only went with her suggestion because she was so persuasive. No one had ever seen Mildred this insistent. She said she had worked in a Greek diner when she was a teenager. It was her job to take the money to the bank every day and make the deposit. She said Mr. Milopoulos, the owner, always gave her the "chremata" bag, as he called it, and one day he told her that chremata meant money in Greek. Well, thanks to Mr. Milopoulos and Mildred's sharp memory, we got that one right! Only one team got the bonus question right, pentheraphobia, fear of one's mother-in-law. I don't have to tell you it was Dutch and Mavis's team. After trivia everyone disbanded, laughing and in high spirits. Pearl always had a way to make people laugh and feel good. Fear of one's mother-in-law? What next?

As THE SHIP NOSED its way into port, I could see that Dominica begged to differ from the other Caribbean islands that share powder-white beaches with crystal sapphire waters. As we glided by, the little capital of Roseau that hugged the waterfront with a carbuncle of houses, storefronts and old stone churches came into view. I was gazing at a serene and colorful West Indian harbor town set against a backdrop of lush green mountains with no beaches in sight. Small houses heaped in a haphazard coziness among the hills of Roseau. Above all else, it was the sight of all the verandas on the upper floors that caught my attention. Beautiful, open-air spaces hung over the streets providing a respite for families to catch a rare breeze behind wooden bannisters of Victorian fretwork designs that also provided some shelter from the frequent rain showers for the pedestrians scrambling along the streets below.

I was toting my bathing suit and towel by sheer force of habit as I descended the ship's gangway and set off to check the place out. What I soon realized was that if I had any intention of swimming on a beach that day, Dominica had quite another adventure in store for me. The cruise ship offered shore excursions showcasing the island's well-earned claim to fame as

"Nature's Island." Options included river tubing, whale watching, snorkeling, and exploring the rainforest with a hike or Jeep safari. I was going it alone, however, and for some reason I was drawn to the notion of visiting one of the beautiful waterfalls. A taxi driver standing next to his van offered me a ride to the Emerald Falls and Pool, promising they were more beautiful than Trafalgar Falls, where the ship's excursions went. The only problem was the cost– a hundred dollars! I asked a few other people from the ship to join us and in no time Felix, the driver, and I had collected an enthusiastic posse of seven fellow cruisers for a trip to the Emerald Falls and Pool. The drive up the scenic roads included fleeting views of the imposing Trois Pitons, the ancient volcanic peaks, sights of pineapples growing naturally next to banana and calabash trees, and charming roadside island houses painted in distinctive Caribbean colors and displaying architecture that recalled French and English colonial influences.

By contrast to these reminders of an older era, Felix showed us the brand-new roads and bridges built by Chinese and Taiwanese investors. He also pointed out the abundance of luscious fruits and oversized flowers growing in this rainforest and laughed as we intermittently splashed through rain showers, which he said is why it is called a rainforest. At one point we all got out of the van and followed Felix to a small hot spring stinking of sulfuric bubbling mud and gas, common enough in this highly volcanic setting.

The entrance to the Emerald Falls and Pool was the typical touristy parking lot with taxis and vans and tour buses vying for the available parking spots just across the way from the hubbub of friendly vendors selling local crafts, packaged spices, and postcards from wooden stalls beneath canvas awnings. Nearby we paid our admission and started the leisurely stroll down the path through beautiful rainforest trees and lush wildlife, commenting along the way on the remarkable absence of mosquitoes. When breathtaking views of the waterfall began to come into sight below, our feet picked up the pace over the stone- and root-covered path. There is something about the sight of water falling with abandon into a beautiful pool that pulls human beings close to it, as if drawn by some unknown primal urge to return to life's watery primordial soup. The bright sun-dappled greens and deep mossy browns of the verdant foliage, festooned with pink flowers dangling from dripping vines, were set against the dark tumbling waters of the falls and looked for all the world like the Garden of Eden. Closer in, people took in the view and then turned around for a photo opportunity with the drooping vines and gushing falls and glistening pool behind them. Some onlookers peeled off tee shirts and shorts, exposing bathing suits, and clambered down the slippery rocks to launch themselves into the calm, inviting water. Watching them, I regretted my split-second decision to leave my bathing suit in the taxi up in the parking lot. With longing, I watched the waterfalls plunging precipitously into the picturesque pool just a few feet from my toes and sorely regretted having come all this way only to forego what looked to be the most wonderful adventure and what would have surely made the best memory of all: a refreshing dip.

It was more temptation than I could resist, and without a moment's hesitation, I simply clambered down the rocks and let myself fall luxuriantly into the warm primeval water wearing my tee shirt, cargo pants, and flamingo-orange Crocs. My hot skin thirstily soaked up the softest, most inviting water I had ever felt. I dunked and paddled out to the cluster of rocks directly beneath the falls, letting my head and shoulders take the splashes directly before the water poured into the pool off my back. Then I immersed my head like a willing convert in a baptism. After getting my fill, I emerged and scrambled back up the slippery rocks and along the dirt path to the awaiting taxi for the scenic ride back to Roseau. At one point, I ran my fingers through my hair and almost gasped at how soft it felt. The pure spring water had left my Brillo-thick hair as soft as puppy down. Someone should bottle that stuff, I thought. I vowed then and there not to wash my hair for as long as I could stand it.

When we returned to Roseau, we were treated to an unexpected surprise. An island carnival parade was in full swing with representatives from the local indigenous tribe dressed in their traditional regalia. A great initiative is vested in preserving the local Carib traditions as Dominica is home to the last Carib reserve in the world. The population of pure Caribs, an original Caribbean indigenous tribe, diminishes every year as members mix increasingly with the island's population at large. The African population of Dominica was represented by a flotilla of colorful jumby walkers, as graceful as they were athletic. They moved along in colorful waves, high up in the air on wooden stilts and covered from head to toe with African-inspired masks and gorgeously appointed costumes. Ravishing island beauty queens waved royally from their thrones atop decorative floats gliding along with regal pageantry. Ambiance for the entire procession was provided by oversized speakers on flatbed trucks blaring music so loud that I'm sure it could be heard two islands over. Young boys and girls tried their skills at walking on child-sized stilts as little pajama-clad boys coaxed colorful handmade wooden carts ahead of them with long sticks. I glanced at my watch and started stepping around people in the crowded street to make my way back to the pier when Wink suddenly emerged from the crowd and caught my attention, waving as he walked up the slight incline. He had Skip, Denny, Mr. and Mrs. Mooney, Ginny, and even Dr. Feerum in tow.

"There you are!" he said like we were seeing each other for the first time in a decade. "We've been looking everywhere for you. We're heading over for our Champagne Snorkel tour right now. Come on, let's go!"

Back at the pier, we boarded the small launch and in no time were heading into the deep and beautiful water where Josiah, our guide and pilot, told us to keep an eye out for whales. He told us about the resident pod of sperm whales that stays in the area, making Dominica the only place in the world where these whales can be seen year-round. Reaching up to seventy feet long, sperm whales are the planet's largest predator and can weigh in at sixty tons. They have a whale-sized brain to match, the largest brain in the animal kingdom. They can dive over a mile deep where they look for their favorite meal, giant squids. If they don't find dinner right away, they have plenty of time, as they can stay submerged for an hour. We strained our eyes across the water anticipating the sight of one of these behemoths, but nothing broke the surface other than raindrops that started to pelt us. Josiah said that, in addition to the sperm whale, many other kinds of whales can be seen around Dominica, including the humpback.

This was definitely a no-frills tour with Josiah taking us around part of the coast near Roseau. Some very well-used snorkel equipment waited in a crate, and a cooler stood at the ready with cans of soda pop and the local Kubuli beer and bottles of water. Ginny registered her disappointment when champagne was not offered on the Champagne Snorkel tour. Josiah grinned widely, exposing a shiny gold front tooth, and explained that the "champagne" part of the tour's title described the bubbly water we would be snorkeling in; bubbles, he added, naturally caused by the underwater thermal activity associated with the volcanic nature of the island. Ginny was not consoled. As Josiah told us stories about growing up in Dominica, he was doing a little fishing while guiding our boat to a lovely beach that could have been an island itself, it was so isolated and secluded. He took this multitasking in stride and laughed about it, saying you learn how to do the work of two when there's only one of you. He stopped the boat in a beautiful shallow near the beach where we tumbled off and waded through clear knee-high water toward the rich black sand, characteristic of the volcanic islands. It was completely empty and pristine, with nary a chair, a towel, or even a beer can strewn aside by prior explorers.

When we reached the sand, we all realized simultaneously that Mrs. Mooney was not with us, and neither was Josiah, for that matter. Looking back at the launch, we watched as Josiah hoisted Mrs. Mooney over the side of the boat and then collected her safely on a small inflatable raft he must have procured from his mysterious collection of accouterments under the trapdoor in the floor of the boat. We could hear her intermittently whimpering as Josiah did his best to get her off the boat and float her to the beach. Mr. Mooney took it good-naturedly, saying she would be happy again once she got back into the casino.

Once Josiah and Mrs. Mooney had reached the

sand, we all donned snorkel equipment and plunged into the water to feel what it was like to swim in a glass of champagne. While we were occupied with our underwater encounters, Josiah was busily preparing a picnic lunch of freshly caught red snapper grilled over an open-pit fire, heaping sides of rice and beans, as well as fried plantain, a kind of banana that needs to be cooked, that his wife had prepared for us. She had also prepared a variety of fresh tropical fruits picked from the trees in their backyard. We savored our time together, enjoying the bountiful repast on a beautiful, deserted beach. As I looked around at my friends from Gilligan's Table, I thought to myself that this could be Gilligan's Island. What if we were suddenly stranded here? I mused silently. When our lunch ended, the three-hour tour was nearing its conclusion and we picked up our things to head back to the motorboat. We all knew that meant wading into the warm and inviting water once again, something we all looked forward to.

There was one slight problem, however. There was no motorboat. It had somehow disappeared while we were enjoying our time on the beach. At first we all thought it was some kind of practical joke. Maybe Josiah played it at the end of each tour. Why not? A three-hour tour, a remote tropical beach that could easily pass for an isolated isle, a group of passengers-cum-castaways with nothing and no one in sight. And no way to escape. We all laughed and congratulated

Josiah on a brilliant finale. Mr. Mooney even suggested he'd reward him with a bigger tip for his imagination.

But Josiah was not laughing. Suddenly, as we started to consider the possibility that this might not be a joke, one of those scattered showers passed through. And when it rains in this island rainforest of Dominica, the water comes up from the ground and closes in from all sides. With no umbrellas or protection, and only a few palm trees offering no cover whatsoever, we were drenched to the bone in minutes. We looked at Josiah.

Now we were the ones not laughing.

Skip and Denny sprang into action, slapping together a makeshift tarp from the raft Josiah had used to float Mrs. Mooney to the beach, and we women huddled beneath it. Mrs. Mooney grimaced, and Ginny pursed her lips so hard they were turning blue.

"I knew this was a mistake when we didn't get champagne in a Champagne Tour," Ginny seethed. She pulled her cell phone out of her bag in an attempt to reach the ship, but there was only static coming through the deluge. I was not thrilled about being stranded on a beach or an isle with rain pouring all over me for who knew how much longer. Pretty soon it would start to grow dark. I was wishing the string quartet performance had not been canceled, because then I would have been safe and sound and, most of all, dry, dressed in my gown sitting in the lovely Paris Lounge right about now, bowing the rich notes of Chopin or Mozart or Ravel. By now, the rain was coming down so hard it was impossible to see past the shoreline. We were screwed.

Dr. Feerum walked around the perimeter of the beach to scope it out for anything that could provide some shelter or a means to communicate with the outside world. He came back with a cracked camera case someone had left in the sand.

Josiah sprang into action and tried reaching a friend on his phone but had to leave a message. He tried two or three more friends who had boats.

Wink walked down to the water's edge and waved a white hankie over his head, trying to catch who knows who's attention. And who goes around with a handkerchief in the first place these days? His shirt and pants were stuck to him like his own skin as the rain ran in thick fast rivulets down his flattened hair. I thought he looked very handsome in a rugged and vulnerable way. We all followed him to the shore and a motorboat whooshed by, close enough for us to see, but possibly going too fast to see us. In any event, Wink determined it was too far out to come for us. We all jumped and hallooed to catch someone's attention anyway, but to no avail as the boat cut a straight slit in the water as it whizzed past and out of sight. Another one followed but didn't stop either, unaware or unconcerned that there were people in desperate need of rescue. Then a third boat zoomed by. By this time the rain had let up and we all jumped up and down screaming and flailing our arms and waving our dripping sunhats to get the attention of the boat. It slowed down and came in a bit closer as if to evaluate the situation. We roared and cheered! It looked like it was coming to rescue us, but then it circled back around and headed along its original trajectory, even faster than before.

By this time, Josiah was frantically trying to make contact with any friend of his that could help out, but he was pretty sure they were all taking a nice long nap after running their own tours that day. He called his wife and asked her to drive to the marina and send over anyone there who had a boat. Ginny and Mrs. Mooney were fuming at Wink, blaming him for suggesting this disastrous excursion in the first place. The men were siding with the women because they didn't have a choice, and Wink stood there helpless and drenched, trying to convince everyone we were going to be okay. "The ship doesn't leave until eleven tonight!" he reminded us optimistically. "And this is a legitimate ship excursion, so the ship won't leave without us in any event," he added. But that only made everyone even angrier. Who wanted to consider the possibility of being stranded there until eleven at night?

I had been thinking about Wink for some time now, apart from all the drama of the mystery on the ship. I had been playing a teasing game with myself, a "what if" in a world where Sorrenta didn't exist and where he might actually have an eye on me. How did I feel about him? I kept putting that thought aside because he was already involved with Sorrenta. But something

I couldn't explain tugged at me anyway. And now, seeing him with his hair matted down from the rain and his clothes sopped and unkempt, one sandal lazily unbuckled and everyone holding him in the crosshairs of contempt for things that were beyond his control, I melted just a little. His eyes still twinkled, and that puckish little smile made him seem so vulnerable . . . and huggable. I couldn't deny the feeling creeping over me that I could actually grow to like this man.

No time for thoughts like that! Suddenly, a strange human utterance came from behind a wall of coconut trees. "Uuuulaboolagalunga!" We all turned to see a paunch attached to a man wearing a crown of woven banana leaves studded with red prickly berries. He was coming at us, waving a crude club in one hand and a rusty machete in the other. As he ran wildly toward the beach crying, "Loooobimbooobimkakabamu!" his makeshift skirt of palm leaves parted slightly, giving us a peep show we hadn't asked for and could have lived without. Suddenly, he looked confused and stopped short when he saw us standing there as if something had gone terribly off script. Josiah looked at the semi-clad man, who nervously twitched his gaze back toward the thicket of trees. The man yelled something in German, but all I recognized was "Helmut!" It sounded like a desperate plea for help as the palm-skirted intruder's eyes continued to search the line of trees. "Helmut!" he bellowed again even louder, looking back and forth from the trees to our little group.

Dr. Feerum started to converse with the man in German. A thin smile spread across Dr. Feerum's face as he broke into a soft chuckle, and we all gravitated toward him for a translation. All of us except for Ginny who stayed put by the shore, pouting, resolved not to get involved. She understood German but was clearly not interested in any entanglements that might delay her release from the beach. Instead, she waved a piece of white paper for a passing boat to notice, giving it more priority than a wasted minute on a derelict compatriot from her neck of the woods.

As Dr. Feerum was explaining to us that this was a film shoot, the fervently-summoned Helmut emerged from the trees with his female assistants, Hilda and Heidi, lugging their video cameras and recording equipment. The girls pointed at us and dissolved into helpless and uncontrollable fits of laughter. Apparently, they had not checked out the beach before sending Caliban down the sand flailing his club and machete at the flying fish, and we had innocently photo-bombed the movie scene they were filming. They nodded and smiled at us as they approached, explaining that they were from Switzerland. When they learned of our predicament, they joined us at the shore to watch for any help that might come along. Skip asked if they had a boat that we could use, and they roared more heartily than ever, pointing at the trees and saying they were staying at the very posh resort beyond the thicket of palms. They said taxis were at the ready just waiting to return us to our ship in no time, taking the overland route.

We looked at Josiah, whose gaze was now fixed on the horizon. We followed his gaze to a little boat that swooped into the bay and came in close enough for us to understand he was going to pick us up. Saying goodbye to the Swiss filming party, we splashed through the water, making a beeline for rescue. Even Mrs. Mooney made a miraculous dash through the surf unassisted, and we all clambered on board safely, offering our heartfelt thanks to the nice man, Billiam, who was our savior and the pilot of this little fishing trawler, *Carib Bean*. Once we were settled in, Billiam passed around a cooler filled with sodas and Kubuli beers and told us he had just been tying up to the dock in the marina when a motorboat raced in with the news that some people appeared to be stranded on the beach at Sibouli. He said, "That boat didn't have enough room for everyone so the captain asked me if I would come after you."

Billiam went on, "What better thing did I have to do right then, I ask you, than to push off and make new friends to join me in cracking open some cold ones?" and he held up a bottle of Kubuli. We cheered and toasted and even thanked Josiah for all his efforts to show us such a wonderful time. As we sped back to Roseau, we passed Josiah's boat drifting toward the shore. Billiam steered *Carib Bean* close up, and Josiah jumped off to reclaim his boat. We all waved as he shot off and left us in his wake.

Billiam dropped us off about a quarter mile from our ship at his marina, directly next to the public fish market. As we were walking the short distance back to the ship, Wink and I kept several paces ahead of the others who were still fuming and not wishing to talk with him just yet. We struck up a conversation, and he confided to me that he might not continue with another contract after the current year. Instead, he was contemplating heading security at a major university in New England and even had an offer on the table. He added that it was really hard to maintain a relationship with anyone when he spent so much time at sea. Unless, he continued, it was with someone who was also working at sea and understood the lifestyle. Just as he turned the subject around to ask what I did for a living we were ambushed by a nail-lacquered hand that reached out and patted Wink on the shoulder blade.

It was Sorrenta. I almost threw up. I wondered if this woman ever worked or if she was really a well-disguised passenger. She seemed to have more time off than I did, and I was a legitimate guest. "Sorrenta!" Wink said. "Where did you come from?" He seemed genuinely happy to see her, which made me feel like there was an annoying pebble in my shoe for no reason I could explain.

She leaned in and kissed him lightly on the cheek. "Wink!" she said, smiling brightly and ignoring me completely.

"Day off?" Wink asked.

"Certo," she answered in Italian. "My day off means poor Wink won't have any dessert with frosting on it tonight in the dining room," she said, laughing. "Instead, you'll have to come later for some special frosting I made especially for you," she added in a sensuous accent while she tapped the tip of his nose playfully with her polished index finger.

"Oh, Sorrenta, have you met Marianne? She's a guest and is filling in for the cellist who plays with the string quartet." I thought it was a little demeaning that he forgot he'd already introduced us in Virgin Gorda. Sorrenta ignored me and suddenly looked very seriously at Wink. "Something is wrong?" she asked, furrowing her eyebrows and pouting in a way that made her lip gloss seem even shinier.

"I shouldn't be talking about it, but yes, something is very wrong," Wink said. Then he told Sorrenta about the missing musician. She was quiet and took it all in. She asked only if Sabrina's room had been reassigned to anyone else and Wink told her it was sealed off as a crime scene. I wondered why she would ask such a question and why he would answer her and chalked it up to one too many Kubuli beers.

When we arrived at the ship, Sorrenta started rummaging through her things dramatically and became visibly distraught. "What's wrong?" Wink asked with genuine concern.

"I – er – I can't find my ship pass again," she said, sounding genuinely mystified. Here we go again,

I thought. Either she really forgot it again or she was one heck of an actress. She turned her handbag upside down and dumped its contents into her lap. This time she was carrying an ordinary-sized beach bag, so it was easier to riffle through. As she dropped each individual item back into the bag, she became more and more frustrated. "I can't believe how I could lose something like that a second time," she said. "This is so embarrassing. Do you see it here? Am I just not looking at it?" she asked Wink. He agreed it didn't appear to be there and suggested she check her pockets. "Not there," she said.

"Well, don't worry," Wink assured her. "I'll make sure you get back on board through the security and then you can have the office make you another new card."

"Oh! That is wonderful," she purred.

"I'm happy to help you out, Sorrenta, but you should really take better care of that card," he cautioned.

When we ascended the gangway and submitted our passes to the security team, Wink made a big deal about presenting Sorrenta to everyone. I don't think anyone would have even asked for her boarding pass if Wink had not mentioned that she had lost it. The security guard on duty shooed her past the station into the ship. It was a drill that was starting to get tiresome. There seemed to be something wrong, and I flirted with the notion that it might be a desperate act for attention. Wink and I parted ways at that point and said we'd try to catch up later. He said he had enjoyed our talk and wanted to continue it another time, but I wasn't sure he really meant it.

THAT NIGHT, I was the first to be seated at Gilligan's Table. Ginny arrived soon after and told me the millionaires would not be joining us. She had just run into Mr. Mooney outside the casino who said his wife was busy inside and didn't want to be disturbed from her gaming so they would order from room service later on. It had been an especially distressing day for her, and she could best recover in the casino. It looked like it might be just the two of us, but then Denny and Skip arrived as Ginny and I began to study our menus. Dr. Feerum didn't come and neither did Wink, who I guessed was enjoying the special frosting Sorrenta had saved for him. Just as we finished placing our orders, two tall handsome officers in crisp white uniforms stood over our table and seated themselves in the two empty seats across from us. At first I thought they wanted to conduct an interrogation about the missing musician. But Giulio, the younger one, informed us that it was "Officers' Night," when the ship's officers scattered throughout the dining room to join the passengers at their tables. I glanced around the room to see dozens of distinguished men and women officers sporting crisp navy or white uniforms, sitting ramrod straight among the slumped and generally older passenger population.

"This is just delightful!" Ginny shrieked. She considered herself something of a "catch" and was eyeing the "older" officer at our table, even if he was still in his twenties. He was not wearing a wedding band, an observation that I was sure was not lost on Ginny. She zeroed right in on him and peppered away with questions about his responsibilities, how long he had been aboard this ship, his career aspirations, and how did the MS *Minerva* compare to other cruise ships in his experience. Apparently very accustomed to and comfortable with older women passengers, the prodigal officer fielded her questions patiently and respectfully as she hung on his every word, dabbing the corners of her mouth to catch any errant smudges of lipstick. The waiter returned without missing a beat and took the two officers' orders and returned just as rapidly with everyone's appetizers.

"Has anything happened on this cruise that you find unusual or of especial note?" I asked, secretly congratulating myself on being so clever and sly.

"Nothing much out of the ordinary, outside of the missing musician," Giulio answered, taking a nibble of the chilled ceviche.

I was stunned at this casual drop of classified information.

"You mean they still have not found her?" Ginny gasped dramatically as she swiped the baton from me and took over, looking directly at Visu, the other officer. Visu explained that he was an officer in the ship's communications department and didn't know much about human resources issues other than the scuttlebutt he heard in the crew bar.

"Maybe it's all just a rumor or a mistake and someone was just left back on shore and missed the ship after an excursion. You think someone is really gone for good?" Skip asked the officers with concern.

"Maybe they were pushed overboard," Denny said, staring at the napkin lying folded and untouched beside his plate. "They say that happens, but you never hear about it happening to someone you know."

"And thank goodness for that," Ginny said dismissively, as if she were delivering a sound scolding.

"Well," Giulio stepped in, "we do know that a woman has not been seen since we left San Juan. She was on board when we arrived there, but now she has not been found anywhere on the ship. It is possible she fell or was pushed overboard, but that's so unlikely we are not really considering either possibility. There are other possible explanations for her disappearance that are much more plausible and less dramatic. This happened once before on a ship I was on, and it turned out it was only a case of mistaken identity because it was one of a set of twins using each other's ship passes and it all got straightened out in the end and everyone was accounted for."

"Meanwhile, out of the kindness of her heart, Marianne is sacrificing her own vacation to play in the string quartet until the missing woman appears or until the cruise ends and the missing musician is found or replaced," Ginny reported importantly, her undivided attention again focused on Visu.

"Yes, the staff and crew already know that, and it is very nice of you, Miss Marianne," Visu said, turning to me and nodding his head like a bow.

"So, where do they go from here?" I asked plainly. "I mean, they are investigating and interrogating, but how do they resolve the situation?"

"Oh, it will be resolved," Giulio said with a confident smile. "These are big ships, and they go to a lot of places but there are enough paper trails and people and witnesses along the way so something will come up and someone will connect the dots. In the case of the twins, it was actually a passenger who connected the dots."

Before leaving the table, the officers posed for photos with everyone at the table and Ginny added a photo of her and Visu to her Facebook page. After everyone else had left, Ginny and I lingered over Baileys and biscotti. "You know," she said, "I think maybe Mr. and Mrs. Mooney are not getting along. Do you see how much that woman gambles? I don't know how he can stand it," she said disgustedly. "Some men find the wrong woman and look what happens to them. She will probably throw all their money away in the slot machines. That's all she does. Gambles and plays bingo. I don't understand why he stays with her when there are much more exciting women in the world."

It didn't take a psychologist to see exactly where this one was going. "Ginny," I said, "I think he has been admiring you." I was testing my theory and she took the bait by looking up cautiously and fluttering her eyelashes coyly.

"You think so, Marianne?" she asked sweetly.

"Why yes, of course! In fact, I am almost certain that if Mrs. Mooney suddenly came up missing on this ship, he wouldn't think twice before popping the question and running away with you and never even thinking about Dovey again."

She smiled and looked straight ahead with a faraway gaze in her eyes. "Oh, well, I wouldn't want that to happen, I mean the part about Mrs. Mooney vanishing and all. But if she ever did just disappear in a cloud of dust . . ."

"Or off the side of the ship," I offered in the most innocent voice I could muster.

She glanced at me in disbelief. "Or off the side of the ship like you say," she continued, gaining momentum. "I would probably make my feelings known to Mr. Mooney. I think we would make an exciting couple. He is very handsome, don't you think?"

"Very handsome," I agreed. "I like the color of his hair. Very aristocratic how silvery gray it is. And so thick. Most men's hair is much thinner, especially at his age. How old do you think he is, Ginny?"

"Well, he is definitely older than I am, but I am not sure he is older than Mrs. Mooney. In fact, I think he looks quite a bit younger than his wife. Don't you think so too?"

I concurred that he did look younger, by several years or maybe even a full decade, than his wife and added that all her smoking wasn't doing anything to help her skin stay young looking. Ginny was lapping up this conversation. "You know, there are people who actually hire hitmen to push other people's wives and husbands off ships so they can marry someone else. Do you think Mr. Mooney knows anyone like that?" At this point I was wondering if Ginny knew any person like that and decided if she didn't already, she would make it her business to find one.

"Do you really think they fight a lot?" I asked in my most innocent voice. It was certainly getting a workout that evening.

"Oh! Talk about fighting!" She was steaming up now. "I heard them arguing, no, even worse than arguing. I heard them fighting about something in their stateroom one day."

"Is their stateroom next door to yours?" I asked, genuinely curious.

"No. They are on another deck. But I just happened to be walking past their room and the door was slightly ajar because the maid had just been in, and they were fighting something fierce!"

This was going into overdrive. I had to slip my hands under the protection of the tablecloth to hug my ribs to keep from splitting up in laughter. Who on earth, I thought, would dream of just happening to walk by someone else's stateroom on a cruise ship when they were staying on different decks altogether? And how clever of Ginny to time it exactly when the housekeeper was about to leave. She must have been studying the comings and goings of the Mooneys and their housekeeping schedule since she came on board to pull that one off.

"Yes," she went on, apparently not realizing how absurd this whole charade was. "I think they are going to split apart!" she said dramatically, her arms flying in opposite directions.

"Oh dear," I said. "That would be terrible! What would poor Mrs. Mooney do without him?"

"Poor Mrs. Mooney, indeed!" Ginny scoffed. "It is obvious that Mr. Mooney is the victim here," she said defensively. "He is the one who worked hard all these years to become a millionaire. And look at her – she gambles it away in the casino!"

"Where would he go then, I mean if they split up?" I asked innocently.

"Well, that's up to us – him, of course," she caught herself. You could just see her imagining Mr. Mooney grabbing his overstuffed saddlebag, jumping on the nearest white horse, picking Ginny up, propping her in the saddle in front of him, and galloping off with her into the sunset. "But he should not waste his life. He is so vibrant! So manly! So potent!"

"So rich," I contributed.

"Yes, he is rich. He deserves a beautiful woman who will appreciate it, I mean appreciate *him*," she self-corrected.

"Well," I stalled for dramatic effect, "I could see you two together if they ever did split up. I mean, you are beautiful and certainly appreciate it, I mean him," I said, trying not to make it too obvious that I was on to her. I was enjoying myself way too much.

"Oh! You really think so?" Ginny asked, batting her lashes and showing me a smile that could frame about eighty-seven front teeth.

"I believe so," I said. "But that's just my opinion and Mrs. Mooney would have to be out of the picture first and then we'd have to see what Mr. Mooney did in that case. You know, Ginny, a man as appealing and rich as he is must have any number of secret admirers back home. I mean, think of all the women who might be thinking the same thoughts you are. Why, he could have a gorgeous secretary, an old flame from high school, his golf partner's unmarried sister, in fact his golf partner's wife for that matter, even the woman who takes in his dry-cleaning order twice a week. All of them might very well be considering what would happen if Mrs. Mooney suddenly and tragically disappeared and Mr. Mooney became available." Ginny thought quietly; her wide grin disappeared, leaving the thin line of her closed lips. She looked down.

"Not that I was implying those other women – or you – would ever actually wish something bad to happen to Mrs. Mooney," I added quickly, patting her hand.

She looked up and said, "Oh, no! That is something I would never want to see happen. Mrs. Mooney is a lovely lady. If we lived in the same town, I am sure we would be very close friends."

"I'm sure you would be too," I lied, still patting her hand.

Later on, after the show that night where a former Olympic medal gymnast performed an entire comedy routine standing on his hands, I joined the "Barn Stomp" party on the pool deck for some line dancing and snacks. The deck was lit up and decorated like a stable with haystacks for seating and checkered tablecloths covering the tables. The waiters wore big cowboy hats and cowboy boots with spurs. Only a few people were dancing to the country music. They were the good dancers who likely intimidated everyone else from even trying. However, the entire show staff was on hand and were paired up to dance in couples. They were all very tall and lanky and athletic and graceful at the same time. I marveled at the four beautiful female dancers and had to conclude they must spend hours in the gym and eat a single slice of cucumber for dinner to maintain their perfect bodies. They were dressed in country and western costumery and did their best to mingle with the crowd between their dance sets. One of the entertainment couples spotted me and the male, Eric, came over and asked me to dance. He was a young New Yorker trying to get a toehold in the entertainment world by working his way through the demanding ranks of cruise ship productions. When he brought me back to my table after our dance, an older gentleman leaning on a decorative post came over to me. We struck up a conversation. He was traveling alone and told me he had been assigned to a table with other solo travelers in the dining room, but he had missed the first night and had never bothered to go down to dinner after that. I told him about our table and invited him to join us and suggested he talk with the maître d' about it. He said he would do that and asked for the slow dance that was just starting up.

While we danced, he told me that his wife had died the year before and they had always come on this ship at this time of year, so here he was out of habit more than anything else. His name was Ralph and he was from Bermuda, which explained his proper British accent and manners. I offered to talk to the maître d' on his behalf, but he said his butler would take care of it and assured me he would try to join our table the following evening. He had planned to travel with his sister-in-law, but she had let her passport lapse and only discovered it when she arrived at the airport. He added with a soft smile that she was ninety-two and probably not going to renew it, so he was officially traveling solo. The band revved up and started a Toby Keith song while more people, loosened up from drinks served in mason jars, hit the dance floor. The night was warm and breezy, and the scents of floral shampoo, tanning oils, and salt air wafted pleasantly across the deck. I ran my fingers through my down-soft hair again, something I had been doing all day long.

I had forgotten about my early shore excursion the following morning and stayed to the very last dance. I chatted easily with people I didn't know, waved at some who looked familiar, and made a point of looking out for anyone from Gilligan's Table but never saw anyone, including Wink, for the rest of the evening. When the last dancers retreated to the inside of the ship leaving the band to dismantle their equipment under a quiet moonless night, I drifted toward the nearest exit and walked the seven decks down to my cabin and fell asleep the minute my head hit the pillow.

SOMETIME IN THE MIDDLE of the night, I got up to use the bathroom. A dull red light was flashing on my desk. I hadn't seen it earlier because I'd carelessly thrown some papers over the phone in my haste to leave the ship that morning. The housekeeping staff never touches or moves personal papers, so they'd been left there covering the phone the whole day. Now half-asleep, I pushed the button and was listening to Pearl's calm and gracious voice. She asked how I was doing and assured me she was available any time if I had any concerns. Thanking me again, she ended and clicked off. Before I had the chance to hit the pound button and erase the message, the machine told me there was a second message. Another message?

I listened as the next message played, and if I'd been half-asleep a moment earlier, I was five-bells-alarm wide awake after hearing what was left there. The same scratchy muffled voice was back, only this time he left these words: "CASTAWAY, OR CAST OVER? YOU DECIDE!" I felt my hands shaking, and thoughts of trying to save the message collided with fear which smashed into the reality that I had to call Wink right there on the spot in the middle of the night. I was trembling so uncontrollably I kept misdialing and had to start over a few times just trying to press the numbers 5111 on my desk phone.

"Hello?" It was Wink, answering on the first ring and sounding as if he were wide awake and had been waiting for my call. Did the man ever sleep, I wondered?

"Wink, it's me, Marianne. I just woke up now and saw there was a message waiting. I mean another message, besides one that Pearl left. It's the scratchy voice again. I'm scared. What should I do now?"

"Don't move, Marianne. I'll be right there."

There was a forceful rap on the door a few minutes later. It was Wink, dressed like it was the middle of the afternoon. He came in and walked directly to the phone. He listened to the message, wrote down some notes, and said he would check out the source of the message. He said he had been able to retrieve the first message but thought it might have originated from off the ship and was not meant for me or anyone at all on the ship. It might have been some kind of weird hoax that wasn't connected to anything aboard the ship and just a coincidence that it came to my room while we were involved in the missing cellist mystery. Now Wink was going to study the message a little further. He told me to go back to bed, but I was fully awake and knew I wouldn't be able to sleep, so he invited me to come to the voice lab with him.

"The ship has a voice lab?" I asked incredulously.

"Well, not exactly an entire lab," he said. "More like some audio equipment. It's all part of what security does, and right now I need to pull out some big guns, well, metaphorically speaking, that is."

I followed Wink to his office and through a back door to a room which held stacks of legal boxes, files, audio equipment, and things I'd never seen before. He pulled up a chair and told me to sit down. He warned me the procedure could be excruciatingly boring and I was free to go back to bed at any time with no hard feelings. Then he transferred the message that was on my phone into a receiver in the voice lab and sent the message through some sort of digital voice decoder. We were listening to a much slower version. The words were spoken very slowly, but unfortunately they were still garbled, and the process had not clarified the voice itself. Wink wanted to see if he could identify the voice to see if it was someone on the ship, and he put the voice sample through a variety of different filters. We listened to one version after another until one version emerged that was hands down clearer than all the others.

The voice was female!

"Stunning!" Wink said. "A woman." We listened several times but could not discern the timbre or pitch of the voice enough to make it identifiable. But it was undeniably a female voice.

"Someone knows what they're doing," Wink said. It could still be a hoax and it could still originate off the ship. He'd have to add another layer of technology, and that would take more time. He turned to me and reminded me about the two events on shore that could have turned out very badly. He asked whether I had seen anyone unusual lurking around the helmet dive orientation area or whether I had seen anyone in or around the grotto at Virgin Gorda's baths. He reminded me that it could be a woman.

He said, "All we know is that this may be nothing or it may be something, and if it's something, you need to stay on high alert at all times. I'm going to tell the others in the quartet as well, but so far no one else has received any threats like this."

I left the voice lab and wondered all the way back to my room if Valetta and Danita were up to something. It becomes macabre when you start to suspect the very people you are trying to help.

Chapter Seven

Day Seven: February 9, Tuesday
Castries, St. Lucia,
Scattered Showers. High: 82°F/2°C. Low 76°F/24°C.

As soon as I returned to my stateroom, I walked out onto my balcony for a look at the small harbor as we entered St. Lucia's capital city, Castries, with the new day. It was morning and the sun was fully up. We were already slowing down, and I could hear noises in the belly of the ship that I had come to associate with its imminent docking. I had scheduled an early excursion and time was already catching up with me. As I scanned the charming little city situated on an immense calm bay flecked with colorful boats, I tried to recall what Dr. Pinot had said about it in his presentation the day before. It was replaying on the lecture channel, so I went back into my room to review it. I appreciated the nuggets of history and background information he provided because I was not going to take a particularly historic or sightseeing excursion. I was booked on the Zipline Adventure, one of Seth's brilliant ideas.

I showered and dressed and ran upstairs for a quick breakfast, returning to my room with just enough time to collect my backpack and camera and some other things. I made sure I had my excursion ticket. As soon as Pearl announced that the ship had cleared immigration, I was one of the first at security, but had to wait before I was allowed to disembark because a woman was boarding right then. She had tawny skin and beautiful long hair done up in a million meticulous braids streaming away from her forehead and down her shoulders and back. She wore a simple and slightly clingy dress that revealed a figure tight from working out, but also soft from enjoying desserts. Her kind face glowed with the confidence of a movie star, so I automatically assumed she was one of the entertainers coming on board. The endless stream of magicians, singers, ventriloquists, comedians, and other so-called headliners that take the stage for some of the nightly shows come on and off the ships on a silent rotation, irrespective of the cruise itinerary. They may join the ship in the middle of the cruise or toward the end and stay on for the beginning of the next cruise. It is one more routine in the endless choreography of scheduling and logistics that takes place behind the scenes. I imagined she was a singer, and I was already looking forward to her show. I admired how she charmed the entire security staff, talking with them like she had known them all her life. I assumed that the entertainers knew the staff from their regular circuits and wondered what it would be like to be a shipboard entertainer going from ship to ship. I pondered a life of singing at night on the stage of a luxury cruise ship and enjoying the days in exotic ports as a guest.

There were enough people going to the Zipline Adventure to require two buses which we boarded quickly, and we were underway in a matter of moments. I didn't see Denny and figured he was on the other bus. The sky threatened rain, and since we were heading into the rainforest, it was inevitable we would get wet before the day was out. I was glad I'd packed one of those pocket-sized ponchos that's folded and squeezed until it's the size of a Kleenex. The excursion description advised us to wear sturdy closed shoes and long pants that might get a little dirty, so I was wearing my sneakers and the only pair of jeans I had brought along. I had never ziplined before and didn't know what to expect.

During the hour's ride to the site, Charmita, our sparking tour guide, told us a lot about St. Lucia with fascinating stories about the places we were passing along the way. First, we saw the big open-air public market with its red-orange rooftops. It was already bustling with vendors and I made a note to try to get there after the excursion. Charmita said that downtown Castries didn't have a museum or much to see because a fire in 1948 had pretty much gutted it. We drove past the imposing Cathedral of the Immaculate Conception, from the end of the nineteenth century, where she told us the interior walls were painted with colorful murals depicting black saints and martyrs to honor the majority population of dark-skinned slave descendants that live on this former slave island. Charmita pointed out a very big tree across the street from the church and suggested it might be over four hundred years old. They call it the Samaan Tree, she said, a name which came about when a visitor asked a local what kind of tree it was and the local answered "Samaan," meaning "I don't know." We all laughed. Then Charmita pointed out a green park inside a fence with an elaborate wrought iron gate. Once named for Christopher Columbus, the park had recently been renamed Sir Derek Walcott Square. Charmita explained that the two statues in the park near a central fountain are of the two Nobel Prize recipients from St. Lucia: Sir William Arthur Lewis, for Economics in 1979; and Sir Derek Walcott, for Literature in 1992. Even more amazing was that these two national heroes of St. Lucia were born on the same day of the year, only fifteen years apart. Who would think that a small Caribbean island could harbor so many fascinating surprises about its history?

In a short while we rode up to Mourne Fortune, or the Hill of Good Luck, and through the Sir William Arthur Lewis Community College campus, named for the Nobel Prize winner who advocated education for his people. Today, St. Lucians enjoy a high literacy rate with their public education based on the British system. All the students from preschool through college wear uniforms to school. School is considered to be their "career" and they are programmed to take it seriously from the earliest grades. What long ago served as soldiers' barracks and officers' quarters were now serving as the classrooms of students at the community college. Other historic reminders we saw of the island's significance were the many cannons, an ammunition storage building, as well as the Inniskilling Monument, which commemorates one of the many battles fought between the French and British for over a hundred fifty years in the harbor below. Both Sir William Arthur Lewis and, more recently, Sir Derek Walcott, lie buried within the college's grounds overlooking this amazing view.

Famous for its natural beauty, St. Lucia is sometimes called the Helen of the West Indies in reference to Helen of Troy's legendary ship-launching beauty. From its origins as a slave-based plantation island growing cocoa, sugar, and coffee, St. Lucia today has a tourist-driven economy. Agriculture makes up part of its economy as well, mostly bananas, although increasingly these islands are diversifying to pineapples and crops that grow closer to the ground to evade destruction by hurricanes. St. Lucia is also an important oil transshipment center, with credit going to American one-time New York Jets owner Leon Hess, who in 1960 built the world's biggest at that time oil refinery in St. Croix, one of the United States Virgin Islands. Oil is collected from Trinidad, Colombia, Brazil, and Venezuela and stored in tanks along the water's edge with capacity to upwards of ten million barrels, mostly unrefined. Leon Hess was a good steward of St. Lucia, rebuilding several of the island schools in 1985 after a destructive hurricane. Charmita told us you can always identify a Leon Hess school in St. Lucia because they are all painted green and white, the colors of the U.S. dollar.

Our bus stopped for a few minutes along a little seaside fishing village. We clambered down the steps to examine the local wares for sale in the colorful stalls lining the street. Friendly locals invited us to buy their island dolls made with the local St. Lucian madras print. They are "reversible" dolls that you can tip upside down and another doll appears under the long and colorful skirt wearing a totally different and equally vibrant national uniform. Charmita had told us that the peaks on a woman's headwrap represent her status. One peak for single and looking, two peaks for married, three peaks for married with children and four peaks for married . . . and looking. We loved Charmita's sense of humor. But this and many of the Caribbean islands have endured times when there were more women than men, especially in the early twentieth century when so many men sought employment with digging the Panama Canal.

The vendors also showcased their necklaces and

bracelets handmade with red jumby beads thought to keep away evil spirits. Piles of ripe and fragrant bananas fresh from the trees were being scooped up by our group, as were the yellow bottles of the famous banana ketchup in several sizes. This was the little village of Anse la Raye, named for the stingrays that once populated the bay beyond the vendors' stalls. A few steps away from the lineup of stalls lay the beach, alive with colorful motorboats or gommiers, named for the traditional dugout canoes, resting on the sand or bobbing in the water. A few barefoot fishermen sat together under a large tent swapping stories as they mended their fishing nets. They had already been out catching fish since the predawn hours. I felt like I was taking a step back in time and wondered what it would be like to live in a sleepy little fishing village in St. Lucia.

WHEN WE ARRIVED at the zipline orientation center, we were greeted with a complimentary fruit punch. No rum, they joked, until after the ziplining. We were given a safety briefing and another ream of mandatory waivers to sign our lives away. This seemed to be the protocol with anything posing a little physical exertion. Then we were outfitted with helmets and goggles and big protective gloves and strapped into a snug harness to connect us to a hook at every line. This was an extensive network of twelve separate ziplines spanning about a mile total.

Once I was hooked up, I wasn't given any time to think about turning back. A little nudge and off I flew like a bird soaring over the trees. Nothing I'd ever felt before came close to the adrenaline rush as the air buffeted past and I looked down at the serene sight of dense tropical jungle below. By the eighth line I was gaining confidence and waving my arms in every direction.

It was at the tenth line that I must have been focusing too much on the scenery below. I had been told you could sometimes spot the national bird of St. Lucia here, the very colorful St. Lucia parrot, or Jacquot, and I was intent on seeing one when my rig suddenly stopped midway across the line with a powerful jerk. It felt like there was a big knot in the wire holding me there. Then I heard voices screaming from the platform behind me to keep going. I turned around to try to explain that I couldn't go forward and realized in horror that someone was coming right at me, full speed ahead. I was terrified. He was shouting and gaining speed as he was careening toward me, and I braced myself for the impending midair collision. I tried pushing myself forward but got no traction, and in a split second he smacked into me so hard the impact broke the hook that connected me to safety.

I had nowhere to go but down, and I dropped off the line and plummeted through what seemed to be millions of trees that fanned out beneath me. My last thought was wondering whether I would land on a nest of monkeys or in a snake pit. Luckily for me, an added security measure was a bungee cord that kept me from smacking into the ground. Not that what I went through was gentle by any means. I crashed through banana leaves and ended up twisting and dangling on the springy cord half-conscious, yet fully aware of the spectacle I must have made. By the time four guides in yellow helmets and fluorescent orange vests arrived to rescue me, I was dirty, scratched, banged up, and confused. They converged around me and went to the task of releasing me from my harness. I was hurting pretty much everywhere. Something was poking into my side and causing me some pain there. The helmet felt tight around my pounding head and I was wishing they would take that off too.

"Are you okay?" the guides took turns asking as they lowered me onto a soft pile of earth. They said they had never seen anything like it, but now they understood the wisdom of the owner installing the bungee cords as a safety measure.

"I think so," I sputtered, wondering if I were missing a tooth. I was trying to breathe. Someone handed me a bottle of water with a straw in it. I took a slow sip and then felt a sharp pain in my left arm. I wiggled my fingers to make sure that arm wasn't broken.

"We may need to take her to emergency," one of the groundskeepers told the others. "I don't know anything on those cables that could stop a flier like that."

I got right up at the word "emergency." Suddenly, I felt remarkably well and did not want to go to any hospital. "I'm feeling okay. Can I just go back to the ship now?"

"Do you think you broke anything?" one of the men asked.

"No. I hurt all over, but it's more from feeling embarrassed and humiliated than from anything else," I tried to convince myself. "How's the guy who bumped into me?"

"He's okay, and so is the girl who bumped into him right after that," the man who had not said anything up to now volunteered. "But they didn't fall or anything."

"Well," I said, "who went before me and why was a knot left in the line when I came through?" No one had an answer. Then one of the guides said there wasn't a knot. I said, "Let me just go to the ship and I'll be okay." They helped me up and with one guide on each side of me, they walked me to the bus and hoisted me up and inside.

I had to wait for the entire group to finish all twelve lines before we could head back into town. I was looking out the window trying to make sense of everything that happened. The one thing I knew I had to face was the possibility that someone had set me up for that accident. I had not even contemplated that my shore-side accidents could be part of a plot to get me until Wink had suggested it that morning. I tried to remember who had been on the bus with me, but nothing rang a bell. I thought about Denny who was on the other bus.

I was looking out the window dreamily as our bus was navigating into the port area and saw the gorgeous woman who had joined the ship that morning. Her shiny hair had a golden aura that made it shimmer in the Caribbean sunlight. I was looking forward to her vocal performance, still imagining her to be a singer. But what caught my eye next nearly winded me for the second time that day – it was the man whose arm she was holding on to. It was Fred! They were smiling, embracing, and nuzzling as they walked along like the happiest couple in the world. So, this must be Stacey, the new girlfriend, I thought. Wow! She is a knockout! A surprising choice for Fred, though, because she was very young. Immediately I began to wonder if they'd first met when he was with Donna in Botswana when I met them. I was trying to rack my brain to remember if I'd seen this gorgeous woman before, but she would have been in her teens or even younger that long ago. Now I was looking forward more than ever to having that drink with them. I also realized with a pang of disappointment that Stacey was not a performer as I'd imagined.

Back in the cabin I took a warm shower and looked at myself in the full-length mirror as I dressed. My skin, usually very pale, was starting to show signs of toasting from all my time in the sun. My hair, dark and thick when I had boarded just a few days ago, was already looking scruffy and starting to fall into a new "do" of its own. A cowlick was taking shape where there hadn't been one before. My brown eyes were surrounded by black and blue welts that were starting to shout at me. I thought it might be time to grab an ibuprofen. Then I noticed all the bruises and scrapes and scratches and welts covering me from my forehead all the way down to my feet. I wondered how much more of this it would take before they kicked me off the string quartet. Grateful that I had got off easy considering all my mishaps, I also accepted that pain would be following me everywhere for the next couple of days. I was convinced there was nothing broken, however. A message on my phone from the ship's medical office simply invited me to check in with them if I required any kind of medical attention. I didn't know how they found out about my accident but thought the hands around here sure worked in mysterious ways. I recalled the words of the guides who had retrieved me from the bungee cord. They said they could see nothing on the cable that had "caught" me. While I was dangling there, I had looked up and realized how high up the cables were and didn't care to hear any details.

I was looking pretty banged up and bruised when I sat down to perform with the quartet for the afternoon tea. Fortunately, most of the passengers were either still out on the island or elsewhere around the ship with only a few coming up to tea. The ones that were present were more interested in the abundant and enticing offerings on the trolleys and tables. Even the little reader was not at her post under her window. So, my less than lustrous contribution to the group went largely unnoticed. The other players were very gentle with me and picked up notes and measures I was only scraping through. I still did my best, even though it felt like there were two rocks in my head competing over which one could smack harder against my skull. As we wrapped up our program, the ship was scheduled to leave, but it wasn't going anywhere. The voice of the purser came on the loudspeaker asking some guests, this time two couples, to contact Reception immediately. The announcement was repeated. Someone was about to miss the ship and the port-side outer deck and balconies started to fill up with curiosity seekers watching to see who would come running up to the ship and if they would make it before the lines were pulled.

Leaving late-returning guests behind at a port is at the discretion of the captain. Latecomers not only inconvenience everyone and risk a late arrival to the next port, but they can cost the cruise line money for extra time in a port. The captain blew the ship's whistle as more and more guests convened on the outer decks, leaning into the railings. People started betting on whether the captain would take off and leave the two couples behind.

But just as the gangway ramp was pulled back into the ship, a vehicle could be seen gaining speed as it raced toward the ship. It stopped at the gate where the four occupants stepped out, obviously took some time to pay and tip the driver, passed through the security entrance and then, seeing that the ship was about to sail and hearing the frantic blasts of its whistle, ran toward it in a madcap dash. They were laden down with shopping bags. The two men looked annoyed and grabbed more and more bags from the two women, who were lagging behind and appeared to be talking with each other. The women gave up running and walked along, scowling and, from the looks of things, shouting at their husbands. This was going to end up being a very bad day for these couples.

As the two men approached the ship, they frantically pointed back at their wives just as the lines were being lifted. One of them tried holding a line back and was nearly pushed aside by the line handler. The ship was poised to sail! The women gave up and one of them dropped her bags and pocketbook and sat down on the tarmac. The crowd from the ship was yelling "Run! Run! Run!" and "Get back up!" and basically having a little fun with the tense moment. It was not fun for the two men, who were coaxing and cajoling their wives to hurry. The husband of the woman who was sitting down ran back and tried carrying her to the ship, but her packages and bags fell from her hands along the way. You could tell they were having an argument.

Would the ship wait, or would we sail without the two couples? People on the ship expressed different opinions – and loudly. "Let's get going! You're holding us up!" was the rallying cry of half the observers and "Go! Go! Go! You're almost here!" was the other half's encouraging war cry. The ship's whistle blasted again, one very long and loud wail. And this time the lines were slipped back down over the pier posts. The ramp was rolled back down to the pier. The ship was going to wait. When the two couples finally boarded, battered, shaken, and angry at each other, a huge cheer and burst of applause erupted from the outer decks. This would become the main subject at dinner for nearly everyone on board. A near-miss with almost leaving passengers behind is grand excitement on a cruise ship.

AFTER ALL THAT DRAMA, I headed back to my room for a little nap before dinner, as a lot of achy twinges all over my body started talking to me. Just as I walked through the door, the phone rang.

"Are you trying to kill yourself, or do I have to worry that someone really is behind this?" It was Wink.

"Oh, you already found out," I said, a slight smirk on my face.

"It's the talk of the ship," Wink said.

"Not anymore," I laughed. I've just been demoted by those couples who nearly missed it altogether. Now everyone will only be talking about that."

"And I know you didn't check in with the ship's doctor, but you should think about it," Wink added, apparently not amused at my attempt to compare my trauma with that of the two near-miss couples.

"I will," I said, intentionally leaving the part vague about whether I would actually go and see the doctor or just think about it. Wink said we would continue this conversation at another time, but something had just come up and he had to get right to a very important meeting and abruptly disconnected. He said he would be missing dinner and to give his regards to Gilligan's Table. I figured Sorrenta had a fresh bowl of frosting for him.

I didn't feel like dinner at all but thought my absence would raise more eyebrows than if I just showed up and kept a low profile. But I had scarcely arrived at the table when I noticed a hubbub of excitement. Mr. Mooney and his wife were not there and everyone else was in a flutter over something. The conversation was moving so fast that nothing was making any sense. When I finally nailed Skip down to tell me what was going on, he said Mrs. Mooney had gone missing the evening before, sometime after dinner and during the Barn Stomp. She had last been seen in the casino. People had searched for her in the casino, on the outer decks, in the lounges, the ladies' restrooms, back in the Mooneys' suite and even at the barn dance out on the pool deck, but she was nowhere to be found. I didn't have to guess what Wink's important meeting was about and felt a little guilty that I had automatically accused him of having plans with Sorrenta. He was no doubt steeped up to his temples by now with not one but two missing people to investigate. No wonder he had been wide awake when I had called him at that ungodly hour in the morning. And yet, I wondered why he had not mentioned Mrs. Mooney's disappearance.

"How did you find out about it?" I asked Skip.

Everyone quieted down and looked at Skip now. "Denny and I were just returning to our cabin when Mr. Mooney came running out of the casino screaming, 'Dovey! Dovey! Where are you, Dovey?' at the top of his lungs. When we asked him what was going on, he told us she was in the casino one minute and gone the next time he turned around. We called security and Wink came running down the hall and took Mr. Mooney back with him."

"We looked everywhere," Denny chipped in. "We even checked all the elevators and staircases, but we didn't see her anywhere."

"Did you see anyone else?" I asked, eyeing Ginny who sat there quietly studying her menu. After her conversation practically wishing something like this to happen, she had to know she was in the crosshairs of my suspicion. I was almost starting to wonder if the voice on my message machine was Ginny's but had been intended for another room altogether. I had to find out what the Mooneys' room number was. I looked around me and wondered if I could trust anyone at all at Gilligan's Table.

"No one that stood out," Denny's voice broke into

my thoughts. "You know how crowded the pool deck was with that party," he added.

"You're quiet," I said to Ginny under my breath when our eyes met at one point.

"How would I know where his wife went?" she whispered back gruffly. "What I said before has nothing to do with what happened. I saw her in the casino last night pulling those levers and stuffing the slots with tokens like a madwoman. She was grasping so hard on the levers I'm surprised anyone could have pulled her out of there."

The waiter interrupted us to take our orders, and when he turned his back on us to return to the kitchen, Ginny defended herself once more saying she had nothing to do with Mrs. Mooney's disappearance. "Do you think I would be here if I had pushed her over the side?" she asked.

"I didn't realize that was what happened to her," I said, just a shade too suspiciously. Ginny scoffed and helped herself to a roll and butter.

"Poor Mr. Mooney," Skip said. "I can't imagine how worried he must be. Mrs. Mooney's such a nice lady. And you can just see how in love they are – er, or were – or, I mean are, I guess."

He looked quizzically at Denny who asked, "Do you think she could have lost all their money in the casino and thrown herself over the side?"

"No," his father answered. "She's too short to climb over the railing. Someone would have had to push her overboard if anything." I sneaked another peek at Ginny who was motioning to the sommelier.

"Maybe she went to the bathroom and got lost on the way back," Ginny offered. "Or maybe she went to the computer room and logged onto one of her online gambling sites. Or maybe she ended up in the gym and thought the screen on the treadmill was a slot machine and tried forcing tokens into the fan vents. I don't know where she is." She grabbed the glass of red wine the sommelier brought her without giving him a chance to set it down. She took a sip.

Suddenly, I noticed Ralph from the previous night's dance quietly sitting at our table. As he'd promised, he had asked to be seated with us. "Hello, Ralph!" I said and turned to introduce him to the rest of the gang. Everyone looked questioningly at the new member of our table. To deflect attention from himself, Ralph asked hesitantly about the couple with the missing wife and what she looked like.

"The wife is small and she's always in the casino," Ginny shot out dismissively. "And where are you from, Ralph?" she asked, only half interested.

"I'm from Bermuda," he answered. "My travel partner forgot to renew her passport and didn't realize it until she arrived at the airport, so I'm here alone as a result of that oversight."

"Oh, that is a terrible oversight," Ginny said. She seemed to be assessing the cloth on his navy blazer to determine whether he had any money. Judging from her increasing attention to him, I gathered the quality of the cloth in his blazer was very commendable.

"Yes," Ralph agreed, "it's most unfortunate. It's been a bit lonely I must admit."

"Is this, um, travel companion of yours, um, a dear friend or a significant other, if you don't mind my asking?" Ginny asked deliberately, closing in as a vulture assesses a corpse.

"I don't mind at all your asking," Ralph smiled good-naturedly, his eyes creased with little lines that made him appear even kinder. "She is my deceased wife's older sister and, frankly, I don't think she will be bothering to renew her passport anymore," he added.

"Your deceased wife's older sister?" Ginny ventured, a smile slowly spreading across her face as she processed this information. "I daresay she shouldn't bother," Ginny agreed, a little too enthusiastically, and nearly heaved an audible sigh of relief.

Ginny turned to face Ralph, all her attention now lasering in on this fresh prospect. She introduced herself eagerly, proffering her forearm weighted down by all the sparkly baubles dangling on her wrist. She reverted to small talk, charmingly inquiring whether Ralph was enjoying his cruise so far and if he had taken any interesting shore excursions.

"Yes," he said, "it's been very nice, but I have been a little preoccupied at every port, wondering if Ida would be joining me there, so I haven't ventured too far. By now, I'm fairly convinced she will not be joining me at all."

"Gee," Denny said, "did you try calling her? They have phones in the rooms."

"No," Ralph said chuckling, "I haven't called but I know her, and I'm fairly assured she will not be coming. Ida is ninety-two, after all. She lives in Charleston and was dreading the flight to Miami to catch the ship. I half suspect she forgot her passport on purpose to avoid the cruise altogether." Ginny nearly jumped out of her seat on hearing this good news.

"That is very interesting," she said, displaying a huge smile and picking up her wine glass in a toasting gesture. "Perhaps you'd like to join me later this evening for a drink at the Mar-teeny's piano bar, Ralph. That is of course if you do not want to go to the casino instead. I'm a very traditional lady myself, and very modest," she added, smoothing the front of her low-cut dress. "I don't gamble or smoke, and I only drink occasionally for social enjoyment."

"Sounds like you're posting your profile on a dating website, Ginny," I laughed, stirring it up. Yes, I am evil when presented with an opportunity like this.

"That's pretty funny," Denny said, picking up on my fun. He added, "You're right, Marianne. These two look like they could be dating."

I turned my attention to Denny who had not shown up for the zipline excursion. I was pretty sure I hadn't seen him with the other bus group either.

"Where were you today, by the way, Denny? I never saw you at the Zipline Adventure. Weren't you going to be there?" I asked.

"They called me in the morning and said the excursion was sold out. I couldn't go because I was on the waiting list, so I went on my own to another zipline place instead. On the way back our driver said that someone actually fell off one of the ziplines in another part of the island. He said he didn't know if the guy lived or not."

"Well," I cleared my throat, "you're looking at that guy," I said while pointing to myself. "And obviously I lived to tell about it. Somehow I got stuck midway across a line, and I fell when someone smacked into me up there on the wire and the hook broke." The table was quiet. For the first time they all looked at me and noticed the bruises on my face.

"Wow," Denny said after a long pause. "You should see your face. It's all bumped and black and blue. That's from today?" As he spoke, I could feel lumps and bumps and a thick lip I hadn't noticed before.

The conversation inevitably turned to the next day's activities, and Denny and Skip were at an impasse. Denny was booked on the same deep-sea-fishing excursion that I was booked on. Skip thought he had booked the fishing excursion and had realized too late that his ticket was for an ATV ride instead. When he went to exchange it, he was told that the deep-sea fishing was overbooked and there was a long waiting list. I remembered how excited the father and son had been about deep-sea fishing on that very first night. I also remembered that I still had Seth's excursion ticket. Since it was already paid for, why waste it? I didn't see why Skip couldn't use it. The three of us planned to meet on the pier in Antigua the next morning before the excursion where I would give Skip Seth's paid-for ticket.

I excused myself as soon as I finished my dessert, a citrus sorbet so tangy and icy I could have gone for another, to be honest. Feeling achier and more exhausted with each passing minute, I headed straight up to my room, determined to go directly to bed.

But the sight of a towel angelfish hanging from the ceiling reminded me that I'd promised to join Angela's solo travelers' group for the evening show, so I brushed my teeth, added a touch of makeup wherever it didn't set me off squealing from pain, ran a brush through my Brillo hair, and headed right back downstairs to the theater. Angela's group was convening outside the theater doors. Angela was extremely tall and sinewy and had begun her ship career as a production dancer. She did not appear particularly happy with her current job, and even less so to see me, greeting me with a deadpan expression. I thought her attitude was highly irregular coming from an employee whose whole function was to be gracious with the guests.

One by one, the other solo travelers clustered around me asking what had happened to me, if I was okay, and even telling me how much they were enjoying my cello playing with the quartet. Two of them went to Angela and asked her to coordinate a solos dinner and seat me with them. I was feeling like a social butterfly with all the attention, and the more it continued, the more obviously Angela scowled. Apparently it was not lost on her. I noticed Ralph standing alone, so I went over and joined him. Angela determined that enough of us were there, so she led the way into the theater and to our reserved section of seats. I noticed she sat as far away from me as possible. I sat next to Ralph and we continued our dinner conversation until the curtains rose.

The show was performed by the talented production staff of singers and dancers, all so beautiful and young that everyone around the ship called them "the kids." They performed a very entertaining show full of dancing from dance-themed movies like *Saturday Night Fever* and *Flashdance* and even *West Side Story*. What Danita had told me earlier was that behind the scenes, one of the female dancers was nursing a sprained ankle and was unable to perform, so the team was lopsided with one less female, the others filling in to cover her role, although I would wager that not one person in the audience was aware of any deficiency in that performance.

Back in my room, the red eye of the telephone message light was yelling at me yet again, so I went to hear my message as a prisoner goes to hear the judge's verdict. Actually, messages. Not one but two. The first was from Fred, inviting me to join Stacey and him for drinks the next afternoon directly following afternoon tea. The next message stopped me cold. There was that same scratchy voice, only this time the message was closer to home: "FALLING FOR SOMEONE . . . OR OVERBOARD?" followed by a menacing snicker and a click to disconnect. I called Wink. Unbelievably, he did not pick up, so I left a message and went to lie down to await his return call.

It didn't come until the next morning.

Chapter Eight

Day Eight: February 10, Wednesday
St. John's, Antigua and Barbuda
Scattered Showers. High: 81°F/27°C. Low: 74°F/23°C.

WINK CALLED ME BACK shortly before 6:30, the phone startling me from a deep sleep. It took me a moment to remember why I'd fallen asleep with my clothes on, lying on top of my bedspread. I must have drifted off while awaiting his return call. Wink said he'd been so wrapped up in Mrs. Mooney's case the night before that he hadn't returned to his room or received my message until three or four in the morning. I told him there was a new message on my phone.

Wink was at my door in thirty minutes, after giving me time to take a shower and get dressed. When I opened the door, there he was, holding two coffees. He listened to the message and forwarded it to the voice lab. He looked worried but told me he was still convinced the calls were either a crank joke or meant for someone else and probably not even intended to come to the ship in the first place. I couldn't tell if he really meant that or whether he was just trying to put me at ease. He stated that they were having a hard time tracing the calls, but they appeared to originate from a cell phone on land. He said there had been no progress in Sabrina's case and told me to be prepared to perform with the string quartet for the rest of the cruise. He was convinced, however, that Sabrina's case had nothing to do with the mysterious messages I had received. He also believed that Mrs. Mooney's disappearance was an isolated case that probably had something to do with her dealings in the casino. He had no reason to believe she had gone overboard and was certain she would be found sooner rather than later. I told him about the conversation I'd had with Ginny when she had mused about taking off with Mr. Mooney if Mrs. Mooney should suddenly and unfortunately disappear off the ship. Wink listened carefully, but said he wasn't concerned; he figured that, knowing Ginny, she'd move on to the next prospect as soon as one appeared. I laughed and said that prospect had already materialized in the form of Ralph, the eligible and well-heeled widower from Bermuda.

We sipped our coffees as we watched the ship glide into its spot along Heritage Quay. Off in the distance, the little city was coming to life as the morning sun glinted on the twin towers of St. John's Anglican Cathedral. Another ship was sharing our pier and blocking our view along one side of the harbor, so all we could see across from us was a mass of humanity peering from thousands of identical glass windows and hanging over the balconies. Between the two ships, something like eight thousand visitors were poised to descend on this small island that day. They would soak up the sun on her beaches or take in her history of sugar mills, slave revolts, and British naval presence. They would drink the local beer and sample the rum and finally sail away with a million tee shirts, postcards and refrigerator magnets. . . and memories. It's true, the little island of Antigua is quite literally ringed with beaches. It boasts three hundred sixty-five of them to be exact, or one for each day of the year, and that's the primary reason it is a popular holiday destination. It is also one of the most popular destination wedding sites in the Caribbean with beautiful resorts ready to accommodate guests and stage weddings as simple or lavish as the couple's hearts' desire. Beneath us, the line handlers secured the ship to the pier as Wink stood up and said he would not be leaving the ship in Antigua but would try to join Gilligan's Table for dinner.

AS PLANNED, SKIP AND DENNY met me on the pier. I handed Seth's ticket to Skip. No one looked twice. We took our seats in the new, air-conditioned bus that left ahead of schedule because everyone showed up early. We were heading toward Falmouth Harbour for some deep-sea fishing on the island's south side with a historic tour of Nelson's Dockyard nearby. We had a nice long ride to enjoy a leisurely conversation.

"Any late word about Mrs. Mooney?" I asked the father and son who were sitting directly behind me.

"We thought you might know more than us," Skip said.

"We were hoping she'd just reappear suddenly. Same with that missing musician," Denny contributed.

I jerked myself into remembering I had to be back on board in time for the afternoon tea performance at four o'clock and was beginning to rue the day I'd volunteered to help. I needed some time to practice a few of the pieces coming up later in the cruise and had been letting other things stand in the way. I calculated I would have at least an hour and a half to practice before show time that afternoon.

Considered the piece de résistance of Antigua's historical sites by any measure, Nelson's Dockyard, a still-functioning Georgian dockyard, was built during the time of King George III, that same British monarch who lost the Thirteen Colonies and eventually his mind. Today, Nelson's Dockyard is a mecca for mega-yachts that converge there for world-class maintenance while their owners, skippers, captains, and guests spend time in one of the Caribbean's most beautiful destinations. The complex wasn't always called Nelson's Dockyard. That name came about during a restoration in the 1950s after it had been abandoned by the British navy for about a century. Begun in 1725, the Dockyard served as the Leeward Islands headquarters for the British navy roughly between the late 1700s until the mid 1800s. In the beginning, it was called simply His Majesty's Antiguan Royal Dockyard. But in the 1950s restoration, it was renamed in honor of the twenty-seven-year-young British admiral by the name of Horatio Nelson who was stationed there between 1784 and 1787. Horatio Nelson, still in fresh memory of his teens, took his post to enforce the Navigation Acts by apprehending American merchant ships in the wake of the American War of Independence. He hated Antigua, griping incessantly of the carnivorous mosquitoes, the torrid climate, and especially the unfriendly Antiguans who never so much as invited him into their homes for tea. In fact, Nelson only left his ship, the HMS *Boreas,* when those unfriendly locals hauled him into court for interfering with their trade. He was prone to seasickness, an unfortunate affliction for an admiral of the seas, and whenever his ship set sail, he reputedly holed up in his quarters for several days awaiting his sea legs. Over and over again, Nelson bemoaned his bad luck to be stationed in "this vile spot and infernal hole."

Meticulously maintained and run with clockwork precision for the legions of tourists today, the complex is a far cry from the eighteenth-century hole where labor came in the way of convicts, slaves, and Irish debtors. They were paid handsomely in rum stored in toxic lead-lined casks, were allowed four half-days off each year, and were deprived of the company of women who were barred from the place. Today the guides will joke that a woman actually owns the joint.

The row of Dockyard pillars is the last reminder of a boathouse and sail loft that were destroyed by a hurricane in 1871. At one time, sails were collected from the ships through a trapdoor to an upper story to be repaired and then returned the same way. The Dockyard pillars should not be confused with the Pillars of Hercules, a stunning natural geological formation nearby, only visible from the sea.

After about an hour of exploring, we regrouped while some in the group took a brief visit through the little Dockyard Museum before heading back to the bus. While we were waiting for the others, I saw a little sign with an arrow pointing behind the museum with the words "Dockyard Bakery." Skip and Denny and I followed the arrow and climbed an old stone staircase to the tiny bakery where an old bread oven displayed some traditional cooking pots made of clay. These were the famous clay coal pots that old-timers across the Caribbean swear made the best food in the world because they heat up slowly over coals, keeping the contents bubbling for hours. The clay coal pots in Antigua are made from a local clay and low-fired in people's backyards. They're called "gads" in Antigua and "yabbas" in other places and are something of a cottage industry.

The bakery's modern glass display case was laden with luscious-looking pastries and chocolate brownies, but what caught my eye was the rack of freshly baked pineapple turnovers. "Yummy," I said as I remembered reading something about Antiguan pineapples somewhere and bought us each a turnover. In fact, these pineapples are so special to Antigua that one appears right on top of the coat of arms. The Antiguan black pineapple is actually more of a dark green than black. It is smaller than most pineapples and exceedingly sweet. The bag full of our pineapple turnovers was warm in my hands and I couldn't wait to bite into one. Back on the bus, I passed one to Skip and another to Denny, and we fell into a state of bliss as we headed toward our awaiting fishing boat. Nothing could go wrong on a day that starts with something this delicious, I thought. I looked at Skip and Denny and decided they must be in agreement as they were eagerly licking the last bits of the divine crust from their fingers.

When our bus arrived at the marina, we split up into small groups to board the charter boats awaiting us. The advisement for the fishing tour was twofold. First, bring plenty of sunscreen because the sun was not only high and hot, but it reflected dramatically off the water. Second, there would be no turning back or refunds due to seasickness or inclement weather once the fishing boats left the pier. We embarked in high spirits on the bright-yellow forty-foot Fiberpool sport-fishing boat named *Fin King* and admitted an eager anticipation to catch the big fish lurking in the surrounding waters.

This boat was equipped to accommodate six anglers, and boasted new navigational equipment, life jackets for all sizes, top-shelf rods and reels, and a full toilet below. There were already two couples on board when the three of us joined. Scott and his wife Arlene were not from our ship and were staying in one of the island resorts. Scott was fishing and Arlene was just along for the ride. They were in Antigua wrapping up a two-week business trip and were heading back to Vancouver the following day. The other couple stayed in the stern and didn't mingle with anyone else. They were both tall and thin, and their faces were protected from the sun by a thick layer of white zinc paste, oversized dark sunglasses, and golf caps with brims pulled down firmly over their eyes. They both wore bandanas that covered their faces from just below their eyes. The rest of us figured they were probably honeymooners and left them alone.

Captain Baby introduced himself and invited us to help ourselves to the beverages in the cooler: bottles of water, sodas, and the local beer called Wadadli, from the indigenous name for the island. At that invitation, the honeymooning woman walked with a noticeable limp to the cooler and helped herself to a bottle of orange soda but did not offer or take anything to her new husband. For honeymooners, they seemed rather detached, never talking or showing any signs of affection to each other. Maybe they were having their first quarrel, I reasoned. The morning sun was already beating down mercilessly as I slathered myself in sunscreen. I kept my sunhat in place, but even with all the precautions, just barely into our excursion, I could feel my skin starting to burn. Skip and Denny talked excitedly, eager to see who would reel in the first big one and debating what it would be. Captain Baby said we'd be reeling in mahi-mahi, blue marlin and wahoo among others. Just ten to fifteen minutes after pushing off, we were in fishing waters and Captain Baby dropped anchor while his one-man crew, Phipps, came around to help everyone. An occasional flying fish caught the attention of one or more of us, and a couple times someone thought they sighted a sea turtle.

Suddenly, without warning, I was taken by a violent seasickness. The boat sloshed in the water, slapping against hard waves while fighting a current. The smell of diesel and fish scales nauseated me, and I had all I could do to keep from throwing up over the side. I grabbed an aluminum bait bucket and clung to it for dear life. I was nearly incapacitated and barely moved the rest of the trip, intermittently clinging to and depositing in the bucket, which Phipps occasionally emptied overboard and then hosed down as he laughed. My misery didn't hold the others back from having a great time in the least. A few tries brought up some small fish the skipper cut up to use as bait, and the others watched and waited, imagining all the big fish that called these waters home. I could hear excited speculations about what they might catch from where

I was sitting, wet and salty and smelly, pretty much functionally comatose as I hugged the bait bucket on the floor of the boat.

I heard one of the guests ask Captain Baby how he came by his name, and he threw his head back and laughed, saying he could have set his watch by that question. He said, "People always ask me that right about now." Captain Baby simply explained that Baby was his real name and pointed at the *Fin King*'s operating license to prove it. He said his parents had ten children before him, equal numbers of boys and girls. All his siblings came in boy – girl – boy – girl sequence. There was even a set of twins in there, a boy and girl, of course. He said his parents ran out of names by the time they were expecting him, and decided they'd call the last baby "Baby" when it arrived, which would serve whether it was a boy or a girl.

A line quivered and Denny gripped and fought for nearly fifteen minutes. His catch was a big blue marlin that fought long and hard. Skip was so excited for Denny that he nearly lost his own rod and reel. When that big fish finally made it into the boat, the uproar that erupted would have made the Rose Bowl cheerleaders proud. Denny stood proudly next to his fish for his official photo op. Captain Baby estimated its weight at a couple hundred pounds before releasing it back to the sea. I was still heaving into the bait bucket, but for everyone else the day was pleasant and the catches were big, as Captain Baby had promised.

Everyone, it seemed, took a turn to reel something in. Scott caught a big wahoo just as Skip pulled in a mahi-mahi. Phipps came over and handed me a rod, gently encouraging me to at least try. I grabbed the rod and wobbled my way up from the floor of the boat, gripping the side bannister and still queasy. Phipps said if anything tugged on the line, he would do all the work and give me all the credit. At one point, the quiet honeymooning guy caught a nice-sized blue marlin he released right after his trophy photo which he posed for without removing his face covering. No one said anything, but it seemed strange. Then the honeymoon woman got her try, and that was when the lights went out for me.

Just as I felt a tug on my line, a rustle and bump caught my attention from the other side of the boat. In the split second it took me to look back over my shoulder, something blindingly bright and silver came at me with such force that I thought another boat had run into ours. I braced for the end of the world as I knew it, and everything went dark. I fell in a heap and drifted into and out of consciousness, seasickness being the least of my problems. I could hear the distant echoes of voices, but I had no idea where I was or, for that matter, even who I was. There was a pervasive and acrid smell I could not identify deep inside my nostrils. My throat was parched, and I felt something very hot on my face, but I was too tired to open my eyes. I realized, gratefully, that I was lying down and did not want to do anything other than lie there unmoving, wherever I was. The voices sounded faint and distant and came and went, and I had not an inkling to whom they belonged, but one seemed more familiar than the others and my ears kept listening for the sound of that voice, even anticipating it when it was silent. Something cool rolled over my forehead and then someone lifted my head and slipped something soft underneath. After a while, the voices seemed a little louder without long gaps between them, and I began to realize that I was coming up from some deep and unapproachable place. I had no conception of time. I only felt the overwhelmingly painful sensation of needles in my throat, and except for the narrow line of cold against my forehead, the heat on my face was starting to rival the pain I was feeling in my throat. My shoulders felt good against the warm floor, and I still did not want to move. Or maybe I couldn't.

". . . emergency on the phone right now," I heard a voice. I tried to wrap my brain around that strange and elusive word: "emergency." It seemed so distant from the place I felt myself in right now: quiet and warm and – except for the needles now giving way to flames inside my throat and a pain in my head welling up enough to distract me from the fire on my face – I couldn't fathom a more comfortable place. The voices continued. I heard that word, "emergency," float through the air again and could not grasp its meaning. Then the voice I wanted to hear spoke up and uttered the word "concussion." That was an interesting word that I turned over in my mostly unconscious mind. Concussion. Some kind of drum? Dr. Seuss hat? Thanksgiving chestnut stuffing? Athletic underwear? I mused over the word dreamily but could not grasp its meaning. I let it drift in and out, still feeling my back secure against a warm solid place. Another cold strip against one cheek, then the other. What was going on here? The voice I wanted to hear said "concussion" again, and this time I wanted to laugh because I thought he meant confusion and I didn't know how someone could get two words like concussion and confusion all mixed up unless they meant the same thing.

When I finally figured out I was in my bed at home and it was time to wake up and leave the crazy dream behind, I opened my eyes and was immediately blinded by a bright light that made me wonder if instead I was on an operating table coming out of anesthesia. Did I have that nose job I was thinking about? I wondered.

"She's waking up," I heard the voice I liked say. It sounded excited and pleased. Then it got a little dark. I opened my eyes again and saw something pillowy right in front of my eyes.

"What are you doing?" I heard another voice say.

"Shielding her eyes from the sun," said the voice I liked. "She can't open her eyes if she has to look straight into the sun," it continued. None of this made any sense to me, but I liked the voice because it sounded strong and soothing at the same time. I strained again and opened my eyes and the pillowy thing was still in front of me, only some cracks were letting in some bright light, so I snapped my eyes shut again. Another sensation of sharp coolness rolled across my forehead. It felt good and took my mind off my parched throat and pounding head. I opened my eyes and heard a faint voice saying, "I'm thirsty," followed by an excruciating pain in my throat. Someone said, "Give her some water," and inserted something in my mouth and propped my head up higher. I felt an instant rush of welcome coolness trickle through a straw and down my throat.

"We thought we lost you, there, lady," the nice voice said. I looked up to see that it was coming from a big friendly looking man I both did and did not recognize. He asked me what day it was, and I could not answer. Then he asked me my name and I said "Marianne," to which he replied, "Poor thing doesn't even remember her name." I thought that was very funny because I did know my name was Marianne, so I started to laugh thinking he probably thought Marianne was just short for Mary Ann.

"It'll be okay, Marianne," the friendly voice said. He was holding my head and giving me more water.

When I was able to sit upright, I realized I was in a boat. I was shown a picture of the marlin that "attacked" me, and someone kidded that it would make a great brochure cover for marketing the charter to other tourists. I glanced over at the honeymooning couple who seemed to be keeping their distance, although at one point the man came over and knelt over my face for a moment. Skip didn't let him come any closer and he withdrew. Even if I weren't so dazed, I wouldn't have been able to see his face because he was so well covered with all that white zinc ointment and the bandana. But something about his earlobe reminded me of something which I couldn't place. I was hot, and still coming in and out.

Back on the bus, Denny and Skip were talking about the tall woman who had caught the marlin that whacked me and her masked husband. The honeymooners, I thought. She was the woman with the limp, and he was the man with the earlobe. Skip didn't see either of them on the bus. Were they from our ship? We didn't know. None of us could remember seeing them before we boarded the *Fin King*.

By the time we returned to the dock, the bus was waiting to take us back to the ship. I was fully conscious by then but hurting all over, and someone said I was probably going to have a couple black eyes in the next few days. Denny and Skip told me I had been knocked out by a two hundred-pound marlin that was fighting hard as the honeymoon woman was reeling it to the boat. It suddenly jumped from the water and smacked into me on its way to a hard landing on the floor beside me. That would explain that awful fish-scale smell in the back of my throat I couldn't get rid of. That would explain a lot of things. When we were safely back on board the MS *Minerva,* I felt fine except for feeling a little punchy in the head. Skip tried to get me to see the ship's doctor, but I assured him I was pretty much my old self and thanked him for all his help. I showered and changed in my room and took my music and headed down to the recital room to get that hour of practice in that I so badly needed.

On the way through the corridor to the recital room, I was met by my entire trivia team heading to the theater. Trivia was just about to start, and they needed me. The game had been canceled the day before, so there was a lot of pent-up anticipation. I quickly glanced at the music in my hands and felt fairly confident I could give it a go without the practice session, rationalizing that I was, after all, on vacation. We sat in our usual places and just as Pearl was picking up her mic to start the game, a general announcement came over the loudspeaker, pre-empting her use of the theater microphone.

"Pardon the interruption, but will the following guest please contact the reception office immediately by dialing 00 or picking up the nearest house phone: Miss Eloise Rudensheimer from Penthouse Suite 1600. Also, will Galley Assistant Raul Pedriguez please call Human Resources immediately. Repeat. Will the following guest please contact the reception office immediately by dialing 00 or picking up the nearest house phone: Miss Eloise Rudensheimer from Penthouse Suite 1600. Also, will Galley Assistant Raul Pedriguez please call Human Resources immediately. Thank you."

First a quiet murmur, followed by an all-out roar of laughter erupted in the theater. Someone was late coming back to the ship. Images came to mind of a wealthy cougar in her deluxe penthouse suite seducing a handsome Latin Lover kitchen assistant and running off with him to Jabberwocky or Runaway Beach in Antigua. The announcement suggested that a wild shipboard romance had gone into overtime on shore. I thought there must be a Harlequin novel in there somewhere. Apparently, this idea struck others as well, judging from the laughter. Pearl kept her composure but was more than usually bubbly and funny during the game. She started by saying she was afraid we were not being fed enough on this cruise, so the theme for the day was going to be food. Finally, a subject I knew something about, I thought!

But once again, I got too excited too soon. I mean, who knew Canola was an abbreviation for Canadian oil? And who knew Twinkies is the American food that could survive a nuclear attack? I mean, who would be thinking about Twinkies during a nuclear attack, anyway? How did Pearl come up with these things? At least we did get the bonus question right, figuring out with all our combined intelligence that the salad some guy named Bob Cobb invented was the Cobb Salad. Ta-Da! But we did score one legitimate point, and that was because Patrick came from Detroit and knew that the first soda pop manufactured in America was Vernors Ginger Ale. He said he grew up on the stuff.

By the time Pearl called our team for our score, we were all but hiding under our chairs from humiliation. Of course, I don't have to say who won – again – and I swore next time I booked a cruise I'd look up Dutch and Mavis first thing I did and beg to join the First Mates. I noticed they only had six people on their team again today and wondered where their missing couple was.

I SAWED AND SCRAPED through the program at tea that afternoon, feeling a little ashamed that I was making so little time to practice. On the other hand, I was a guest and I wanted to make the most of my time with other activities during the cruise. I looked around at one point and noticed the little girl reading in her usual spot under the window. I made a mental note to find out more about her. I had long since given up trying to remember where – or if – I had seen her somewhere before, but she was a striking character and stood out as the only kid that made time to read. I couldn't see the title of the book she was reading and would have liked to know that too. At the conclusion of high tea, Fred and Stacey came up to me while I was still seated with the quartet and reminded me of our Happy Hour date. Since the Paris Lounge switched from high tea to Happy Hour at 5:00 PM, we were already where we had to be. Mario offered to return my cello to the rehearsal room, allowing me to join Fred and Stacey straightaway at a small table near the window where the little girl had been reading her book through the recital. Now she was nowhere to be seen.

I learned that Fred and Stacey had met within the past half-year and that Stacey had never known Donna. In fact, Stacey had never been to Africa, let alone Botswana, so she and Fred did not meet while on our safari. Stacey was part English and part East Indian and said her family came from the southern Caribbean island of Trinidad. She grew up in Canada, where her parents relocated when she was a child. She went on to medical school to become a hand surgeon. I said I was surprised about her East Indian ancestry, coming from a Caribbean island, but she explained that East Indians and other Asians have a very strong historical and cultural connection to the Caribbean, particularly so in Trinidad, whose East Indian population was imported to fill the labor gap left after the African slaves were emancipated. She said anyone who visits Trinidad will see the proof of an East Indian culture from the presence of all the curry and roti restaurants there. She even said Bollywood movies are all the rage in many neighborhoods.

Trinidad wasn't on the itinerary for this cruise, but Stacey was making me want to visit there some day. And just when I thought St. Lucia was a standout for boasting Sir Derek Walcott for its Nobel Laureate in literature, she said Trinidad had its own Nobel Laureate, Sir V.S. Naipaul, and encouraged me to read

A House for Mr. Biswas. I was hooked just hearing the title alone.

She said Port of Spain, the island's capital, is a very cosmopolitan center with skyscrapers and modern buildings. At first Spanish, before it went to the British, Trinidad was supposed to be the gateway to a legendary City of Gold the Spanish called El Dorado. Even the English explorer Sir Walter Raleigh passed through Trinidad searching for El Dorado, but instead of a city of gold, he stumbled across the largest natural pitch lake in the world, the tar from which was later used to pave the streets of America's biggest cities. She said today Trinidad has a thriving economy built on black gold and chemical processing. And the shipment of that oil in those millions of oil drums inspired some musicians to start beating on them, which led to the island's iconic steel-pan drum music.

Stacey was a wealth of knowledge about her ancestral home island, and I already knew how smart Fred was. I had to be very delicate about inviting them to join our trivia team because once they met our motley crew, they'd figure out it was a trap. I complimented Stacey on her knowledge and said she'd be a whiz at trivia. She and Fred looked at each other and chuckled, saying they had only missed trivia today because Fred had a conference call with his company right at that time, but they'd already committed to joining a team starting tomorrow. They'd been invited by a very nice couple, Fred explained, Dutch and Mavis, who said one of their couples had to back out a couple days ago to join the bridge class at that time which left a vacancy on their team. Fred and Stacey had agreed to fill the void. Fred said he had met Mavis and Dutch over drinks one night and learned they were both nuclear scientists. Damn! Dutch and Mavis had already snapped up Fred and Stacey right from under my nose. This really was a blood sport. And I was starting to crave the taste of blood.

THAT NIGHT I FELT much better at dinner. We were all there except for Mr. and Mrs. Mooney. Everyone was curious about my big-fish encounter and admired my two fresh and new inky-black eyes that were now also marbled with red and green streaks. Wink wanted to hear all the details, of course, and asked Skip and Denny to point out the honeymooning couple that had caught the big marlin, but Skip said he had not seen them on the ship and couldn't identify them in any event because they had been slathered in zinc cream and hidden by hats and sunglasses and bandanas the entire time. They hadn't shown any concern when I had been smacked by the fish and had somehow quietly disappeared into the landscape as soon as the boat returned to the marina. Wink took it all in.

The conversation inevitably shifted to the next day's destination: Tortola. Another British Virgin Island, very close to Virgin Gorda, where we had stopped on our first port day. No one at Gilligan's Table had been to Tortola before, but Ginny had to tell us of a place she knew about near the harbor in Roadtown, the capital. She said it was a little purple building surrounded by beautiful pink and white bougainvillea flowers and aptly named the Bougainvillea Clinic. She said it was the secret destination of movie stars who went for a "nip and tuck," as she put it, and then turned to explain to Denny that that meant a facelift. She said celebrities went there to have their secret surgery to avoid the paparazzi.

"So, are you thinking of having some cosmetic work done?" Ralph asked innocently.

"You think I need to have plastic surgery?" Ginny pounced on him like a cat on a canary. "I'll have you know, what you see on this face is natural beauty. I do not need any artificial beauty enhancements." She framed her face with her hands as she fluttered her eyelashes dramatically.

"Calm down, Ginny," Ralph cajoled. "I was just pulling your chain. But if you were considering straightening your nose or smoothing your furrow, I'd offer to pay for it." He was obviously having fun.

"I never!" she said as she lightly brushed her manicured fingers over her nose and forehead. But before she could start a tirade, a blast of marching music blared through the dining room and the lights went out as a procession of chefs and waiters wearing high caps and aprons and fluorescent-white uniforms proudly strode through and fanned out across the dining room. The only light in the entire room came from the flaming baked Alaska desserts they were holding high on silver trays. The diners applauded as the maître d' took the microphone and introduced the entire kitchen and dining staff. Each baked Alaska made its way to a table, promising the most special and dramatic dessert ever offered on a cruise ship at sea. And coming in direct trajectory toward our table, dressed in an immaculate white tunic with a crisp white linen napkin over her forearm and a blazing mile-high baked Alaska held proudly above her head, was none other than Sorrenta. Smiling wildly, she blew a kiss directly at Wink as the sounds from the marimba band increased to a fevered pitch. She deposited the baked Alaska dramatically on our table directly in front of Wink as if he were the only one sitting there. She seemed so excited to see him that she might have jumped in his lap if she hadn't been on duty. She probably wished she could have jumped out of the baked Alaska.

"Did you frost this yourself?" Wink asked.

"Certo!" she beamed and took up the serving knife to slice pieces for everyone. She placed the plates in front of each diner and then leaned over Wink and whispered loud enough for all of us to hear, "And I will see you later!"

Wink smiled but seemed to dismiss it once she turned around and left. We returned to the conversation about Tortola and discussed the long list of shore excursions available on the island, concluding that it must be very big and diverse compared to the others we had visited. We had all planned different excursions in Tortola. Denny was heading for the Sage Mountain hike and beach trip. Skip was taking the escape to Jost Van Dyke, a laid-back island named for a Dutch pirate and famous for its beach bar. He promised to while away the day lolling in a beachside hammock with a bottle of strong rum in his hand while listening to the live calypso band playing at the famous Foxy's. Ginny was booked on a tour of the historical sites around the island and looked forward to some shopping at Sunny Caribbee after that. She asked if Ralph happened to be on the same tour, but he was taking the island boat tour with a stop at Marina Cay. That reminded me of the book I had borrowed from the library the first day, so I asked him what there was to see there.

Ralph said Marina Cay is a tiny islet off Tortola so small you can walk around it in an hour. It was uninhabited until a young American navy man, a wannabe author, moved to Tortola with his new bride and bought Marina Cay. This was during the Depression. The couple had to build their own house with limited resources, bringing everything in on their tiny skiff, and recruit some help from the local friends they made at a time when the majority of the population in the Virgin Islands was comprised of African slave descendants and you could count the number of whites on two hands. They enlisted a poet, for example, to build their roof. Sometimes the cultural differences prompted misunderstandings that led to serious rifts that impacted the building of their house. Everything presented a hurdle, and the largest was digging a cistern because the ground was solid coral and rock. They had no end of close calls with unexpected and dangerous visitors. In the midst of it all, the woman's mother arrived unannounced one day and when she saw the conditions under which her daughter was living, she immediately declared war on her son-in-law. Things went out of control from there. His name was Robb White, and he actually became a famous writer. He authored lots of adventure books like *The Lion's Paw, Up Periscope, Deathwatch, Torpedo Run* and many more, some of which were made into movies. Robb White wrote a memoir titled *Two on the Isle* about the young couple's time on Marina Cay. In the end, he was recalled by the navy and the couple left the island. Eventually they split up. That was when they learned they had never owned the island, even though they'd paid for it.

I was chastising myself for not having read the book, which I had been hoarding from the first day when I took it out of the ship's library. I hadn't even opened the cover and couldn't remember truthfully if it was on my dresser or on the coffee table. Everyone was fascinated and Wink asked what there was to see on Marina Cay these days.

"I'll know when I see it," Ralph replied. He had

never seen the place before. He expected to see the Robb White House still at the top of the island, possibly renovated as a small bar or hotel. He was fairly sure there was a Pusser's store as well. "It's pretty hard to avoid those in these islands," he added, chuckling.

I said I'd heard about Pusser's but couldn't understand why someone would call their business such an ugly name. Ralph explained it was the way they pronounced "purser" in the pirate days. He said the purser is the person in charge of all the money and finances on a ship. I remembered the captain introducing the chief purser the night of the captain's gala and had always meant to find out what that meant. I thanked Ralph for closing that gap. Ralph added that while Robb and his wife, Rodie, eventually separated, their daughter followed in Robb's footsteps as an author: Bailey White of *Mama Makes Up Her Mind.* I marveled at the layers of coincidences I was already discovering in these islands in the short time I had been here and imagined an infinite world of fascinating connections beyond. Unanimously we agreed that Ralph's was the most interesting choice of activities at Tortola, and we made him promise to come to dinner the following night so we could hear all about it. Then we asked Dr. Feerum what he was planning to do.

Dr. Feerum said it was hard to top Ralph's choice, but he was going to go scuba diving at the wreck of the *Rhone,* which made us look at him in stunned silence.

"Gee, Dr. Feerum," Denny was the first to break

the silence. "I had no idea you were certified to dive."

"Yes, it comes with the territory of being on these islands so much. I got scuba certified about twenty years ago and I've always wanted to dive the legendary wreck of the *Rhone*," he said, leaning back and folding his arms behind his head.

"You think you'll see bodies?" Denny asked.

"Not exactly," the professor said. "But I'm hoping to see a teaspoon."

He said that there were only twenty-five survivors of a total on board of one hundred forty-five crew and passengers, but many of the bodies were buried at Salt Island where the wreck occurred. There were so many victims because the ship was sailing through a hurricane, and back in those days, they strapped the passengers to their beds to reduce the chance of injury from falling. I was stunned, imagining how helpless that would make me feel, being strapped to a bed knowing the ship was going down. Everyone else must have been imagining the same thing because we were all quiet, waiting to hear more.

Dr. Feerum said the Royal Mail Steamer, RMS *Rhone*, was a 310-foot steamship that started its career in 1865 plying the Atlantic between Southampton and Brazil. It was an iron-hulled ship that could sail at speeds to fourteen knots at sea. In addition to carrying mail, it accommodated three hundred passengers. The RMS *Rhone* had some innovations in its design, including the second bronze propeller ever put on a ship. It also had the technology to recycle water for its boilers. He said it came to be called "Unsinkable *Rhone*" because it had evaded trouble along several of its transatlantic sailings. But it was deployed to a Caribbean route in 1867, and that's when its luck ran out.

"On October 29th," Dr. Feerum said, "the barometer dropped. The master of the ship, Captain Frederick Woolley, was concerned but dismissed the possibility of a hurricane because it was past the hurricane season. He would not live to learn that the storm that overtook them was a hurricane after all.

"The *Rhone* was supposed to bunker at the coaling station in St. Thomas, but an outbreak of yellow fever there forced them to refuel at Peter Island instead, where they found themselves alongside another mail packet, the RMS *Conroy,* in a violent storm. The two ships' captains decided to put all the passengers together and transferred those on the *Conroy* to the Unsinkable *Rhone,* whereupon the *Conroy* headed away in the storm, only to end up foundering at Tortola. The *Rhone,* now with passengers from both ships strapped to their beds, stuck fast when the anchor chain suddenly caught on a head of coral and had to be cut loose to release the ship. That chain is still in Great Harbour at Peter Island, by now home to millions of generations of sea creatures," he added.

"Anchorless, the RMS *Rhone* tried to sail to safety, but the second half of the hurricane struck the ship only two hundred fifty yards from the safety of Dead Chest Island. A sudden shift of strong winds smashed the *Rhone* against Black Point Rock at Salt Island with such violent ferocity that Captain Woolley was jettisoned overboard. His teaspoon is still in the wreck, and that is what I am hoping to see." He said the ship broke in two pieces and exploded when the searing water from the boiler met the cold ocean water, sinking the vessel to a depth of eighty feet.

I had a whole new appreciation for the professor. On first impression he did not come across as an adventurous type, but the facts disproved that impression. We all clamored for a recount of his *Rhone* diving adventure and forced him to promise to join the table the following night at dinner.

Wink said he had a lot on his plate what with two missing passengers and he would not be leaving the ship in Tortola, but then he remembered that one person had not yet submitted her plans to the group. He turned to me and asked what those plans were. I told him I was going to ride a horse on Sage Mountain. He smiled and said, "That is good to know. Shadow runs that operation. He is a good man, and he keeps his horses clean and healthy." Then he added, "They are very tame and gentle. See if he'll let you ride Starlight."

We left the dining room in high spirits after polishing off the baked Alaska and sharing our stories, and everyone agreed to extend the evening by attending the nighttime show all together. We met in front of the theater door about fifteen minutes later and settled into an empty row. We were expecting the singers and dancers to appear in another full-fledged production as advertised in *The Tides* and all over the ship's marquees. But when the curtains parted, we saw a lone ventriloquist perched on a high stool holding a dummy dressed as a very old man. Bald, glasses, red suspenders, and drab gray pants drawn up to its chest, the dummy expressed a wry sense of humor from the moment it opened its mouth. Within minutes of the act we were holding our sides in laughter, easily forgetting that the ventriloquist was talking for the dummy. During his performance, he brought out additional equally hilarious dummies that drew us in as though they were autonomous individuals and had lives of their own. The dummies even talked to each other and conversed in unison with the ventriloquist, leaving the audience spellbound in disbelief that this three-way conversation with three distinctly different voices was all coming from one person. He even interjected a phone call at one point, and the audience burst into applause when a voice came through a phone from across the stage. Then he played on cruise-themed humor by weaving some of the things that had happened on the ship right into his script. He was not only talented but wickedly funny. At the show's conclusion, Pearl invited everyone upstairs in the Paris Lounge for a Twisting Party with Beatles music and two-for-one drinks for any drinks ordered with a twist.

It had been a long day and I opted to go back to my room and get some serious sleep before my horse ride the following day. Incredibly, another message was lurking behind the malevolent blinking eye on my phone. I listened while the scratchy voice warned: "YOU'RE FISHING FOR TROUBLE! GO HOME!"

For once I was so tired I didn't care. All I wanted was sleep. I dropped the phone on the receiver and crashed on top of my bed.

Chapter Nine

Day Nine: February 11, Thursday
Tortola (Road Town Harbor), British Virgin Islands
Showers: High: 80ºF/27ºC. Low: 71ºF/22ºC.

TORTOLA WAS THE OTHER British Virgin Island on our itinerary besides Virgin Gorda, which had been our first stop where I got lost in the grotto. It seemed to share the laid-back and leisurely pace of its smaller sister, Virgin Gorda. Colorful island houses with bright contrasting shutters peek-a-booed playfully behind lush green and vibrantly colored plants and flowers. A marketplace near the harbor sprawled for blocks, offering a mind-boggling array of sundresses, tee shirts, towels, ties, beach bags, caps, sandals, headwraps, and hair-braiding services as well as handcrafted items, toys, masks, spices, rum cakes, candies, beaded necklaces, paintings, prints, and seashells. The town bustled with cars and tour buses competing for space on the roads that connected government buildings, restaurants, services, and tourist attractions like Pusser's and Sunny Caribbee's.

I found my group and we headed up to Mount Sage in a small van. Imagine my surprise when I learned that my excursion companions were Stan and Mildred from my trivia team. Outside of our team association, we hadn't come to know each other, and I was looking forward to spending the next few hours with them. But any more familiarity was not going to happen on the ride to the stable. Our jolly driver, Walla, was as high-spirited as they come, brandishing a machete and shaking his head as he laughed heartily while revving up his car. He lurched forward abruptly, and we all took a sharp breath and sat up straight. Walla assured us that he was the island's best driver, and he would introduce us to some of his island's bounty. He then proceeded to stop along the way and used his machete to hack down samples of the roadside fare growing from the trees. Breadfruit, mango, papaya, soursop, sugar cane, starfruit, sugar apples, coconuts – there seemed no end to the variety of delectable tropical fruits this island grew. He cut them into wedges or slabs or slices and offered the juicy samples from the blade of his machete along with napkins at every stop. No one starves on Tortola and no one gets thirsty either, because of the rum, he told us. He threw his head back and laughed loud and hard as he lurched and squealed off to the next stop, brandishing his machete outside the window with one hand while he steered with the other.

When we arrived at Mount Sage National Park, Walla handed us over to Shadow, introducing each of us by our first names to the very thin man who would guide us through the forest on his horses. Shadow had gray dreadlocks cascading down his back and was wearing a faded knit cap in red, green, and yellow stripes. He greeted us with a kind expression that exuded wisdom and complacency. I thought in another setting he might have been a bodhisattva and wondered to myself if Rastafari was similar to Buddhism.

As if on cue, Stan asked about Shadow's knit cap with green, gold, red, and black bands knitted in, saying he had seen similar caps being worn by locals in these islands. Mildred added that she ran across them in the tourist shops and some had long braids attached. As Shadow walked with us to his stable, he told us that green, gold, red, and black were the symbolic colors of Rastafari. He said Rastafari originated in Jamaica in the 1930s as an interpretation of the Bible, and adherents consider themselves Christians. He said Rastafari emerged because descendants of black Africans, who had been displaced by the slave trade and brought against their will to labor in the Caribbean plantations, sought to remember and perpetuate their African origins, to find solidarity and identity. More than a religion or worldview, Rastafari came to be associated with black consciousness and a positive identity for black people. The religious movement arose during a time when Jamaicans and, by extension, other black Caribbean islanders still under the yoke of British colonialism, yearned to express themselves with a new and positive identity that connected them with their proud African roots, rejecting the notion that blacks were an inferior race.

Pausing, he added that the word "Rastafari" was derived from Haile Selassie's name, before he was crowned emperor of Ethiopia. That name was Ras Tafari Makonnen, Ras meaning prince. Rastas believe the Bible was originally written in the Ethiopian language and depicted the black race as the chosen people. He added that Ethiopia was called Abyssinia in those days. Rastafari has no large unifying church, no central leader, and just two commandments: love of God and love of neighbor. Rastas follow a diet of natural food, homegrown whenever possible, and avoid pork and seafood. Many are vegetarians, even avoiding sugar and salt. Rastas reject alcohol, tobacco, and hard drugs like heroin or cocaine, but do smoke ganja or weed during their religious gatherings, fulfilling a sacramental ritual. They meet in small groups, play drums, chant, and sing Rasta songs, sometimes to tunes from Christian hymns, which makes for a Creolized version of African and Christian beliefs.

"Music has played a dominant role in spreading awareness of Rastafari," he told us, "mostly the popular styles of ska and reggae. "But," he added, "most Rastas themselves don't listen to reggae."

"What about all that hair?" Stan asked. "Does that carry religious significance?" He was referring to the dreadlocks men wound up and stuffed into the knit caps, or let fall down their backs.

"Growing long beards and long hair for men probably started as a way of imitating Haile Selassie," Shadow said. "The dreadlocks symbolize Rastafari. However, they can be a stigma since people who don't understand Rasta might think us unkempt and unclean, but actually the opposite is true."

By this time, we'd reached the stable where we found four horses awaiting us. Shadow said his other horses were on the trail with another group guided by his son. The horses looked very healthy and content and were groomed and clean. They were already saddled as he'd come by a little while earlier to prepare them. Sizing us up, he gave the biggest one, white with some dappling he called Prospect, to Stan. Mildred got the black horse, Indira. I got the smallest horse, a roan with a star-shaped marking on her forehead. "Starlight," he said to me, "is who you'll be riding. I offered her to a little girl in the other party, but she said she was an experienced rider, so I gave her Mustang instead and she trotted right off." I thought immediately of the little reader from our ship and wondered if he was talking about the same girl.

We mounted the horses and Shadow carefully adjusted the saddles and stirrups for each of us, taking his time and making sure we were safe and secure before he mounted his own horse. He led us along the beautiful paths through this national park of eighty-six acres that was established in 1964 and boasts the highest point in all the Virgin Islands, British and U.S. combined, at 1,716 feet. As we trotted along, we took in the sumptuous vegetation and beautiful mahogany and white cedar trees growing all around us. Shadow said, "Okay, I've told you a bit about myself. Now it's your turn to share something about yourselves with me."

Mildred started by saying she and Stan had been married for nearly forty-five years. They were from Indiana originally but after retirement moved to Florida's panhandle where they had been the past four years. They had two grown children and two grandchildren with one on the way. All the grandchildren were their daughter's kids. Their son wasn't married and probably never would get married at the rate he was going. Shadow asked why they came on a cruise to the Caribbean and she laughed and said, "Why does anyone come on a Caribbean cruise? To enjoy beautiful beaches and wildlife and nature without cell phone interruptions." They had been on a half-dozen cruises since retiring, but still kept busy enough with their hobby to spend most of their time on land. Shadow asked about their hobby, and Mildred said Stan could better explain. Stan had been lagging behind us, but now he goaded his horse to get closer to Shadow. The horses were complacently trotting along as the light danced through the trees, casting freckles of light all over the forest. The overall effect was relaxing and rejuvenating.

"We grow organic herbs and spices and sell them to small neighborhood restaurants," he said. "We started doing it for a hobby, and technically it still is because we're not making much money. But it gives us a fun project and we get a kick out of going into a little place in town for lunch or dinner knowing we're enjoying a meal spiced with herbs that came from our own backyard. We call our little company, if you can even call it a company, Milstan Herbs, obviously a combination of our first names."

"I like the sound of natural, organic herbs," Shadow said. "You'd have no trouble marketing your product to the Rasta community here." Just then, we pulled our horses up to a spectacular lookout point that opened up gorgeous views of indescribably beautiful deep green foliage tumbling over the mountain into the sapphire water below, and we traded cameras back and forth to take photos of each other against this beautiful backdrop. The horses were calm and sure-footed, familiar with the paths from years of walking along them.

As we rode under the dappled shadows of the verdant canopy, Shadow pointed out the different indigenous trees and plants and told us some things about the island like the famous Bomba Shack and its monthly full-moon parties on the beach and a place where Spanish treasure was commonly believed to be buried. He also said there was a 400-year-old rum distillery still making some very strong rum at Cane

Garden Bay. He said it was rustic and very home-spun yet produced some of the purest rum anywhere – with some of the oldest equipment. Not a lot of it, he clarified, but very good. The Callwood Distillery was the oldest continuously operating rum distillery in the entire British Virgin Islands. The family that acquired it in the 1800s and still operates it today grows its own sugar cane and presses it immediately upon harvesting it to make a very pure and uncontaminated rum that bigger operations cannot offer.

"The interesting thing about Cane Garden Bay," he continued, "is that there was a sugar plantation there that belonged to a Quaker family in the 1700s."

Quakers in the Caribbean? I thought. I had an image of the Quaker Oats man from the cereal box with that big black Quaker hat on his head, lying in a hammock beneath a couple of palm trees, an umbrella drink in hand, and his bare toes dipping into the water lapping at the shore beneath him.

"Seriously," Shadow continued, "the real history is that while there were Quakers in these islands, they weren't much wanted around here because they were against slavery, and the whole economy depended on the free slave labor. Many of those emancipation-touting Quakers were prosperous planters who had slaves of their own.

"In fact," he continued, "Quakers from Tortola contributed in ways that spread their influence far beyond these islands. Did you know the architect who designed the United States Capitol Building was a Quaker from Jost Van Dyke?" Mildred, Stan, and I gasped in united disbelief!

"His name was Dr. William Thornton and he was a physician by training, but he apparently was a wannabe architect too," Shadow said. "His design for the U.S. Capitol Building won a competition offered by Thomas Jefferson. He was born in Jost Van Dyke in the 1700s to a Quaker family and earned his medical degree in Scotland. At one point, he led a failed movement to resettle freed black Americans in Sierra Leone in West Africa. Dr. William Thornton also served as the first Superintendent of the U.S. Patents Office."

I asked if there were any monuments or statues of Dr. William Thornton in the British Virgin Islands. Shadow chuckled and said there was a monument of sorts, one that floated. It was a sailboat converted to a floating bar named *Willie T.* He considered this a moment and added, "If you think about it, it's probably the biggest honor for anyone born in these islands when you consider how important tourism is to the local economy."

After nearly two hours, we turned our horses around and took a lower but parallel path back to the stable for a different but equally satisfying view of Mount Sage. This time we were on a quiet road where only an occasional car whisked by, but the horses took it in stride. Shadow asked me to share my story. But just as I started to talk, out of nowhere a car, blaring its horn wildly, squealed by so fast and close it nearly hit me. In an instant, Starlight started taking me on an uncontrollable ride down the road at a full-tilt canter. She was running so fast I could see her nostrils flaring. I was hanging on for dear life as she clopped down, neighing and bucking and shaking her head back and forth. Foliage was brushing against me and thwacking me on the arms and on my helmet. I barely dared to look ahead for fear of getting poked in the eye with a protruding branch. I could hear Shadow calling to Starlight from a distance but to no avail, although his voice seemed to be getting nearer. I pulled back on the reins, but it wasn't enough – she was seriously spooked. And, truth to tell, so was I. I could still hear Shadow shouting and the clip-clop of his horse approaching hard on our heels, which was of some comfort. But Starlight could run! She left the road and was now heading down the steepest path I had ever seen.

Petrified, the only thing I could see was Starlight's mane flailing wildly in front of me and alternating glimpses of forest and ocean and sky and ground. What added to my fear was a huge clap of thunder that riled the horse up even more. As rain started to pelt down, she was neighing louder and racing down that path like a house afire. I was bouncing helplessly in the saddle, but I managed to hold onto the reins until it felt like my fingernails were carving my own skin. I didn't dare scream for fear of spooking Starlight even more, but I was sure she could hear my heart pounding right out of my chest. She slipped on a wet stone but caught herself from falling and continued to tear on at a maddening speed. I could feel the saddle starting to slip underneath me and felt myself gradually bouncing and slipping over to my left side. I judged I was probably listing about twenty degrees off center and sliding down a little more with each passing minute. I tried to calculate how long it would take before I would be parallel to the ground and then completely upside down beneath the raging horse. Then I realized with utter astonishment that the bit was no longer in her mouth but had somehow come loose and was bouncing all over her nose. I didn't know if I felt sorrier for the horse or me, but I was not going to let go of the reins. I could no longer hear Shadow's voice over the noise of the steadily increasing rain and thunder. We were in a full-fledged thunderstorm now and I was drenched and fearing exactly what I knew that horse was fearing too – lightning! I tried saying something to soothe Starlight, but she raged on and seemed to be gaining momentum and speeding up like a runaway train.

The horse galloped through a deep puddle, and I felt the shocking splash of muddy water spray over me from my face to my shins. I had long lost any hope of my camera surviving, if it was even still in my fanny pack which for all I could remember I hadn't bothered to zip it back up the last time I opened it. I don't know how it happened, but I looked down and saw my hands clasped tightly enough to draw blood, but they were holding nothing. I had lost hold of the reins somewhere. I dared not look down at Starlight's legs because I knew with utter terror that the reins would be flailing around, causing her to panic even more and threatening to trip her. Then, all of a sudden, she stopped short and I flew off her like a stone in a medieval catapult. I landed with an excruciating thud and felt every bone in my body screaming. I tried to breathe, but I was totally winded and had to wait patiently until my breath came back to me. I could hear noises above the din of the rain and thunder, and when I felt brave enough to open my eyes, I saw Shadow coming toward me with a look of agonizing concern on his face. He told me to stay still and not move.

He said that the car looked like it had been aiming at me, and he was thunderstruck when it actually grazed Starlight. He said in all his years guiding the horses, no one had ever done anything like that. He was angry at himself for not getting the car's license plate, but he did recognize it as a rental car.

By this time, the other group, which included the little reader and her parents, had returned. They dismounted and entered a taxi that was waiting for them. Their guide, who was Shadow's son, went to round up Starlight. Shadow stayed with me and made sure I was okay. I was pretty shaken up and bruised, but it didn't feel like anything was broken. Thankfully, the helmet had protected my head from injury when I had flown off the horse. Shadow said Starlight was his gentlest horse and she had never so much as reared her head, so he was as stunned as anyone to see her so spooked. As we walked back to the parking lot, he asked me something that shook me to my core: "Do you have any enemies here?" I immediately thought of the latest phone threat.

"I'm beginning to believe I might," I answered, and told him a little about the events on board.

"I know all the people who own the car rental companies," he said, "and I will try to find out who rented that car. Here is my card. You can call me later, when I hope to have some information. I don't know who was driving that car, but I know it wasn't anyone who lives on this island," he said.

I took his card and thanked him. Then I piled into Walla's awaiting cab with Stan and Mildred for the ride back to the ship. This time Walla was careful to negotiate all the potholes and sharp turns as gently as he could to avoid causing me any further pain.

BACK ON THE SHIP, Mildred and Stan showed up for trivia just when I did. They said they were there to keep an eye on me and asked if I'd been down to see the ship's medic. Of course, I had not. We joined everyone else, already seated and chatting. The game was starting up in three minutes, so I quickly told everyone about Stan and Mildred's herb business and hastily asked everyone else what they did. Before they could share their stories, however, Pearl called for everyone's attention and announced that the questions today were geography-based. It dawned on me that no one on the ship actually knew what I did for a living, and I wondered how much longer I could keep my story under wraps.

Pearl's first question was, "Which African country used to be called Abyssinia?" Mildred and Stan and I looked at each other and gave the thumbs-up in unison. We knew we had this one in the bag, remembering Shadow's account of Ethiopia's earlier name. We were in a gridlock over which was the world's longest river, half of us voting for the Nile and the other half for the Amazon. We wrote down the Amazon but turns out it is the Nile. There were a lot of objections and challenges from the teams, but Pearl reminded us that trivia is not a democracy and her answer stood. We did slightly better than our average, with over half the answers correct. I was almost proud when Pearl asked for our score and it was respectable. Barry got us a point knowing that the national emblem of Canada is the maple leaf, and Karla knew that the River Liffey flowed through the center of Dublin because she had just read a mystery set in that city. But my attention was called once again to the number one team, boasting one hundred percent of the answers. As I glanced over at Mavis and Dutch's corner of the room, there sat Fred and Stacey. Fred caught my eye and waved. Blood sport!

I WAS DREADING having to forfeit a nap for afternoon tea, but I felt better after a warm shower. Dressed in my black dress with a pink and turquoise scarf, I felt revived and ready for showtime. I discovered more bruises and battle scars and scrapes and scratches and even blisters on my hands from holding onto the reins so tightly, but other than that, I was okay. The long gown would cover my legs, and whoever saw my arms would probably think my bruises were from the zipline fall or the fish encounter. I was starting to accumulate a rap sheet of accidents.

When I sat down with the string quartet, we were just a few minutes from starting up. The girls were giggling and chattering about something and Mario was looking on with a smile. Apparently, there had been a showdown between Pearl and the ventriloquist the night before. The girls explained to me between giggles and fits of laughter that, because of the female dancer with a sprained ankle, the production show could not take place as advertised the night before. So, Pearl phoned the ventriloquist who was scheduled to appear another night to commandeer him to take the stage instead. This is accepted practice on ships and all entertainers are accustomed to filling in on unscheduled nights for just such emergencies. But when the ventriloquist did not appear backstage at the specified time, Pearl stormed up to the room and banged on his door demanding to know why he was not backstage. Surprised, he answered that he had no idea he was supposed to be there. She said she had called earlier and gave him the message. That was when he cleared his throat and asked specifically to whom she had given the message. Pearl had to admit she'd left the message with his dummy, and the ventriloquist said that was the problem. The dummy simply hadn't conveyed her message to him! Bristling, Pearl demanded he suit up and get himself and his dummy to the stage in three minutes – or she would show him who was the real dummy!

I was worried about keeping up with the rest of the quartet that day because we were playing a medley of tunes with which I was less familiar: classical versions of Gospel, Negro spirituals and folk songs, many of which were new to me. I surprised myself, though, with how much I enjoyed the program and how well it went, even as I was sight-reading much of it.

Once again, the little girl occupied her favorite spot under the window. She had dark hair that was cut in a straight line across her forehead, and the rest of her hair fell in lofty waves to her shoulders. Today, instead of reading, she was busily typing on her tablet. She seemed to be able to occupy herself whether her parents were around or not, and I did not see them anywhere. Two or three times I caught the girl glancing at the quartet and was almost certain she was looking directly at me. Most kids that age would be reaching out to play with other kids their age, but this little girl was able to amuse herself independently. She seemed to be deep into her own world, oblivious of everything except the music surrounding her. She was totally engrossed in whatever she was writing and rarely looked up. Yet, for some reason, she preferred the ambience of our music to the DJ's loud party music on the pool deck. She reminded me of myself when I was that age. I decided to make a point of talking with her after our performance, but she was gone in a flash before I'd even collected my music.

THAT EVENING, everyone at Gilligan's Table was anxious to hear about Ralph's and Dr. Feerum's excursions, but our spirits were dampened with the news that Mrs. Mooney was still missing. Mr. Mooney joined the group but seemed agitated and distracted. When he saw all the bumps and bruises and scratches on my arms and face, he nearly flew out of his seat. He didn't realize that my injuries had occurred over the course of several days from an accumulation of mishaps. "You look downright awful!" he bellowed. "You look like you were caught in the middle of a herd of stampeding rhinoceroses."

"I probably look worse than I feel, but it's been a pretty exhilarating cruise, I'll say that much," I said, trying to keep some semblance of humor.

Mr. Mooney ordered his customary burger and fries, but barely touched them and left before the waiter passed around the dessert menus.

Everyone else listened raptly to my story and

murmured sincere expressions of concern. "I think someone is trying to kill her," Ginny said.

Dr. Feerum said he always thought riding horses was a dangerous endeavor and couldn't understand people who thought scuba diving was dangerous. I took the opportunity to ask if he had seen the teaspoon, and he proudly confirmed that yes, he had, and that his dive had been perfect in every respect.

Ralph volunteered that his time at Marina Cay had been splendid. He was able to see firsthand the old house that Robb and Rodie White had built and was amazed at the above-ground cistern. He added that he had enjoyed a wonderful daiquiri at the bar there while sitting at a small table overlooking the rocky little beach.

As dessert was winding down and the conversation started to lull, Wink tapped me on the shoulder and asked me to tell him the details of the horse-riding escapade. "Did I get a glimpse of who was in the car?" he asked.

"No, it happened too fast," I answered. Then I suddenly remembered that Shadow believed it was a rental car and told Wink, "Shadow said he will do some island sleuthing." I fished out Shadow's card from my purse and handed it to Wink as we headed to the theater for the evening's show.

That night, no one was expecting the treat that awaited us when the stage curtains rolled open. Instead of announcing the entertainer from behind the stage, Pearl appeared on the stage herself wearing a beautiful floor-length African gomesi, with peaked shoulders over wide elbow-length sleeves and an obi-like sash tied in a beautiful bow at her waist. The purple and gold African-inspired pattern of the sash contrasted with the sophisticated red and gold of her lavish gown. She paused, looking as regal as an African queen, as the audience gasped at the sight of her against the dramatic stage setting of exotic animals in a wild and natural African savannah. The music bloomed and blossomed in a way that buoyed her voice and rarified the air in the theater. Every eye was on her as Pearl mesmerized the audience with one achingly beautiful African song after another sung in a number of African tribal languages. Some were very sad and haunting and accompanied by what sounded like a reed flute. Others sounded flirtatious and rhythmic, with the beating of hands or sticks on African drums. Anyone could see that this was Pearl's night as she shared her talents and her African heritage and culture.

Toward the end of the show, she briefly explained that she had started her career path singing in the Methodist church in her hometown in Jamaica and added that many of the soulful songs she grew up with were African in origin and had been carefully preserved and passed down from the slave era. When she finished her last piece, everyone stood up to acknowledge her performance with a regaling standing ovation. Pearl bowed and left the stage as Roy appeared on the stage to invite her back out for another round of applause before announcing more fun to follow upstairs. He said a fortune teller was waiting in the Paris Lounge to reveal our futures with her tarot card readings. The audience nearly stampeded into the elevators to race upstairs.

Wink looked at me and said, "I know you want to go upstairs as much as I do, so we'll have our talk right here and now. I'll make it brief: No more excursions unless I go with you. Period, end of story. If you don't, I will cancel all the remaining excursions you have booked, but in any event I will personally take you snorkeling when we get to Grand Turk. I can't leave the ship tomorrow, so you're on your own in Old San Juan, but I don't want you going on any ATV's, fast catamarans, ziplines, horse trails, jet skis, snake charmings, crocodile hunts, bungee jumps, hang gliding, or anything else, okay?"

I got the message. And, truth be told, I secretly welcomed a little alone time. "I don't think I have the stamina for any of that anyway," I said. "I was just going to walk around Old San Juan and do a little souvenir shopping."

We joined our Gilligan's Table group, already assembled at a little cocktail table in the Paris Lounge. Annie, fortune teller, was already moving from table to table, laying out her cards and telling the fortune of one of the guests in each group. She was outfitted with a mic so the whole lounge could hear her, and of course everyone craned their necks to see her working in action. Judging from the reactions of her "victims," she was exposing their secrets one after the other. Things took an interesting turn when she came over to our group and zoomed in on Dr. Feerum, who was vigorously gesturing "No!" as he saw her single him out. But she persisted and, calmly smiling, spread out the deck of cards at our table right in front of him. Narrating in her mic for the entire lounge to hear, she started by saying that this man definitely was running away from something, and she went so far as to suggest that he might be in the Witness Protection Program. The room was set to laughing. Annie said Dr. Feerum had recently endured some disturbing and life-changing event, perhaps a jury trial of some sort, that had set him off in a new and unexpected direction. She picked up some cards and said he was looking for something – or someone. He was searching near and far, and it was that search that had brought him to this cruise. His longtime relationship had suddenly ended over something she wasn't sure about, but she thought he may have been unfairly accused of something, possibly a crime he did not commit. She joked about taking the cruise as part of the Witness Protection Program as the murmur of chuckles swelled over the room. His partner had suddenly disappeared, she explained, and he was actively trying to find her in a desperate attempt to explain himself and try to reconcile. The fortune teller picked up more cards from the pile and said he may be closer to his partner than he realized. According to his tarot cards, it was likely that she was somewhere in these islands, but this close partner may be a brand new one, not the one that got away. She predicted his search was about to end.

When Annie got to this point, Dr. Feerum's cheeks and ears flushed bright red. In a dramatic gesture, Ginny untied the scarf on her neck and swabbed his sweating forehead and cheeks. From his uncomfortable expression, it appeared that the fortune teller had nailed his story in this climactic confrontation. She was amazing. The crowd was wild with excitement and a general buzz of voices filled the venue. I knew Dr. Feerum wouldn't want to fill me in on his story after this. But if he feared he would be fielding questions from curious passengers for the rest of the cruise, he had only to wait for Annie to move on to her next "victim," whose story was even more gripping. It only took that long for everyone to forget about Dr. Feerum and start licking their chops anew.

I BRACED MYSELF for whatever was awaiting me inside my stateroom, but there was no blinking red light on my phone, so I flipped the TV on to Dr. Pinot's lecture and started dressing for bed. Just as I realized I had mistakenly picked up Ginny's scarf and brought it back with me, the phone rang. I picked it up, assuming it was Ginny. "STOP HORSING AROUND! GO HOME TOMORROW!" the scratchy voice said.

"Who are you?" I demanded. I was looking for a button on the phone to record the message. The voice repeated the same message, as though it were a recording. "STOP HORSING AROUND! GO HOME TOMORROW!" Then it clicked off.

I called Wink who was at my door in a shot in his pajamas and robe. Two seconds later, Ginny showed up looking for her scarf. I handed it to her, but instead of going back to her room, she lingered. There I was in my nightgown and there was Wink in his pajamas sitting on the edge of my bed at 12:36 AM. I figured it was all the proof Ginny needed to believe there was something going on between us. I turned around and looked at Wink with a "What next?" kind of expression. He picked up a pen and the pad of paper with the MS *Minerva* insignia and told Ginny point blank to leave because he and I had something important to discuss. But Ginny would not budge. She wedged her way into the door to my room and stood there demanding to be a part of the conversation. She was angling for gossip and didn't care if it was about Wink and me, or about the missing cellist, or anything else. She had to be the first one to receive the hottest news. She was the lioness after the fresh kill. She sat down in the only chair.

Wink started in. "You said this time the voice answered when you picked up the phone?"

"Yes. There were no messages waiting for me. I had put my things down and was dressing for bed when I realized I'd grabbed Ginny's scarf. Right then the phone rang, so naturally I thought it was Ginny and I picked up without thinking. It wasn't Ginny but the gruff voice was there instead, telling me to go home from San Juan tomorrow. I panicked and asked, 'Who is this?' to stall while I looked for a button on the phone to record the call. The voice repeated the same thing again, and I'm pretty sure it was prerecorded because there was a gap between 'go home' and 'tomorrow' both times. I think the caller never expected me to answer and just played the message two times instead of giving me any additional information." Wink was writing something down. Ginny asked if it was the cellist's abductor leaving the messages, but Wink held up his hand to stop her. He ignored her completely.

"And it was the same voice as before?" he asked me.

"I knew it!" Ginny interrupted. "I knew you were getting the threats for Sabrina!" She pointed at me and said, "Wasn't I right in warning you not to wear her gowns?"

Now I was ignoring her. I answered Wink. "Yes, definitely the same voice." I was trying to think of the exact wording of the message, but it wasn't coming to me just then.

"How many of these messages have you received, Marianne?" Ginny pried. Wink and I ignored her. She added, "How many accidents have you had on this cruise, Marianne? Are you always so clumsy? My God,

I have never seen anyone so black and blue. Every day it's something else. And you are working so hard, too. You need to think about everyone around you very carefully and make a list of them to see who is doing this. Did you ever think that someone was setting you up? These messages are coming from someone who wants to distract you. Wants you off the ship, but not dead for some reason. You are standing in the way of their getting something and time is running out for them."

Wink and I looked up at her in disbelief. There might be some truth to what she was saying. I had never thought about listing everyone on the ship in order of my degree of acquaintance with them to consider any potential motives for wanting me off the ship – not dead and off the ship, but just off the ship and out of the way. Wink was thinking the same thing. He said, "Let's start the list, Marianne."

Ginny got up to go, adding that she wished us both well, which I figured she left as a mysterious coda for us to take any way we wanted.

Wink stayed for a very long time, taking notes while we considered every possible motive of everyone on that ship who knew me at all, from Fred and Stacey to the trivia team members to everyone at Gilligan's Table to fellow solo travelers I'd talked with to the people I had met on shore and on the excursions. Wink had me thinking about them all and did his best to suggest possible motives for each one on the list. We came up dry with everyone. To be honest, the only person I even halfway considered an adversary who might want me out of the way was Sorrenta, who showed up every time I was with Wink. But I didn't want to mention her because it might give Wink the impression that I was interested . . . or even jealous. I left that one for him to bring up, which he never did.

Chapter Ten

Day Ten: February 12, Friday
San Juan, Puerto Rico, USA:
Scattered Showers: High: 83ºF/28ºC. Low: 73ºF/23ºC.

I WAS ACHING by morning. It had been a very long night with Wink working until the earliest hints of daylight. I'm sure Ginny had drawn all sorts of wild conclusions about us and, well, Wink and I probably did at least a few things in that time that might justify her suspicions. It was late, we were there together and, well, it's hard to resist the gentle rocking of a ship as it slices through the water on the way from somewhere to somewhere else. What can I say? It's a romantic setting. We added wine to the mix, and before we knew what was happening, the list Wink was working on was cast aside and we tumbled headlong first on the couch and then . . . I'll just say we woke up in each other's arms and leave it at that.

I lingered in bed, trying to reconstruct all the scenarios we were establishing with possible suspects and motives for anyone wanting me off the ship. And it just kept boiling down to the same thing: someone wanted me off the ship. But even as I thought about that, my mind kept slipping back into the warm and irresistible feeling of Wink's arms around me.

Sorrenta! I sat up with a jolt, suddenly wide awake. The thought of her and Wink together stabbed me like an ice pick. I almost started plotting ways to get Sorrenta off the ship and out of my way.

A FLOOD OF BRIGHT sunshine entered my room, and once I walked out to the veranda and saw the magnificent sights of Old San Juan, I couldn't resist watching the entire sail-in until we were snugly in our space along the pier. As the ship glided past the immense fortress of El Morro sitting high atop its craggy bluff and surrounded by a long and massive wall, I contemplated the centuries of history and the fact that this city became such an important Spanish stronghold in the New World by dint of its location. After rounding the point with El Morro and its lighthouse, the ship slipped past a red portal in the massive old wall and sailed by a grandiose old building peeking out from behind the wall a short distance beyond. I could see a jumble of buildings in various stages of repair and exhibiting a diversity of architecture that ranged from Spanish colonial to Art Deco. As we slipped into our berth on the pier, the city stirred to life below. I couldn't wait to explore Old San Juan.

I did not forget my promise to Wink, and frankly didn't have much energy or inclination for more than a little sightseeing and souvenir shopping. Within the hour of the ship's arrival, I was strolling through the charming streets of Old San Juan.

The streets were narrow and cobbled with old, blue-glazed bricks. They were being washed with buckets of water splashed over them and swept clean by the fastidious merchants preparing to open their shops, bakeries, and restaurants for the day. The heavy shuttered windows of the gracious old stone buildings in the Spanish style shut out the searing Caribbean sun. Passing breezes slipped through wrought-iron railings that hugged second- and third-floor balconies that offered city residents a pleasant respite from the heat. Plants and flowers in big clay pots, with flowering tendrils cascading down, adorned these balconies. Impregnable wooden doors of massive proportions that could have been centuries old sneered at passersby with their priceless brass doorknockers, knobs, and handles wrought in an earlier age. Faded tiles meticulously hand-painted with delicate flowers, birds, and religious images added patina and interest to ochre and lavender painted buildings. Every so often, a big wooden door left open on the street front afforded a glimpse of a charming inner courtyard like a secret jewel inside a plain box.

The streets were already busy with morning traffic squeezing through the narrow passages and store owners opening their doors as I tiptoed carefully over the beautiful, blue-glazed cobblestones on my way to Plaza Colon. Named for Christopher Columbus, this central gathering spot commemorates the Italian admiral with an imposing statue gazing down from high atop a blazing white column, the tallest statue of Columbus in the world, I remembered reading somewhere. The entire plaza lies under the eternal watch of old Fort San Cristobal, also named for Columbus, looming over the plaza from the precipice above.

Coffeeshops, kiosks, restaurants, and artsy stores beckoned couples and groups pouring out of the cruise pier, enticing them through their doors with alluring aromas and beautiful curios and signs that claimed the "First," the "Best," and the "Original." Even with a satisfying breakfast in me, all the competing and irresistible aromas permeating the air made me hanker for something else. I turned down a street called Calle Fortaleza, marveling at the beautiful old tile work on the building exteriors and admiring the hand-painted tiles with street numbers on the building fronts. Painted tiles certainly seemed to stand out as a feature of this Spanish colonial city. Balconies of wrought iron in no end of elaborate scrolls, curlicues, and other intricate patterns bespoke the Moorish influence on Spanish design and architecture in this one-time Spanish stronghold in the New World.

Puerto Rico remained under Spanish control from the day Columbus trod its soil on his second New World voyage in 1493, until 1898 when it fell from the clutches of Spain. After the USS *Maine* exploded in Havana Harbor in Cuba on February 15, 1898, the so-named Spanish-American War erupted, ending Spanish dominion over the Philippines, Cuba and Puerto Rico. In 1917, Puerto Ricans were granted American citizenship by an act of Congress and were free to come and go between the island and the mainland without a passport. Since then, Puerto Ricans have been migrating back and forth, following the tides of economic opportunity while bringing along a willing, able and educated workforce. With a population of about three million in Puerto Rico, more than five million Puerto Ricans live in the United States, where they account for nearly two percent of the U.S. population. The Commonwealth of Puerto Rico is neither a nation nor a state, but rather an unincorporated territory of the United States. Since 1952, its citizens have had their own constitution, governor, and legislative body. Pressure to push toward statehood manifests in occasional referenda, some with surprising results like the one in 1993 when, given the choice of commonwealth status, statehood, or independence, the majority voted "none of the above!" Puerto Ricans use the U.S. dollar and can choose between English and Spanish because both are the official languages. Americans traveling to Puerto Rico feel like they are "coming home" when they see branches of the U.S. Post Office and familiar brands like CVS and Walgreen's. The Puerto Rican national parks are run by the U.S. National Parks Service, and stateside national park passes can be used for admittance to many of the popular tourist sites in Puerto Rico.

Calle Fortaleza took me past stores, some with familiar national brand names and others that were local. A plaque on the door of one establishment boasted that it was where the daiquiri had been invented and promised the best piña coladas in the Caribbean. Barrachina's seemed to be a popular gathering spot, even in the morning. I continued down the busy street between a row of narrow buildings until the street ended at a large wrought-iron gate. A massive blue-gray building with white window trim stood on the other side. I remembered seeing it as we sailed into San Juan that morning. This example of architectural grandiosity was the oldest still-serving governor's residence in the Spanish New World. It was once part of the city's earliest fortress, the Fortaleza, built in the sixteenth century, but in the tradition of many old Spanish fortresses, it was placed in the wrong spot to the chagrin of the early city fathers, who were forced to admit their error too late. Damage control followed with the construction of the city's second fortress, this time placed high on the bluff overlooking the channel entrance to the harbor and named Castillo del Felipe del Morro, or El Morro, meaning bluff because it stands atop the bluff at the entrance to the harbor.

Backtracking a block to return to Calle Cristo, I looked to my right where tourists and locals were starting to fill colorful umbrella-covered tables for coffee, lunch, or anything in between. But what caught my attention was the top of a small and old structure at the end of that little cul-de-sac. I walked over to check it out and the heavy gates opened to a very small chapel, with ancient oil paintings, gold relics, and silver candlesticks inside. A docent explained that this was the Chapel of the Christ of Good Health. Apparently it was built by an officer in the military who had witnessed a terrible accident in 1753 when young men were racing their horses on a certain feast day. One of the horses took his rider on a flight over the precipice and the officer, on witnessing the disaster, made a sudden and fervent prayer to God that he would erect a chapel on this spot if God saved the young man's life. The horse died, but miraculously its young rider survived. The officer made good on his promise and built the Christ of Good Health chapel where, over the subsequent centuries, people left valuables to the Christ of Good Health in hopes of cures and healing and restoration after injuries, sickness, and disease. The docent said the original oil paintings were created by Puerto Rico's most famous artist, José Campeche. The other relics, silver and gold, represented Milagros, or miracles, just like the original miracle of the young man surviving the accident.

I left the chapel and continued along Calle Cristo past Fortaleza and the governor's residence until I was stopped by an imposing staircase leading up to the entrance of San Juan Bautista Cathedral. The city of

San Juan was named for St. John the Baptist, but the city wasn't always called San Juan. When Christopher Columbus came around in 1493, he named the entire island San Juan and the harbor Puerto Rico, or "rich port." In time, mapmakers switched the names around on the maps. San Juan Bautista is the city cathedral. It sits up high over a small plaza fronting a road that connects the church, with a direct path, to the San Juan Gate a couple blocks down at the waterfront. The San Juan Gate is framed in bright cherry red, a sight hard to miss during a ship's sail into San Juan Harbor. The massive ancient wooden doors stand wide open for easy pedestrian passage between the city and the waterfront boardwalk, hugging the old city wall on one side, and providing panoramic views of the harbor on the other. The city's icons, the garitas, the cylindrical guardhouses spiking the walls and fortresses, pop out at every vantage point to offer striking backdrops for photos and selfies.

During colonial times, ships were prohibited from entering the harbor after sunset. Ships already in the harbor were barred from disembarking after sunset when the San Juan gate was closed, so sailors had to wait the night through on the ship. But as soon as the gate reopened at sunrise, the voyagers made the short pilgrimage through the San Juan Gate up the narrow Calleta de San Juan to the church to offer thanks for their safe passage. Today that church, the San Juan Bautista Cathedral, is known mostly as the third and final resting place of Puerto Rico's first governor, Juan Ponce de Leon. Yes, that same Ponce de Leon who was always searching for the elusive fountain of youth. While he never found it, he did come across some indigenous adversaries on an expedition to Florida, providing them some target practice. He died from injuries sustained in that battle after reaching Cuba, where he was buried. The first time.

Subsequently, a descendant of Ponce de Leon had his remains exhumed and moved from Cuba to the Church of San Jose in San Juan, about three blocks away from San Juan Bautista Cathedral. Finally, he was moved again from the Church of San Jose to San Juan Bautista Cathedral where he rests in an enormous tomb, hopefully for good.

I stopped to admire some sculptures in the tiny park fronting the cathedral. They appeared to be made of brass and depicted playful characters like cats and penguins that looked like they came from a children's book. A pale peach colored building, brightly contrasted by its turquoise awning, shutters, and balustrade, caught my attention. A man on the corner was selling ice cream from a little pushcart. People were already occupying the benches in the little park, and I walked toward a pale ochre building of the same medieval architectural style as the church with a sign identifying it as "Hotel El Convento." I walked up the slight incline and through the large medieval doors and found myself in a beautiful old hotel lobby; I feasted my eyes on centuries-old, threadbare tapestries, bells, and sconces on the walls, and yet more splendid tile work. No one seemed to mind that I was availing myself of all this beauty, even though I was not a guest of the property. There was a flurry of activity in one of the high-ceilinged rooms which a team was decorating for a wedding, judging from the masses of beautiful white flowers they were arranging on the white-clothed tables.

The aroma of coffee tantalized my nostrils and I couldn't resist taking a seat in the airy atrium and ordering some. I was looking forward to tasting Puerto Rican coffee and had read somewhere that it was President Franklin Delano Roosevelt's favorite coffee, the only coffee he served for breakfast in the White House. I took a sip and couldn't help but agree with President Roosevelt. I left the Hotel El Convento and continued my trajectory along Calle Cristo to the intersection at Calle San Sebastian which I crossed diagonally. Opposite me high up on a column stood a statue of Juan Ponce de Leon, apparently right up there with Columbus as national heroes go in Puerto Rico. A plaza abutted the side of another large and very old church. It was surrounded by scaffolding, and an illustrated narration on banners running along the side explained that the church was undergoing renovations. This was the Church of San Jose, where Ponce de Leon was first buried when his remains were brought from Cuba at the direction of a descendant who was a member of the clergy. This was the church that Juan Ponce de Leon's family actually attended and supported, and the second oldest church in the Spanish New World, predated only by the Cathedral of Santa Maria la Meñor in Santo Domingo.

Clearing the plaza and the Church of San Jose, the next thing that caught my attention was a solitary column, bright terra cotta red against the cloudless sapphire sky. I had reached the Five Century Plaza with its eye-catching centerpiece. A few people stood at the base of the forty-foot-high totem taking photos from an ant's-eye view at its base. I was reminded of the apes that converged on the monolith in that old science-fiction movie, *2001: A Space Odyssey*. The Five Century Column was erected in 1992 to commemorate the five centuries since Christopher Columbus had first set foot in the New World and stood as a tribute to all the original First Nation tribes in the New World. Thousands of intricately carved clay tiles, or tesserae, covered the entire totem, each representative of a distinct First Nation tribe. The column displays Puerto Ricans' pride in the mix of blood that runs through the veins of their population, predominately Spanish, black African, and indigenous Tainos.

Beyond the 500-year totem, I caught a breathtaking view of El Morro, the great fortress on the bluff overlooking the sea. Its limestone and sandstone walls were eighteen to forty feet thick, and the structure capped a rolling green lawn of twenty-seven acres alive with families flying colorful and whimsical kites. A vendor truck nearby displayed kites along with caps, magnets, and cold soda pop. An enormous green iguana lumbered over from the nearby expansive green and looked around before disappearing into some bushes. The iguanas are not indigenous here, but they say there are now more iguanas than people and may have been introduced from Panama when the canal was being constructed.

After taking in the riveting views of the fortress grounds and nearby chapel dome of the city cemetery, I turned around to start heading back to the ship. Along the way, I stopped in front of a massive white wall with a posted sign that told me this was the Casa Blanca. I had stumbled across the house that was built for Juan Ponce de Leon in the sixteenth century, a house he never saw because of his untimely death. His family and descendants occupied the estate from the 1500s until the Spanish-American War. Inside the massive gate, I took in the expansiveness of this palace-sized house with horse stables, rows of rooms containing original weapons and furniture, and views of the city below from the upstairs windows. Outside, the grounds were equally impressive with gorgeous landscaping that merited a leisurely stroll with more exceptional views of the San Juan Gate, the city walls, and garitas against a backdrop of the dramatically blue sea.

When I left the Casa Blanca estate, I noticed

a curious statue, so I strayed slightly off course to investigate. It portrayed a group of people walking in procession. The story goes that in April, 1797, Sir Ralph Abercrombie made a cameo appearance intending to capture San Juan with several thousand men. When the Spanish governor of San Juan saw sixty-eight enemy ships approaching, he knew his rag-tag militia of a few thousand peasants, criminals and assorted convicts could not repel the British forces. So, he appealed to the bishop for some divine intervention. The bishop organized a religious procession, knocking on the doors and urging all the housewives to join his march and bring along anything that clattered, clanked or kept a flame. From a distance in the dark, the British interpreted the sight and sounds of all these women pounding and rattling their pots and pans and waving candles in the air as newly arrived reinforcements. Apparently the ruse worked, and on May 1st the British left San Juan, even abandoning their arms and ammunition on the shore. The Spanish considered it another Milagro, or miracle, and the Rogativa statue commemorates the religious procession, the rogativa, that saved San Juan.

Only steps down a small incline, I found the San Juan Gate and walked through to enjoy the beautiful stroll back toward the ship. I could see the water glinting and dancing to my right, and glimpses of statues in tiny parklike settings in breaks in the wall to my left. This path opened up to an enormous fountain representing all the races that make up the population of Puerto Rico, fittingly called the Fountain of the Races. The way back to the ship was a wide strolling boulevard, the Princess Way, or Paseo de la Princesa. Alongside it, stalls were busy with vendors selling homemade nougats, handmade jewelry, and hand-painted wooden toys.

I stepped inside the CVS once I was safely back in view of the ship. There was nothing I needed, and by now we were only a couple days from going home. But the familiarity drew me in, and you never know what you'll find in these places. I found Skip and Denny. They had been traipsing around the city and had come upon a local guide who offered to take them on a short bike ride outside of town. When they asked me to join them, I couldn't resist, envisioning a pleasant ride on a bike along a countryside road.

We returned to Plaza Colon where we found the guide, Ollie, and met the rest of our posse. A van transported us to Loiza, a little town east of San Juan that is known for the Bomba, a dance to drums that has African roots. We selected our bikes, strapped on helmets, signed another ream of waivers, and headed for the trail. We weren't too far out when the path started to go slightly uphill. I've always kept myself in decent shape and was glad of that fact now because some of the other riders were already starting to flag and fall behind. One man actually got off his bike and pushed it for a way up the hill. His wife rode back to join him, remonstrating that had he been in better shape and stuck with his regimen back home, he would have been able to keep up with the group. He responded by telling her that all she ever did was work out and that if she would ever do anything besides that, they might actually find one or two things in common to do. They were playful with their back-and-forth bantering, and others chipped in lightheartedly and took one side or the other or added quips about their own marriages.

After a while, our path narrowed and only an occasional pedestrian came from the other direction. One girl in our group, about thirteen or fourteen years old, was on the lookout for monkeys up in the trees despite the guide's solemn pledge that there were no wild monkeys to be seen. Still, she rode along, barely touching the handlebars and looking straight up into the trees, convinced some monkeys would come out just for her to see. Her mother was a few bike lengths behind her, chatting with another biker. We passed along the waterfront and little houses and local stores and slathered on more sunscreen and drank more water as the sun rose higher in the sky. We made an ice cream stop at a little kiosk, sitting on a couple of old benches or on the sparse ground covering or rocks. I sat with Denny and Skip and another couple from Australia who, we discovered, were also from our ship and sat at the next table in the dining room. They wondered whether our table was an extended family. We spent about twenty minutes resting before mounting our bicycles once again and turning back in the direction we had come.

Ollie was directly in front of me this time and we all ambled back down the path in single-file order, reversing our direction to head back to the bike depot. Suddenly, the monkey girl got excited when she thought she saw a monkey in a tree up ahead. She swerved out of the queue, came directly around me and inserted herself squarely between me and Ollie with barely a wheel width between us. Then, as suddenly as she had done that, she started screaming and pointing excitedly at her imaginary monkey . . . and stopped short. What happened after that may best be described by the sequence of unnatural sounds that ensued when I took a hard left to avoid smashing into her, blew my front tire on a jagged piece of rock and went flying over a barbed-wire fence, landing ass over apple cart in a goat pasture.

I was more angry than injured thinking about what Wink would have to say. Those familiar words "not again" started spinning round and around in my head. Skip was by my side in an instant and in a couple minutes I was back on my feet, Skip pulling the bike up next to me. "Looks like you're not going to be riding this thing any time soon," he said. He asked if my head was hurting and said my head had hit the ground with a hard thud. I assured him I was okay, reminding him about my bike helmet, even though the mention of a thud sent my hand over my skull, automatically searching for any sore spots. Ouch! There it was, a large bump on my forehead where my head had made contact with the ground. But if I didn't touch it, I felt reasonably okay. I felt a little nauseous but didn't say anything about it.

On the bus ride back to Old San Juan, Denny and Skip said they were going to take advantage of the long day in port and had booked an afternoon excursion to El Yunque, the national park that was a rainforest. They offered to accompany me back to the ship, but I opted to return to town to do some shopping. I was feeling better, even though that bump on my head was starting to throb. I figured walking around a bit would do me good. This time I took a different street, one that was a block apart and ran parallel to Calle Fortaleza, the street I had taken earlier that day. Calle San Francisco afforded a beautiful stroll with more little restaurants, many with outdoor seating under bright umbrellas right on the sidewalks, and more storefronts and coffee shops. Signs along the way boasted the island's best mofongo, Puerto Rico's national dish based on plantain, a kind of banana that needs to be cooked that never quite caught on in the States outside of ethnic neighborhoods.

A little farther along, the street widened to become a large oblong park with trees and benches and kiosks and a thousand pigeons scrabbling after crumbs left on the pavement. A couple of coffee kiosks with shaded seating tempted locals and tourists to take a relaxing break. This square, the Plaza de Armas, was once used for military drills and was bordered by important government buildings, including the imposing city hall building. A fountain spewing water with statues representing the four seasons anchored one end of the plaza, while nearby, people took turns posing on a bench next to the bronze sit-by-me statue of Tité Curet Alonzo, a Puerto Rican composer. When it was my turn to sit for a picture, no end of hands reached for my camera to do the honors.

I started to think about where I might stop to pick out a souvenir or two, so I took the little street to exit the Plaza de Armas and before I knew it, I found myself squarely back in front of the San Juan Cathedral. My eyes went longingly to the welcoming door of the Hotel El Convento a few steps away, and I thought of its breezy inner courtyard and divine Puerto Rican coffee. As I headed straight through the hotel's gracious door once again, I suddenly felt a new rush of nausea and dizziness. I half-wondered if that rap on the head was starting to talk to me. By now, a searing headache was radiating from the large bump on my head. I blamed the hot sun and counted on a little time in the breezy and delightful courtyard to put things to right. I walked down the corridor and turned into the courtyard and took a seat on a bench under a flowering frangipani tree. A three-man band was striking up some notes as a scant audience of a dozen or so patrons at a half-dozen tables looked on.

As I was sitting there, assessing the severity of my pounding head, a tall young woman walked across the courtyard toward me, welcoming me back to the Hotel El Convento. She had seen me there earlier and said she was happy to see me again. As she watched my fingers feeling around the growing lump on my forehead, she asked if I was all right. I looked up at her face for the first time and was caught by complete and utter surprise. I blamed my eyesight, the heat, my headache, the growing dizziness and nausea that must be contributing to the sight of Sorrenta's face in front of me. I blinked and stared but the face didn't change. I did not understand what was going on and fairly shouted, "Sorrenta! What are you doing here?"

Chapter Eleven

Still in Old San Juan, Puerto Rico

THE WOMAN FROZE. She appeared shocked. She said she was not Sorrenta and shook her fist at me threateningly! Then she looked at me again. Could she tell my head was splitting like someone had just introduced an axe to my skull? Her expression softened and she disappeared briefly and brought back a clear glass of water with some ice and a lemon slice in it and handed it to me. I took it with both hands, not trusting myself to hold it with only one hand, feeling very shaky. In a calmer voice, the young woman said I looked unsteady and offered to sit with me. I gestured at the empty space beside me on the bench. I asked her what her name was. She looked at me and tears welled up in her eyes. She was about to say something when a matronly woman who had been watching the whole scene came from behind the bar and asked who I was. The young lady explained to the older one that she had seen me come into the hotel earlier in the day, and now

I had returned looking very pale and unsteady and she was sitting with me until I felt better. The matronly lady smiled and patted my shoulder. "You are from the cruise ship, then?" she asked.

"Yes, Señora, the *Minerva*," I said. "My name is Marianne."

"You look like you have had some rough seas on your cruise, Marianna?" She said this as she was scanning the bumps and bruises on my face and arms. Her eyes were evaluating me like a concerned mother.

"In a way, you could say that," I said, with a little chuckle, and told them briefly how I had been stuck on a runaway horse on Tortola the day before and had taken a nasty bump on the head from a bicycle fall just a short while ago.

The older woman then looked at the Sorrenta look-alike and said, "Poor girl, she was left dazed and confused in a coffee shop two weeks ago when a couple staying here at the El Convento brought her back with them. She had only the clothes on her back and no memory at all of who she was. She still does not know her name. We are keeping her here with us until we can find her family or until someone who knows her comes for her. She has not shown any recollection of anything until you mentioned the name Sorrenta to her."

Suddenly the nameless young woman convulsed and shook her fists in the air. Tears welled up in her eyes again. "Never call me that! Never! Never!" she shouted at the ceiling.

"My name is Señora Villanesca," the matronly lady said, extending her hand and holding mine firmly. "Do you mind talking with our friend, Marianna? Perhaps there is something else you might say that will prompt her memory. She seems to trust you. Talk about anything you can think of. We all have been talking with

her, but nothing has helped. We hope we can find out who she is before she is taken to a sanitarium."

I said I would be happy to talk with her, but I only had two hours before I needed to be back on the ship to play with the string quartet. As soon as I said the words "string quartet," the young woman looked up at me, her expression revealing her complete attention. I asked her if she knew what a string quartet was. She responded with a look of deep interest but said she did not recognize the term. She asked me to tell her more. I started to tell her about the instruments in the string quartet, pantomiming how each one was played. I don't know what made me do it, but I suddenly asked her if she knew someone named Sabrina who played the cello.

What happened next could not be described as anything short of another Milagro, or miracle of Old San Juan. The young woman stood up, clutched herself with closed fists and let forth a torrent of tears. It was as if she realized for the first time in her life who she was. "I'm Sabrina!" she gasped between breaths. "I'm Sabrina! And I play the cello in the string quartet with

Danita and Valetta and Mario, my friends!" She was shouting with a mixture of discovery and relief, with a twinge of anger. "I am Sabrina!" she exclaimed again as she melted into tears and fell headlong into Señora Villanesca's comforting arms. A couple sitting at the bar turned and looked, but Señora Villanesca gave them no mind while a bartender handed them piña coladas. They continued to watch this drama unfold, leaving their piña coladas untouched.

"Thank you, thank you," Señora Villanesca said to me. Then she held Sabrina and let her cry, simply telling her, "It's okay, Sabrina. You're going to be okay."

Señora Villanesca seated Sabrina back on the bench and went to the reception desk to say something to the attendant. A few moments later, a waiter appeared rolling a polished wooden tea table laden with pastries and sandwiches and a silver coffee urn. Señora Villanesca drew up a chair and invited Sabrina and me to dig in. The sandwiches were delicious, and I helped myself to grapes and cheese and little sweet cakes. The Señora poured us some of that delicious Puerto Rican coffee and we began to talk.

"Can you remember anything about being Sabrina?" I asked Sabrina gently.

"No, not really much more than what I already told you," she answered. "I am so tired." I could see she was emotionally drained.

"What do you want to do, Sabrina?" Señora

Villanesca asked. Sabrina replied that she wanted to wait until her ship returned to Old San Juan so she could rejoin her friends and continue playing her cello with the quartet.

"I think your ship is back in town right now," I said. "And before you say you don't have your boarding pass, just come along with me and I will get you back on board."

"Oh, thank you," Sabrina said. She asked Señora Villanesca if she could go back on the ship with me, and the Señora said to go with God's and her blessings, but to promise to return and visit her friends at El Convento the next time the ship stopped in Old San Juan. Sabrina arose and hugged Señora Villanesca and then went to the reception desk to say goodbye to the woman and man working there. While we were alone, Señora Villanesca confided that when Sabrina had been brought to the Hotel El Convento, she had a serious bump on her forehead. The couple that brought her from the Cuatro Sombras Café said the staff there had found her slumped over in a deep sleep in a corner of the café right before closing. Señora Villanesca had never told Sabrina about the bump on her head and had not let her look in the mirror. I thanked her for the information and made a note to tell Wink about it just as Sabrina returned saying, "Let's go to the MS *Marina!*"

When we were asked to produce identification at boarding, I showed them mine and said confidently,

"She's with me!" just exactly as Wink had done to get Sorrenta on the ship. For anyone who was not looking closely, Sabrina looked enough like Sorrenta at first glance, plus I had loaned her my sunglasses to assure an extra buffer of anonymity. Security was used to the drill with Sorrenta and easily let Sabrina aboard, admonishing her to be more careful with her card.

Safely on board, I brought Sabrina to my stateroom and called Wink, who was at my door in a flash. Almost predictably, as soon as Wink walked through the door, his first reaction was a double take. "Sorrenta?" he said, looking confused, at which I nearly jumped in front of him to prevent Sabrina from shaking her fists as she'd done at El Convento. I introduced them, and Wink remarked that the likeness between the two girls was uncanny. I shushed him and gave him a quick jab in the ribs with my elbow.

I winced when Sabrina looked at herself in the mirror, but thankfully the bump on her forehead was barely noticeable.

Sabrina was springing to life now that she felt safe and was back in familiar surroundings. As her memory started to return, she was actively reconstructing the last things she remembered. When the ship came to Old San Juan last time, she left it in the late morning to pick up a few things at the Walgreen's across the street and to call her mother in Mexico City. Her plan was to return immediately to the ship to practice her cello.

But while she was talking with her mother on

the phone, Sorrenta had appeared out of nowhere and hailed her. She was surprised to see Sorrenta, as they'd not worked together in several months and had not kept in touch. Sorrenta was working on the sister ship, the MS *Athena,* which was also visiting San Juan that day. Unlike the last time they were working on the same ship together, Sorrenta seemed cheerful and happy to see Sabrina. Sorrenta invited Sabrina to join her for a coffee and the women walked down the street and settled into a quiet corner inside the Cuatro Sombras Cafe. The last thing Sabrina remembered was enjoying a very tasty cup of coffee, while nestled into a cushioned chair, when suddenly everything went blank. The next thing she remembered was being stirred awake by a server who gently shook her and patted her face. She must have been passed out for a while because when she came to, it was dusk and Sorrenta was gone. So were the ships. I made a mental note to tell Wink later about the bump on Sabrina's forehead.

"Sorrenta must have put something in your coffee to knock you out like that. Otherwise, why would she have left you there alone?" Wink was thinking fast, trying to piece the puzzle together as Sabrina talked.

She went on, "It was already dark and when they woke me up, Sorrenta was gone and I was alone. The staff at Cuatro Sombras said they were closing the café and I had to leave. Luckily, there was an older couple in the café who saw all this. They were heading back to the hotel and offered to take me with them. That is how I ended up at the Hotel El Convento, where Marianne found me today."

"So," I interjected, "Sorrenta was so jealous of Sabrina that she had to get her out of the way to open a clear path for you, right Wink?" I was way ahead of myself, regretting that question almost as soon as I had blurted it out.

"What are you talking about, Marianne?" Wink asked, turning to me with his full attention. "I'm not the least bit interested in Sorrenta. Never have been. What would that have to do with anything, anyway? I will admit she used my influence to get on the ship when she didn't want to use Sabrina's boarding card, which she clearly had with her."

I couldn't believe that Wink had missed Sorrenta's brazen overtures. I thought that jealousy as the motive seemed to fit the puzzle, with Sabrina looking so much like Sorrenta, but I kept my mouth shut. Sabrina supported Wink, saying jealousy could not have been a motive because she was not interested in Wink and was not in any competition for him. In fact, she had a boyfriend, Tomaso, who was probably frantically worried about her by now because they used to email every day up until she had been knocked out. She wanted to get her laptop so she could email Tomaso and assure him she was okay.

"Did Sorrenta say anything while you were drinking your coffees at Cuatro Sombras?" Wink asked, directing the conversation back to the beginning of Sabrina's escapade while her newly emerging memory was fresh. "What did you two talk about? Did you say anything that might have set her off to knock you out and leave you there?"

Sabrina thought. She said the conversation had been cordial. Catching up with small talk. Who was working on which ship, who got promoted to what, who was rooming with whom, who broke up, and if any new engagements had been announced between crew members. Stuff like that. "But then," Sabrina added, rolling her eyes and pushing her hair back, "Sorrenta started asking me about the recipes again and just wouldn't let it go. We even ordered more coffee because she wouldn't drop the subject. We were there so long I had to use the restroom. She pressured me and pressured me to sell the recipes to her, even doubling and tripling her offer. Finally, I told her for the last time, NO! I am not giving or selling you my recipes!"

"The recipes?" Wink and I asked together as we looked at each other. "What recipes?" I asked, genuinely mystified.

Sabrina explained that while the women were working together on the MS *Athena* on their last contract several months back, Sabrina had told Sorrenta that her grandmother had entrusted her with her own mother's rare recipes for rich Bavarian desserts and special frostings. Sabrina's great-grandmother had inherited them from her father, Sabrina's great-great-grandfather, who had been a well-known baker in his day in a little town near Hamburg, Germany. When Wink asked how it was Sabrina's family hailed from Mexico City, Sabrina explained that her maternal ancestors immigrated to Mexico from Hamburg with many Germans during the reign of the Austrian Emperor of Mexico, Maximilian I, back in the mid-1800s. My head was reeling from all the gaps in my knowledge of the captivating history of this part of the world.

A few days after her conversation with Sorrenta and on Sabrina's birthday, she continued, Sorrenta brought a bottle of German dessert wine and a cake she had made to Sabrina's room to celebrate. After emptying the bottle together and polishing off the cake, Sorrenta asked to look at the recipes and Sabrina brought them out. Sabrina explained that Sorrenta leafed through the hand-written recipes, many smudged with old butter spots and dried batter smudges left as testament that the beloved recipe cards were actually used by the old Bavarian baker. As Sorrenta read them, she became intensely and passionately interested and asked if she could buy them from Sabrina. Sabrina said no, they were family recipes and would remain with her. She would never sell them to anyone. Sorrenta tried and tried. She became very demanding and unreasonable. She pleaded and finally offered to copy them all down by hand, but Sabrina said no, absolutely not. Her grandmother had given them to Sabrina in trust and she would never break that sacred bond. Sorrenta stormed out of the room, slamming the door violently. For days she was sullen and dark, avoiding Sabrina altogether. That was why Sabrina had been surprised to see Sorrenta hailing her and in such high spirits in front of the Walgreen's in Old San Juan that day.

"So, it was Sabrina's recipes she was after," I said, as if the obvious needed clarification.

Wink remembered that Sabrina's card had been scanned both off the ship and back on again the day that Sabrina had disappeared in San Juan. She left the ship at 11:27 AM and re-boarded at 3:14 PM, according to the security records. Wink thought out loud: "If Sabrina did not go back on the ship at 3:14, then who used her ship pass card to get back on the ship?" It was looking like Sorrenta had used Sabrina's card to gain entry to the ship. Most likely, she had entered Sabrina's room with the card to get the recipes. Once she had them, she left the ship and deliberately avoided another scan of the security card to make it appear that Sabrina was still on board. Sorrenta then went across the pier and boarded her own ship, the MS *Athena*. Both ships sailed from Old San Juan on time and without incident within a half hour of each other that day.

"But just maybe Sorrenta didn't get what she wanted," Wink said. "Otherwise, why would she have come back to rejoin the *Minerva* in Virgin Gorda?" He added that it wouldn't have been difficult because the *Athena* was stopping at Virgin Gorda the day before the *Minerva* arrived, and all Sorrenta had to do was switch ships: leave the MS *Athena* in Virgin Gorda with a personal excuse, stay overnight in a local hotel, and join the MS *Minerva* the next day.

"So, when Sorrenta suddenly appeared at the Baths the day we were in Virgin Gorda, she was actually coming to join our ship," I reasoned. "She was not taking a beach break." I mentioned her oversized satchel with enough clothes in it for a week, and Wink said he had noticed that too.

Then he added, "Only she was coming for personal reasons because she was not on the work manifest. The security detail could have reasonably assumed she was taking passage to an upcoming port to catch one of our other ships, which staff does all the time. No one would have been the wiser."

Sabrina suddenly shrieked, "My grandmother's recipes! I left them in my room! Sorrenta stole my recipes!"

But Wink calmly explained his theory that Sorrenta probably didn't get the recipes. If she did, why would she want to return to the *Minerva* in Virgin Gorda? He asked Sabrina how well she had hidden the recipes. Sabrina said after Sorrenta saw that she kept the recipes in an empty rum cake box in the refrigerator, she removed the recipes from the box. She left the rum cake box in the fridge with a stack of worthless decoy recipes and receipts from purchases in the various ports of call. She'd left the real recipes in a place that was unlikely for anyone to find: in a large envelope she duct-taped to the back of the nightstand that was pushed tightly against the wall next to her bed. Wink was fairly confident that Sorrenta had taken the cake box from the refrigerator and left the MS *Minerva* assuming she had the old recipes. Then, once she got onboard the MS *Athena* and actually opened the box, she would have realized immediately that she only had the worthless decoys. Sorrenta's work was not done, and it was with that realization that she must have decided to leave the MS *Athena* in Virgin Gorda and join the MS *Minerva* there the next day, knowing that Sabrina was still in Old San Juan and not on the ship.

"Wait a minute!" I said. "Do you think she actually found the good recipes and is just staying on board to test them out on you?" I couldn't think of another reasonable explanation for all that frosting she kept offering Wink. Well, except maybe one.

Wink replied that it was far more likely she was using her frosting and feminine wiles to seduce him into letting her into Sabrina's room so she could have another look around for the real recipes. That room was still considered a crime scene and sealed off, and the only person with access to it was Wink. I asked Wink if Sorrenta had ever hinted about going into Sabrina's room, and he said she had not only hinted, but had out and out requested it. She told him the evening after she'd met up with us in Dominica that she had loaned a pair of shoes to Sabrina that she needed. Wink let her in briefly and waited for her to grab the shoes from the closet. She lingered there for a while and then turned to him and suggested some fun ways to put that empty room to good use right then and there. She added that since he was the only one with access to the room, there was no need for a Do Not Disturb sign. She was using feminine wiles and every other stall tactic she could think of. Wink said he never fell for her ploys but looking back, he was wondering how he could have missed her motive to search that room so much.

Sabrina insisted on getting into her room to see if her grandmother's recipes were still in their hiding place. Wink escorted her to the room where she found the recipes still snug in the envelope taped securely to the back of the nightstand, just as she had left it. She checked inside and they were all there. She also grabbed her laptop and gathered a few articles of clothing from her closet. When we returned to my room, we all agreed it was best to keep Sabrina under wraps until the next day. She could stay on the pull-out bed in the sleeper sofa in my room, which Wink set up right then. Wink said I could bring Sabrina meals from the Lido deck or order them from room service. She could sit on the veranda or in my room but was not to leave the room under any circumstances. It was essential that she avoided being seen by anyone. Bottom line was, we had to keep her hidden until we had a plan.

As I regretted having to miss my trivia team while they bungled and botched their way through another one of Pearl's legendary mental obstacle courses, Wink and Sabrina and I hatched a plan of action to smoke out Sorrenta. We did it in record time, too, because with all the t's crossed and i's dotted, I was able to make it, dressed and powdered, right in time for my high tea performance. I thought the music on this program was going to be my biggest challenge, as I was never comfortable playing jazz pieces, which was today's music fare. But the hardest part about sitting there with the rest of the string quartet was having to keep the secret. Their colleague was safely on board and I could not breathe a word of it. High tea was as festive as ever, with petits fours and macaroons and jelly rolls lavishly served. As soon as we finished performing, I explained to the group that I needed to borrow the cello overnight to practice the Spanish classics on the next day's agenda. No one thought twice when I lifted the heavy cello and brought it back to my room where Sabrina could practice while I went to dinner. She was as excited as a schoolgirl to be playing her cello again, and the program of Spanish classics was her absolute favorite. Suddenly I realized I had just performed for my last time with the string quartet. I could heave a genuine sigh of relief and pat myself for a job well done, or at least a decent effort. I ordered Sabrina's dinner from room service and waited with her for it to arrive.

That night at dinner, I learned that Mrs. Mooney

was still missing. Wink and Mr. Mooney were absent from the table as well. I was doing my best to appear as normal as I could under the circumstances and restraining the urge to spill the beans about Sabrina. When Ginny said she saw me walking with Sorrenta toward the ship, I was very relieved she had been too far away to catch up with us and get a closer view. I only hoped Ginny wouldn't run into Sorrenta in the next twenty-four hours and say she had seen us walking together in San Juan. Something like that could spark Sorrenta's suspicions.

I deflected Ginny's observation and, turning my back to her, spoke directly to Dr. Feerum. "Will you be diving again tomorrow at Grand Turk?" I asked him.

"As a matter of fact, yes, I will be going on a shark dive," he answered. "The water at Turks and Caicos is about the clearest water anywhere I've been, with indescribable corals and seahorses and luminescent fish so bright you don't need a mask to see them."

"That's cool," Denny said with approval. "I'm going parasailing," he added enthusiastically.

"What about you, Ralph? What do you plan to do tomorrow?"

"I'm looking at my lovely lady and wondering what she wants to do and then if I can accompany her," he said, looking at Ginny.

"Ohhh!" Ginny said, beaming. "I think we will spend a day on a glorious Caribbean beach and maybe have one of those umbrella drinks and do a little shopping and maybe have a little lunch if there's a place for a meal."

"Oh, there's a place for a meal, all right," Dr. Feerum said. "Jimmy Buffet's Margaritaville restaurant is right there on the beach near the cruise complex. You can order anything you want for a drink or lunch."

We were asking Dr. Feerum more questions about Grand Turk when a bluster of excitement caught everyone's attention and we looked toward the entrance of the dining room where Wink and Mr. Mooney and his wife bustled past the maître d' toward our table.

"Hurrah!" we cheered joyfully at seeing Mrs. Mooney alive and well and back in our fold. One by one we stood up and clapped as the couple approached us. People sitting at other tables started to clap as well, although they probably did not know why.

"Dovey's back!" Mr. Mooney announced with a boom in his voice. "She's back and we found her, thanks to Wink and his amazing detectives." Mrs. Mooney looked a bit dazed as Wink and Mr. Mooney helped her into her seat, one at each elbow. We were all bursting to know what had happened. The story came out that a housekeeper assigned to clean one of the ladies' rooms discovered Mrs. Mooney bound and gagged inside a locked stall. They could not tell us more because of the pending investigation. But Mrs. Mooney was safe and that was all that mattered.

I took a dessert back to the room for Sabrina, only

realizing later that I had selected one with frosting. I was sure Sorrenta had frosted it, but I made certain not to tell Sabrina that, and thankfully she didn't ask. She was tired, but grateful to be safe. We talked for a while and I filled her in on the lost-and-found Mrs. Mooney. Just as we turned out the room lights and started to fall asleep, Sabrina sat up and said she remembered something. The telephone rang while I was at dinner and when she answered it there was a very long pause, then a voice saying to go home. Sabrina recalled something like: "NO MORE MONKEY BUSINESS! GO HOME!" and then some evil laughter. Sabrina said she was sorry she'd answered my phone without thinking when she was supposed to be in hiding and all, but it was just a reflexive response and she had acted on impulse.

At least she spared me the angst of hearing that horrible voice again.

Chapter Twelve

Day Eleven: February 13, Saturday
Grand Turk, Turks and Caicos Islands,
Sunny: High: 80ºF/27ºC. Low: 67ºF/19ºC.

FROM MY VERANDA, the spectacular beach at Grand Turk beckoned with a million sapphire waves, all edged with white lace, rolling up against miles of white-sand beach with the regularity of a billion heartbeats. As if the scene needed any more reminders that this was the Caribbean, palm trees dotting the shoreline obligingly did the honors. Sparkling clean and ready as a fantasy, this tropical playground was the ideal place for our last leisurely day of surf-and-turfing in some of the world's clearest water. The last stop on our Caribbean cruise brought the MS *Minerva* into calm waters where blue waves lapped merrily against the shiny white hull. A short tender ride conveyed us from the ship to Grand Turk, the biggest island in the archipelago known as the Turks and Caicos. Blessed with some of the world's nicest beaches, the equally blue sky above might shed a raindrop or two about fifteen days out of the year on average. Ours was one of the three hundred fifty days when only an occasional cloud drifted lazily across the blazing lapis-blue sky. Variously an administrative ward of Bermuda, then The Bahamas, and finally Jamaica until 1973, today the Turks and Caicos is an Autonomous Overseas Territory of the United Kingdom, meaning a part of the Commonwealth, that greets over a million tourists a year and uses the U.S. dollar as official currency with an unapologetic tourist economy. There are eight main islands and about three hundred cays, spits, and rocks divvied up in two groups, the Turks and the Caicos. The name Caicos probably was an indigenous name or word, but Turks likely came from the name of a common cactus called the Turk's Head that looks like it is wearing a bright red Turkish cap, or fez. Conventional belief maintains that Christopher Columbus's first footfall in the New World in October of 1492 happened on the Bahamian island of Guanahani, which he claimed in the name of the queen of Spain and re-christened San Salvador in his next breath. The Turks and Caicos challenges that assertion, claiming that Columbus's own log describes the geography of Grand Turk, not San Salvador, and would like to set the history books straight about where Columbus first landed. The debate rages on.

The islands came to the attention of some enterprising Bermudians who, sailing nearly a thousand miles from home, found and harvested salt at

Grand Turk and Salt Island. Soon they were bringing African slaves to work the briny salt pans, extracting the salt and transporting it to Bermuda for storage in salt cellars before selling it to a ready market of buyers, mostly in the American colonies. Salt was such an iconic feature of the Turks and Caicos that white salt piles on the beach were depicted on an early flag of the Turks and Caicos. However, the artist must have missed the lesson about Caribbean climate, drawing a door to make one look like an igloo. It took decades before the beach igloo was removed from the flag of Turks and Caicos!

One of the surprises about Grand Turk was displayed in the outdoor exhibit featuring a replica of the Friendship 7 Spaceship, with a model of an astronaut and exhibit commemorating Astronaut John Glenn's dramatic splashdown on February 20th, 1962, in nearby waters. The Mercury Program astronaut landed near Grand Turk just under five hours after his rocket launched him from Cape Canaveral and into history as America's first astronaut to circle the Earth. After three swings around our planet, his capsule was rescued from the blue waters near Grand Turk, forever after to be called the "Area Hotel" by NASA Mission Control and subsequent astronauts passing over the Turks and Caicos.

As we'd been planning, Wink and I boarded the tender together to spend the day snorkeling. I looked around the tender and, to my relief, Sorrenta was nowhere in sight. She had no idea that Sabrina was on the ship. She had no idea how this day was going to end for her. She was probably scheming a last-second plot to get Wink to let her into Sabrina's room one more time. Wink and I chatted lazily about our plan for Sorrenta that afternoon and after examining the Friendship 7 exhibit, we headed down to the shore to stake out a couple of chaise lounges.

Minutes later, we were swimming in our masks and flippers among a small group of fellow ship passengers. I had never seen water so clear and was not prepared for the abundance of purple fish, orange fan corals, sea cucumbers, brain corals, and even jellyfish, all magically and peacefully coexisting in a harmonious living tapestry under the shimmering beauty of the transparent blue. At one point, someone looked up and very excitedly announced there was a barracuda swimming below us. I swam down to see it, my eyes leading a 360-degree circle that the rest of me followed, but it eluded me. I came back out to ask Wink if he'd seen it and he pointed in the general direction where it was last seen. We looked for the barracuda a little while longer, but in vain. We swam and played in the water for a couple of hours, halfway making up for the fact that we couldn't spend time together the night before. We gravitated far enough away from everyone else to have a tiny patch of the ocean to ourselves, and in time surrendered to an excitement that the barracuda simply couldn't provide, frolicking with reckless abandon for a while and then clasping hands as we skimmed smoothly together over colorful schools of fish, swaying fan corals, brain corals, starfish, and all manner of other beautiful creatures going silently about their daily routines in that warm, clear water.

After a while, we reclaimed our lounge chairs and Wink went to the Margaritaville to bring back some lunch. It was then I decided to go back into the water and look for that sneaky barracuda. I hopscotched over some brain corals and seashells and plunged in indulgently, surrendering to its feel on my skin as it enveloped me.

I submerged, surveyed the water around me and saw nothing unusual. I came up for air and then descended for another look, and that's when I spotted the barracuda taking refuge behind a shelf of coral several feet away. I wanted a better look, so I went down again and glided closer to it. All of a sudden, I felt a strange sensation on my neck. Then I felt a searing pain across the front of my throat, and my hand automatically went to the pain where I could feel some broken skin. It seemed like there was an awful lot of blood in the water around me, and I knew blood could attract sharks. I thought I might be fainting and fought to stay alert.

Suddenly, I felt arms pulling me up and taking me to the shore. They felt strangely familiar, and I assumed it was Wink who was rescuing me. But as soon as we got to the shore, my rescuer deposited me gently on the sand above the waterline and disappeared. Dazed and confused and still bleeding, I did my best to hold the wound, but felt myself wafting in and out of consciousness. I don't much like the sight of blood, especially when it's coming out of my own neck. I thought about the person who had rescued me and couldn't understand why he had disappeared as soon as I was safe on the sand. His face was hidden from my view, so all I got was a view of his ear.

It wasn't long before Wink came back and ran over as soon as he saw me. He placed the bags of lunch he'd just purchased next to me. He sat down beside me on the sand as blood streamed down my front, smearing my bathing suit and dripping into the sand. I half-raised myself on my elbows and asked him, "Do barracudas carry rabies?"

"What happened this time, Marianne?"

I told him about looking for the barracuda and how something suddenly tore at my neck and someone pulled me out of the water and left me here on the sand.

"I can't leave you for fifteen minutes." Then he added, "But to answer your question, I highly doubt that barracudas carry rabies. It's just a superficial wound, so I don't think you'll need stitches or anything. Just sit here for a few minutes and it will probably dry up and scab on its own. Do you have a bandage with you? I don't think I have any."

"Yes, there are some in my beach bag, I'm pretty sure. I put a few in there and can't believe I haven't used any of them until now." We went back to our chairs where I searched in my bag and found a bandage that Wink carefully opened and pressed over my wound.

"It's probably my gold necklace that attracted it," I said, running my finger over the gold chain I'd been wearing since I bought it on the Ponte Vecchio in Florence, Italy, several years before. "I've heard of barracudas going after things that shine and sparkle. I think they are attracted to sparkly things."

"You're kidding," Wink said. "I never heard of that. Maybe it's an old wives' tale. We can ask the enrichment speaker. What was his name again?"

"Dr. Pinot. But I've heard this from other people who have been on cruises to the Caribbean. I even have a friend who said her kid's piano teacher came to the Caribbean one time and almost lost a finger to one of those underwater buzzards when it went for her sparkling wedding ring."

"Well, I think you'll survive," he said as he assessed the situation. Then he turned and looked out at the water saying, "Tell me again how you got out of the water."

"Someone swam over and lifted me out of the water and carried me back to shore where you found me. I thought it was you. I didn't get a view of much more than his ear. His face was turned away, and he didn't say anything. Besides, I was a little preoccupied with the blood gushing out of my neck."

"I understand," Wink said. "Let's have some lunch

and you think about it and tell me anything else that comes to mind." He handed me a foam plate and took one for himself. Then he opened the steaming bags, allowing the irresistible aromas of spicy fried seafood to permeate the air around us. Suddenly I was famished.

"So, what's your story, Marianne?" he asked as he doled out portions of captain's platters with tartar sauce and fries with ketchup onto our plates.

"I already told you my story and it really hasn't changed since then, Wink," I half-lied because I'd only told him about being jilted by Seth that first day of the cruise. I still hadn't told him about my brief earlier marriage or my unusual livelihood.

"That's right," he said. "I remember you were jilted at the airport. Well, it could have been worse," he said, reaching for some ketchup packets and tearing them open before squirting them over his fries. "You know, there are couples that take a cruise specifically to break up. Well, at least one of them knows it's going to happen. Usually, it's the guy. He books the cruise, pays for both of them, and within the first one or two days he simply announces to his wife or girlfriend that it's over and for whatever reason he's moved on. Then typically a huge fight ensues, loud enough for half the deck to hear and ugly enough for fellow passengers to take sides, usually with the jilted woman. The guy disembarks and flies home alone somewhere around day three or four on a pre-booked flight, leaving her to lick her wounds. People rush in to help, so she gets a lot of attention out of the deal and sometimes a new boyfriend in the bargain. Everyone loves getting involved in a shipboard soap opera, much like the one you are experiencing right now."

"I guess any guy would be smart to get out of Dodge after doing something like that, or she'd probably find enough accomplices to help her throw him overboard," I grinned. "Well, maybe Seth did me a favor. But what about you, Wink? You really haven't told me anything about yourself."

Just then, a beach vendor came along with icy-cold beers and sodas in a big cooler strapped over his back. We bought a couple of each and continued enjoying our lunch.

"How did you end up with a job like yours?" I resumed.

He shook his head and smiled wistfully as he crammed a crispy breaded shrimp into his mouth and chased it with a long swallow of the local Turk's Head Lager.

"I was head of security systems for one of the maritime container companies, like Maersk or Crowley or Hapag-Lloyd, but much smaller," he started. I had seen those names on containers on the docks of our ports and knew what he was talking about.

"I was on a cruise with my wife for a very-much-needed vacation. One night at dinner, we got into a conversation with a table full of guests about modern-day piracy. You know, the Somalian pirates targeting cargo container ships. Since that was my bailiwick, word started to run through the ship that an expert on modern-day maritime piracy was on board. It didn't take long for the cruise director to approach me and ask if I could give a little talk or moderate a Q&A session on the subject during the cruise. Nothing elaborate, he said, because I hadn't come prepared for that. I agreed, and he announced to the guests that I would give some comments on modern-day piracy and take questions. One thing led to another, and before you know it, I was talking nearly every day to a packed theater.

"Then, about halfway through the cruise, the cruise director had to leave the ship for an emergency back home. The assistant cruise director could not step in because she had just broken her foot and was bed-bound awaiting disembarkation at the next U.S. port. The general manager had noticed how popular my talks were and asked if I could step in, not as a full-fledged cruise director, but more as an emcee, just for the remainder of that cruise. Announce the shows, make some general announcements over the ship's public address system, and so forth. They would direct me. They comped me the entire cruise in exchange for helping out. I guess it was during that gig that I realized how much I liked life at sea. And I liked it a heck of a lot more on a luxury cruise ship than on a cargo tanker.

"But before the end of that cruise, and it was twenty days long, the cruise line needed a security director for the entire fleet, and they tapped me once again. I took the offer on a trial basis and loved it. In less than a month, I had moved in. Well, not quite literally moved to Miami, but I was the head man in charge of ship security, spending about half my time on the ships and the rest of the time at the headquarters in Miami. I only got home to Charleston about once a month, and it put a real strain on the marriage. My wife didn't want to leave our house or her family in Charleston to move to Miami, so we put off any decisions about moving for a couple of years. But it was harder and harder because I was going back home less and less frequently and eventually, of course, I had to rent a place in Miami. Then she got seriously ill and within a year she was gone. It all happened so fast. She never complained, so I didn't know things were as bad as they were. Then suddenly one day when I was on a ship, they called me to the chief purser's office for a telephone call. Toughest time in my life."

"Oh, I'm so sorry," I said.

"When things were looking grim, we always thought she'd get better, but she just couldn't rally. She always sounded optimistic and told me to focus on my job. It was an awful blow to lose her, and I miss her every day. That's why I winced at your suggestion that I was interested in Sorrenta," he snorted, looking directly at me. "Sorrenta's a work associate and nothing more. To be honest, I resented her overtures and would never capitulate to anything like that. But all the same, people working on these ships can be very lonely," he went on. "Many of them have to leave families and children back home to work a six-month contract. It's really brutal. I never forget about that, so I am always gracious and kind to everyone."

"Did you move permanently to Miami after your wife . . .?" I didn't say the word.

"Not right away. I was really busy and didn't want to take the time to pack and move since I was renting a small house in Coral Gables. I rented the Charleston house to some friends of one of the captains. Then one time I had the holidays off, let's see, that'd be about three years ago, and went back to Charleston for a month. I stayed in the guest room of my own house and got to know my tenants. They were two very smart sisters. Sisters, not nuns. Twins, to be more accurate. They were working on a book together on the connection between Charleston's Gullah Geechee culture and the island of Barbados. When one of them went home for the holidays, the other stayed in Charleston to interview someone for their book. Her name was Caralyn and that's how I got to know her. We hit it off almost from the start, but by the time I went back to work, Caralyn and her twin sister, Maralyn, had submitted their manuscript and Caralyn was going home. I invited her to stay on in the Charleston house, this time without paying rent, and we became an 'item,' you might say. I tried to get to Charleston more often so we could spend time together there, but it wasn't enough to hold things together. Caralyn made a halfhearted attempt to move to Miami with me, but as soon as she and Maralyn landed another book deal, they moved to Juneau to start their research there. I had to admit things weren't going to work out with Caralyn, and I've just been focusing on work ever since. I finally sold the Charleston house last summer. I have since bought a condo on Key Biscayne from a captain who retired and moved back to Italy."

"Too bad their book wasn't about Florida," I said.

Well, I thought. Here we were, two people in limbo with quite a bit in common. Wink's explanation maybe did a bit to accelerate my interest in him. I looked over at him, mentally making an assessment. He was about eight or ten years older than I was. He was good looking in a "take me as I am" kind of way and didn't seem to make any special effort to stand out. He was the kind of guy who was steady and stable, but not flashy or sexy like Seth. He didn't dance as well as Seth, or care for that matter. I liked his style.

We sat there for much of the rest of the day between taking dips, mostly talking about Sabrina's abduction, and added some finishing touches on our plan to expose Sorrenta later that afternoon. We had long since established that Sabrina's case had nothing to do with the phone threats left for me. Wink kept repeating that the threats were a separate issue, that the messages were probably not even meant for my room in the first place. He was still working on it but was more preoccupied with Mrs. Mooney's case. He said there was something about her disappearance and sudden discovery that didn't add up, and he had put in some calls to check a theory he was entertaining. I found this very curious and asked if he could tell me more.

"Mrs. Mooney was found by a housekeeper who went to do a routine cleaning in a ladies' room in a very well-trafficked part of the ship," he told me. "When the housekeeper arrived, a sign on the door said, 'Cleaning in Progress.' The door was locked, but staff never locks the doors while they are cleaning. This was the housekeeper's first clue that something was irregular, and she immediately called her supervisor who came to the scene and called security.

"When we arrived, we unlocked the door and discovered Mrs. Mooney in one of the stalls," Wink explained. "She said she felt weak and had not eaten anything since being taken captive days earlier, but I couldn't help noticing a very potent smell of garlic on her breath. Later I asked room service to supply me with a summary of the meals delivered to the Mooney's stateroom in the last three days and there had been not one, but two meals delivered to their stateroom barely two hours before we found Mrs. Mooney. One of those meals was a garlic chicken stir fry and the other was a burger and fries. I think we both know who the burger and fries were for."

"Yes, and that would leave only one person who could have eaten the garlic chicken stir fry, explaining Exhibit C, the garlic breath." I giggled while scooping

312

up a crispy conch fritter. After taking a bite, I asked, "So you think Mr. Mooney knew all along that she wasn't missing and . . ."

". . . and was complicit in the whole thing." Wink answered my question before I finished asking it. "Absolutely! To add fuel to my theory, Mr. and Mrs. Mooney are now demanding a total refund for the cruise, claiming restitution for all their pain and suffering. I have put out some feelers to see if this might be a pattern for them."

"Wow," I said. "So, it was staged. Then, what was the motive? How would it have gone down?"

"Easily," Wink answered the second question first. "When both parties are in it together, they work as a team.

"Mrs. Mooney is a professed gambling addict. Her husband literally brags about it. She spends all her time in the casino unless she is eating or sleeping. If she is any good – or really lucky – she may beat the odds. Sometimes people actually do, and in about one case in ten million, they might even win enough to pay for their entire cruise. It's not likely, but it's something a die-hard gambler might actually go for. I reviewed her gaming history on this cruise, and it was about average. One night she walked out of the casino with over $5,000."

I gasped. "Couldn't she have paid for their whole cruise and still had some shipboard credit left for a couple of watches in the boutique?" I asked.

"I didn't finish," Wink went on. She walked out of there with $5,000, but she had gone into the casino that evening with $10,000. Like most gamblers, she wins a few and loses a few, and in the end she probably makes out with a few extra dollars from playing the slots. But even if she wins anything this cruise, it's almost a guarantee she will lose it all – and she still might – the very last night. Happens often enough."

"So, you are saying because it was nearing the end of the cruise and not likely that Mrs. Mooney would win enough at the casino to pay for their cruise, the couple staged her disappearance? This was their Plan B?"

"Are you a private eye, Marianne? Tell me you've been holding out on me and you are a professional detective," Wink mocked. We both laughed as we swallowed some more Turk's Head Lager from the cold glass bottles.

"So, tell me how this went down," I said, dipping a fry into a puddle of ketchup on his plate.

"Mrs. Mooney simply stayed in her room whenever Mr. Mooney ran around the ship saying she was missing. She would of course come up missing everywhere else on the ship when they both knew she was hiding safely in their room. Security staff always gave Mr. Mooney ample notice before coming to their room, which worked to their favor by giving her enough time to sneak out and hide somewhere for an hour or so until security came and went and the coast was clear to return to her room. Then she stayed safely in her room while Mr. Mooney cried wolf about her being missing. Until yesterday, that is. That's when she taped up the Cleaning in Progress sign she had swiped from a housekeeping trolley earlier and locked the entire bathroom. It probably never dawned on Mrs. Mooney that the housekeeping staff follows a tight cleaning schedule, and she most likely never expected a housekeeper to go to the effort of checking who was supposed to clean the bathroom on that shift, or to call security at the sight of that sign and the locked door. And you know what else?"

"Tell me she was so lightly bound and gagged she could have pulled it off herself," I said.

"She could have put it on herself, too, and probably did. It wasn't even duct tape, just a little used masking tape that was barely even sticky anymore. Even a ninety-pound weakling like Mrs. Mooney could have pulled it off."

"Amateurs!" I exclaimed. "Can you prove it yet?"

"Pretty much, but there's a little more I'm looking for. In any event, they will be turned over to the authorities when we arrive in Miami, although they won't have a clue about that until we get there. Mum's the word, okay?" I promised, but at the same time I thought that dinner with them would be a little sad, knowing what awaited them in the morning. In spite of their weirdness, I had grown fond of the eccentric couple.

Back on the ship that afternoon, Wink and I escorted Sabrina and her cello to the dressing room directly adjacent to the theater on Deck 5. Wink had called the members of the string quartet and asked them to meet us there a half hour before tea for something very important. They arrived while Sabrina was dressing in the closet. They kept asking at the same time what the meeting was all about. Wink announced that Sabrina had been found in Old San Juan and was safely back on the ship and that their little string quartet family was once again whole and reunited. As if on cue, Sabrina emerged from the closet wearing a beautiful red gown and faced her friends for the first time in a couple of weeks. Valetta and Danita shrieked with delight, running over and throwing their arms around her neck as Mario wrapped his lanky arms around all three girls.

Batting off a million questions at once, Wink said the story of how Sabrina was found would have to wait because as of this afternoon, Sabrina was officially back on the crew manifest and would resume her position as cellist with the string quartet. He did say that I had helped to discover Sabrina in Old San Juan. Then, in an unexpected gesture, he thanked me for helping out, at which point the quartet members took turns expressing their sincerest gratitude and kind compliments about my efforts to help out and my musical talents. With only a couple minutes to spare, we rode the elevator up to the Paris Lounge where the quartet members busied themselves with their music stands and chairs, and then opened their program with the beautiful "Malagueña" by Albeniz. With hours of practice since rejoining the ship the day before, Sabrina dove right into her part, sparkling all the way through. From her expression, she was elated to be back doing what she loved to do.

Wink had predicted that Sorrenta would show up to oversee the trays of her pastel-iced petits fours and ultra-frosted chocolate eclairs. He also knew she would join him as soon as she saw him. For the occasion, he had selected a table front-and-center to the quartet. Expecting her to sit in the chair closest to him, he had moved one of the place settings closer to his own to bait her into taking that particular seat: the seat with the best unobstructed view of the string quartet!

Sure enough, Sorrenta entered the room as two waiters rolled polished mahogany carts piled to the ceiling with irresistible desserts, each variety frosted with unique colors, textures, toppings, and swirls. Predictably, Sorrenta helped herself to the seat Wink had reserved for her, focusing on him and never once bothering to look over at the string quartet. Wink engaged Sorrenta in small talk and she immediately went into flirting overdrive, which I could see from where I was waiting behind a column. It was funny now, watching her antics and knowing Wink wasn't interested in her in the slightest. She was probably buttering him up just to get into Sabrina's room, I thought. It wasn't until after Wink dropped his teabag into the teapot as a signal to me that I walked casually to their table and sat down on the other side of Wink, close enough to startle Sorrenta. I said to Wink nonchalantly, "Hey! Fancy meeting you here. Mind if I join you?" Sorrenta was visibly shocked and discombobulated as she processed what was happening. Gradually, she was realizing that if I were sitting at the table, then I wasn't playing the cello, meaning someone else was. Slowly, she focused her gaze on the quartet and for the first time saw Sabrina playing her cello!

Sorrenta stood up and howled a blood-curdling scream that stopped everyone in the room cold. Teacups froze in midair. Forks stopped midway to mouths. Knives about to smear jam on scones clattered to the floor. Tortes and tarts and cucumber sandwiches slid off silver trays as thunderstruck waiters loosened their grips and watched the scene before them unfold in fascination and amazement. Only the quartet, warned to anticipate this moment, played on like the musicians that continued to perform even as the *Titanic* was sinking. Relishing the irony of the moment, they spontaneously struck up the notes for the tune of "Send in the Clowns."

I thought it was a brilliant touch and gave them extra points for class and improvisation.

Wink arose calmly and escorted Sorrenta back to his office where a fiery interrogation was followed by Sorrenta's vehement argument that ramped up to a fury of vitriol, finger-pointing, accusations, and staunch denial of any plot to steal Sabrina's recipes. Wink said he had proof she had planned and carried out Sabrina's disappearance to the extent that she had dropped some sleeping pills in Sabrina's coffee that day in Old San Juan, had smacked Sabrina in the forehead with a sandwich board when she started to come to, had stolen Sabrina's ship card to board the MS *Minerva* when she was not authorized to board, and had entered Sabrina's room unauthorized to look for the recipe box. He said when she got to her ship later and realized the recipes she had stolen were decoys, she made a plan to return to the *Minerva* at Virgin Gorda a few days later.

Ignoring her denials to everything, Wink asked her why she would go to so much effort to obtain Sabrina's recipes. Sorrenta melted in a puddle of tears saying she wanted to quit working on the ships so she could spend time with her family back in Italy. She wanted to write a cookbook about desserts, but she didn't want it to be like all the other cookbooks out there. Hers had to be different. Once she had seen the recipes in Sabrina's collection, she knew they were stand-outs. They were truly historic and rare old-world recipes that would bring back flavors the modern world simply never knew; flavors without synthetic additives used in modern ingredients, flavors without funny-tasting low-fat substitutes, flavors without fake sugars that leave an unpleasant aftertaste, flavors without genetically modified creams and butters that were nothing more than engineered and highly marketed spreads. The recipes called for the purest of ingredients combined in the most unexpected ways, blending textures and tastes that she had never encountered before. The world would literally have gobbled up her book and she would succeed in her goal of getting rich. And she knew she couldn't write the cookbook without Sabrina's grandmother's treasured recipes.

The world would have to wait.

When Sorrenta dejectedly admitted to everything Wink had enumerated—dropping sedatives in Sabrina's coffee while she was in the restroom and smacking her forehead with a sandwich board in the Cuatros Sambras Café in Old San Juan that day — Wink had no other option but to confine Sorrenta to the ship's brig until he could turn her over to the authorities in Miami. Suddenly she changed her story, screaming that the sedatives she used were from Sabrina's own Walgreen's bag and saying Sabrina fell and hit her own forehead in the bathroom at the café. She accused Wink of framing her and resisted the security officers as they escorted her from Wink's office to the brig. For once she was helpless, her charming wiles unable to rescue her.

Later Wink told me she could chill in the brig. I said, she'd more likely frost.

I was dreading Gilligan's Table that night, knowing how happy the Mooneys would be, and also knowing the unfortunate fate that awaited them in Miami. But on arriving back at my room, an invitation waiting on my door reminded me that this was the night Angela had asked the string quartet to help her host dinner for her solo travelers' group. I put on my trusty black dress and topped it off with a bright scarf in pinks, oranges, and violets and headed to the dining room. Angela was already there as the solo travelers started to arrive. By now, many of them had formed friendships and were entering in couples and groups of three. The nature of traveling alone begs of connecting with others with similar interests to do things together and have built-in dining partners. Usually it works, and sometimes lifelong friendships are formed through the effort.

I greeted Angela, who didn't even bother looking at me. I found that a little off-putting and wondered if she'd meant to tell me not to bother coming tonight since Sabrina was back on board. But to be truthful, under the circumstances, more guests knew me than Sabrina, and Angela would have been aware of this. Besides, the name cards would have been set in place that afternoon. The rest of the quartet members arrived as a group and split up to mingle with the guests. Angela was very cordial with them, I noticed. She apparently didn't like me for some reason, and since you can't win 'em all, I ignored her pouts and pressed on.

Our quartet was spread out among three tables of

eight guests each. Danita and Sabrina sat together at one table, Mario and Valetta sat at another, and there was my place card at Angela's table. I found that curious, considering the icy reception I was getting from her. We were seated directly opposite each other, so we could each focus on our "half" of the table. I had seen how this worked on officers' night and was starting to get into the groove. I could almost imagine myself as a staff member of a cruise ship, figuring I would probably opt for the social hostess role over any other. As the waiters and sommeliers came and went bringing our courses and drinks, we settled into conversations with our table mates. Of course, everyone wanted to know how it was that Sabrina had suddenly turned up so that I was just as suddenly out of a "job" with the string quartet. Then, out of nowhere, one of the guests, Mrs. Cahill, a recent widow who had come on the cruise she and her husband had booked before he died, said to me, "Well, they can use a friendly social hostess around here. You should apply for that position," forgetting that Angela was two seats away from her. It was small comfort to know that Angela wasn't singling me out. Apparently, she was unpleasant to nearly everyone.

Just as Mrs. Cahill realized her regrettable faux pas, the entire table went for a lame attempt at damage control, murmuring, clearing throats, and changing the subject. No one stepped in and said what a fine and gracious social hostess Angela was, however, because it would have been too obvious a save, and because, quite frankly, it would have been a lie. For the rest of the dinner, Angela glared at me whenever she looked across the table. I soldiered through dinner, dessert, and coffee, half wishing I'd just gone to Gilligan's Table instead.

Whew! When I was finally done with that scene, I went alone to the show. A bald magician in a bright-red jacket held the audience in thrall as he pulled doves from his sleeves, swallowed razor blades to scary music, bantered with the audience while soliciting a twenty-dollar bill that disappeared easily and turned up again miraculously inside an unpeeled orange. After his show, guests lined up to congratulate him. The man in front of me said to him proudly, "I figured out one of your tricks," to which the magician calmly replied, "Then I will have to kill you," to the delight of everyone within earshot.

The party moved upstairs, and I followed like the happy lemming I had willingly become over the course of the cruise. The band was in high gear, cranking out favorites from genres and eras across the board. Latin, sixties, disco, hip-hop, swing, you name it. It went nonstop. During the band's breaks, Angela took over as DJ and didn't seem to be in much better spirits. The dance floor was packed solid, and suddenly I remembered I had not selected a dance partner for the Valentine dance contest the following night. I decided to audition some dancers on the sly to see if anyone offered the best prospect for winning. I started with

Roy, the assistant cruise director, when he tapped my shoulder. We glided out to the floor with a fox trot when, for some reason, an expression of anger fairly erupted over Angela's face as we passed her.

I danced two Latin rhythms with Dr. Feerum and some disco stuff with Wink. Of the three men, he was the most fun to dance with, but the least qualified to place in a contest. I had to admit that of the three, Roy had the best prospect of winning the contest. I asked him to be my dance partner for the Valentine contest, knowing full well he would have to decline. But he surprised me by accepting my offer gladly, saying we could enter the contest but would be disqualified from winning any prizes because of our "work" status on the ship. His, of course, was official and mine was unofficial. I didn't mind in the least. It was all about the honor, I said, and we agreed to meet ten minutes before the contest was to start the next night. Armed with the results of my informal auditions, I found Angela and informed her that I'd found a dance partner for the contest and filled out an entry form and handed it to her. When she saw I had listed Roy as my partner, she reared up and snapped quickly that he was not eligible. I said neither of us was eligible to accept any prizes, but that couldn't stop us from entering the contest.

If a face could turn into a storm cloud, it was happening before my eyes.

Chapter Thirteen

Day Twelve : February 14, Sunday
En Route to Miami, USA
Weather updates will be given in the morning by the cruise
director and midday by the captain.

VALENTINE'S DAY. The last day of the cruise. I woke up to a beautiful view, sipping coffee on my balcony as the sun rose over the glinting sea. I was alone again, as Sabrina had moved her things back to her room after tea the day before. Her room was no longer a crime scene since she was safely back on board. I watched the sea below as a group of flying fish skittled across the surface. I wondered if they were considered a flock or a school. Either way, pelagic birds skimmed a few feet above them, grazing for breakfast.

I pondered how I would spend my last day on this most remarkable cruise. It was my first day of being totally free to do completely as I wished with no obligations, and the sheer relief was surprisingly welcome. I had visions of attending Dr. Pinot's morning talk about Caribbean Castaways, stopping by for the merengue dance class, playing trivia for the last time with my friends, and of course joining Gilligan's Table for our last supper. Relieved of my cello-playing duties, I was not certain if I could fit the afternoon tea into my busy last-day schedule, and not convinced that I really wanted to. Then, the high point was going to be the Valentine dance contest. I would wear my red dress confidently, knowing Roy and I would place, if not win, even though the trophy bottle of champagne would go to someone else. Fair enough.

After breakfast, I headed out to the pool deck. Ginny and Ralph came over and invited me to join them for miniature golf on the sport deck. It was still early enough to squeeze in a friendly game before heading to the theater for the castaway lecture, so why not? The miniature golf on the MS *Minerva* was an elaborate setup, intended to amuse and entertain all ages. Designed with a sea creature theme, players had to aim the ball into the partially obstructed mouths of a whale, a dolphin, a sea turtle, an octopus, a manta ray, and even a lobster. We squealed with the fun of hitting the ball and mostly missing the mark, and Ginny and Ralph told me of their plans to continue seeing each other after the cruise. In fact, Ginny was going to fly directly to Bermuda with Ralph from Miami for the weekend and looked forward to meeting his three sons and their families.

The rest of the day blurred by with Dr. Pinot,

who told us the real story behind Robinson Crusoe, followed by a fun merengue dance class that Roy taught with Angela's assistance. Dr. Feerum came to dance with the unpartnered women. Minga was still in the group and he spent most of his time with her. Stacey and Fred showed up and they were so good, Roy asked them to demonstrate to the whole group. I wondered if they were going to enter the dance contest because they would offer some real competition. After the class, they pulled me aside and we said our farewells and promised to stay in touch. Stacey said they were planning to visit her cousin in Trinidad and Tobago in the fall and would love me to meet them there and join them for part of the time. I said yes, by all means, send me the details and count me in!

I was really looking forward to our last game of trivia and didn't care any more about scoring because the game itself was so much fun and I had come to enjoy the lively company of our pathetic team. When Pearl announced the theme to be home-made solutions, I predicted a total crash and burn. And as it turned out, it was anything but the disaster I had foreseen. Every time there was a question about the healing or therapeutic properties of herbs, Mildred and Stan were right there with answers straight from their herb garden; they really knew their peppermint, cilantro, rosemary, and lemon balm. When the questions were about do-it-yourself repairs, the do-it-yourselfers, Karla and Patrick, stepped up to the plate with all the right answers. Questions about home cures for wounds and pains were the everyday stuff of Kate and Barry, who helped their daughter run her yoga clinic and natural healing spa. Garlic, onion, honey, and coconut oil seemed to come in handy for all kinds of everyday nicks and scratches. And Meredith brought it home by knowing which home beauty secrets were used by which celebrities. I hadn't really contributed much to the answers, so the team gave me the honors of reporting our score to Pearl: 100 percent! We aced it! High fives flew in all directions, and when I announced proudly that our team had gotten all the answers correct, Dutch caught my eye from way across the room and gave me a thumbs up! But then again, we weren't the only 100 percent. We had to share our limelight with First Mates, of course. Blood sport.

At five o'clock, the theater doors opened, and guests stuffed themselves inside for the matinee starting at quarter past five. This was the grand finale for the cruise where the full entertainment team, including singers and dancers, band, and string quartet, all came together for one final performance of dances and songs from around the world. At the end, Roy introduced a member of the laundry department, Datu, from the Philippines, who was dressed in a tuxedo recalling the '50s. He brought the house down with his rendition of Sinatra's legendary "My Way." The audience rose in unison to a standing ovation as his last words rang out. Cruise director Pearl came onstage dressed in a stunning sequined purple dress, her dark hair piled in braids on her head in a very seductive looking updo. She thanked everyone for sailing with the MS *Minerva* and invited us back again soon. She said pretty soon we'd be back home dropping our towels with no one there to pick them up after us. We'd have to shop and cook and serve ourselves and wash the dishes afterwards. And if we went to a restaurant, we'd have to pay. The audience laughed and applauded with the reality of her statements. We were all well aware that the cruise provides a bubble of fantasy that, even for a few days, lets you forget about the humdrum routines of home.

Then the house lights were lowered, giving way to neon-colored strobe lights that beamed and crisscrossed throughout the theater. A rainbow caused by a thousand colorful balloons emerged from the ceiling and floated downward as hands reached up instinctively to bat them around. The band struck up "We Will Rock You" as an endless procession of chefs, waiters, sommeliers, housekeepers, engineers, launderers, entertainers, office staff, concierge staff, pursers, destination members, and the ship's full complement of officers marched enthusiastically down the theater aisles like a huge sports team taking a victory lap, following two crewmen holding the ship's banner and waving to all the guests amidst a fog of lightning caused by all the cameras and cell phones. Everyone was up on their feet, energized by the surge of smiling staff and crew filling up the stage one neat row at a time. When everyone was in place and the stage could not accommodate one more body, the captain and general manager made some brief comments to thank the guests and acknowledge the hard-working crew.

Pearl took back the microphone for a very special announcement to thank one gracious and talented guest who stepped in to help out when she was asked. She called me to the stage where the string quartet members came forward to present me with an enormous bouquet of flowers and a bottle of champagne as Sabrina fastened around my neck a silver necklace depicting a cello leaning up against a palm tree. Pearl said she looked forward to welcoming me back on the MS *Minerva* for a future cruise and hoped I could have a restful vacation the next time. Everyone laughed and clapped, and Pearl invited the audience to stay and join in the lively tradition of dancing to the *YMCA* song, even inviting guests to come down to the stage, while the officers and crew filed back out of the theater as confetti and more balloons dropped from the ceiling. The whole house stood up and followed the lead of the singers and dancers on stage and other staff members who were scattered throughout the auditorium. When the *YMCA* song ended, Pearl invited everyone to join the band on the pool deck for the big Valentine's party and dance contest, all starting at eight o'clock.

Just as Pearl was signing off, the theater was overwhelmed by a noisy racket of bells, whistles, buzzers, whistles and alarms erupting from down the hall. Word started spreading fast that someone had hit the big jackpot in the casino! As the theater emptied out, the corridors buzzed with this new shipboard excitement as speculation and gossip flew from one mouth to another with people wanting to know more. Who won? How much? Was it true? I managed to squeeze into the casino for a peek between the huddled masses of curiosity seekers and there, sitting at the roulette table looking dazed but smiling, was Mrs. Mooney. She had just beat the odds and won $50,000! She really was the one in ten million Wink was talking about. She could easily pay for their cruise now. Too bad they had already staged that Plan B abduction, I thought.

THE DINING ROOM was packed by the time I arrived and was decorated with everything Valentine. Seductive red lighting replaced the usual subdued lighting, and tables overflowed with red and white carnations, roses, and babies' breath. Cupids on the light sconces held garlands of flowers threaded with hearts and arrows. A huge table laden with chocolate hearts, chocolate fondue, and chocolate sculptures greeted guests upon entering the room and elicited oohs and aahs as they were escorted around it to their tables. The waitstaff was formally dressed in white with scarlet ties or scarves.

Everyone at Gilligan's Table was in high spirits, congratulating Mrs. Mooney for her big roulette win and bubbling to ask her a thousand questions. The Mooneys were jubilant, basking in the attention of their incredible windfall. Drinks and toasts preceded our dinners and continued through the appetizer course. Strolling musicians dressed like Venetian gondoliers serenaded the tables with romantic music from guitars or squeaked out polkas and Venetian ballads on accordions.

When dinner finally arrived, it was a Valentine delight, with choices of surf and turf, and Chateaubriand for two. Valentine cards had been left at each place setting for each person to sign and give to someone else at the table. During the meal, I received four of the table's cards: from Skip, Dr. Feerum, Wink, and Ginny. I was sure the Mooneys sent theirs to each other. I figured Denny sent his to Ginny. I sent mine to Wink. There was no end of chocolate offerings for dessert, including a sumptuous profiterole dripping with chocolate sauce. As we ate, the conversation turned to everyone's plans after the cruise. The Mooneys were already booked for another cruise to start immediately. They were literally taking their suitcases from the MS *Minerva* to the MS *Helen of Troy* to embark on another cruise, only this time the itinerary would take them through the Panama Canal. Wink and I exchanged glances knowing that things might not go quite as planned for them the next morning. Skip and Denny were going to return to Cleveland and move Denny into Skip's house. Denny was going to start his Coast Guard job and get right to work. But both of them were going to put their heads together to invent a suitcase that closed itself. They'd been trying all day to pack and decided that what the world needed was a self-closing suitcase, so their plan was to invent one, patent it, and sell it on the TV shopping channel. Dr. Feerum said that during the cruise he had been offered a book deal. After returning home, he would repack and head to the South Pole with a National Geographic team to start his book on penguins. He added that he didn't intend to do very much scuba diving there. Denny asked if he was going to keep looking for that lost lover the fortune teller had talked about, but he smiled and said his search may be ended and that the fortune teller might have been correct in forecasting that his new love interest was closer than he thought. Ginny announced to the table that she and Ralph were flying to Bermuda together, straight from Miami the next day. While she was talking, two roving musicians returned to our table, and a waiter set champagne flutes at every place while a sommelier startled half the dining room when he popped a champagne bottle and started to pour the bubbly all around Gilligan's Table. To add to the moment, Ralph dropped to one knee and asked Ginny if she would marry him. He held up a small box and opened it so she could see the golf-ball size diamond inside.

"Oh, Ralph!" Ginny spouted in genuine surprise and gushing delight as she plucked the ring out of the box and fitted it over her finger, "Yes, of course, Darling!" She waved her sparkling ring at us and kissed him on both cheeks. Everyone cheered as the waiters struck up a jubilant chorus of "For They're a Jolly Good Couple" that didn't really suit the occasion, but it was the thought that counted. More toasts chink-chinked all around.

Then Wink looked at me and asked, "And you, Marianne? What are your plans after the cruise?" To be honest, so much had been going on that I hadn't thought much about it. Besides, I would be happy enough to get back home and hunker down to my old familiar workaday routine. Before I could say anything, the little girl who liked to read books during the afternoon teas came to our table holding a book. She stood next to me and asked me for my autograph. She said she knew I was her favorite detective author, Hope Dares, the minute she saw me that first night when she wanted to be seated at our table. She had read all my books, the popular girls' detective stories known as the Hope Dares Detective Series. The book she set before me to autograph was *Hope Dares the Durango Detective.*

"Why, this is my favorite of all my own books," I said, surprised to see it was her choice. It was not the most popular in the series by any means, possibly because it was a tad sophisticated for the average preteen reader. The girl explained it was her favorite too and she had brought it along to re-read during the cruise. I looked at her with renewed interest. "Why do you like it so much?" I asked, thoroughly curious.

"I liked how all the adults overlooked Bunchy, and it was Bunchy who ended up solving the mystery," she explained. "I like how she staged the whole mystery by herself too."

Well, she certainly had read the book, I concluded. I thought back for a moment. Yes, Bunchy was that precocious little Machiavellianette of my own perverse invention who had outsmarted all the adults by masterminding a convoluted mystery and solving it before the adults even knew what was happening around them. Bunchy was always leaving a trail of clues and traps for others to untangle. She was also a master at creating paranoia over events that were pure happenstance or unrelated coincidences that had nothing to do with the mystery. Blindsided, the adults fretted and second-guessed themselves, blurring evidence and naming random suspects. No one ever suspected Bunchy of this degree of nefarious genius because Bunchy was just a kid.

"Well, you know my name, but I don't know yours," I said.

The girl smiled widely, "I'm Ivy Welles. You'll need to know that to autograph it, I guess." Obviously she was not new at this. She asked, "Will you please write, 'To Ivy - from one trickster to another,' and then sign your name?"

I remembered this girl now in a sudden flashback. A year or so ago, she had approached me at a book signing in either Wilmington or Providence or Newark and had asked me to sign one of my other books with the very same inscription. She had short hair back then, I remembered, and different glasses. Since about the middle of the cruise, her longish hair had been pigtailed in tight cornrow braids and adorned with colorful beads, the way they do it up at virtually every port stop in the Caribbean where local women offer "licensed" braiding service. Ivy thanked me as I handed her the signed book and she turned around to rejoin her table.

Everyone at Gilligan's Table stared at me dumbfounded. Maybe awestruck is more accurate. Suddenly, they all broke out in applause, joined by people at some nearby tables who had witnessed the whole thing. Wink said I had really tricked him. He asked why I didn't let anyone know who I was, and I replied that I just wanted to travel out of any limelight. The last thing I wanted was to get involved in any mysteries during my vacation, and here I was at the hub of at least three during my twelve days on the MS *Minerva*. I admitted, however, that I couldn't resist getting involved when any mysteries presented themselves because they provided such irresistible fodder for future books.

THE BAND WAS ALREADY thumping out some calypso and soca and reggae music to a packed dance floor when I arrived at the pool deck, all dressed in red, a few minutes before eight o'clock to meet Roy. This Valentine's Day party had the Venetian carnival for a theme. High cocktail tables with red and white tablecloths and balloon bouquets were set up with canapes and party favors, including Venetian-style carnival masks. I selected a mask with an oyster-white face and coal-black eyeliner, thin aubergine lips drawing up into a sardonic smile, and a tear drop falling from one eye. A long table near the bar was well supplied with champagne flutes and bottles chilling in ice buckets. Waiters were popping champagne bottles and filling the flutes as fast as the guests sidled up to the table. An intricately carved ice sculpture of a huge Valentine surrounded by winged cherubs with arrows served as a centerpiece with subtle red lighting coming from within. Everyone was in a jubilant mood as smiling waiters whisked by with trays of chocolates truffles, macaroons, and chocolate-dipped strawberries held high above their shoulders. Most couples were mingling or dancing as officers and staff watched from behind the railings on the upper deck. Here and there an isolated couple could be seen sharing a quiet moment together in the shadow of a column.

I wandered around greeting people I'd met on the cruise and met new people besides. It's always easy to reach out to fellow passengers on a cruise because, chances are, you'll never see them again. People have been known to bare their souls and confess sins to total strangers on a cruise, admit to misdeeds they wouldn't divulge to a priest during confession. More often than not, however, they run into each other again, either on another cruise or in the most unexpected places and times. In fact, while you often hear people say that you'll never see anyone you meet on a cruise after it ends, the opposite happens often enough and enduring friendships spring from chance meetings on cruises, as if there were some bigger cosmic reason for two people who would otherwise never meet, to book the exact same cruise on the exact same ship sailing the exact same itinerary.

The carnival masks made it easy to slip in and out of conversations with total strangers. The thought crossed my mind that this was the night Seth and I had planned to win the dance contest, the big night I was secretly expecting him to present me with an engagement ring. Well, hopes of anything like that had long been dashed, but I had no regrets. In fact, with each passing day, Seth slipped farther and farther back in my memory. I felt like I was better off as things had turned out, and for the first time had an inkling of new adventures awaiting me beyond new horizons. I was getting excited!

Before the contest started, the music changed from the island beats to more traditional ballroom fare. Masked couples were heading toward the band to dance to the rhythms of swing and waltz and even a tango. Naturally, I was happy to join them when Dr. Feerum tapped my shoulder and led the way. His mask of the Pope was pushed up on his forehead. As we were enjoying a bolero, someone wearing a white mask with a long, hooked beak cut in. I was fascinated by the mask that was modeled after the eerie-looking ones doctors wore during the era of bubonic plague. I danced with the tall stranger as the band segued from a merengue to a cha-cha, and I noted how good a dancer this stranger was. Better than good. He moved in a familiar way and I wondered where he had been all cruise long, suspecting he was one of the dance hosts. I asked him his name, but he put a finger to his lips and gave no reply. I could only see his hairline and an ear, and I wished I could pull his mask off to see his face as well. But once the cha-cha ended, he bowed chivalrously and disappeared in the crowd as abruptly and mysteriously as he had appeared. Somehow, I had the feeling I'd seen him before, but these thoughts were interrupted when Roy waved me over to the contest table.

I joined Roy and we got our contest numbers from Angela, who was obviously having a very bad night. She seethed at me, almost throwing my number decal at me and simply allowed Roy to take his own. With a voice that quavered threateningly with an accompanying display of spit wads shooting from her teeth, she reminded us that we could not take any prizes even if we did place in the contest, which we could fairly well expect would not happen if she were a judge. Since she didn't offer to help us with our numbers, we simply applied the decals to each other's backs.

When I mentioned that I thought Angela really had some hostile feelings toward me, Roy said not to bother myself thinking about it. He said her attitude might have something to do with the fact that he and Angela had been an item for quite a while until he had broken it off during their last contract together on another ship. They weren't supposed to be working together now, but the original assistant cruise director went AWOL in Barbados on the last cruise, and they flew Roy in to take over until a replacement could be found. He said he was heading to the sister ship, the MS *Athena*, as soon as we returned to Miami the following day. Ever since he came on board, Angela was trying to reconcile with him, but when she saw he was no longer interested, her attitude deteriorated. She was on probation at this point and would probably not be asked to continue with her contract after this cruise. I thought back on Mrs. Cahill's negative comments about her that night at dinner.

The contestant couples squared off as Angela took the mic and announced the Valentine's dance contest to the entire party. She sounded anything but enthusiastic, and one couple, the tall man in the mask that had just danced with me, and his partner, backed out at the last minute. That left only four couples. Besides Roy and me, there was Stacey and Fred who I knew would give us some serious competition. Dr. Feerum and Minga formed the third couple. I'd never really focused on them before, but they did make a nice-looking couple. Dr. Feerum was "moving on" with Minga, it was pretty easy to guess. The fourth couple was one I'd seen dancing before but didn't really know. Angela introduced them as Paul and Patty from Seattle. The contest was just for fun with a couple of ship tee shirts and caps and other low-stakes booty for all the contestants except, of course, Roy and me. First place couple got that bottle of champagne. The rules were simple. All the couples danced together for a solid five minutes as the band played, morphing from swing to Latin to disco to ballroom and so forth. At the end of the five minutes, one couple would be eliminated by audience applause. Paul and Patty were out first. That left Dr. Feerum and Minga dancing against Roy and me and Stacey and Fred. The second round was tough because there was no discernible difference in the applause for all three teams. We had all tied and had to go to a face-off round. On the next try, Dr. Feerum and Minga were edged out by an indiscernible margin, leaving Roy and me to dance against Fred and Stacey. Once more, there was a tie and after two more tries the applause was so close that Angela had to break the tie. She chose Stacey and Fred who triumphantly walked over to the table to claim their bottle of champagne. No one could argue that she didn't do the right thing, and

I wanted to assure her there were no hard feelings on my part. But she disappeared in a flash as soon as the contest ended.

The band started in with a line dance, and several dozen people flocked to join a boot-stomping rendition of the reggae cowboy. Roy and I thanked each other. Before parting ways, he asked for my contact information, and if there was some way we could continue a correspondence after the cruise, possibly looking ahead to a relationship. I thanked him and said I might be starting a relationship with someone else and he nodded as if he knew what I was talking about. We said good night as I headed back to my room to finish packing.

As I was turning the corner on the staircase at the ninth deck, someone jumped out of the corridor and grabbed my hands from behind and tried tying them behind my back while I fought to free myself. All my shouts went unheard, swallowed up by the blast of the music coming from the band on the pool deck. When I craned my neck for a look at the person, all I could see was a mask. An oyster-white face with coal-black eye rims, thin aubergine lips, and the teardrop spilling from one of the eyes. It was the very same mask I had worn earlier before the dance contest started! I'd left it at the contest table before we danced. Why would someone attack me while wearing my own mask? Was this some kind of cruel joke?

My masked assailant was dragging me to the outer

deck. He was tall and thin and incredibly strong. I tried kicking but I risked falling down completely, without balance from my restrained arms. I shouted again, but only in vain. If anything, the music from the dance was ramping up in volume as a boisterous electric slide line dance took form on the pool deck. I panicked as I felt myself being dragged closer to the edge of the deck. Black water roiling beneath me came into full view. Whoever had a hold of me was determined and wanted me gone – of that I had no doubt. I struggled desperately to pull myself away and wished beyond hope that someone would come through and discover us. Then, we both slipped on something wet, probably melted ice cream, and landed in a heap together on the floor. That gave me just a second to pull away, but I wasn't fast enough. A gloved hand grabbed my ankle and pulled me back down where I continued to resist my unknown enemy. All my attempts to make noise by thrashing loudly or shouting were drowned out by the thumping of the drums and the stamping of the line dancers from the party upstairs. In a desperate act that can only come from a surge of adrenaline, I kicked my assailant as hard as I could. What escaped from my target was a grunt that was too high-pitched to come from a guy. At first I thought it might have been my own voice, but the grunt was followed by an almost inaudible groan. It was distinctly female. This was some strong gal, I thought! But what did she have against me, to fight this hard?

As our struggle intensified, we were both inching perilously close to the railing. On this deck, the bottom rung did not meet the floor and the six inches or so might be just enough for a very slim person to squeeze through – or be forced through. I was starting to see my entire life roll out before my eyes. On the sea, a swath of brilliant light over the black water beneath me reflected the full moon above. I wished my hands were free so I could yank that mask off my attacker's face to see who she was. Desperately, I aimed another kick at her; although I couldn't see her, my foot met its target and elicited a harrumph so distinctly female, I realized she wasn't even trying to hide or disguise her voice anymore. I jumped back up in the split second it took her to rally from my kick, but she jumped right back up with me. I kept wondering who would want to kill me this much. Suddenly, the ship took a very hard bump, slapping down on the water, and I took the opportunity to trip her. Instantly she fell and I was standing right over her, her hand within easy reach of my ankle. Wham! Down I came again. Between gasps I shouted into the dark, "Who the hell are you and why the blazes are you doing this to me?" My actual language might have been stronger. There was no answer, but I felt her grip loosening as I felt myself being pulled away from the railing.

"What th-" a voice said. "Are you okay, Marianne?" The voice belonged to Skip. He had been bringing a basket of fresh laundry down from the launderette for

Denny to pack. I could smell the dryer sheet perfume permeating the clothes that were still warm from the dryer. He'd dropped the laundry basket to rescue me, and now the laundry basket lay dumped on its side with a pile of clean clothes nearby, with some pieces already scattering in the strong wind.

"I've got to get to Wink!" I half shouted through my parched throat as hot tears escaped from the corners of my eyes. I thought I could taste blood in my mouth. I tried running ahead, but Skip held my arm firmly while he picked up what laundry he could gather.

"You're not leaving my eyesight one more time," he said emphatically. I tried tugging and pulling against his strong grip on my arm, but I had no choice but to let him lead me down a flight of stairs to his and Denny's room where Denny was focused on packing their two big suitcases and talking about that self-closing suitcase he wanted to invent. Their TV was tuned into the lecture channel where the morning's lecture about castaways was in replay, with the volume turned nearly up to screech. Skip switched off the TV and invited me to sit on the sofa while he poured me some water and called Reception to page Wink. Wink was at the door within minutes, followed soon after by the security team.

"Do you have any idea who he was?" they kept asking.

"I'm pretty sure it wasn't a he, but a she," I answered. "Tall and lanky and very determined. But it was dark, and she was wearing a mask from the pool deck party, so I didn't get a good look at her. But from the voice, I am sure it was a woman."

Wink walked me back to my room and sat on the sofa for a while. I'd left piles of clothes around the room, intending to pack at the last minute. A sweater was heaped over the phone on the desk, and I picked it up and tossed it haphazardly into the open suitcase on the floor. Instantly, we both saw the red light blinking a new message. Wink picked up the receiver and put it on speaker. We listened to the familiar gravelly voice we now knew was coming from a female. "THE GAME'S NOT UP UNTIL YOU LEAVE – GET OFF EARLY!" Wink replayed it, then forwarded it to his voice lab.

"I'm pretty certain that is not the same voice as the one I just heard," I said resolutely.

Wink stood there perplexed, deep in thought, standing over the phone. "This has nothing at all to do with Sabrina," he said. "Up to now I wasn't convinced they were meant for you, but now I am second-guessing myself."

I pointed out that the messages usually made reference to a shore-side mishap and recalled the allusions to falling, fishing, and monkey business in three of the messages.

"That's the stickler," Wink said. "I'm really stumped, but at least tomorrow you'll be safely off the ship and I'm fairly certain you will make it safely home." But just to be on the safe side, he went around the room checking inside the closets, then got on his hands and knees to look under the bed. He walked into the bathroom and moved the curtains and towels around and even checked the balcony. "You'll be okay," he said. "There's no one else here."

He walked toward the door, then on second thought turned around, detouring around my half-filled suitcase and stepping over a pile of clothes I'd pretty much dumped on the floor right out of the drawer to pack later. He sat down on the bed and patted the blanket next to him, so I went over and sat down. Taking me in his arms, he held me close and tight, not moving. I could tell he was trying to calm me down, but the effect he had on me was anything but calming. We sat together that way for a very long time as the clock on the nightstand ticked away. For the first time, I realized that the clock in my room ticked out loud. I wondered that it hadn't kept me awake all night the entire cruse. As we sat together unmoving, I mentioned that I still had to pack and get my suitcase outside my door by midnight. Wink laughed, assuring me the housekeeping staff makes hourly sweeps through the corridors the entire night before disembarkation, and told me just to call Reception as soon as I placed it outside my door.

As if on cue, Kulit rapped at the door. He let himself in and appeared embarrassed when he saw the two of us sitting together on the edge of the bed. I could just imagine the stories that sight would unleash in the crew bar later that night. I could hardly fathom the trove of colorful and lurid stories the staff and crew could tell from working on a cruise ship and wished someone would compile them all in a racy, steamy and juicy book someday – an automatic best-seller. Kulit reminded me that my suitcase needed to be out in the corridor by midnight and I assured him I would do my best. I also handed him a gratuity envelope I'd stuffed earlier in the day and thanked him for all he had done for me and his impeccable service. He thanked me, bowing profusely as he closed the door after him. I opened a can of Sprite and poured it into two glasses over ice and handed one to Wink. We turned the ship TV station on and watched a few slides in the rebroadcast from Dr. Pinot's castaways talk. That immediately brought to mind Gilligan's Island and, inevitably, Gilligan's Table, and the subject of Mrs. Mooney's disappearance surfaced anew.

Wink explained that immediately after their windfall, Mr. Mooney had run down to the purser's office to withdraw his claim for a refund. Suddenly, they'd forgotten all about the pain and suffering from her "abduction," but apparently weren't concerned about the imposition it caused for the ship's crew. Wink was in the middle of all kinds of research and legalities and it would probably take him the rest of the night to sort it all out. In any event, he had to go and leave me to my packing. He asked me to call if anything came to mind.

After he left, I focused on my suitcase with resolve to get everything in it and get it out in the hallway before one in the morning and as I worked, I noticed that the contents seemed to expand in spite of the fact that I hadn't bought more than a small gift or two the entire time. I began to agree with Denny and Skip that a self-closing suitcase would be a very useful item, hoping they would hurry up with their invention. I'd be the first to buy one and could have used one right then. I would definitely buy stock in their company. I jammed everything in the suitcase, zipped the expander open, closed it, and rolled it outside of my door. Then I called the reception desk and told them I had just deposited my suitcase in the hall. They cheerfully assured me someone would be by to collect it.

When I finally fell into bed, I was doomed to a sleepless night. All night I tossed and rolled. Sleep was not coming, and I couldn't blame the caffeine from all those Valentine's Day chocolates I'd enjoyed with dessert. The night stretched before me while my mind was on fire with endless thoughts, recollections, theories, images, and impressions. I only drifted off long enough for a very short dream. It was more of a vision than a dream, really. A scar. A little scar I knew, and now it was coming back to me. In an instant, I was wide awake. Suddenly, I knew where I had seen that scar before, and suddenly I knew I had seen it three times on this cruise. My thoughts collided in a frantic effort to piece together the scenario that I was certain would not only identify my attacker but could also explain everything that had been going on.

The next morning, I was wide awake and showered

and dressed before 6:30. I called Wink. When he didn't pick up, I remembered that he was probably putting the papers in place to turn Sorrenta and the Mooneys over to the authorities. I left a message. I had no plans for breakfast or to leave my room until I heard from Wink. Precisely at five past seven, the phone rang. It was Wink. I told him to look up the name Phaddeus Lexeth Oop on the ship manifest. He did so and confirmed that the name was there – Mr. Oop was a guest on our cruise, on my deck farther toward the front of the ship and across the hall. He was traveling with a companion. I told him that Mr. Oop was in fact Seth! Last night, when I remembered that I had seen that unmistakable earlobe scar three separate times, I suspected that Seth was on the ship. Wink said we had to act fast before Seth and his new girlfriend disembarked.

Wink ordered me to get right down to his office. The door fairly blew off its hinges as I flew out of the room.

Chapter Fourteen

Farewell from the MS Minerva: February 15, Monday
Miami, Florida, USA
Scattered Showers: High: 81ºF/27ºC. Low: 68ºF/20ºC.

I BYPASSED THE ELEVATORS which were already crowded with guests and their luggage trying to figure out which deck was open for disembarking. Pearl's voice over the loudspeaker filled the halls, reminding all passengers to settle their accounts by 7:45 and clear all rooms by eight o'clock. I arrived at Wink's office just as he was returning to his desk. He had just met with Customs and Immigration to arrange the handover of Sorrenta and the Mooneys to the authorities who were waiting inside the terminal. Sorrenta had had enough time to figure out that she was in heap-big trouble for her part in Sabrina's disappearance. The Mooneys, on the other hand, had probably slumbered peacefully in a cloud of dreams about their big win and their next cruise, but these alleged millionaires were about to find out there would be no cruise in their immediate future. They were also about to discover that Mrs. Mooney's big win in the casino the night before had been rigged. Mrs. Mooney had won nothing at all – the whole thing had been staged to see if they would withdraw their claim for a full refund for their cruise, which they did. Wink had researched the couple and had learned that they had a rather impressive rap sheet for scamming and skimming. When their casino wins could not pay for their cruise, they staged scenarios that sent them running to file for refunds. In this case, Wink hedged a bet that they would withdraw that claim when their casino winnings were enough to pay for the cruise. The authorities were awaiting them, and the Mooneys would learn that not only would they be held accountable to pay for their cruise in its entirety, but they would also be digging more deeply into their pockets to get them out of the fix they brought on with their staged abduction.

Pearl's velvety voice came over the airwaves again, calmly reminding everyone to vacate their rooms by eight o'clock so housekeeping could clean everything up in time for the next group of guests. She would invite guests to disembark very soon, according to the color of their luggage tag. Meanwhile, the staff captain's gruff voice came over the loudspeaker to inform everyone that the ship was in the process of bunkering, and no one was allowed to smoke on any of the outside verandas or decks while the ship was taking on fuel.

Wink showed me his computer screen where I

saw the name Phaddeus Lexeth Oop III under a photo of Seth. I said, "Yes! That's Seth." I theorized it was probably Seth's new girlfriend who had attacked me, imagining her to be tall and lanky like Seth. It was worth investigating, I said. Wink agreed and said we had to act fast.

"We've got to keep them from disembarking until I can question them. We know they are still on the ship." He asked me if I knew who Seth's new girlfriend might be, and for the first time, I had to admit I'd never even considered who Seth had traded me in for. I guess it didn't matter, at least not until now. I didn't have a clue. But if she was tall, as I'd imagined, she would fit the description of the person who had attacked me the night before. Wink scrolled down Seth's information and his roommate's name popped up. "Her name is Whitney Beth Berkeley and she goes by Beth," he said.

The name did not ring a bell, and I found that curious. Knowing Seth as well as I thought I did, I would have expected him to run off with a mutual friend or someone he had talked about or mentioned from his past. We all have former girl- and boyfriends, after all. Or maybe she was a work colleague, or even one of the mothers of his two kids. But the name Beth Berkeley was a flatline, completely new to me. Wink showed me her photo and I nearly shot up from my seat. Here I was expecting Seth's jealous new girlfriend to be tall, lanky, and athletic as hell. This darling petite little petunia smiling up at the camera like a schoolgirl was anything but! She probably weighed 103 pounds. She was a doll! She looked friendly and nice. She was downright cute, to be honest. I figured I would have dated her if I'd been a guy. I said to Wink, "She is absolutely not the person who attacked me! Maybe Seth had nothing to do with my attacks. But then, who did?"

Wink asked me to recount the three times I had seen the scar on Seth's earlobe, and I told him the first time was when I was dazed after being smacked by that fish on the fishing charter boat. He had stood right over me; while his face and eyes were covered, I saw his earlobe, but I was too confused and hazy to make a connection. The second time was when he rescued me from the barracuda. I only got a view of his earlobe and not his face, but I was more preoccupied with all that blood spurting from my neck to make any sense of it. The third time was at the Valentine deck party less than twelve hours earlier when the man with the plague doctor mask came over and asked me to dance. There the scar was again, but it didn't register until it all came back to me in my dream last night. Wink rang up Seth's room, but there was no answer. The couple was probably at breakfast or heading toward the gangway.

Now Pearl's voice was coming through the air inviting the first group of passengers to disembark, those holding green luggage tags. She asked everyone else to wait patiently in any public part of the ship so as not to crowd the gangway and slow things down. The next group to disembark would be the red luggage tags. Wink did a little search and learned that Seth and Beth were in the group immediately to follow red, the yellow tag holders. He called security and told them to hold off on disembarking yellow tags until he got down there. Then we bolted for the gangway. Green and now red luggage tag holders were filing off the ship wearing raincoats and toting umbrellas as thunder started to roll above. Several couples emerged from the door and lined up against the railing, waiting for the yellow tags to be called. I could see Seth clearly now, although he was wearing a cap he must have purchased in Saint Lucia pulled down over his forehead, his eyes covered completely by sunglasses. His face was not smeared with white zinc cream and he didn't have a bandana over it. Beth, considerably shorter, stood by his side with a bright and innocent smile spread across her face. I liked her already, and never mind what happened with Seth, anyway. He was history.

Wink approached the couple and spoke to them. He pointed in my direction and Seth looked up at me. He didn't appear surprised as he walked toward me, removing his sunglasses and leaving Beth at the railing with their carry-on bags.

"Yeah," he said quietly when he was standing in front of me, one foot twisted behind the other ankle. I wondered if that was supposed to be an admission of guilt or an apology or what someone says when they are clearly busted. I decided it was a stall. I didn't break in but let him marinate in the awkward silence.

"Well," he started back in, ever the man of few words, "you're probably surprised I'm here after all," he said, shoving his hands in his tight jean pockets.

Ya think? I thought but remained silent. Let him squirm, I figured.

"I just didn't want you to know I was – er – we were – er, Beth and I were here too, so we wouldn't ruin your time." What was he thinking? I was questioning my own sanity for dating a guy who could be this dense. I restrained from responding, as I was starting to enjoy the sight of him so out of his comfort zone trying to explain himself. It was going from absurd to comical.

"Oh, you probably wonder about Beth," he said, fast running out of logic.

There's a newsflash, I thought.

"We met online at the ship's own chat website some time before the cruise. I was searching for opinions and ratings of some of the shore excursions and we ran across each other looking at the same excursions. She was booked on this cruise too. She'd just broken up and was coming alone. During our online chats, we realized we already knew each other from way back. We both went to grade school together as kids. Beth and I were close friends back in those days. We actually went out together when we started junior high school, but then both our families moved away from Lansing. We lost touch after that. When we saw each other's pictures and realized we could be together again, we decided to follow our hearts. Then the decision was whether to come on this cruise together knowing you would be here too. I didn't want to ruin your time, so we decided to come but to stay out of your way, disguise ourselves if we had to, and let you have your cruise while we had ours. I – we – never wanted to hurt you, Marianne," he said, and I did feel a twinge of sincerity there. Then, as if to cheer me up, he said, "We even got engaged! Last night during the Valentine's party."

I wondered if he had given Beth the same ring that was meant for me.

"Was that before or after you came over to dance with me?" I spoke up for the first time. I admit to a little swipe of the cat's paw in my voice.

"It was right after," he said quietly. "I wanted to tell you, Marianne, and let you know we'd been here all along and hoped things went okay for you. I thought it would be the right thing to do, but I lost my nerve. I guess I haven't had much nerve this whole time. I'm really sorry about this, Marianne." He turned to go back to Beth, but I stopped him.

"So, is that why you backed out of the dance contest?" I asked. "So you could propose to Beth instead?"

"Well, not really. It was because you were competing too, and we didn't want you to know I was here."

Then as he started to walk away, Wink broke in. "Hey, Buddy, before you slip away, what do you know about the physical attacks on Marianne?"

Seth turned around, this time with a completely serious and concerned expression on his face. "What are you talking about?"

"Marianne was physically attacked in the dark on the ship on three separate occasions."

"What? I had no idea. I would never, ever hurt Marianne," he said earnestly. He turned around and planted himself squarely between Wink and me, re-entering the conversation with his full attention. He did not sound defensive, but adamant. "If someone was trying to hurt you, Marianne, I promise I wasn't involved, but I would like to find out who it was. Beth and I were very careful to stay out of your way so you wouldn't have to think of me – ah, us – the whole time." Then he thought for a moment and added, "And if I were out to harm you, Marianne, then you tell me why I would have rescued you from the barracuda that day on the beach at Grand Turk."

Good point.

"Well, then, who was the tall person with you the day that marlin or tuna or whale or whatever the hell it was slammed into me and nearly knocked out my lights for good?"

Seth thought back to that day without asking me how I knew that was he. "I don't really know," he said. "She was on the excursion alone and so was I. Beth gets really seasick, so she took a nature trail hike that day."

Smart choice, I thought.

"I barely talked with that woman. Besides, she had a strong accent, so I couldn't understand her. I never even got her name."

I recalled how she had limped over to the cooler to help herself to a drink, but did not offer one to him, and how I concluded at the time that they were not a very affectionate couple for newlyweds.

"We were just fishing from the same part of the boat and when she caught that marlin and it slammed into you, I was surprised she didn't go right over to apologize. Much as I wanted to, I simply couldn't go running over to help you or you'd know I was on the cruise. I did go over at one point just to make sure you were okay. I knew you were in good hands with that big guy cradling your head like that, so I made myself scarce as soon as we got back to the marina." Then he added, "It wasn't the same thing as when you were out swimming alone with that barracuda biting you and no one else around to help you out of the water but me."

God, I thought, trying to keep up with him. Men can be so annoying even when they are trying to help.

"Would you know that woman from a lineup, Seth?" Wink asked.

"Probably not. She was smeared with white zinc cream and wearing huge sunglasses and a big hat and that bandana covering her whole face. I didn't pay her much attention except I followed her cue and covered my own face to disguise myself when Marianne suddenly boarded our charter boat. Marianne and her friends weren't even supposed to be there, but the couple that was meant for our boat overslept and missed the excursion completely so we had the space for two more. I tried the whole time to stay under wraps."

"Well, except for that telltale scar on your earlobe," I said. Seth laughed uneasily and ran his thumb and forefinger over his right earlobe, never taking his eyes off me. They were kind and admiring. This was the Seth I had known.

Just then, Pearl's voice announced that all the yellow luggage tag holders were free to disembark.

"Well," Wink said, "I guess that means you and Beth can go now."

Seth said, "Before we go, I'd like to introduce Beth to you, Marianne. If it's okay. I think you'd really like each other. I mean, after all this – er – um – well, you're both really nice women." He motioned to Beth who rolled their carry-ons as she came to join the action, still smiling, and handed Seth's roller to him. We met briefly and cordially, and I had to admit Beth was really nice and honestly, more compatible for Seth than I could ever be. I congratulated them and they smiled and walked down the gangway hand in hand.

"Well," I said, "I guess that still leaves us up in the air about the identity and motive of my attacker on the ship and the origin of those messages. I can't stand leaving a mystery unsolved."

Pearl announced that gray luggage tag holders could go next. With my gray tag I was free to go any time now, but something kept me from leaving just then. I had to try one more time. We returned to Wink's office.

"Describe her again, as you remember it," Wink coaxed.

"Tall, strong, lanky, obviously athletic and very powerful. And now we know she has an accent, if she was in fact the same person fishing with Seth that day," I said. I was wracking my brains trying to remember any woman who was tall and spoke with an accent who might have it in for me. I kept coming up dry. I also could think of no motive now that Seth and Beth and any supposed motives of jealousy were out of the way. This was really stumping me. I asked Wink if he'd ever been able to trace those threatening messages that were left on my phone. He said the best they could come up with was a source from somewhere in Delaware. He honestly didn't think they were meant for me or anyone on the ship and had long since ruled out the idea that they had anything to do with the attacks.

I asked him if he had the transcripts from those messages handy, and he pulled them up on his computer screen for me to review. As I looked at them, something clarified for me so suddenly that I wondered at myself for missing it earlier. The sinister messages recalled similar threats in my book, *Hope Dares the Durango Detective*. It was the same book that the little girl, Ivy, had asked me to autograph for her the night before. I thought about how the little kid, Bunchy, had masterminded and organized an entire mystery with an unsuspecting victim, and then single-handedly solved it to win a very distinguished mystery competition. Suddenly the metaphorical clouds parted, and everything made sense. On a very strong hunch, I said to Wink, "Please bring up the information for Ivy Welles, that little girl who asked me to autograph my book the other night." In an instant her face was on Wink's screen alongside photos of her parents.

As we looked at the photos, Wink told me that Ivy had asked questions and was very curious about me. "About me?" I asked, puzzled.

"Yes. She is very precocious and was curious about the things you did on shore. She inquired nearly every evening at the excursion office about your plans for the following day. No one ever questioned that because she is a kid, and they gave her the information freely." Wink only knew about this because he had overheard the conversation on one of those occasions. Ivy tried to go on the same excursions I was on, but her parents had pre-booked other ones. It didn't stop her from looking into the ones I was on, however, which apparently was of importance to her. I wondered why Ivy would be so preoccupied with my movements on shore. The daisy wheel on Wink's computer stopped and the information opened up. Just as I'd suspected, the family was from New England. Delaware. Before I said another word, Wink was on the phone with security giving them instructions to stop the Welles family from disembarking.

I asked Wink to see if Skip and Denny were still on board. I had a suspicion about them I wanted to check out as well because Skip always seemed to be there for me just in the nick of time. In a flash, Wink called security and put a hold on their disembarkation too. Then I took another leap and asked Wink to bring up on his computer two women from the crew manifest, both tall and very athletic, who spoke with accents. The images of Natalia, a staff dancer from Belarus, and Fedora, the gym director from Croatia, filled his screen in side-by-side mug shots. I envisioned both of them slathered in white zinc with bandanas on their faces, and Natalia crystallized as the dead ringer for the angler who caught that fish, the woman I thought was a honeymooner. I asked about the dancer who had sprained her ankle during the cruise, and after checking with the medic's office, Wink confirmed that it was Natalia. Bingo! We had a match! Furthermore, she had reported the sprain shortly after her first encounter with me. I guess I didn't do so badly defending myself, I thought.

In less than twelve minutes, security had rounded everyone up and the entire party was sitting in the reception area. Wink asked them whether they knew each other, and they admitted they had all met during the cruise but hadn't known each other beforehand. He asked if they knew anything about a plot against one of the other passengers. They squirmed uncomfortably. Only Denny spoke up saying he knew of no such thing, and Skip quickly gave him a nudge in the ribs with his elbow. Suddenly, I came through the office door holding up a sheet I'd asked Reception to print for me. It was an online announcement for the annual Agatha Christie Trick A Detective Writer competition, named for one of the world's all-time greatest mystery writers.

"Well, I never would have suspected this! I can't believe I almost didn't figure it out. But here you all are. Thank you very much for a roller-coaster ride I was not expecting on this cruise. I will never forget it! Now that the game is up and I've figured it out, the ball is in my court."

Everyone laughed uneasily when they realized I had just uncovered their plot and trumped them as the winners in a high-stakes competition. The annual Agatha Christie Trick a Detective Writer contest was conceived in the spirit of Agatha Christie's own mysterious disappearance on learning that her husband had fallen in love with someone else in December of 1926. At the time of her disappearance, no one could figure out if it was real or a publicity stunt. The contest invited avid detective and mystery book readers to stage a real mystery around their favorite detective writer without the writer's knowledge. The rules allowed pretty much anything short of critical injury or death. Also, pressing charges by either party would automatically void the contest. The mystery had to be clearly plotted out and submitted in its entirety before its execution. If the framed mystery writer did not figure it out by the end of the game, the game host could win $25,000 – a lot of money for a ten-year-old. If, however, the mystery writer figured out and solved the mystery before the deadline, she or he could win twice that amount, or $50,000. The winner was always announced in October on Agatha Christie's birthday.

With her parents looking on in stunned silence with expressions of both horror and admiration, Ivy admitted that she had submitted an online contest entry on the first night of the cruise when she saw me at Gilligan's Table when her family had almost been seated there with us. Later, Ivy brought Natalia and Skip in on her little conspiracy. She explained that Natalia's role was to shake me up a little bit with a couple of tussles on the open deck, and then Skip was to show up in time to rescue me before the struggles got serious. Taking her cue from Bunchy, Ivy said she could depend on unrelated events that would confuse me and create a setting for paranoia and second-guessing. This would predispose me to even more distractions leading to more mishaps and accidents. It was a masterful stroke, I thought, and right out of Bunchy's playbook . . . and my own imagination.

Ivy set the game's deadline to be the moment of

her own disembarkation, when she swiped her ship card at security for the last time. Since Ivy had not yet disembarked, and I was standing in front of her and her accomplices with the whole thing figured out, I was the winner. All I could say to everyone was, "Close, but no cigar!"

Wink asked me if I wanted to press charges, but I told him no, I did not. No harm had been done, other than the fact that they had scared me half to death. Besides, pressing charges automatically voided the entry and canceled my opportunity to win $50,000. I thanked Skip for saving me all those times and he chuckled, saying he only agreed to help Ivy knowing I would figure it out and take it all in good humor. He went on to assure me that he never planned on taking the hundred dollars Ivy promised him for his part, even if she won. He said he knew it would never come to that because he had every faith that I would solve the mystery before the deadline. "And you did!" he said, pointing at me with pride.

All I could think about was that Ivy had offered him only a measly hundred dollars from a possible win of $25,000! A brilliant little entrepreneur on top of everything else!

I told Natalia she was underappreciated as a staff dancer on a cruise ship and should really consider a career as a stunt actor. She'd probably earn much more money and get the chance to rub elbows with celebrities. She could move to a mansion in Malibu. She said she would not have accepted Ivy's hundred dollars either. I didn't believe her. When I congratulated her on that big fish catch, she said that hitting me with it wasn't part of the plan and apologized that it had hit me so hard.

I thanked Skip again for coming to my rescue on the boat, but he also said it wasn't part of the plan and reminded me that he was only on that charter because I had given him Seth's unused ticket. Good point. So, the whole fishing incident was an example of a completely isolated coincidence borne of distraction from my own paranoia over the confrontations on the outer deck and the mysterious messages, all of which suddenly reminded me of one more thing.

"Just answer me this, my little trickster," I said, facing Ivy, "how did you voice those clever messages and send them to my room all the way from Delaware while you were right here on the ship? Did you have some help from the ventriloquist?"

Ivy didn't deny sending the messages and went right into high-tech mode explaining about some voice converter app she used to transform her little girl's voice to that of a man's and went on to explain that her cellphone on the ship was communicating to her computer back in Delaware and she was able to outsmart the system and make it look like the messages she taped and sent to her home computer from the ship were coming from Delaware. Her parents looked at her in amazement, not fathoming when she could possibly have done all this, outside of the dead of night. I don't think they were aware of all the writing she did during high tea while she sat alone under that window every afternoon.

I was already lost in her technobabble and said half-jokingly, "Did you get all that, Wink? Maybe you should recruit Ivy. In any event, it just goes to prove that every new computer and cell phone and electronic device should come with a ten-year-old to show the rest of us how to work the dang thing and you can skip the warranty."

Everyone laughed again.

"So, to summarize," I said, on a roll and going with it. "The motive behind those threatening messages was simply to scare me into disembarking before the cruise ended to prevent me from figuring out the mystery in time." Ivy nodded in agreement. "The run-ins on the deck with Natalia were meant to scare me and put some teeth into the messages." Ivy kept nodding. "This worked to create a setting for paranoia and distract me from realizing I was 'framed' as a dupe in this mystery game," I concluded. Ivy was still nodding. "Brilliant!" I exclaimed. "Right out of Bunchy's playbook." But I reminded Ivy that Bunchy was my own creation and it would take getting up pretty early in the morning to trick me with my own trick. Ivy stopped nodding.

Then I explained to her that according to the rules of the contest the game was now squarely in my hands. I was taking rightful ownership as apparent winner since I had figured out the mystery before the stated deadline, and by the contest's own rules she was required to concede. Everyone else served as a witness, and Ivy was bright enough to understand and accept the determination. Now I would be the one to receive notification as the grand prize winner in October. It got me to thinking, however, that no matter how good you are, no matter how hard you work to get to the top of your game, there's always someone younger coming up the ranks nipping at your heels and trying to catch you off balance. For now, at least, I was still on my perch.

As Ivy walked out of Wink's office between her parents, each holding one of her hands, she looked back at me once more. I marveled at the brilliant little trickster who had almost trumped me at my own game. I was satisfied knowing that once she submitted her card for its final scan and walked down the gangway for the last time, the game belonged to me by the parameters she herself had defined.

I turned once again to Natalia. "I'm just curious about something, Natalia. You scared me enough with those first couple of tussles on the deck. But, honestly, you really almost got me for good last night," I said. "That was some roughing up. It felt like you were trying to kill me. Don't you know you risked losing the entire contest by pushing it that far?"

"Last night?" Startled, Natalia looked up. She was either incredulous or a damn good actress. "I was in the crew bar last night," she said. "You can ask Javier and Kalu. I was there with them until midnight when we had to report to baggage-handling duty. I did not come up to the outer decks or mingle with any guests at all. I don't know what you are talking about."

"Well, I almost saw my life fast-forwarding in front of me with the view of that water under the ship coming closer and closer. If it hadn't been for Skip coming through right then, I wouldn't be here right now. If that wasn't you trying to push me overboard, then who was it? And why did Skip just happen to come by in the nick of time?" I asked, turning to Skip.

Wide-eyed and jumping from his seat, Skip spoke up. "I honestly was just coming back to our room with the laundry. It was a total coincidence that I ran into you like that, unlike the other times. In fact, I didn't even know it was you until I came right over. I hadn't expected to see you there with Natalia because there was nothing scheduled for us last night. After finding out it was you, I figured Ivy must have added it later and I didn't get the memo in time. I don't always check my email."

Besides appreciating everything they went through to play out this complicated plot, I was also starting to realize the degree of danger I had been in the night before. Apparently, there was another attacker acting independently of Ivy's contest scheme.

Wink gave the okay for Skip and Denny to disembark, and from all their talking and gesturing, it was clear that Skip was filling Denny in on everything.

Wink also told Natalia that she could return to her duties.

"Whoever it was," I said, "it was definitely a tall and lanky woman. She never said a word, but she did grunt and emit other sounds of pain, and I heard enough to know she was female."

Wink ruffled papers. He made chicken scratchings on one of them. Then he looked up and said, "Is there anyone, crew, staff, or passenger, that you just have a bad feeling about?"

"Angela!" I blurted.

"The social hostess?" Wink laughed, almost incredulous.

"Angela is an ice pick," I said. I told him about her reaction when Roy had agreed to be my dance partner and what Roy had said about her imminent dismissal and the random comment of the guest at our dinner.

Wink opened another file in his computer. "Aha!" he said, as if discovering something. "Let me try asking someone in the know." He made a phone call, and in a few minutes, Pauline, the calm and collected human resources director, joined us in his office.

"Yes," Pauline confirmed, speaking professionally. "Angela was placed on probation at the end of the last cruise. She knew very well that her attitude must improve or she would be terminated and replaced. Angela had tried to get Roy to submit a testimony of her good behavior back when they were a couple, but things had deteriorated, and Roy could not endorse

Angela in good conscience. The more he refused, the more she persisted and clung to him until he finally pulled away for good and ended it. Still, Angela refused to let go and it was her growing realization that Roy wasn't interested in her that fueled her sour attitude that impacted her work and her impression on the guests.

"At one point after the break-up, Roy took a shine to one of our guests. He started a correspondence with that guest after she left the ship, but Angela broke into Roy's email and sent the woman a very uncomplimentary letter, signing it from Roy, and then blocking her replies and erasing her email contact from his list. Roy was furious with Angela when he found out about it, and things only went from worse to catastrophic. But she still never gave up on him. You might say she is the jealous type," Pauline concluded.

Oh, do tell! I thought to myself.

Wink asked if there was anything that might connect Angela to the attack the night before in addition to the grunts and squeaks I heard during the tussle. Suddenly, I thought of the mask! Wink called security who went straightaway to her room. There, on the side of the desk, was the mask with the teardrop and aubergine lips. Another search on the ship's cameras in her corridor showed Angela, wearing the same black pantsuit she had worn to host the dance contest, walking to her room and through the door wearing that mask! The time showing on the film was a few minutes after Skip appeared with his laundry basket, which was caught on another of the ship's cameras. Wink said it looked like a closed case and asked if I wanted to press charges. Again, I said no. I wanted to close the entire chapter on all the mysteries that sprang from this cruise and only look back to the fun times I had, which were mostly the times I spent with Wink. Anyone could see that Angela would get her severest comeuppance with her imminent termination.

I had one final question for Wink. "Aside from the two deck fights with Natalia," I asked, "were you able to establish whether any of my other accidents were orchestrated by that little genius-devil trickster?" Then I added, "Please don't tell me 'Poison Ivy' was evil and conniving enough to stage all those shore-side mishaps. I'd rather think I am a klutz."

Wink laughed. He said getting lost in the Baths grotto wasn't something anyone could have planned, and neither was the defective bell dive helmet I'd been issued in St. Bart's. He said we were all stranded on the "Gilligan's Island" beach in Dominica and I could not take any credit for bringing that one on myself, let alone the rest of us. He said the ship was still looking into the zipline accident in St. Lucia, but the outfit had followed all the safety protocols. What happened there seemed to be just an incredibly unlucky event, but the bungee cord safety measure they'd implemented worked exactly as it was intended to and saved me from further injury.

Wink had contacted Shadow in Tortola who told

him that the rental car that spooked my horse was traced to some tourists rushing to the hospital after one of them had a nasty encounter with a poisonous manchineel tree and was burning in pain. They were lost and panicking and didn't mean to spook my horse along the way. The bike mishap in San Juan was caused by the misguided preteen looking for a phantom monkey where there wasn't one and I just happened to take the hit there. Finally, he said no one can predict when a barracuda will bite anyone underwater.

"Definitely in God's hands, not Ivy's, if that's what you were thinking. She's a smart kid but probably at her cleverest just setting you up to wallow in your own paranoia. Just like your own character Bunchy did in your book," he concluded. Finally, he looked up at me with a goofy smile and said, "Admit it, kid, you're just the victim of some pretty bad timing . . . and maybe you're a bit of a klutz."

Wink asked Pauline to stay in his office and help him while security rounded up Angela. He said I should get off the ship and get to the airport. Angela was in their hands and they could take it quite handily from there. He said he'd try to finish up in time to catch me curbside at the taxi stand before he transferred to the MS *Athena* across the pier.

I HAD ONE LAST THING to do before disembarking. I went to the cruise director's office where Pearl was calmly looking over a ream of papers and spreadsheets on her desk and talking with various members of the performance staff making plans for the next cruise that was to start that same day. I tapped on the wall just inside the office and everyone looked up. I went over to Pearl who stood up to greet me, smiling broadly. I reached out to hug her and she immediately reciprocated with a bear hug of her own. I said, "Thank you, Pearl. I am going to miss you and everyone here. You certainly lived up to your promise. It was the most unforgettable cruise of my life."

Pearl gave me an extra squeeze and released me, looking down the six or seven inches that separated us from being at eye-level with each other. She had the loveliest smile. She thanked me again and said she always observed that no experience in life is ever wasted, and she had a very strong feeling about me, that we would be seeing each other again . . . and sooner than we might think. I said I was really hoping so. We wished each other well and I headed to the gangway.

Cleared of the ship, I stood at the curb in the very long queue for a taxi. Finally, it was my turn and as the taxi driver loaded my big suitcase into the trunk, I placed my carry-on bag down so I could pull out some cash for a tip. Wink came up just then to join the queue for a cab to his next ship on the other side of the Port of Miami.

"How did you come up with all that?" he asked.

"I'm still shaking my head over how you pulled that whole thing together and figured out that contest before they scanned their way off the ship with potential for a tidy little prize."

"Well, it certainly has been an adventure," I said, summing up the entire cruise.

"I expect to read about some of your exploits in your next great detective book," he added. "I've never heard of the Hope Dares Detective Series, but I've already downloaded all eight of the books on Kindle and will start reading the first one tonight alone in my room with a glass of red wine."

"Or maybe a mug of hot chocolate," I laughed. "Thanks for all you did and for making the cruise so memorable."

Wink set his carry-on next to mine. He tweaked my nose playfully and said, "You still have that complimentary cruise coming to you, and you should take them up on it and come back so we can do this again." I was hoping he would ask me for my email or phone number, but instead he took my face in his hands and planted a big kiss on my lips. I have to say, I took it in a very good way.

I reached out to him, hoping for one more kiss that was more meaningful and longer lasting, but his cab stopped right then, and the driver emerged to take his suitcase. I grabbed my carry-on and tumbled into my taxi and off we went. I waved at Wink one last time as we swooshed away, but he was loading his suitcase in his own cab with his back to me. As my taxi left the Port of Miami, it swung by our sister ship, the MS *Athena*, the ship Wink was heading over to. I could only imagine the new set of adventures that awaited him there and wished with all my might that I could join him.

AS I WAS SETTING my suitcase on the scale at the American Airlines check-in counter, my phone rang. It wasn't from anyone I knew and only said "restricted number." I answered. I immediately recognized the pleasant and composed voice of the ship's human resources director, Pauline. She thanked me again for providing the information about Angela and apologized for everything I had gone through because of her. Then she changed the subject.

"Because of what has just happened, we are going to be without a social hostess for the new cruise that starts today. So, I am wondering on the very slim and off chance, if you would like to come back and fill in that position for the duration of the cruise. You are already familiar with how things work here, and you're a natural for the position, judging from the positive guest comments that are still coming in. It's only a two-week cruise and by the end we should have Angela's replacement ready to take over . . . unless you will want to continue on a more permanent basis by then." Then she added a correction.

"Excuse me," she said. I could hear her smile over the phone. "Things are changing in front of me as we speak. I am just learning now that we are actually going to fill the MS *Minerva's* position today with the MS *Athena's* social hostess, Diane, who is transferring over to our ship right now from the other ship. You already know the two ships are across the pier from each other. Diane was scheduled to join this ship in two weeks anyway, so she will take over today instead. That means, if you are interested, you can go directly to the MS *Athena* instead of coming back here. They are sister ships and almost exactly the same in every way." Then she added, "I think Wink is heading over there right now, so at least you will know one person when you arrive . . . if you are interested in taking up this offer, that is."

If there was anything that could have made me happier in the world right then, I didn't know what it was. My heart was so light, I didn't even notice the weight of my overstuffed suitcase when I lifted it back off the check-in scale. I rolled it out to the taxi curb and headed straight back to the Port of Miami and this time the MS *Athena*. As soon as I was settled into the cab heading back to the Port of Miami and the MS *Athena*, I opened my carry-on to tuck my phone inside. A big white sheet of paper was lying on top that I did not remember putting there. It was then I realized I had someone else's carry-on bag. Apparently Wink had switched our carry-ons at the taxi stand . . . but maybe not by accident. When I picked up the paper, there was all his contact information, including his email, Miami address and telephone number. And scrawled across the sheet were three words: *To be continued?*

I smiled and dialed his number.

CPSIA information can be obtained
at www.ICGtesting.com
Printed in the USA
LVHW110740160422
716377LV00019B/156